The End of the Civil War

❧ A Drew Steele Civil War Mystery ❧

E.E. "Doc" Murdock

H.O.T. Press

Published by
H.O.T. Press
Los Angeles, CA
www.hotpresspublishing.com
Publishing fine books since 1983

ISBN: 0-923178-17-1
ISBN - 13: 978-0-923178-17-8

Acknowledgments

I am indebted to the members of the Ojai Writing Workshop who provided valuable feedback as I worked through the many drafts of this book. And of course, without the help of Zoe, this book would not exist.

The End of the Civil War

Chapter 1

*H*e couldn't sleep. He got up and dressed and went into his office where he stood for a while looking out of the big window behind his desk. The sun was just coming up across the San Francisco bay, but it would be hours before it could break through the thick morning fog.

He lit a lamp and sat down at his desk. He picked up yesterday's *Bulletin* and reread the story about the group of Confederate fighters who were still holed up in a remote mountainous region of North Carolina. Most of the country's newspapers had been describing them as fanatics, confused pseudo-patriots continuing to fight for a hopeless cause even after the peace treaty had been signed by both sides. On the other hand, the Southern newspapers were promoting the idea that they were loyal soldiers of the South, unwilling to give up their dream of a free nation. Steele wasn't so sure either concept was true: what if they were being directed by Southern leaders who wanted to keep hope for the Confederacy alive?

His thoughts were interrupted by someone banging on the door. "Steele, open up. It's me."

Rudd? What was he doing up and around so early? Steele got up and went to open the door.

Rudd rushed in waving a piece of paper. "Wait 'til you hear what's in this letter, Steele. It's about the war-crimes trials."

"Well, good morning to you too, Rudd," said Steele, smiling at his old friend's exuberance. "But isn't it a bit early for you?"

Rudd flopped down in the guest chair and fanned himself with the letter. "It sure is. The boss sent messengers to wake all of us reporters up as soon as he opened this letter. He told us what it was about and said we should all go out and see what we could find out about it. I ran all the way over here to tell you, seein' how you study about the war all the time."

Steele went back to his chair behind the desk. "I would expect your newspaper to get a lot of letters about such a divisive issue as the war-crimes trials. Why the urgency?"

"Yeah, we do, but this one isn't the usual ramble. It's from some guy named Ramsey who claims to be a general. And he's threatening to take hostages."

That name gave Steele a start. Hadn't there been a General Jacob Ramsey in Tennessee, one of Bennett's subcommanders? Could it be the same man? He held out his hand. "Let me see the letter."

"Well, uh, the boss said we weren't supposed to show it to anybody. How 'bout if I read it to you? He didn't say anything about reading it out loud."

"Fine, then read it. That's a copy, isn't it?"

"Yeah, I made a copy when nobody was looking. How'd you know?"

"It's never been folded as a letter would be." Steele opened his journal and picked up his pen. "Read."

Rudd took out a pair of wire-rimmed spectacles and cleared his throat. "It starts out like this: 'The war-crimes trials currently taking place in the Federal capital are inherently illegal. They must be stopped. Take heed. For each Confederate officer brought before that tribunal, there will be one hostage taken. For each Confederate officer executed, there will be one hostage executed.'"

"Wait," said Steele, holding up his hand. He finished copying down the words and took a few seconds to reread them. The letter writer was referring to the historic war-crimes tribunal that was going on back in Washington The series of trials were intended to punish Confederate officers who were accused of committing atrocities during the Civil War. Maybe the letter writer personally knew somebody on trial back there. Perhaps a friend or relative. Steele dropped his hand. "Continue."

"It says, 'This unprecedented and illegitimate tribunal portends to punish loyal officers of the Confederacy who were only carrying out their orders.'" For effect, Rudd looked at Steele over the top of his spectacles, and then continued: "It goes on to say, 'You have been warned.' And at the bottom of the letter, there's this great big signature, C. J. Ramsey."

Steele was sure he had read that name somewhere. Maybe there had been a Confederate general by that name. "You could read the signature clearly? It was C. J. Ramsey?"

"Yeah, do you know somebody by that name?"

"I believe there may have been a Confederate general named C. J. Ramsey. Are you sure you copied the letter exactly?"

"Sure. I'm good at that. People tell me things, and I write 'em down. Exactly."

Steele looked at what he had written in his journal. The letter was brief and to the point. No extra flourishes, no unnecessary repetitions. The letter-writer was used to writing formal letters, and he was confident of his ability to communicate through the use of straightforward language. It did sound like the writing of a military mind. However, despite the reference to "loyal officers of the Confederacy," it seemed unlikely a Confederate general would write such a letter to a San Francisco newspaper. If he was serious about the taking of hostages, why not send the letter to those in charge back in Washington? "Who delivered the letter?"

"Some guy left it at the front desk. The girl didn't know him. She said he didn't speak English."

"A Mexican?"

"That's what the girl thought."

"What kind of paper was the letter written on?"

Rudd shrugged. "I think it was just regular white paper, not fine stationary if that's what you mean. Is that important?"

"Of course. Everything is important. What was the handwriting like?"

"A big flowing script. Everybody in the office commented on that."

"Were there any words crossed out? Any corrected mistakes?"

Rudd glanced at his copy of the letter, thinking. "As I recall, not a one." He looked up at Steele. "Hey, that's kind of unusual isn't it?"

"It means there were probably prior drafts. The letter writer planned the contents of the letter carefully. He wanted his message to be very clear, without any potential for confusion. Did the letter ask your newspaper to publish it?"

"Nope. It didn't say anything other than what I read to you."

Steele sat back in his chair to think what the letter-writer's purpose could be. Why hadn't he made any demands? Maybe he was just trying to get the newspaper's attention. "If there's anything to the letter's threats, you will undoubtedly get another letter with more details."

Rudd thought about that. "Well, maybe. But isn't it possible this Ramsey guy is just another Rebel chowderhead? Out to make trouble."

"If the letter really was from a Confederate general, it should be taken seriously."

"Do you think he could be? A real general, I mean?"

"I'm fairly sure there was a general by that name who participated in the war. I may be able to find his name in a document I have." Steele got up and went to his file cabinet. He removed a thick stack of unbound papers and brought them back to his desk.

"What've you got there?"

"It's a draft of a book about some of the Confederate officers who took part in the war. The author sent it to me for my opinion."

"Is this Ramsey guy in there?"

"It includes information about most of the Confederate high-ranking officers." Steele leafed through the book, which was organized by region. In the Tennessee section, he found the reference he was looking for. "Here it is. General Jacob C. Ramsey, commander of the 2nd Tennessee infantry regiment. It says he was known as the 'Butcher of Shelbyville.'"

Rudd let out a low whistle. "The Butcher of Shelbyville? That sounds ominous."

If the letter writer was the same man, it was ominous. Steele remembered hearing about that general when he was working in the Union field hospital in Tennessee. Wounded men who were brought in from a battle near Shelbyville were saying they were lucky to be alive because the Confederate General they were fighting against was "The Butcher," a General who ordered his men to kill any Union solider they captured.

Rudd sat forward to look at the book. "So there *was* a Confederate general named Ramsey. Does it say anything else about him?"

"It says that near the end of the war he was quoted as saying he would personally shoot down any man who tried to surrender to the North."

Rudd let out another low whistle. "Shoot his own men? Sounds like a real fanatic."

"The author of this book goes on to speculate that it could have been that very statement that caused a revolt of his men and the eventual mass Confederate surrender at the battle of Crossville."

"Crossville? Where's that?"

"Near Chattanooga. Back then, Chattanooga and the Tennessee River area near the Alabama and Georgia state lines was known as the gateway to the South. The Confederates were trying to hold it at any cost."

"So this Ramsey was there?"

"Apparently. This book says that after Crossville, he was demoted to the rank of lieutenant general and re-posted as commander of the Hackleburg prisoner-of-war camp."

"So he lost his rank and got stuck in some backwater place. But why would somebody like that be writing threatening letters to my newspaper?"

Steele searched the book's war prisons section for references to Hackleburg, and soon found exactly what he was looking for. "Listen to this. It says Hackleburg wasn't a real prison, just a fenced in perimeter with no buildings or shelter of any kind."

"Uh oh, wasn't Andersonville like that?"

"Yes, and the commander of the Andersonville camp has now been arrested for war crimes. This General Ramsey might be wanted by the tribunal for similar war crimes. This book suggests Hackleburg was almost as bad as Andersonville. It says the prisoners reported that they only survived the cold by scraping out holes in the ground and using their dead companions to cover themselves. They said they were barely fed enough to survive. They ate rats, insects, even worms."

Rudd made a sour face. "Christ! Hard to imagine eating . . . stuff like that. So this General Ramsey was the one in charge of that prison?"

"Apparently he was. If he's wanted by the war crimes tribunal, it might explain the threats in his letter."

"But why did he send the letter to a San Francisco newspaper? Do you think it means he's out here in the West now?"

"If you were wanted as a war criminal, where else could you go?"

Rudd nodded thoughtfully. Then he said, "You know, he could be right here in San Francisco. Wouldn't that be a story? A Confederate general on the run, right here under our noses."

"He'd be smart to stay away from large cities. But if he is in the West, and he wants publicity for his cause, the San Francisco Morning Herald, the largest newspaper west of the Mississippi, would be the one he would choose."

"But the letter was hand delivered. Doesn't it mean he could be here?"

"It *is* important that the letter was hand delivered. It means he was close enough to send a messenger. The letter mentioned the taking of hostages. Has your newspaper reported any recent kidnappings?"

"Naw. My boss asked if anybody had heard anything like that. Nobody knew about any kidnappings, at least not any that's been reported around here. That's why we all thought it must be a crank letter. But the boss said to ask around, just in case."

"You should check the other branches of your newspaper. Maybe someone has seen or heard something about a Confederate general on the run somewhere in the West."

"Now wait a minute," protested Rudd. "I'm not telling anybody anything. So far, I'm the only one who even knows the letter might be from a real Confederate general. It's my story, and I plan to keep it that way." He jumped to his feet and jammed on his hat. "I'll go do some nosing around about this General Ramsey, but I'm not gonna tell anybody why I'm asking. This story could be the break I've been waiting for, my chance to get off the society page and break into crime reporting."

Chapter 2

Steele listened to Rudd's heavy footsteps going down the front stairs. He turned in his chair to look out the window. The fog was lifting a little, but the sun had not yet broken through. He tried to imagine a Confederate general, hiding in the West, writing a letter to a San Francisco newspaper. Would he make such a threat before taking a hostage? Why would he warn everyone in advance? It could mean he's already taken a hostage. But if he had, why hadn't he made specific demands?

He pushed aside the journal and looked toward the door. If a Confederate general *was here* in the West making threats related to the ongoing war crimes tribunals, what did he hope to accomplish? Surely the government was not going to stop the war crimes trials just because somebody out west was threatening to take hostages. Unless . . . the hostages were very important. Maybe he should go down to the newspaper office and talk to Rudd's bosses. But why would they believe him if he told them somebody important was about the be kidnapped? And even if they did, what could they do about it?

Steele closed the war manuscript and stood up. Nothing to do but wait to see what happens next. Maybe the newspaper would get another letter. He decided to keep to his usual schedule. He'd spend the morning at city library, studying, as he did every morning.

He put on his coat and started down the stairs to the street. But he was still troubled by the fact that the letter writer had made no demands. He hadn't even asked the newspaper to publish the letter. It had to mean something else was going to happen, something important enough to get the attention of the U.S. government. And if this General Ramsey really did intend to stop the war-crimes trials, he would have to act fast. Steele decided it wouldn't hurt to drop by the newspaper office, just to see if they were taking any further action about the letter.

The moment Steele walked into the newspaper building, he could see that something was up. Despite the early hour, the place was not deserted; on the contrary, there were even more men in the newspaper office than usual. They were rushing to and fro, many of them in shirtsleeves instead of their usual buttoned-up suits and starched collars. The door of one office was ajar and inside Steele could see Rudd, among others, gathered around a desk where a man in a dark suit sat reading from a small piece of paper. Steele recognized the paper: it was a Western Union telegraphic message. Everyone in the room was asking questions, all at the same time; questions about where it had happened, about when, about demands. Steele realized Ramsey *had* acted fast. Was it another message from Ramsey saying he had carried out his threat to take hostages?

Steele went into the office and stood behind the group of reporters.

The man sitting behind the desk threw up his hands and looked at the others. "He isn't asking for any money, so what the hell does he want?"

Steele tapped Rudd on the shoulder.

Without looking back, Rudd pushed away the hand, saying, "Just a minute. I'll be right there."

"Rudd, it's me," whispered Steele.

Rudd looked back. "Oh, Steele, it's you. By God, you were right. You said we'd get another letter."

"Who's that?" shouted the man behind the desk. He turned the message face down. "Get him out of here."

The others turned to look at Steele.

Rudd pulled Steele forward to stand in front of the desk. "Mr. Gilson, this is Drew Steele, the detective I told you about. He's the one who told me the first letter might be from a Confederate general."

Steele had heard of Gilson, the editor of the newspaper. He had a reputation as a man who drove his employees hard, but got results. Gilson was staring at him, frowning.

Steele met his stare. "So the letter *was* from General Ramsey?"

"That's right," said Gilson. "How'd you know?"

Steele glanced at the reporters who were all watching him, waiting for his answer. He moved through them to the edge of Gilson's desk. "Maybe we should talk about this in private."

Gilson abruptly stood up, glaring at Steele. "What? Are you telling me what to do in my own office?" His angry eyes were the eyes of a man who expected to be obeyed.

Steele waited calmly.

Finally, still scowling, Gilson turned to the others. "All right, everybody out except Rudd. I gotta talk to this man. Go write something vague about rumors of a kidnapping, but don't file anything until you hear from me."

"What should I tell the layout people?" asked a nervous-looking man.

"Tell them to wait," shouted Gilson. "And don't any of you say anything to anybody outside this office. Got it?"

The reporters mumbled their acquiescence, and filed out the door.

As soon as the reporters were gone, Gilson pointed to a chair in front of his desk. "All right, Steele, let's have it."

"I assume there has been another message," said Steele, sitting down. "And I assume that if you know it came from General Ramsey then he must have used his title this time." But even as he asked the question, Steele wondered why Ramsey would have used his title in a second message if he hadn't used it in the first one.

Gilson sat down and leaned across the desk, pointing at Steele. "Hold on a minute. First I want to know what you know. Who is this maniac, this Ramsey? You think he was a real Confederate general?"

"He really was, Mr. Gilson," said Rudd. "Steele looked him up in a book."

"I didn't ask you, Rudd. I asked Steele."

"There was a Confederate general named Jacob Ramsey," said Steele. "Did he sign the new message with the title of a general?"

"He sure the hell did." Gilson reached down to touch the message, but didn't turn it over. He put both hands on his desk and leaned even closer to Steele. "Listen here, Steele, I have to know if this so-called general is serious. What's he up to? I mean if he—"

"Something more has obviously happened," interrupted Steele. "More than a threat this time."

"He's got Mr. Kane," said Rudd. "He sent a telegra—"

"Shut the hell up, Rudd," said Gilson. "I don't know anything about Steele here. You say he's a detective, but what makes you think he won't go to the other papers? They'd pay a lot for a story like this."

"He wouldn't do that," protested Rudd. "He's a . . . a detective."

"So detectives don't want to make a buck?" Gilson turned back to Steele, studying him.

Steele stared back, thinking about the implications of such a kidnapping. If Ramsey had somehow captured Edward Kane, the rich and powerful owner of many businesses in the West, including the Morning-Herald newspaper chain, then the general had taken a hostage that might well be significant enough to get the government's attention. Edward Kane wasn't merely a well-known San Francisco businessman; he was known throughout the country. He was even rumored to be considering a run for the U.S. Senate. What better hostage to put pressure on the federal government?

"All right, Steele," said Gilson. "Rudd here thinks we can trust you. But if we pay you to help us, I don't want you talking to any of the other papers. Or to anybody else. Agreed?"

"Of course," said Steele. "I never talk about my cases."

"I don't know if I'd call it a case," said Gilson, frowning. "I mean, this man may be bluffing. We don't know if he really has Kane."

"What did he say?"

Gilson picked up the telegraph message. "Only one line. 'I have Kane.'" He handed it to Steele. "It came in early this morning. What kind of man sends a one-line message like that? I mean, what the hell does he want?"

"What telegraph station was it sent from?"

"San Diego. A little town down south. Near the border."

"Have you checked with that telegraph office to learn who sent it?"

"Yeah, sure. They say some Mexican brought it in, already written out. In English. The guy dropped it off along with the money for the fee to send it. By the time they'd read it, the Mexican was already gone."

"You say you're not sure he has Kane. Does that mean you don't know where Mr. Kane is?"

Gilson shrugged. "He took his family down there for a little vacation. To take the baths. That's what I heard. Maybe he's still down there somewhere, enjoying his vacation."

"Have you tried to get in touch with him?"

"Of course. We wired our branch office in San Diego. They said he took off with his family in a rented carriage."

"When was that?"

"Two days ago."

"And they haven't heard from them since?"

"Well, no. But maybe they found those hot sulfur baths they were looking for. They might be staying out there."

"That would be something of a coincidence, wouldn't it?"

Gilson frowned. "Yeah, I guess so. So you think this Ramsey guy really does have them?"

"You should act on that assumption. Have you sent somebody out to look for them?"

"Of course, but nobody seems to know which way they went."

Steele paused for several seconds, thinking, then asked, "Was Kane's presence in that part of the state known? Was it advertised?"

"Sure. Everything Mr. Kane does these days is pretty well known. All the other papers report everything he does. So do we."

"That's my beat," said Rudd, perking up. "I try to keep him in the news."

"Rudd's job is to make him look good," said Gilson. "The other papers are not so kind. They seem to think a businessman shouldn't be getting into politics."

"The point is," said Steele, "it would have been easy for someone to find out he was going down there."

"Yeah, I guess so," said Gilson, looking downcast. "So what happens next? I suppose there'll be another message soon. With his demands."

Steele thought about that. Why *hadn't* Ramsey made any demands? He must be planning to ask for something in return for Kane's safe return, presumably something to do with the war-crimes trials. If so, why hadn't he stated his demands in the telegraph message? "Let me look at the original letter you got from him," said Steele, holding out his hand.

Gilson opened his top desk drawer and took the letter out. He handed it to Steele and got up to pace nervously back and forth behind his desk.

"No envelope?"

"Nope," said Gilson. "Just this one piece of paper."

Steele could see the handwriting was bold, as if the letter writer was bearing down hard. Before reading the letter, Steele studied the paper. It was thick, high quality bond. He held it up toward the window to look at the watermark. "It's from the Wheatman Mill, in Boston."

"So it came from back east," said Rudd.

"All paper comes from back east," said Steele, still examining the paper. "Or from London. There are no paper mills in the West as yet."

"Oh," said Rudd.

"It's stiff, unglazed paper, but notice that it is somewhat frayed along one edge."

"Does that matter?" asked Rudd.

"No, but what does matter is that the handwriting avoids the frayed edge. It means the fraying occurred before the paper was written on. The paper was carried on its side, probably one of a packet of papers carried in a bag. Or in a saddlebag."

"A traveling man," said Rudd.

"That's right. Ramsey probably carried a packet of this stationary with him all the way from Tennessee, possibly on a horse. He planned to do some writing so he brought ink and fine paper with him."

"Interesting," said Gilson. "But how is it going to help us find Mr. Kane?"

"It isn't, but it can help us to understand Ramsey. For one thing, it might indicate he had this whole thing planned before he headed west."

Gilson stopped pacing and threw up his hands. "So if he carries his fancy paper with him all the way from back east and writes out a real formal sounding letter, why doesn't he say what the hell he wants us to do."

Steele thought about that as he read the letter. It was exactly as Rudd had dictated it, a warning, and a threat to take hostages. If nothing else, Rudd was good at copying. The letter mentioned the war-crimes trials going on back east, but made no demands. Now Ramsey had his hostage, an important one. So why hadn't the telegraphic message demanded a trade of prisoners? Or a halt to the trials? Suddenly, Steele realized the implications. "He's going to do something else," he said, almost to himself.

Gilson stopped his pacing to look at Steele. "Something else?"

"Like what?" asked Rudd.

Steele looked from one to the other. "Something more dramatic, to show he's serious."

Gilson sat back down behind his desk. "What do you mean, serious? You don't think he'd hurt Mr. Kane?"

"I expect he will keep Kane alive," said Steele, handing the letter back to Gilson. "But when it comes to hostages, it's hard to predict what can happen. Do you remember Quantrill's band, the border raiders who fought on the Confederate side during the war?"

"Sure," said Gilson. "We published several stories about him and the trouble his gang has been causing ever since."

"Quantrill often took hostages. In sixty-four, as the end of the war neared, Quantrill raided a small town in Missouri. As they left, they took a young girl as a shield, but they left behind one of their gang, a boy who had been wounded. The town sent word they would begin to cut off the boy's fingers, one by one, until the gang brought back the girl. Quantrill sent back a reply that for each finger of the boy cut off they would receive two from the girl in return."

"Holy Christ," whispered Rudd. "What happened?"

"They went ahead and hung the boy. The girl was never seen again."

"Well, that was war," said Gilson. "But it's over now and this is Mr. Kane we're talking about, one of the most important people in the country. They wouldn't dare do anything like that to him."

Steele suppressed the urge to confront the man about his quick dismissal of the people who had suffered in the war, but he suspected that Gilson, like most everyone else, just wanted to forget such reminders of that dark period. "I agree it is unlikely that a rational mind would seriously hurt, or kill, such an important bargaining chip," said Steele. "Nevertheless, he is—"

"A bargaining chip?" said Gilson, jumping up again. "You think Mr. Kane is nothing more than a poker chip in this game?"

"I'm merely trying to think about how Ramsey would see it," said Steele calmly. "We can only hope the general's thoughts are still rational."

"Rational? How can you call that man rational? Taking hostages. Sending threats. And for what? The war is over and done with."

"Hostage taking and bargaining for their release was a common practice during the war. If he still sees himself at war, he will—"

"Wait a minute now, the war *is* over," interrupted Gilson. "Doesn't that madman know they lost?" He started to pace again.

"What should we do?" asked Rudd.

Steele watched Gilson pace, wishing the man would sit down and try to be a bit more calm. Finally he said, "It doesn't look as if we can do anything. We have no way to contact Ramsey."

"So we just wait?" said Rudd.

"I'd like to go to San Diego and ask some questions," said Steele. "Maybe somebody down there knows where the Kane family was heading."

Rudd turned to his boss. "What do you think, Mr. Gilson? Can I take Steele down there?"

Gilson looked at him for several seconds before sitting down and putting his face in his hands. "Damn, damn," he mumbled. He looked back up at Rudd. "All right, go ahead. Don't forget to fill out a travel voucher. But listen, Rudd, keep me informed whenever you get near a telegraph. I'll let you know if we hear anything more from this madman."

"Uh, so it's okay to hire Steele?" asked Rudd. "I mean should I get some money from the cashier?"

"What?" said Gilson. He was staring toward the window. "Right, yes. Get going. Go!"

Chapter 3

*A*fter agreeing to meet Rudd at the train station in one hour, Steele headed for the street vendor alley that had recently sprung up off of Washington Street. He found the man who sold war surplus uniforms by the bale to use as rags and asked him to dig out a fairly clean Confederate uniform in his size. The man was surprised, but did as he was told. "You gonna wear it?" he asked as he handed it over. "What are you , some kind of Rebel sympathizer?" Steele ignored the question. He paid for the uniform and hurried back to his office.

Once there, he went into the small sleeping room that adjoined his office and pulled his old army backpack out from under the bed. He quickly stuffed in some clothes and the Confederate uniform. Before closing the backpack, he carried it out to his office where he opened the bottom drawer of the file cabinet. He took out his multibladed folding knife and put his foot up on the drawer to carefully place the knife in its well-hidden pocket inside his left boot. Next, he took his small Remington revolver out of the cabinet and unwrapped it from its oiled rag. He took a moment to admire the well-designed little weapon, using the rag to wipe away a fingerprint before he put the gun into its special holster inside his right boot. He grabbed a box of shells for the Remington and tossed them into the backpack before closing it. He swung the pack over his shoulder, took one last look around the room, and left.

After going down the stairs to the street, he stopped to look up at his office window. He had the oddest feeling that he might never return to that building. He shook off the thought and continued on down the street.

The few pedestrians that were out on the street that early seemed fairly cheerful despite the chilly fog that still lay over the city. Steele realized he also felt cheerful, and more alive than he'd felt in a long time. It had been quite a while since he'd had the mix of apprehension and eagerness that came just before he headed into a dangerous situation. He had to admit he liked the feeling.

At the station, Steele waited next to the train's engine as it began to build up steam. When the engineer began clanging the bell and the conductor started shouting his last warning, Steele began to wonder if Rudd was going to make it. But just as the train began to move, Rudd came along the platform, trying to hurry, but barely able to drag his large suitcase. Steele ran to take it from him. He helped Rudd aboard and threw the large suitcase up to him before swinging up onto the steps of the moving train.

As they went up the aisle looking for seats, Rudd kept up a constant chatter about the lack of enough coaches and the poor design of the Union Pacific's passenger cars. When Steele had to help him get his big suitcase up into the overhead rack, Rudd was somewhat apologetic. "It's a little heavy, I know. I couldn't decide what clothes I would need down there so I just threw in a whole bunch of stuff."

Rudd wanted the aisle seat, "To keep an eye on things."

Steele took the window seat and settled in to watch the scenery pass by. The rolling grass hills were starting to dry out. The newspapers were already starting to talk about the danger of wildfires after the especially wet rainy winter.

Rudd took out his pipe and searched each of his overstuffed pockets before finding what he was looking for, a small pen knife. He began to scrape away inside the bowl of the charred pipe. Once he had finished the job, he tapped the pipe against the heel of his shoe to empty it onto the floor. Then he filled the pipe with tobacco and lit it before turning to Steele. "Well, what do you think? Will this Ramsey guy really kill Mr. Kane? I mean, what if those politicians back east aren't willing to trade any of those war-crimes Confederates for Mr. Kane?"

"Ramsey hasn't asked for a trade."

"Yeah, I guess that's true, but what else can he want?"

"If he wants an exchange of hostages, he would have said so in his telegraph message. Being the commandant of a prisoner-of-war camp, he must have participated in prisoner exchanges. Therefore, we must assume he knows the procedure."

"You make it sound like there are formal rules."

"During the war, there were rules. They became formalized over time. You see, hostage taking was a common tactic throughout the war. Both sides used it. It wasn't widely publicized because neither side wanted to admit they were doing it. Usually, they took army officers or politicians as hostages, but near the end of the war, Southern civilians were also taken as hostages to protect the Union forces as they marched through the South."

"I remember reading something about hostages in the war," said Rudd. "Didn't some mother write to President Lincoln about her son who had been taken? Wasn't he going to be hung? As I remember, the press played it up as a sad case, real unfair."

"That's right," said Steele. "The letter was from a mother whose son was a low-ranking officer on a captured Confederate privateer ship. The North considered all hands on such ships to be pirates and therefore subject to execution. When the Union announced that all members of the crew would be hung, including the junior officers, the South retaliated by going into Richmond's Castle Thunder Prison and removing Union prisoners of the same approximate age and rank as the captured privateers. They said if any of the ship's crew were executed by the North, they would execute the Union prisoners."

"Did they?"

"Yes. All of the ship's officers were hung. And of course the South responded in kind."

"They hung Union prisoners of war?"

"They did. It started a practice of hostage taking and revenge executions that became commonplace throughout the rest of the war. Both Lincoln and Jefferson Davis approved it as a necessary evil of war."

Rudd shook his head. "Terrible. And you think this General Ramsey was involved in that?"

"Apparently he still is."

As the train steamed southward along the west side of the bay, Rudd pointed out the window. "Good thing we aren't going to Sacramento. We'd have to go all the way around the bay. Union

Pacific's too cheap to build a bridge. They're holding out until the state does it for them."

He then launched into a long description of the current level of government graft and corruption, but Steele was only half listening. He was more interested in the many tall sailing ships that were anchored in the bay waiting to unload their cargo. The ships reminded him of the day he and Stacy had sailed from the New York harbor, heading for England. Once they arrived in London, it hadn't taken Stacy long to get involved in the British fight for women's rights, leaving him with little to do. For months, he had spent his days in the local libraries, reading about medicine, advances in armaments, and the many new scientific discoveries that were being made on the Continent. When he'd told Stacy he was going back to America, she at first tried to talk him into staying. But eventually she had agreed that he should get back to his work. She said she would come home as soon as she could, but now, after six months, she still hadn't returned and her letters mainly talked about "the movement," as many women were now calling it. She said they were making such great progress she couldn't leave yet.

"Hey," said Rudd, "did you hear anything I was saying?"

"Sorry, I was thinking about Stacy."

"Oh, have you heard from her? When is she coming back?"

"Soon, she says."

Rudd looked doubtful. "That's what she always says. I say a woman should be with her man."

"She has her work there."

"And that's what you always say. Well, I say it's time to eat. We had to hurry so fast to catch this train, I didn't get any breakfast. Let's hike up to the food car." He stood up.

"You go ahead. I'm enjoying the scenery."

Rudd leaned down to look out the window. "Not much scenery out there, I'd say. And as soon as we get past the bay, there's gonna be even less. Nothing but dry grass and maybe a few cows. But suit yourself, I'll be back soon."

When Rudd didn't return for some time, Steele suspected he'd found a better conversationalist in the food car. Grateful for the peace and quiet, Steele gazed out the window, enjoying the gradual changes in scenery as the train rolled on southward. The trees along the bay soon gave way to the openness of grasslands and rolling hills. Occasionally there was a small farm, marked off by a row of young trees. He thought about how different it was from the thickly-wooded hill country of Tennessee where he'd spent most of the war years working in the Union field hospital. Steele remembered a wounded soldier who had come into the hospital talking about a big battle in the woods down near Chattanooga. While Steele dressed his wound, the soldier had described cannon fire so intense the woods had caught fire. He was sure some of his friends had been pinned down by the Confederates in those woods and burned to death. Could General Ramsey have been the commander on the Confederate forces in that battle?

Steele's thoughts were interrupted when Rudd returned with some dried fruit, bread, and cow cheese. "Try some of this cheese," he said. "It's good. They've got better food on this train than they've got in some restaurants."

Steele accepted some of the food and ate it as he continued to stare out the window.

Between mouthfuls, Rudd resumed his nonstop talking, jumping rapidly from one topic to another, starting with the excesses of the railroads, and then moving on to the corruption and ineptness of the Washington politicians.

Steele assumed Rudd was going to talk all the way to San Diego, but as soon as he finished his meal, Rudd wiped his mouth and his mustache with a large white handkerchief and sat back with a big sigh. Soon, he was asleep and snoring.

Steele took out his journal to make a few notes about the case. There was one thing about the threatening telegraph message that puzzled him: Ramsey's first letter had been a carefully worded explanation of his intentions. Everything about the letter indicated the writer was a careful man. But the second message was both abrupt and vague. And it was signed as General Ramsey. Why would he reveal that he was a general in the second message, but not in the first one? The message's one line about having Kane seemed designed more to create fear than to convey information. Why such a dramatic change in tactics? Steele would have expected a seasoned military officer to exert more control, to tell the recipients how they were expected to react. He turned the page of his journal and began to write.

> *General Ramsey is acting somewhat unpredictably. He threatened to take hostages, probably because he considers the men being tried in the war-crimes tribunal to be hostages of the North. That would imply that he wants to trade Kane for one or more of them. But he sent his letter to a newspaper, not to the tribunal. That may mean he also wants publicity. But he didn't ask the newspaper to publish his letter. So what does he want?*

Steele stopped writing to look out the window. They were passing through a very small town. It had only a church and a tiny train depot to accompany its five homes. Two young boys on horseback waved as the train sped through.

He looked back at the words he had written and added one more note.

> *Ramsey wants something more than a hostage trade.*

Next, he took out his drawing pad to draw a likeness of what he thought General Ramsey might look like. He decided the man would probably be tall, with a narrow, angular face. He would, of course, have a full beard, as almost all Confederate officers did. He gave him the neatly trimmed gray beard of Robert E. Lee. Ramsey's letter had shown him to be a thoughtful man, but his war record showed him to be guided by an unyielding ideology. Steele gave him the high forehead of General Albert Sidney Johnston, another ideologist.

Steele completed the drawing, except for the area around the eyes. The eyes were always the hardest. When he had been a student in Paris, his art teacher had told him that the eyes were the window into a person's soul. That teacher always said, "Get the eyes right, and the portrait will be right." But Steele couldn't decide how to portray Ramsey's eyes. He suspected the General would have angry eyes, eyes that searched for a man's weakness. But there would be something else in those eyes, something that truly characterized him. He decided to leave that part of the drawing unfinished. He looked at the hollow space where the eyes should have been. Would he ever meet the man? If so, he would finish the drawing then.

To pass the time, he began to draw some of the other passengers on the train: first an old man who was sleeping in one of the seats across the aisle, his head leaning against the window, then a young girl two seats ahead who kept popping up to look back at him. As he drew, he smiled at her and made faces to keep her looking at him. Unfortunately, the mother eventually noticed what was going on and made her sit down.

After several hours, Rudd woke up yawning and stretching. He glanced over toward Steele. "Hey, that's pretty good," he said, pointing at the drawing. "Who is that, your little sister?"

"I don't have a sister," said Steele. He pointed toward the little girl who was again peering over the top of her seat at them.

Rudd smiled and waved at her which caused the little girl to quickly duck down again.

He turned to Steele. "I'm hungry again. Shall we head for the food car?"

Steele shook his head. "You go ahead."

"Suit yourself." Rudd went off down the aisle mumbling to himself about skinny people never knowing when it was time to eat.

Steele turned back to the window, enjoying the fact that the tracks passed close to the Pacific Ocean. It was a crisp, clear day with almost no clouds and he could see a few small islands far out to sea. A few people sat on the sandy beach, watching the waves come in. It seemed very peaceful. But then, why shouldn't it be? The people of California had been little affected by the war. The state's role had been mainly support, providing gold and silver ore, although it had sent some troops to the Arizona Territory to help keep the war from spreading west out of Texas. Steele took out his journal and drew the rough outlines of California and Arizona. Then he drew a straight line across the bottom to indicate the Mexican border. He knew the border was quite long, without any rivers or other natural boundaries to mark it. He looked at that line. The telegraph message had come from San Diego, a small town near that border. Could Ramsey be hiding on the other side of that imaginary line?

Rudd came back just as the train slowly rolled into the San Diego station. Before the train had even stopped, Rudd had grabbed his suitcase and was headed for the exit. Steele put away his drawing pad and grabbed his backpack to follow.

"They told me the newspaper office was right down the street from the station," said Rudd over his shoulder. "If you can call what they have here streets. Nothing but dirt paths."

Steele saw that the town was laid out around an old Spanish mission. The mission was in bad shape and mostly abandoned, although one outbuilding seemed to still be in use.

As they walked past it, Rudd pointed and commented: "Looks like that old mission has been here for a hundred years. One end of it is falling down."

"Actually, it isn't quite one hundred years old," said Steele. "The first mission was built in 1769, but it was attacked and burned by Indians. This is the new mission, built in 1776."

Rudd looked at him, frowning. "You memorize all that stuff? Your head must be filled with those kinds of facts and figures."

"I've read several books about the history of the Spanish missions. It's interesting reading."

"Okay," said Rudd, "now I know this mission was built in 1776. Hey, that was the same year the Declaration of Independence was signed. I bet those Spanish missionaries who were building this place didn't know about what was going on back there in Philadelphia and how it would affect them later."

"Actually, they were well aware of the Revolutionary War and it's implications. Spain was Britain's enemy at that time so they were very supportive of the American patriots who were fighting the British. But later they became very concerned when the Americans began to move west toward Spanish territory. When they heard about the Lewis and Clark expedition to explore the West, the Spanish sent an armed force to try to intercept them. Luckily, they never found them."

"More memorized facts," mumbled Rudd. He fanned his hand in front of his face to wave away the dust kicked up by passing horses. "Looks like they don't get much rain here. But it's warm isn't it?" He smiled and took off his hat to glance up at the sun. "I like it better warm." He put his hat back on. "Long as it doesn't get too hot."

They soon found the newspaper office. It was one of only a handful of businesses in the small town.

Rudd led the way into the office and went straight to the messenger's station in the corner of the large room "Got anything for me? I'm John Rudd."

"You're supposed to see Bailey," said the young man, pointing. "First room on the left. He said to send you in as soon as you got here."

At the office, Rudd tapped politely on the sill of the open door. "Are you Bailey?"

A heavy-set man with watery eyes looked up. "That's me, editor and office manager. You Rudd?"

"Yeah. The boy said to see you."

"You'd better put your bags down and listen. No time for introductions or any of the other niceties. We got trouble."

"Trouble?" asked Steele.

"You the detective?" said Bailey, looking Steele over.

"That's right," said Rudd. "His name is Steele. He's working for us. For the paper I mean."

"All right then, sit down and listen." He rubbed his temples as he spoke. "Your General Ramsey *has* got Mr. Kane. Kane's wife and daughter just got brought in. Some rancher picked 'em up out by Mesa City, a little town a ways east of here. Seems they kidnapped Mr. Kane and dumped Mrs. Kane and her daughter way out in the desert so it would take 'em a long time to hike back to civilization."

"Are they hurt?" asked Rudd.

"No, they're fine. They're at the hotel, getting some rest."

"So they took Kane, but let his wife and daughter go," said Steele. "Interesting."

"Why do you say that? They're not going to kidnap women, are they?"

"Near the end of the war, both sides held women and even children as hostages. It was effective because it created more public outcry than male hostages."

"Effective?" said Bailey, frowning. "You make it sound like clever strategy."

Steele turned to Rudd. "We need to talk to them. Let's go."

"I expect they'll be pretty tired out," said Rudd. "Maybe we should let them rest for a bit. In the meantime, we could get something to eat."

"I'm sure they are tired. But Mrs. Kane will understand we're trying to help get her husband back as soon as possible."

Bailey told them how to find the hotel and on the way, Steele asked, "Do you know Mrs. Kane? Is she a woman of strong constitution?"

Rudd's eyes widened. "What are you thinking? That they're going to kill Mr. Kane?"

"As I said to your boss back in San Francisco, it seems unlikely that they would kill such an important man. As long as they hold him, they have bargaining power. What I am suggesting is that this may go on for some time. It will be hard on his wife."

"Yeah," agreed Rudd. "And his daughter too. Cute little girl, last time I saw her."

At the hotel, Steele asked for Mrs. Kane's room number. He was told they were in the hotel's finest suite, at the end of the hall. Steele led the way there and knocked on the door. A woman's voice told them to come in.

Steele opened the door and looked in and saw a prim, dark-haired woman in a blue and white dress sitting in a chair in front of the window, looking out.

"Excuse me, Mrs. Kane?" said Rudd.

The woman turned slowly. She looked tired. "Yes?"

Rudd stepped forward and took off his hat. "I'm John Rudd, Mrs. Kane. Do you remember me? I work at the San Francisco office."

She looked a bit confused. "San Francisco? I'm afraid I don't remember you."

Steele stepped forward and offered his hand. "Mrs. Kane, my name is Drew Steele. I'm sorry to hear what happened to you. Would you mind if I asked you a few questions about it?"

She turned to Rudd, unsure.

"The newspaper hired Steele here to help get your husband back," said Rudd. "He's a detective."

"A detective?" she said, turning back to Steele. "A police detective?"

"No, I'm a private investigator. So far, the newspaper has decided not to bring in the police. For your husband's safety."

"We'll get him back," said Rudd. "Don't you worry."

She nodded and turned to Steele. "What kind of questions?"

Steele pulled up a chair next to her. "They said your husband was kidnapped out in the desert. Can you tell me where it happened?"

"I'm not sure where it was, exactly. We went for a carriage ride in the afternoon, my husband, my daughter, and I. We were somewhere out in the desert when a group of men came up from behind us on horses."

"Terrible," said Rudd. "It must have been very frightening. Why, if I would have been there, I'd have—"

Steele silenced him with a raised hand. "Mrs. Kane, can you tell me which direction they took him."

"It was south. My daughter commented on that. They took us off the main road, up into the hills, then they took my husband away in our carriage and left us there."

"Terrible," said Rudd. "Just terrible. To leave a woman and child alone out in that desert. Unthinkable."

Steele gave him another look to shut him up and took out his notebook. "Just a few more questions."

"Uh, I think I'll go check the telegraph office," said Rudd. "I'd better send a message to Gilson to tell him we're here."

After Rudd had left, Steele asked, "How many men were in the group that took your husband?"

Mrs. Kane looked toward the ceiling, remembering. "Uh, I don't know for sure. Maybe four or five."

"Were they Americans? Mexicans?"

"I'm pretty sure there was only one American. The others looked like Mexicans to me. My daughter was sure they were, but they all had cloths over the lower part of their faces. One of the men had evil eyes. He kept looking at my daughter."

"Did the American speak?"

"Yes, he was the one giving the orders. He was very . . . harsh. He told one of his men to take hold of our horse, to lead it. We went very fast on a rutted dirt road. I was afraid the carriage was going to turn over at any minute, but my husband was very brave. He kept telling us not to be afraid."

"Did the man have a southern accent?"

"Yes, now that you mention it, I think he did. Do you think they were Southerners? Mr. Bailey suggested they might be former soldiers who won't admit they lost the war."

"Could you tell how old he was, the man with the Southern accent?"

"Oh, not very old. A young man, I think. But the others did what he said. One of the Mexican-looking men acted as if he was going to strike my daughter when she refused to get out of the carriage, but the leader told the man to get away from her."

"And then they rode off with your husband?"

"Yes. They tied his hands and they drove the carriage away with him in it. That was the last we saw of them."

Steele noted the sequence of events in his notebook. "Did they give you any instructions about what to say when you got back?"

"No, not a word. They just left us there. We starting walking back to town, but it got dark. I thought I heard some dogs howling, but my daughter said it was coyotes. It frightened me, but she said they wouldn't hurt us."

Steele was surprised to hear the men hadn't given Mrs. Kane any instructions. Why no threats or demands? Apparently they wanted to keep everyone waiting and wondering.

Just then Rudd returned to the room, followed by an attractive young woman with blonde hair. She went immediately to Mrs. Kane's side.

Steele stood up.

"This here is Mr. Kane's daughter, Helen," said Rudd, smiling broadly. "It's been quite a few years since I last saw her. But she's still just as pretty as ever."

The girl stepped forward to firmly shake Steele's hand. She was not smiling and she looked directly into his eyes.

Steele tried not to show any reaction to such an unusually aggressive action by a young woman. He shook her hand firmly, as he would a man's.

"Rudd here tells me you're the detective Gilson hired," she said. "I think they should have at least checked with my mother before doing that." The girl was scrutinizing him closely, still staring directly at Steele.

It was clear that the girl was challenging him, and Steele wondered why. Rudd was right about one thing: she was very pretty, and obviously no longer the cute little girl Rudd had described. She was thin and seemed to be in good physical condition. She would stand out on any street in America, not only because of her beauty, but also because she was dressed like a man, wearing a man's white shirt and tight fitting blue cotton pants, like the ones the miners wore up at the Comstock. But what was most noticeable about her was her startling blue-green eyes. They never strayed from Steele's face, as if she was critically evaluating him

Finally, she turned away to confront Rudd. "You'd of thought that with my father's life in the balance they could have at least found somebody with more . . . experience."

"Oh no, you're wrong about that, Miss Kane," said Rudd. "Steele here has a great deal of experience. In the detective business, I mean. He was even in the war, as you can see." Rudd touched his own cheek.

The girl turned back to Steele. "Oh, that. I thought it might be a shaving scar."

Steele was surprised at her sarcastic comment. It was yet another suggestion that she considered him too young to be an experienced detective. Such aggression was especially surprising for a woman who was still quite young herself. He judged her to be only about twenty, possibly even younger.

"Now, Helen," said Mrs. Kane. "Mr. Steele is only trying to help us. He's been asking me some questions. Maybe you can help me answer them."

"Is that right?" said Helen, frowning. "What does *Mister* Steele want to know?"

"I was just asking your mother about the men who kidnapped your father. She tells me one of them had a Southern accent."

"Of course he had an Southern accent," she said. "They were Rebels weren't they?"

"But dear," said Mrs. Kane. "How can we be so sure?"

"Why else would they be doing this? We all know their type. Father's newspaper has been published articles about their kind, Confederate officers who talk like the war is still going on. Giving speeches. Making trouble. They should all be rounded up and slapped into prison. Or hung. That would take care of the problem once and for all."

"The officers of the Confederacy were soldiers," said Steele, "carrying out their duty. They felt their cause was just."

"Their cause. That's what they all say." She stepped close to Steele and fixed him with her now almost-green eyes. "Just following orders? Well, which one of them gave the order to kill my brother at Ellisville? Not one man in his unit was allowed to surrender. Not one survivor. That's what your fine Southern gentlemen officers did."

Steele was taken back by her ferocity, but if that battle had resulted in the death of her brother, her anger was understandable. Steele had read about that incident and knew the details. "Your brother was with Hillman's rangers?" he said softly.

"That's right."

"I'm sorry. Let me explain what happened there. Hillman's unit had been ordered to move across a swampy area near the lake. The Anna Valley was foggy that morning. The large force of Confederates were taking up positions around the lake and didn't see your brother's unit until they were practically on top of them. I'm afraid your brother died in one of the many tragic accidents of warfare."

"Tragic accident?" said Helen heatedly. "You're wrong. It couldn't have happened that way. My brother was a hero."

"Maybe we should let bygones be bygones," said Rudd stepping between them. "We should focus on getting your father back."

"I'm sure your brother was a hero," said Steele, leaning around Rudd. "They all were. But Rudd is right, our task now is to get your father back."

Helen jabbed Rudd in the chest with her finger. "All right, let me ask you this. Does your *mister* detective have a plan to get my father back? Yes or no? If he does, I want you to ask him just exactly how he plans to do it."

Before Rudd could answer, there was a loud knock at the door. Rudd turned away from the girl to hurry toward the door, but before he got there, it opened, and Bailey rushed in, excited and out of breath. He was waving a piece of paper. "We got another note." He stopped to catch his breath. "And this time it was pinned to the chest of a hung Negro soldier. It says Kane is next."

Chapter 4

*A*fter Bailey sat down for a moment to calm himself, he began to explain. "Some rancher found the hung guy down by the border. A black pony soldier. Young guy. Been dead for a while. He had this note pinned to his chest. It starts with that line, 'Kane is next.' They underlined the word *next* twice." He turned the note so they could all see the underlining. "Then it tells us what we have to do to get him back." He looked at Mrs. Kane. "I'm sorry, ma'am. But it says they want to negotiate. That's hopeful, at least." He looked at Steele. "Isn't it?"

At first, no one in the room spoke. Mrs. Kane, leaned against her daughter and the girl began stroking her mother's hair. "At least it means he's still alive," she whispered.

"May I see the note?" said Steele.

Bailey handed it to him. It only took one glance to see that the note was very different from the San Francisco letter.

> *You will be sorry if you do not do exactly what we tell you. Now you know we mean what we say. You have been warned. If you do not do what we say Kane will suffer for it.*

It had obviously been written by a different person. The first letter the newspaper received had been carefully written in a large bold hand. This one was more of a scrawl. Also, the tone of the first letter had been calm and serious, as if written by a disciplined man. The note he held in his hands contained vague threats and warnings, and it had several strikeouts indicating that it had been written hastily without prior drafts. He read on and then looked at Mrs. Kane. "It says a hostage negotiator is to come alone to the exact spot where Kane was taken. It says, no family, no law, and nobody associated with the military."

"Let me see it," said Rudd, taking the note out of Steele's hands. "Hey, the handwriting looks different."

"It is different," agreed Steele. "But the paper is the same, from the same packet. Notice the identical fraying along the edge."

Rudd scratched his head. "The same paper, but somebody else did the writing? What does that mean?" He handed the note back to Steele.

"I'm not sure," said Steele. He reread the note. The idea of two different writers, both signing as General Ramsey, didn't make sense. There was not even a mention of the war-crimes tribunal. "Notice the signature," he said, holding up the note for the others to see. "General Ramsey."

"What does that mean?" asked Helen. "What are you talking about?"

"The first letter was signed as C. J Ramsey."

"Maybe something happened to Ramsey," suggested Rudd. "Maybe he got hurt or something."

"It's possible General Ramsey has become incapacitated and is unable to write," said Steele, "but the tone of the note sounds as if the writer was acting on his own, not simply writing what Ramsey dictated."

Helen frowned. "Are you saying there are two different men sending us letters? Why would they do that?"

"I'm afraid we won't know that until we meet with them."

Helen turned to Bailey. "Well, why are you standing here? Get going."

Bailey looked startled. "Me?"

"Yes, you. He's your boss. You owe him that much at least."

"But I wouldn't know what to do," protested Bailey. "I don't know how to negotiate."

Steele could see that the man was afraid. A fearful negotiator would not be very effective. "I'll go," he said.

The others turned to him. "You?" said Helen. "I don't think so. Bailey will do it. It's his job."

"What my daughter means," said Mrs. Kane quickly, "is only that Mr. Bailey has more . . .experience in such matters."

"Me?" said Bailey. "I have no experience at all in this kind of thing. They told me Steele was in the war, and he knows all about this Ramsey guy."

"The message says they want someone who wasn't in the war," said Helen.

"It says someone not associated with the military," said Steele. "I worked in an Army hospital, but only as a volunteer."

"That's right," said Bailey. "Steele knows these types. Me, what do I know about soldiers and such? During the war I was out here in California, the whole time."

"If I may suggest something," said Rudd loudly. When everyone turned to look at him, he said, "This is why we hired Steele. Because he knows about these things. Why just yesterday he was telling me all about hostage taking, about how it was a common tactic all through the war."

"Fine," said Helen. "Then let him go. If nobody else around here is man enough to do it, let the detective go. After all, that's what we're paying him for."

"I'm ready to go right now." Steele turned to Mrs. Kane. "Do you think you can draw me a map of where those men intercepted you?"

"Oh my," said Mrs. Kane, "I'm not sure I know where it was. My husband was driving the carriage and I'm not very good with directions."

"I can find it," said Helen. "I'll show you."

"But dear," said her mother. "You haven't even slept. You must be very tired."

"I'm not tired. Father's life may depend on this."

"Perhaps you should just draw me a map," suggested Steele.

"No. You'd get completely lost out there in the desert. I'm taking you."

"The message said no family," Steele reminded her.

"I know that, don't I? But I can at least get you on the right road. No law against that, is there?"

Steele turned to Rudd. "Can I borrow your handkerchief?"

"You want my handkerchief?"

"During the war, the hostage negotiator came in under the white flag of truce."

"Oh, yeah. I've got it right here," said Rudd, pulling it out of his back pocket. He glanced at it before folding it up carefully. "It's a little . . . soiled. You want me to go get a clean one?"

"This will do."

Helen gave her mother a hug and led the way out to the street.

Bailey hurried off to arrange for a carriage.

"I'll go get my suitcase," said Rudd.

"Why do you need your suitcase?" asked Helen. "You're not going."

"Oh yes I am," insisted Rudd. "This is my story and I'm going wherever Steele goes. My boss told me. I'm supposed to represent the newspaper."

"You can wait for us here," said Steele. "Stay near the telegraph office, in case any more information comes in."

Rudd looked disappointed. "Well, if you say so. But make sure you remember everything that happens so I can put it in my story." He hurried up the street toward the newspaper office.

"If Steele says it, Rudd does it," muttered Helen under her breath.

Soon, Bailey returned with a one-horse carriage drawn by a strong-looking gelding. Helen immediately climbed onto the seat and untied the reins before turning to look at Steele. "Well, are we going or not?"

Before Steele could climb up beside her, Rudd came running back up the street. "I brought you some food," he yelled. "And something to drink." He held up a large basket.

"I already put in two canteens," said Bailey.

"Yeah, but I got beer," said Rudd. "It'll get mighty hot out there." He opened the lid of the basket to show Helen the large variety of foods he had purchased.

"I guess we won't go hungry," she said.

"That's right," said Rudd. "Better to have too much than not enough, I always say."

Steele helped Rudd load the food and the beer into the back of the carriage. Rudd put a hand on Steele's shoulder. "You take care of yourself out there."

"I will." He shook Rudd's hand.

"And keep an eye on that girl," Rudd whispered. "She's mighty pretty, but she's a bit . . . headstrong."

As soon as Steele climbed up on the seat next to Helen, she cracked the whip and the big black gelding took off fast down the street sending pedestrians scurrying for their lives.

Rudd yelled after them, "Hey, be careful." He shouted something else, but they were already too far away to hear it.

As they quickly picked up speed, it was clear to Steele that Helen did not plan for him to be in charge of any aspect of the trip. No matter, he thought, once they arrived in Mesa City he could rid himself of the troublesome girl and go to meet the kidnappers alone. He wished he could have gone without her. She was too unpredictable. She might try to get involved, risking not only her own life, but his.

Helen pushed the horse even faster. There were several near misses with other oncoming carriages and once they were beyond the town limits, she used the whip even more. Soon, the road began to climb. Helen continued to hurry the horse, mindless of the steep grade.

Steele could see that the horse was growing exhausted. "Slow down," he said. "You're going to wear the poor animal out."

She ignored him and snapped the reins over the horse's back. When the road grew even steeper, the horse began to falter. Finally, they made it over the top, but as they went through a low-lying sandy area the horse slowed and came to a stop. He would not move, no matter how much Helen used the whip.

"You pushed him too hard," said Steele. "Now we'll have to stop and rest him."

"I knew you'd want to rest sooner or later. I knew you weren't man enough for this job." She again struck the horse with the whip. In reaction to the pain, the horse took a few steps forward and then stopped again.

Steele realized he had to act or they would never get where they were going. He reached over and took the reins away from her.

She slapped at his hands and tried to take them back, but Steele calmly tied them off and stepped down. She spat curses at him for several seconds, but then suddenly stopped, scowling. "All right. I'll go on by myself." She began to untie the reins.

Steele quickly got both hands around her waist and lifted her out of the carriage. "The horse needs rest," he said, looking into her angry eyes, "even if you don't."

She pushed his hands away and struck at his chest. "How dare you put your hands on me, you . . . you nobody. I'm the daughter of one of the most important men in this state, one of the most important men in the country. How dare you touch me?"

"We are going to rest the horse. Stay out of the carriage." He took hold of the horse's bridle and led it through the sandy area, slowly at first, but soon taking up a steady jog, encouraging the horse with gentle whispers.

Helen hurried to catch up. "Do you think we're going to walk all the way with this stupid animal? Its job is to take us out there, to save my father. You should do your job and let the horse do his."

Steele didn't reply. He kept on moving, murmuring to the horse to calm it. He could only hope that if he jogged along with the horse for a while, without any weight in the carriage, it would recover.

Helen walked along behind, muttering to herself.

After a while Steele spotted a grove of thick-trunked palm trees a short distance to the north. He led the horse toward the trees, hoping they were a sign of water. When he arrived, he discovered a tiny pond. The water was only a few inches deep, but it looked drinkable. To be sure, he scooped up a handful and tasted it. It was slightly warm and smelled of sulfur. He held the horse back while he took several more small drinks. He decided that it didn't taste all that bad, if you could ignore the smell. He released the horse and let it drink. He sat down in the shade of a palm tree to wait for Helen.

She soon arrived, red-faced and out of breath. She stood above him, her hands on her hips. "You might of let me know you were going to turn this way. I could have gotten lost out there."

"I was keeping an eye on you," said Steele quietly, "to make sure you weren't falling too far behind."

"It's not my fault," she complained, sitting down and taking off her shoes to inspect her feet. "It's these damn shoes. I've got blisters."

Steele smiled. "Those shoes *are* quite fashionable."

"Oh very clever. I know what you're implying. How was I supposed to know we were going to walk all the way?"

"If you hadn't driven the horse so hard, we wouldn't have to walk."

"Right, right, blame it on me. If you would have made sure Bailey got us a better horse we wouldn't be sitting here while my father is still in the hands of that madman."

"Let's give the horse a few more minutes and I think he'll be ready to go on."

She pushed her hair behind her ears with both hands and looked up at the sun.

Steele watched her, thinking how pretty her face would be if she would just relax a little. But he understood that she was worried about her father; apparently it was just her nature to react to that worry with anger.

She glanced his way. "What are you looking at?"

"Are you hot?" said Steele gently.

"Of course I'm hot," she said, looking away.

"Try soaking your shirt in the water before we start again."

She didn't reply so Steele got up and took off his shirt. He didn't glance her way, but he knew she was watching him. He pushed his shirt under the surface of the water and left it there while he went to check the horse's harness.

"How did you get that scar on your back?" she asked.

He looked back over his shoulder at her. Her face wasn't so red as before and she at least seemed to be showing a little interest in something besides her feet. "The war."

"The same time as you got that one on your cheek?"

He tightened the belly strap under the horse. "No, earlier in the war."

"The Rebels shot you in the back?"

"That's right."

"Probably shot you while you were running away."

"Yes, I was running away."

"Figures." There was a long silence before she asked, "Did it hurt?"

He came back to sit down near her. "Are you asking if it hurts to get shot?"

She shrugged and broke off a bit of grass at the stem. She put it in the corner of her mouth and looked at the ground. "I was just making conversation."

Steele realized he should have been more responsive to her legitimate question. She was chewing on the piece of grass, seemingly lost in thought. "It doesn't hurt as bad as you might think. It's fear that causes the worst pain, the fear of dying."

She looked up at him. "You thought you were going to die?"

He held her gaze. "Many times."

"You got shot many times?"

"No, but there are times when you think you are sure to be shot. Or hit by artillery shells. Sometimes things happen that make you think . . . your time is up."

"And you felt like that, sometimes?"

"Yes."

She looked down and didn't say anything for a while. Then she turned back to look at him for a long time, as if she was studying him. "What's your first name?"

"Drew."

"All right, Drew. If you were weren't a soldier, what were you doing there?"

Steele looked away. "That's always a hard question to answer. I was a student, studying in Europe, and everybody at my school was fascinated by the news of war in far away America."

"You were educated in Europe?"

"My mother's idea."

"They sent you all the way to Europe? To where? Paris?"

"My family was living in London at the time. I went to a school in Paris for a while, and then Rome."

She looked away. "So many places. Paris. Rome." Then she turned back to confront him. "I could have been educated in Paris too, if I wanted." She took the stalk of grass out of her mouth and pointed it at him. "So, if you are such a fine gentleman, educated on the continent, how come you're just a detective?"

"Just?"

"You know what I mean. If you got such a fancy European education, why are you risking your life doing this kind of thing?"

Steele thought about how to answer that question. Why indeed? How do you explain the allure of adventure and risk? Finally, he said, "What would you have me do?"

"If you really were educated in Europe, I'm sure my father could find you a good job. He owns plenty of other businesses besides the newspaper."

"I like what I'm doing. And I'm good at it."

She frowned. "That's not a real answer. You just don't want to tell me. You probably think you're better than me, just because I'm a girl."

Steele shook his head. "No, I—"

"Don't shake your head at me. I know you continental types. Well, I'll have you know I was educated in the best schools of the East, a lot of them."

Steele tried to keep from smiling.

"You can smile if you want to, mister silent detective. But you're not the only one who knows things. I'm smart too."

"I'm sure you are. If I said anything to imply—"

"I only dropped out of those stupid eastern schools because they thought the most important thing for a young girl to learn was how to be a lady. It was stupid and I told them so. What difference did it make what sex I was?" She looked at him, waiting, as if she expected him to answer her question.

Steele tried to think how to respond. Finally, he said, "There are some differences between the sexes but it needn't—"

"Just what I would expect you to say. You men all think alike."

"I don't think like that."

"Well, anyhow . . ." She didn't finish her thought. She stared at him, as if she was trying to figure something out. Finally, she turned away.

Steele remained silent and broke off a stem of grass to chew on, just as she had. They both sat there, chewing on their grass in silence until she said, "So you left your fancy school in Europe to come here. To see the war."

"That's right."

She hesitated and then said softly, "I can understand that."

He looked at her. "Can you? Most people can't."

"Well, I can," she said firmly.

He wondered if she really could. He assumed she meant that she understood a yearning for adventure, but for most people war was not an adventure, once they got a real taste of it. Even grown men tried to get out of harm's way, if they could. It was not logical to stay near danger when you didn't have to. So why had he continued to follow the battles, even after being wounded? He had wondered about it so many times he had given up trying to find a logical answer.

"What are you thinking about? Are you remembering the war?"

"Yes, I still think about it. Quite a lot, actually."

"And that's why you study it? The war I mean. Mr. Rudd told me you study about the war all the time."

He stood up. "We'd better get going." He moved to the water to fish out his shirt. Without wringing it out, he slipped it over his head. Even though the water in the tiny pool had been a little warm, the shirt felt cold against his skin. It sent a slight chill down his back, but he knew he would be grateful for the cooling once they were out in the hot sun again.

Helen stood up and dusted off the back of her pants. Steele watched her, noting her fine figure. And now that she was being more friendly he could begin to wonder if there might be some possibility that they would get to know each other better, after her father was safe. But he quickly pushed away the thought. Time enough for that later.

She turned to smile at him. "I'm ready."

"I still think you would be cooler if you soaked your shirt in the water, as I did."

"All right," she said with a shy smile. "But I don't exactly have anything . . . on under it. You'll have to look away."

Steele went to inspect the horse's harness again, even though he had just done it a few minutes before. He waited there patiently, but soon began to wonder why she was taking so long.

"I'm ready now," she said, very close behind him.

He turned to look at her and saw immediately that the water had made her lightweight white shirt nearly transparent. He couldn't help glancing down at the fine fullness of her breasts and the obvious outline of her darker nipples. He quickly looked away.

"You looked," she said, frowning.

"I assumed you were dressed."

"I am dressed, but the water made my shirt . . . so you can see through it."

Steele was still turned away from her. "Yes, I noticed," he said, smiling to himself.

"A gentleman wouldn't have looked." Her voice seemed a bit challenging, but not as angry as before.

He turned back to her and she quickly folded her arms in front of herself. "That's true," he said, looking into her eyes. "I shouldn't have looked."

She dropped her arms to her side, but he forced himself to keep his gaze on her eyes. They were more blue than green out there in the desert and he made himself concentrate on that fact.

"All right," she said with a shrug. "We'd better go."

Now what was that in her voice? wondered Steele. Was it disappointment? Had she expected him to try something? To take her in his arms? Not likely with her father's kidnappers waiting ahead. Maybe it was just some kind of test.

She turned and headed for the carriage. She climbed up onto the seat as Steele went around to the other side and got up next to her. When he untied the reins, she said, "I suppose you are going to insist on being the driver now. Being as how you are the man."

"You can take the reins if you like," he said, still trying not to look down at her chest. "But keep the horse under control. A steady pace will get us there quicker than if you wear them out."

She glanced at him and then back to the road ahead. "I think I know how to drive a horse."

The irritation was back in her voice. She snapped the reins and the horse responded. While she concentrated on controlling the horse, Steele was finally able to get a good look at her. Seeing her like that, in a thin wet shirt, without the facade of a man's appearance, he could see quite clearly that she had all the attributes of a handsome woman, even if she was a bit . . . troublesome. She glanced at him, and then back toward the horse. He was glad to see that she was no longer trying to cover herself. Apparently, she was no longer concerned about what her wet shirt was revealing. He had to admit he was a bit disappointed to see how quickly that shirt was drying.

Chapter 5

*B*y the time they reached the tiny town of Mesa City, the sun was getting low in the west. The livery stable was easy to find as it was one of only three businesses in the town, the others being a general store, and the usual town bar. He told the old man at the livery stable that he needed to rent a horse.

"Two horses," said Helen.

Steele turned to her. "I think I can find the place from here. You can just tell me where they left you."

She shook her head. "No, I have to show you. Besides, you're a city man. You'll probably fall off the first time the horse shies at a snake or something."

She was smiling as she said it, so Steele assumed she was kidding. "All right, but we have to move fast. It's getting dark."

"You'll be the one trying to keep up. My father owns lots of horses. I grew up on a horse."

Steele transferred the water, a bit of the food, and two bottles of beer to the saddlebags on the larger of the two horses. Then he quickly got up into the saddle. The horse shied and began to back up, but Steele managed to get it under control.

Helen smiled and started to say something, but refrained and got up on the other horse. Steele could tell she was very comfortable there.

They started out of town, heading south. Steele glanced back to see the old man still standing in the street, watching them go.

He pulled in close to Helen's horse. "There are not many roads out here. All you have to do is get me on the correct one, then you can turn back."

"They took us up into the hills. I can go part way up there with you."

"No," insisted Steele. "The note said no family. You have to go back to Mesa City and wait for me there."

She didn't reply but simply spurred her horse ahead. That kind of response worried Steele. It would complicate things considerably if she got in the way.

When they reached an intersection with a rutted road that led up into nearby foothills, she stopped. "This is it. They took us up there."

Steele got down off his horse to inspect the ground. He could see the carriage tracks leading up toward the mountain and the same tracks coming back down again. But which way had the carriage turned when they came back to the main road? There were too many other tracks to be sure. He looked toward the south. It wasn't far down to the Mexican border. Is that where they had taken Kane?

He remounted. "All right, Helen. I'll go on up. You go back and wait for me in Mesa City. Send a telegraph to Rudd and Bailey. Tell them I've gone to meet the kidnappers. I'll come back for you as soon as I've heard their demands."

"How long should I wait? I mean, what if you don't come back?"

"There is no reason for them to hold me. I'm not valuable as a hostage. The only reason they would ask for a negotiator is to discuss terms. They will send me back with those terms."

"All right," she said, frowning. "But I still don't know how long I should wait."

"I should be back before morning. If I haven't returned by then, you can go back to San Diego.

"No, I didn't mean it like that," she said reaching out toward him. "I'll wait for you." But then she pulled her hand back. "I mean, I'll stay until . . . I hear from you."

"Go ahead and turn back now. I'll wait until you're out of sight before I head up."

"All right," she said, but she didn't do it.

Steele waited. It was clear there was something else she needed to say, but he was worried about how dark it was getting. "You'd better get going. You should try to get back to town before dark."

She hesitated, and then said, "Well, all right then. Be careful."

"I will."

She reached out to touch his hand. She held the touch for a moment, and then she turned her horse and spurred it into a fast trot back toward town.

Steele watched her until she rounded the next bend and disappeared. Then he started up the road, maintaining a steady pace, watching for any movement ahead. He took out Rudd's white handkerchief and tied it to one of the reins, as he had seen done at Burkesville when the Union negotiator had gone forward to propose a Christmas peace.

He started up the road, going slow, inspecting the ground as he went. There were some fresh hoof prints, and occasionally he could still pick out the carriage tracks. As he climbed higher, the road began to curve around low ridges. The ground soon changed from sandy desert to rocky composite. He stopped when he saw that the road ahead led into a tight valley marked by rocky outcroppings on both sides. That was where they would be waiting.

He went forward, slower now, keeping both of his hands on the reins so they would be in plain view. Suddenly, two men came riding out from behind the rocks. They were both Mexicans, both dressed in nearly identical dark pants and colorful, but faded, shirts. They were both wearing wide-brimmed *sombreros*. Steele was surprised to see that they had not covered their faces. Mrs. Kane had clearly said all of the men had hidden their faces behind kerchiefs. Something had changed and Steele didn't like the implications of it. Why were they no longer afraid of being recognized?

Steele stopped and waited, his hands in the air. Soon, a third man came out from behind the rocks. He was not Mexican, but his face was tanned dark. Steele judged him to be about thirty years old. He was wearing a gray shirt and gray pants that could have once have been part of a Confederate uniform, but they were now so faded it was hard to tell. He sat in the saddle with such an erect posture Steele wondered if he might have been a military officer.

The three men approached, each of them with a pistol in hand. Steele kept his hands in the air as they reined in their horses in front of him. His horse shied back and the American said, "Hold your horse, damn it."

Steele took the reins with his left hand, keeping the other hand in the air. The man had a Southern accent. Was he the man Mrs. Kane had described? His accent seemed familiar. It might have been high-country Tennessee, or maybe southern Kentucky.

The man said, "You got no gun?"

Steele shook his head and didn't move.

"What's in the saddlebags?"

"Nothing but food."

"Check it out, Jose."

One of the Mexicans got down off his horse and cautiously approached, keeping his pistol pointed at Steele. He opened the first saddlebag and looked in. He pulled out an apple and happily bit into it. He left it in his mouth as he went around to check the other saddlebag. He pulled out the two bottles of beer. He took the apple out of his mouth and grinned. He held the bottles up for the others to see. "*Mira, cerveza.*"

"Time enough for beer later," said the American. "Get his reins."

The Mexican took out a ragged piece of rope which he tied to the reins of Steele's horse. He tied the rope to the back of his saddle and started down the road, happily munching on the apple as he pulled Steele's horse along behind him. The other Mexican rode close by, his pistol trained on Steele.

The American took the lead and the rest followed in one line. Because of the dust, some of the men tied kerchiefs over their faces.

After they had gone a short distance down the road, they turned onto a narrow trail that traversed the side of the hill, gradually heading downward. Steele could see that it was too narrow and shallow for regular horse traffic; it was probably a game trail. But there were quite a few fresh hoof prints and some fresh horse droppings on it. The three men must have come on that trail to avoid the main road.

The trail led around the side of the hill through a scattering of boulders before turning down more sharply to meet the main road. It was deserted, but the leader stopped and held up his hand. They all waited in silence. What were they waiting for? There was no sign of anyone coming, but still the leader didn't move. After a few more minutes, two riders came around the bend, riding fast. As they drew closer, Steele saw that the lead rider had ahold of the reins of the second horse. The second rider was wearing a white shirt and dark pants. Steele knew immediately who it was.

They arrived in a cloud of dust. "Look here what I found, Sergeant," said the man who was leading Helen's horse. "And she's a sweet little package too, just like you said she was."

Chapter 6

Steele noted that the newly arrived man also had a Southern accent, and that he had addressed the first man as sergeant. Had they been in the war together?

"She was following him, Sergeant. I caught her coming up the hill."

"You shouldn't have done that, Miss Kane," said the sergeant. "Now I'm going to have to take you with us."

Steele tried to catch Helen's eye, but she wouldn't look at him. He hoped she would remain silent, but he knew that wasn't likely.

She shook her head and glared at the sergeant. "I'm not going anywhere with you. I demand you tell this man to let go of my horse."

Steele urged his horse forward. "Send her back, Sergeant. You don't want her along."

"No, I want to go," insisted Helen. "In fact, I demand to go. Take me to my father. I have a right to know if he's all right."

"Shut up, both of you" yelled the sergeant. He nodded to the man who held her horse. "Bring her along." He rode on, refusing to look back.

The other man followed, pulling Helen's horse along behind.

"Be reasonable, Sergeant," called Steele. "Ramsey's note said no family. She's Kane's daughter. Send her back."

"I'm not going back," said Helen.

"I know who she is," said the sergeant over his shoulder. "Just keep quiet and maybe you'll get out of this alive."

Helen turned away, refusing to look at Steele. She waved her hand in front of her face because of the dust that rose up from the horse that was leading her.

Steele untied the white handkerchief from his reins and tried to ride up to give it to her., but one of the Mexicans pushed his horse in between them and shook his finger at Steele.

The other Mexican rode up close to Helen. "Hey, *señorita*," he said. "You *muy bonita*."

"Go to hell," said Helen, turning away.

The Mexican smiled and shook his hand as if he had burned it. "Ooh, *she muy caliente*. I like."

The sergeant looked back and yelled, "Keep away from her!"

The Mexican dropped back, still grinning.

"And you stay away from her too," he yelled to Steele. "Everybody just keep away from her, damn it." He picked up the pace and the others spurred their horses to stay with him.

Steele suspected the sergeant was trying to reach the Mexican border before dark. If Ramsey was waiting there, and he sent Steele back with his demands, maybe he would let Helen go with him. But Steele knew that hope was a slim one: now that she had gotten herself caught, Ramsey might well decide to keep her as an additional hostage.

After the sun went down, the night seemed to come quickly. The horses instinctively slowed and soon it was so dark Steele could barely make out the lead rider up ahead. They went on slowly until a narrow quarter moon rose in the east, making the road stand out a bit more clearly. Their pace picked up a little and Steele paid close attention to the distance they were covering and the lay of the land.

Soon, they began to descend and after a few more minutes they splashed across a shallow river. Steele wondered what river it might be. In the past, he had looked at maps of the southern California, but he didn't remember seeing any river close to the Mexican border. It must mean they had already crossed into Mexico.

Once across the river, they turned off the road onto a barely discernable trail that gradually curved eastward toward some distant hills. Was that where Ramsey was?

After a few more minutes of riding, they started up into a pass between the rock-covered hills. Under the faint moonlight, tall tree-like cactuses cast long strange shadows. They were like silent sentries with upturned arms, watching the group pass.

It was rough country, dry and remote, and it was becoming rockier as they rode higher up into the hills. From time-to-time, little swirling gusts of wind and dust sprung up out of nowhere, but they soon dissipated. Steele looked ahead at the outline of the rocky peaks. It looked like a good hiding place for a military commander; high ground was always easier to defend.

Soon, they topped a ridge and there was the flash of a lantern high up in the rocks. Steele immediately slid off his horse.

"¡*Alto!*" yelled the closest Mexican. He pulled his pistol.

Steele ignored him and stepped off the trail next to a huge cactus. It had broad, pointed leaves that spiked upward and outward from a center stalk.

The sergeant turned his horse and came back. "What the hell do you think you're doing?"

Just relieving myself, "said Steele, beginning to unbutton his pants.

"Get back on your horse. Now!"

"I'll just be a moment," said Steele. "The beer."

One of the Mexicans laughed.

"You can piss from your horse," insisted the sergeant.

"Not in front of the girl." Steele moved behind the cactus and allowed his stream of urine to splash noisily against it.

"Well, hurry it up for Christ's sake," said the sergeant turning away. The two Mexicans apparently thought Steele's stopping was a good idea because they also got off their horses and headed for the bushes.

"I have to go too," said Helen, getting down and moving toward some low bushes on the other side of the road.

"Jesus," said the sergeant. "Can't any of you hold your water?"

The Mexicans finished and got up on their horses again. Both of them stood up in their stirrups to try to peer through the darkness to see what Helen was doing.

Steele used that distraction to quickly reach down and take out his pistol. He made a furrow in the sandy soil with the toe of his boot and dropped the pistol into it. Then, as he re-buttoned his pants, he used the bottom of his boot to cover it and smooth out the soil.

Back in the saddle, they all waited for Helen. She came back to her horse, buckling her belt.

"Let's go, let's go," shouted the sergeant.

They were only back underway for a few minutes when they heard a voice that came from the rocks above. "That you, Sergeant? Did you get him?" The voice had a deeply southern accent.

"Yeah, it's me. We're going in," said the Sergeant

"All right, I'll signal," said the voice.

A light appeared, swinging back and forth and a short distance ahead another swinging light responded.

As they rode in, Steele was surprised to see the size of the encampment. There were rows of canvas tents all along the north side of the camp. Steele counted twenty-four of them, in three neatly aligned rows of eight. Several campfires were burning between the tents with groups of men sitting or squatting around each of them. All of the men were wearing worn and faded gray Confederate uniforms and each uniform seemed to fit the wearer perfectly. Steele realized these men were wearing their own uniforms, clothes they had worn for a long time. Were these men Ramsey's former soldiers, brought all the way from Tennessee? Were they still following their general, even though the war was over?

Between the tents, long muskets were leaning together in tight circles, bayonets mounted and ready for action. The weapons were all Enfields, standard Confederate Army-issue muzzle-loaders. It was as if the time that had passed since the end of the war had been an illusion and an entire Confederate unit had somehow been moved from a Civil War battlefront all the way to western Mexico. The scene gave Steele an odd feeling, as if he too was back in the war again, riding straight into a Confederate camp.

He glanced at Helen and saw that she was also looking at the Confederates. She turned to him with questioning look on her face, as if he could provide an explanation. But of course he could not. He didn't know how, or why, these soldiers had been brought there, but he had to accept the reality of what he was seeing. It meant Ramsey was not a lone wolf, writing letters to newspapers just to make trouble. There was more to this than the taking of a hostage in hopes of exchanging him for someone held by the government. In the sparsely populated West, this many armed men constituted a formidable army. How could they have traveled all the way from Tennessee without anyone noticing? They must have come on their own, individually or in small groups. It meant they knew where they were going. How was that possible? Was there some kind of secret network in the South that was able to recruit this many men? And why were they here in the West? An army was for fighting, but there was nobody to fight. There were no cities within hundreds of miles. If Ramsey had some plan to continue fighting the Civil War, why would he put together his army in far-away Mexico? That thought led Steele to wonder if this General Ramsey might be quite mad.

After they rode past the last of the tents, they approached a small log cabin. The cabin looked old, but it had a front porch made out of new-looking wood. A short distance past the cabin, there was another crude building made out of rough logs. Two Mexicans with rifles stood on either side of that building's door. Was that where they were holding Kane?

Farther up in the valley, Steele saw more campfires, but no tents. Men were also gathered around those campfires, but they were too far way for Steele to determine who they were. Was another armed group bivouacked up there?

As they neared the log cabin, the sergeant turned to the two Mexicans. "That will be all, men."

Without comment, the two men headed toward the campfires at the upper end of the valley. Steele realized the camp in the upper valley must be the Mexican's camp. Apparently, they were being kept separate from the Confederates.

The sergeant brought them to a stop in front of the cabin. It was too old to have been built recently by Ramsey's men. It must have been built by the Mexicans. But for what purpose?

Two Mexican guards were waiting on the porch, one on each side of the front door. They were wearing tan uniforms, military in style, but without emblems or insignias to indicate rank. They had fancy black collars and wide black leg stripes, very different from the uniforms the Mexican Army wore. Were they some kind of militia? Steele wondered if the Mexican government knew about it this camp hidden in the hills of northern Mexico.

The sergeant called to the two guards and they picked up their rifles and came forward. Steele recognized their rifles; they were new-looking Winchester rifles, the latest version of the Henry lever-action model. But when they got closer, Steele realized they were not the usual Winchesters; could they be the new version, the military version of the Winchester known as the Improved Henry? Steele had read an article about the new weapon in a British magazine. But it said the entire production had been shipped to Spain for use in their fight against Peruvian and Puerto Rican separatists. How could those guns have made their way from Spain to Mexico? And why would the two Mexicans be armed with such formidable and expensive new weapons while the Confederates were still using the old Enfields?

The sergeant pointed at Steele. "Take this man in to see the commander."

Steele got down from his horse, but waited to see where they were taking Helen.

The sergeant got down and went to her. He held out his hand to help her down from her horse.

The captor is now playing the Southern gentleman, thought Steele. It was a good sign. The sergeant was apparently going to treat her well. But would others in the camp be so polite? On the trail, the Mexicans had been very interested in her. She was, after all, young and quite attractive, and there didn't seem to be any other women in the camp.

The sergeant took Helen's arm and tried to lead her away, but she pulled free. "What do you think you're doing?" she said. "Let me go. Drew, do something."

"Where are you taking her?" said Steele.

The sergeant took out his pistol and pointed it at Steele. "I told you to go inside."

"Tell me where you're taking her."

"Don't worry, she won't be hurt. Now get going."

One of the Mexican guards had come down from the porch and was prodding Steele with his rifle. Steele ignored him and kept his eyes on the sergeant. "Do I have your word as a Confederate soldier that she will not be unharmed?"

The sergeant locked eyes with him. Finally, he said, "You do."

Steele looked at Helen. "Go with him, but make sure he tells anyone you see that you are under his protection, that he has personally guaranteed your safety."

"Why can't I stay with you?" she said. There was fear in her eyes.

"We have to do what they say," he said gently. "Try to be calm."

"You're telling me to be calm? This man is taking me away to do who knows what and you're just going to stand there and say be calm?"

"Are you two through?" said the sergeant. "I already told you she would be safe. Now get going." He gestured with the barrel of his pistol toward the cabin.

"Can she see her father? Will you take her to her father?"

"I told you to go inside. Get moving."

"She has the right to see her father. We have to know that the hostage is safe and unharmed. Otherwise the negotiations cannot continue."

"Fine, I'll take her to her father in the stockade. Satisfied?"

Steele nodded. "We have the sergeant's word that you will be safe, Helen. Go with him to see your father."

She frowned, but allowed herself to be led away.

"*Vayamosnos,*" said the Mexican, again jabbing Steele with his rifle.

"You feel like eating that rifle?" said Steele.

"*Que?*"

Steele pushed the gun away and went up onto the porch. The guard followed and reached past him to push open the cabin door.

"*¡Vayamos!*" The guard pushed Steele into the cabin. Inside was another Mexican, wearing the same pseudo-military uniform. He stood up as they entered and looked at Steele with undisguised curiosity. Steele noticed two doors in the room. Another Mexican guard stood in front of one of the doors. There was a battle flag on the wall with the words "2nd Tennessee" below a line of gold stars.

The guard tapped on the unguarded door and Steele heard a deep voice from inside say, "*Entre.*"

The guard opened the door and pushed Steele in.

Inside the room, a big, broad-faced man was seated behind a wide table. He wasn't Mexican. He was light skinned, with deep-set brown eyes and dark hair. He had a thick beard that was long, but well-tended. Despite the warmth of the night, the man was wearing a light blue Confederate general's frock coat. Was this General Ramsey? Steele had expected him to be older. Strangely, the man's shirt collar had only the two-star insignia of a lieutenant Colonel.

The man looked up from some papers he was reading. "Has he been thoroughly searched?"

The guard shrugged.

"Well, search him, damn it."

Steele stood still while the guard carried out a thorough search. He found Steele's money, and grinning, put it into his own pocket. He pulled up Steele's pant legs and looked into both boots, but luckily he didn't notice the well-concealed secret pocket that held the small knife. The guard turned back to the officer. "*No armas.*"

The officer pointed to the chair in front of the table. "Sit down. Take off your hat in my presence."

When Steele did not remove his hat, the guard stepped forward to grab it off of his head. He threw it into the corner. Then he took up a station next to the door.

As the big man at the table looked him over, Steele looked around the room. There were four large wooden boxes stacked against the wall. He recognized them immediately as rifle boxes, even though all of the markings had been painted over with thick black paint. Probably more of those brand new Winchester rifles. In addition to the rifle boxes, there was one very large crate made out of extra heavy wood. Steele suspected it might contain some other kind of weapon. A small cannon? He wondered how a band of Mexican militia could have come into possession of so many new weapons.

The man pushed away the papers and looked Steele over.

"So you're the one they sent. What's your name?"

The man had a slight accent, but it wasn't foreign. It might have been from Oklahoma or Texas.

"My name is Steele. I was sent by Mr. Kane's newspaper."

"Are you an employee of that newspaper?"

"No, I am a private investigator. And you are?"

"You know who I am. You may address me as General Ramsey. So they hired a private detective to be go-between."

"You're wearing the collar insignia of a Colonel," said Steele. "Not a general."

"That's neither here nor there. I'd advise you to just shut up and listen. I could have you shot right now, as a spy."

"I was sent here to negotiate."

The man leaned back in his chair to look Steele over. "Don't suppose you were ever a soldier?"

"No."

"Didn't think so. Why'd they hire you? You know Kane?"

"I don't know Mr. Kane. But I would like to speak to him before we begin negotiations."

"Negotiations he calls it." The man laughed a loud gruff laugh. He looked toward the Mexican guard   "This here detective says he's ready to begin negotiations. *Negociaciones*." He laughed again, still loud, but he cut it off quickly. "What's that accent I hear? You from the Northeast? Boston? You one of those fancy Boston types?"

"I grew up in England. In London."

The man raised his eyebrows. "London, you say. Well, well, looks like we got us a real fancy go-between here. From England, no less."

"And you also have an accent," said Steele. "But I don't believe I ever heard it in the South. From Texas, perhaps?"

The man stopped smiling. "You don't need to know where I'm from. You'd better just mind your manners and do exactly what I say or else you may never get to see your precious London, England again. You say you want to begin negotiations? Let me tell you somethin'. There aren't any negotiations to be done here. I'll let you know what I plan to do with Kane when I'm good and ready."

"Before we go on, Colonel, I would like to speak with General Ramsey."

The man frowned and sat forward in his chair. "What's the matter with you, mister? You deaf or something? I already told you I'm Ramsey. You deal with me or I'll turn you over to my men. They'll just shoot you and dump you out in the desert for the coyotes."

"I am here to negotiate on behalf of Mr. Kane's family. I would like to speak to General Ramsey."

The man glared at Steele.

Steele calmly met his eyes.

"You got a lot of balls for somebody in your situation. Why do you think you need to talk to Ramsey?"

"I was told to negotiate only with General Ramsey."

"Ramsey's not in charge here anymore." The man banged his big fist on the desk. "You're in Mexico now, not Tennessee. I'm in charge here and you'll do what I say."

"I can see that you're in charge, Colonel. But I also saw the General's Tennessee battle flag on the wall out there. Let him assure me that you are now in charge of his men and we can begin negotiations."

The Colonel sat back. "There you go again. *Negociaciones*. I already told you there aren't going to be any negotiations. I'm going to lay out what we want and your job is to go back and tell them. They give it to us and they get Kane back. Otherwise, he's a dead man."

"I will carry your demands back, as soon as I talk to General Ramsey and have his assurances that Mr. Kane is safe."

The Colonel shook his head. "Stubborn, that's what you are. Just plain stubborn." He turned to the Mexican guard. "*Llévelo al* Ramsey."

"Si, Coronel," said the Mexican, saluting.

The Colonel turned back to the papers on his desk without returning the salute.

The guard led Steele out of the room and to the other door. He opened it pushed Steele in.

Inside the room, a gaunt older man was sitting hunched over in a chair in front of the window, staring out into the night.

The man turned in his chair to look Steele over.

Steele stepped forward and saluted. "General Ramsey, I presume?"

The man stood up and pulled back his shoulders. He instantly changed from a hunched over old man to a formal, erect army officer. The only thing that remained of the old man was the tired look on his face. "And you are?"

"My name is Drew Steele. I was sent to negotiate for Mr. Kane's release."

The General walked up close to Steele and looked him up and down, as if he was inspecting one of his soldiers. He had strange, very light blue eyes, and closely-cropped graying hair. He wasn't wearing any kind of uniform, but his shirt was collarless with a bibbed front, the type worn by most officers of the Confederacy.

The General looked past Steele. "Thank you, soldier, you can go now."

"*Pero, General,*" said the Mexican, "*Coronel Medina dijo—*"

"I know what Colonel Medina says, but this is still my office and I am telling you to wait outside."

"*Pero, General.*"

"Dismissed."

The Mexican shrugged and left the room, closing the door with a bang on his way out.

The general turned his attention back to Steele. "Where did you get that scar, young man?"

Steele remained still. If Ramsey wanted to inspect him, as he might inspect a soldier, Steele was willing to go along with it. "In the war, General. An exploding shell."

"Yes, it looks like it could have been caused by shrapnel. Where was that, son?"

"In Tennessee, sir. Near Hoover's Gap."

Ramsey seemed surprised. "You were there? I was near there, at Chattanooga."

"Yes, sir. I know."

"You've heard of me?"

"I heard about the battle of Shelbyville."

The general walked back to the window to look out for a few moments. He picked up his coffee cup from the sill but didn't drink from it. "Shelbyville. Were these my men you were speaking to, son?"

"No sir. Wounded Federal men."

"You were a Union soldier?"

"No, sir. I wasn't a soldier. I was working in a Union Army field hospital."

"I expect the wounded men did not speak fondly of me."

"No sir, they said they . . . that is, the battle was not spoken of kindly."

The general turned back to face him. "Go ahead, you can say it. They referred to me as the butcher of Shelbyville."

"I've heard that expression. Yes, sir."

"Shelbyville," whispered Ramsey, a far-away look in his eyes. "Seems so long ago now." Then he refocused on Steele. "So you were not a soldier."

"No sir. Your note said not to send anyone in the military."

"My note?"

"The newspaper received a note telling me where to go. It said not to send the law or anyone who had been in the military."

Ramsey thought about that for a moment. "A note, eh. Son, I'd like you to tell me everything that has happened." He looked back toward the window. "Would you mind if I sat down? I'm having a bit of trouble with my leg." He reached down to touch the front of his right leg. "An old wound."

"Of course, sir," said Steele. "Please sit down."

"I'm afraid there is only the one chair. You can sit by the window, if you want."

Steele went to sit on the window sill, facing the general.

"Now you say you received a letter from me?"

"Yes, sir. It was signed with your name, but I suspected it wasn't from you. The handwriting was different from your original letter. And the tone of it wasn't the same."

"You are referring to my letter to the newspaper?"

"Yes sir. I read your original letter. It was what prompted Mr. Kane's newspaper to hire me."

"I see," said Ramsey. He stared into his coffee cup. Then he looked up. "Would you like a cup of coffee? These Mexicans don't make a bad cup of coffee."

Steele shook his head. "No thank you, sir."

"I don't know where the Mexicans get such good coffee," said Ramsey taking a sip. "Toward the end of the war we couldn't get coffee at all. The Union blockade you know. But the boys made us some as best they could. They'd use dried beets. Roasted beets. It didn't taste much like coffee, but we all pretended it was good." He looked up at Steele and smiled. "I'll bet you Northern boys didn't have to go without coffee, did you?"

Steele merely smiled back at the general. The old man was calm and soft spoken, but Steele reminded himself that this was a Confederate general. His actions in the war had made his enemies fear him. From what Steele had read, even his own men feared him. "Sir, in your letter you referred to the war crimes trials going on back in Washington. Do you know someone being tried back there?" He watched the general for a reaction.

"Trials," scoffed Ramsey. "As if that illegal tribunal could conduct fair trials. Those trials have nothing to do with the war. It is the North's lust for revenge, and the weakness of politicians, doing whatever the rabble wants, just to get re-elected."

"Nevertheless," said Steele, "you have rekindled the old specter of wartime hostage taking. Mr. Kane's wife is very distraught."

"Yes, yes, I'm sure. It is always hard on the families." He took another drink from his cup. Then he looked up at Steele. "A man like you should understand such things. Such actions are often a necessity . . . in war."

The general seemed somber, but Steele saw no pity in those eyes. "The war has ended, General. Mr. Kane's family has no stake in your personal fight."

The general's eyes flared. "You are mistaken, son. This is not *my* personal fight. This is my country's fight, our continuing fight for freedom, even if the fighting on the battlefield has ended. What the Federals are doing to my country proves the war has not ended. They are denying us our dignity, our liberty. It is the patriotic duty of every Southerner to fight to the death for liberty. I am merely doing my duty."

Steele knew better than to argue with a man who used terms like patriotic duty and liberty. Was the kidnapping of Kane an old soldier's reaction to what he saw as injustice? A way to fight back at the Union, even after the Confederate Army had laid down its weapons? Steele again wondered if the general might be a bit mad.

"I take your silence as disagreement," said the general. "I understand. You were not a soldier, despite your attempts to pretend to be one with your standing at attention and calling me sir and such."

"I apologize if that seemed deceptive," said Steele quickly. "But I do respect your rank and your war record. I was sent here to do a job, to negotiate for Mr. Kane's release. I am trying to do that job to the best of my ability."

Ramsey studied him for several seconds. "You seem to be an intelligent young man, but you will never understand the duties of a soldier."

"I accept that. During the war I was in or near many battles, but I was not a participant. Since the war's end, I have been studying about it. Reading whatever I can find about it."

The General smiled. "A student of the war, eh. I should have known that would happen. People are writing books, are they?"

"Yes, sir. Many."

"Do they mention me?"

"Some do."

"Not favorably, I expect."

"They mostly just report the campaigns you were involved in."

"I see. And do these books talk about tactics and strategy? Do they say why the war ended?"

"They say the Confederacy ran out of resources. An army can't fight without resources."

The general sat forward to shake his finger at Steele. "Nonsense. You shouldn't believe everything you read in books, Mr. Steele. Resources don't matter. What matters is the courage of the men. And tactics. When you are out manned, you change tactics. Aren't the Apaches out-manned? Do they have anywhere near the resources of their enemy, the U.S. Army? No, but they fight on using different tactics. They hide in the mountains and come down only when the time is right. They understand that a guerrilla force can move fast and take what they need from the enemy population as they go."

Steele thought about what the General was saying. Was he merely an old war horse, arguing about the tactics of battle? Or was there something else behind his words? As a negotiator, Steele would be expected to take back the general's demands. Was he also using him to take back some other kind of message?

The General frowned and shook his head. "Forgive my outburst, Mr. Steele. I know you are not here to talk about the war."

"Yes, sir. I am here to learn your terms."

Ramsey was again looking past him, out the window into the darkness.

Steele leaned toward him. "General? Your terms for Mr. Kane's release?"

General Ramsey turned back to face Steele, his eyes gradually refocusing. "Yes, yes, I heard you. Well, young man, I'm afraid we have a problem."

"Colonel Medina?"

"That's right. He has placed me under . . . call it house arrest. While he waits for his own reinforcements. He and I . . . shall we say, have some differences."

"Differences? You mean differences in strategy?"

"I don't wish to go into that, Mr. Steele, but it boils down to who will lead, and to what end."

"He plans to lead your combined forces?"

"As I said, I cannot speak of that. I have probably said too much already. Your problem concerns only the disposition of the hostage."

"So, you no longer have authority over the hostage?"

"For the moment, that is true."

"But your men? I assume those men camped out there are your soldiers. Are they not still under your command?"

"Are you suggesting armed overthrow?"

"Isn't that how the Colonel took over from you?"

"Not exactly. We are in his country. We are surrounded by his compatriots."

"But you must have come here knowing that."

"Such is the nature of alliances, my boy. You say you study the war? Then you should know war is changing. To understand the future of warfare you will have to come to understand the art of alliances. As Napoleon put it, alliances of the weak against the strong can yield the greater power. However . . ." He paused a moment. "Alliances can be . . . complicated." He glanced toward the door, and then he smiled. Besides, the new weapons are kept in Colonel Medina's office."

"So you are not willing to confront him?"

Ramsey had a bemused look on his face. "Apparently you are a man of action, Mr. Steele. But there is no need for violence. This is only a temporary setback. The Colonel and I will resolve our differences."

"General, you have an entire camp of armed men just outside this building. If those soldiers are still loyal to you, you could take control any time you want to."

"I take your point, Mr. Steele. But if you are suggesting my men are not loyal to me, you are mistaken. We have been through a lot together and I believe in them. And while I do think the Colonel's plans are . . . foolhardy, we are, as I said, in his country. There are times to put heated words aside and wait for rational thought to prevail."

"And while you wait for that to prevail, Medina's reinforcements are coming. Do you really think he will turn control of this camp over to you when those reinforcements arrive?"

"I think you are now going beyond your duties as negotiator, Mr. Steele."

Steele decided to take a different tact. "Medina is using your name for his own purposes. He signed your name to that letter."

"Did he? How clever of the man. He probably signed my name because it was my plan."

"There was another note."

"Was there?"

"The note was pinned to the chest of a dead soldier. Medina had him hung."

Steele tried to assess the look on Ramsey's face. There was a reaction, but it was hard to tell what it meant. "You didn't know that, did you, General?"

"Do you expect me to believe everything you say, Mr. Steele?"

"I think you can tell that I have been completely honest with you up to this point. Why would I lie to you now? Medina hung an innocent soldier to make a point."

"No soldier is innocent," said Ramsey with a wave of his hand. "If he fights for the Federals, he must expect . . . the consequences."

"The soldier was an Indian fighter, from Nevada. A black man. He was too young to have even been in the war."

Ramsey took another drink of his coffee before he spoke. "These things happen . . . in war."

"This was not a combat death, General. It was ordinary murder, committed in your name. He does not have your goals. He cares nothing about your cause, your country."

Ramsey again turned his angry eyes on Steele. "Are you trying to bait me, Mr. Steele? If so, it will not work. What did you expect? Perhaps Medina did execute an innocent man. Many innocent people have died in this conflict already. You said you saw combat in Tennessee. Then I'm sure you saw many such things, or worse."

Steele looked into those unblinking, unsympathetic, eyes. They were not the eyes of a tired old man. They were the eyes of a predator, looking for vulnerability. Now he would know how to finish the eyes in his drawing of the general. This man could kill if he deemed it necessary, if it furthered his cause. "As you said, General, my job here is to secure the release of Mr. Kane. From my brief conversation with Colonel Medina, I believe Mr. Kane would be safer in your hands than in his. Therefore I am willing to help you regain control of your valuable hostage. Tell me what's going on. Why did Medina build this camp here? And why did you come here to join him?"

"You are not in any position to help me, Mr. Steele."

"If that is so, then there is no harm in explaining the situation to me."

"There is nothing you can do."

"I see that Medina is in charge and you are not. In my opinion, that endangers Mr. Kane."

Ramsey looked at him for several seconds. Finally, he said, "Let me be clear, Mr. Steele, I am only willing to answer questions relevant to . . . what I might call our *temporary* alliance. I do want to regain control of the hostage, as you said. He is . . . important to my goals. If our temporary alliance is successful, you will again resume your role as merely the go between. Agreed?"

"Agreed."

"All I can say is Medina is my liaison with . . . important people in Mexico."

"He sounds Texan, not Mexican."

"He is from Texas, but his family is from this area of Mexico. They emigrated here from Spain. As I understand it, they once held vast amounts of property here, on both sides of the border."

"So he has his own interests in this. Is the Mexican government involved?"

"No."

"But somebody must be supporting him. Those new Winchester Henry rifles are quite expensive, not to mention the guards he has surrounded himself with. I assume they are not loyal to any cause. Therefore, they must have been hired by Medina."

"Let's get back to the issue of the hostage. There is something you can do. After you leave this office, try to get word of my situation to my men. If you can tell them I am being held prisoner in here, they will come free me. Then I will let you go back to California with my demands."

"Which are?"

"Tell your employers I will release Mr. Kane in exchange for my son."

"Your son?"

"Yes, my son. My only son. He is being held by the war crimes commission. He is threatened with execution merely because he is my son. But he knew nothing about my . . . actions at the Hackenburg prison camp. He was a line officer under my command, simply doing his duty there. After the hostilities ended, he was on his way back home when they took him. He is entirely innocent of any so-called war crimes."

Suddenly, Steele understood. Ramsey simply wanted to trade Kane for his son. But why had he come all the way to western Mexico to take his hostage? And why align himself with Medina? There was something else to it, but for now, Steele knew what he had to do. He had to help Ramsey regain control. Then the General would send him back with that one demand: his son for Kane.

"All right, General, I understand. But there is an additional problem. Kane's daughter, Helen, came here with me."

"That wasn't very wise, Mr. Steele."

"I told her not to come, but she followed me and was captured. Does your offer apply to both Mr. Kane and his daughter?"

Ramsey thought about the question.

"If you value your son's life, I suggest you stop thinking about her strategic value and agree to exchange both of them."

"All right, Mr. Steele, it is agreed. If you can get word to my men and I am able to regain control of this camp, you can go back and tell them I will release both Kane and his daughter in exchange for my son."

"All right. I will try to get to your men. What about the sergeant who brought me in here? Can he be trusted?"

"Of course he can. He was with me at Chattanooga."

"Then I will try to get to him. Which is his tent?"

"He is in the tent nearest this cabin. I wish you Godspeed in that effort, Mr. Steele. But you must act quickly. Colonel Medina has a much larger force of his militia coming from Hermosillo. If they get here before—"

Suddenly the door opened and Medina stepped into the room. "Just what I would expect from you, General. You are plotting with this man. This is treason."

The general stood up to confront him. "How dare you listen at my door, Colonel?"

"I knew you'd try something like this, Ramsey. Up to now, I was satisfied just to place you under house arrest. But this is an act of treason with a Yankee spy. I can hang you for this."

"You can't do anything to me, Medina. My men will stop you. This man told me what you have been doing. You murdered an opposition soldier without cause. You have been acting unilaterally, using my name, without my authority. You never intended to negotiate for the release of my son."

"Shut up, old man. I am placing you under arrest as a traitor. From this point on you have no authority to tell me anything. You are in my country now. The rest of my men will be here within a few days. Then I will hang you and take charge of your ridiculous army. Guard, take them both to the stockade. *A la estacada. ¿Entienda?*"

The Mexican looked confused. "*¿El general tambien?*"

"*Si*, both of them."

Chapter 7

Medina walked away and the Mexican guard pointed his pistol in their general direction. He said, "*Vayamos*," but he didn't seem very sure of himself.

"It's you who are acting traitorous, Medina" shouted the general. "I am your superior."

Medina ignored him and headed back to his office.

The general tried to follow Medina, but the Mexican guard stepped in front of him. He pressed his pistol against the general's chest, but it was the Mexican who was trembling, not Ramsey. The general pushed his chest harder against the barrel of the gun, defying the Mexican.

The outer guard had risen from his chair and was watching the scene intently. He slowly raised his pistol and aimed it at the general.

Steele stepped forward and touched Ramsey's shoulder. "General, you are making these men nervous. Let's go along with this for now, before they do something we'll all regret later."

The general looked at Steele for a long moment, but then he shrugged and pushed the Mexican's pistol away. He headed for the door. As he passed Medina's office door, he yelled, "You're making a big mistake, Medina. My men won't stand for this."

The general led Steele and the Mexican guard out the door. The two guards on the porch jumped up, surprised. One of them asked, "*¿Qué pasó?*"

The guard shrugged and pointed to the stockade. "*El general. La estacada.*"

With one of the guards leading and another close behind, they were herded to the log stockade and pushed inside. The only light was what little came in through the cracks in the log walls.

The general sat down on the dirt floor grumbling. "That son of a bitch. I'll have his head."

"You may not get the opportunity, general. Medina might decide to have you killed before morning, before your men wake up."

"He wouldn't dare."

"He's committed now. But where is Kane and his daughter? I thought they would be locked in here too."

"I think there are some other rooms farther back. I've never actually been in here before."

"I'll go look for them. Stay close to the door, General. If anyone comes, call out."

Steele began to feel his way back farther into the darkness. He felt his way through a large empty room and then at the end of another room he found a door. But when he tried to open it, he felt something blocking it on the other side. He put his shoulder against it and pushed.

"Stay back, I'm warning you." It was Helen's voice.

"It's me, Helen. Let me in."

He heard something being moved and the door opened. He squeezed through. There was a terrible smell in the room. "Are you all right?"

"I'm all right, but father is sick. He's lying down over there."

"Who is it, Helen?" The man's voice sounded weak.

Steele could barely see him in the darkness.

"It's Steele, father. The detective I told you about." She turned back to Steele. "So, did you finally decide to come rescue us?"

"I'm afraid I'm also locked in here."

"Oh, fine. The big detective ends up locked in, just like us."

Steele ignored her sarcasm. "What's the matter with your father? Did they hurt him?"

"No, it's his stomach. Something they've been feeding him, or maybe it's the water. He's pretty sick."

"Let me talk to him."

She took his hand to lead him across the dark room. Her hand felt hot and damp. He stopped her and brought her close to whisper, "Are you all right? They didn't hurt you or anything?"

She put her hand against his chest. "They didn't hurt me. They just locked me in here and left me. After a while I went searching for my father and found him hiding back here. I blocked the doors to keep them out, but we haven't seen or heard anything. There isn't any bathroom so I'm afraid it's kind of smelly back there."

She led Steele back to her father and she was right, the smell of the man's illness was very strong. But Steele ignored it and kneeled down next to him on the dirt floor. There was just enough moonlight coming through the cracks in the log walls for Steele to see that her father was lying flat on his back. "How are you feeling, sir?

"Like crap. Take my advice, Steele, don't eat anything they give you. And don't drink the water either."

"We may not have any choice about drinking the water. We may be here for a while."

"My daughter told me about this General Ramsey, and about how you came here to negotiate for my release. But if you're in here with us, it would seem the negotiations are not going well."

"The negotiations are not the problem. The general is willing to exchange both of you for his son who is being held by the war crimes tribunal back in Washington. The problem is that a Colonel Medina has taken control."

"But you were supposed to negotiate with General Ramsey," said Helen. "Who is Colonel Median?"

"All I know about him is that he's wearing the uniform of a Confederate Colonel."

"Medina," said Kane. "That must be the man who came out of that log cabin to look me over when they brought me in here. Big fellow?"

"That's him. He has a force of Mexicans with him."

"Well, he can't be working for the Mexican government. They wouldn't dare do this to me."

"Yes, sir. But Medina has formed some kind of militia that may not be known to the Mexican government."

"Yeah, I saw them. Mexicans in strange uniforms. And I also saw a bunch of men in Confederate uniforms. What the hell is that all about?"

"I think they were men that served under General Ramsey during the war."

"Real Confederate soldiers? What the hell are they doing clear out here?"

"They've formed an alliance with the Mexican militia. I don't know to what end."

"Damn it, let me talk to this Medina. Maybe he at least understands money."

"I doubt he is after money. He seems well supplied. Somebody is providing him with new and very expensive weapons."

Kane lay back and let out a big sigh. "These damn Rebels. First it's the war, and now it's the Mexicans. Don't understand money, don't listen to reason, and then they feed a man poison food."

"Father, let him explain," said Helen. "You're always interrupting."

Kane reached out to take Steele's sleeve. "My daughter says you've got a head on your shoulders. Can't you do something?"

"As long as General Ramsey is willing to exchange you and Helen for his son, I think we should work with him, at least long enough to complete the exchange."

"So you're saying we have to cooperate with them."

"We have no other choice. For the time being, anyhow."

Helen touched Steele's shoulder. "But Drew, how can you ask us to cooperate with the man who ordered the kidnapping of my father?"

"To paraphrase Mr. Shakespeare, trouble creates strange bedfellows."

"He was educated in Europe, Father. He likes to show off."

"But I see his point, Helen. If there was only some way to talk to this General Ramsey."

"That won't be hard, Mr. Kane. I'm afraid he's also locked in here."

Kane sat up. "What? He's here? I can't let him see me like this."

"That's not important now," said Steele gently. "If you will wait here I'll bring him back."

"No, no, if I'm going to talk to the man who kidnapped me I want to be standing up. I'll go up there. Help me."

Steele and Helen helped her father to his feet and they made their way to the front of the stockade. They found Ramsey sitting next to a crack in the logs at the front of the stockade talking to the Mexican guards. They seemed to be ignoring him.

"Stay back," whispered Steele.

Steele went up to the general and whispered to him: "General, could you come away from there for a moment?"

"Yes, what is it?"

"Could you come a bit farther away from those guards for a moment."

"Might as well. I'm wasting my time talking to them. They don't seem to understand a bit of English."

Steele led the general back into the darkness to where he had left Kane and Helen. "Mr. Kane, this is General Ramsey."

Ramsey held out his hand. "I'm sorry I was not there to greet you when you arrived, Mr. Kane. I was in a difficult situation myself."

"Yes, Steele here was telling me about this Medina fellow."

Helen stepped in front of her father to confront Ramsey. "So you are the evil man who ordered the kidnapping of my father. How could you do such a thing?"

"Ah yes, you must be the daughter." He reached out to take Helen's hand. "I'm sorry dear, I didn't even know you were in camp until Steele told me. But you must believe me, your father would never have been harmed, not while I was in charge. He was only to have been here with us for a short time. I talked to a few of the wives of hostages during the war. I always tried to reassure them, to help them to understand the ways of war."

Helen shook her finger in his face. "The ways of war? General, your so-called hostages are real people, good men like my father. It's cruel and inhuman."

"Your anger is understandable, Miss Kane. The necessities of such matters are often beyond--"

"Excuse me," said Steele. "You can continue your discussion if you want to, but I'm going back to that other room. It was a dirt floor back there. I might be able to dig my way out."

"Yes, you do that, young man," said the general. "If you get out, go directly to my men."

"Now wait a minute," said Kane. "I say if you can get out of here, you should run straight for the border." He turned to Ramsey. "Steele told me about your son. If Steele can get word to my people in San Francisco, they'll use all the power of my newspaper to free your son."

"The important thing is to regain control of this camp," said Ramsey. "Then we can deal with that issue."

They all looked at Steele, waiting for a decision. A hostage trade would be the best way to free Helen and her father, but that depended on Ramsey. If Ramsey was killed, Medina's terms might be very different." I'll go to the general's men. It's our best chance."

"Good lad," said the general.

"Then head back north as fast as you can," insisted Kane. "If you are working for my newspaper then it means you are working for me. I say get out of here as fast as you can. We can't trust this man. We can't trust any of them."

"No," said the general, "if you are successful, you should stay here until I am back in command. That's an order."

"I will try to contact your men, General, then I will go back across the border as Mr. Kane said. I will carry your terms to his newspaper. Your son in exchange for both Mr. Kane and his daughter."

"Then I'm going with you," said Helen, moving close to Steele's side.

"You should stay with your father," said Steele.

"You think I can't help? I can do anything you can."

"Stay with me, Helen," said Kane. "I need you here with me."

"Stay with your father," said Steele. "Wait for the exchange to take place."

"You can't tell me what to do. I'll stay, but only because my father asked me to."

"You all stay up here near the front," said Steele. "Keep an eye on the guards while I try to dig my way out."

Steele felt his way back to the room where he'd found Helen and her father. Once there, he moved to the back wall and took his knife out of its boot pouch. He opened the largest blade and began to dig. It was hard work, but after digging through the hard-packed floor, the dirt got a little softer. He was soon able to dig enough of a hole to get his hands under the wall. He pulled more dirt out from under the wall and then got onto his back to try to squeeze out. It was a tight fit, but he was able to wriggle his way out.

He quickly crawled away from the building and into the bushes. Staying low, he worked his way up into the hills. When he was above the tents, he stopped to look down at them. The general had said the sergeant would be in tent closest to the cabin. He crawled down the hill toward that tent, but then he heard voices and stopped. Two soldiers were sitting next to a campfire. He would have to cross right in front of them to get to the sergeant's tent. He could only hope the soldier's eyes would be adjusted to the firelight rather than the darkness beyond. Steele slowly began to crawl toward the back of the tent. The two men by the fire were talking in low tones. One of them poked at the fire with a stick.

When Steele made it to the sergeant's tent, he took out his knife and made a long slit in the canvas, trying to make as little noise as possible. He put the knife back into his boot and stuck his head through the slit. It was completely dark inside. It smelled like leather and men's sweat. He could hear men breathing. How many? Maybe three. One was snoring softly. He pushed his way through the canvas and crawled inside.

"Whose there?" came a voice out of the darkness.

"It's Drew Steele, the hostage negotiator. General Ramsey sent me."

A match flared and Steele found himself staring into the barrel of a large pistol held by the sergeant who had brought them into the camp. Two other men sat up from their sleeping mats, blinking. One of them jumped up and lit a lantern.

"I just came from your general," whispered Steele. "Medina is going to kill him."

"What?" said the sergeant. "Why would he do that?"

"He's planning to take over. He's going to kill General Ramsey tonight while you are all sleeping."

"You expect us to believe that? Why didn't the general say anything to me?"

"Medina has been keeping him under guard in his office. Tonight he threw him into the stockade. I just escaped from there. The general told me to come here to find you. We have to get him out of the stockade before Medina comes to get him."

For several seconds the sergeant didn't respond. He still had the pistol pointed at Steele's chest.

Just then, the two men who had been tending the fire pushed through the tent flap. "What's going on," said one of them.

"Keep it quiet," said the Sergeant. "This man says Medina's put the general in their stockade. Says they're gonna kill him."

"Let's go get him out," said the man holding the lantern.

The sergeant cocked the hammer of his pistol and pointed it at Steele's head. "Listen you, I don't know what you're up to, but we're gonna go right down to that stockade and see for ourselves. I'll be right behind you with this gun pointed at the back of your head. If this is a trick, you'll be the first one to get it."

With Steele leading the way, they formed a line behind him and headed for the stockade. But as they went past the cabin, the Mexican guard stood up and yelled.

The sergeant ignored him and pushed Steele forward. But before they made it much farther, Medina came out onto the porch. He had a Winchester rifle in his hands and he was followed by two of his guards who were also holding rifles. "Hey," he shouted, "where do you men think you're going?"

"This man says you got our general locked up in your damn stockade," said the sergeant. "We aim to go see for ourselves."

"You men will go back to your tents immediately."

"No, we ain't goin' back," said the sergeant. "Like I said, we're gonna go down there and see what's what. Don't try to stop us."

Medina pointed his rifle at the sergeant. "I'm giving you men an order. Go back to your tents. This is your last chance."

The other Mexicans also lifted their rifles. In response, the sergeant's men leveled their old Enfields at the Mexicans.

Steele began to edge slowly to one side.

"You ain't my commander," said the sergeant. "We don't take orders from no Mexicans."

The words were barely out of the sergeant's mouth when Medina fired. The sergeant went down and the other Confederates fired in response.

Steele didn't wait to see if Medina had been hit. He dove to the side, rolled once, and came up running. He heard the distinctive thud of the old Enfields, followed by the fast repeating cracks of the Mexican's Winchesters.

Steele ran toward the hillside, hoping the smoke from the old muzzle-loaders would hide him long enough to make it.

Confederates in night shirts and long underwear began to pour out of the tents. "The Mexicans are attacking," yelled Steele. "Your Sergeant has been hit."

One of the soldiers stopped, confused. Steele heard a shot from a Winchester and the solider was hit in the throat. He fell back against his tent with both hands clutching at his bleeding throat, as if he was trying to strangle himself.

Steele ran through the rows of tents, dodging the sleepy Confederates, until he made it to the hillside. There he stopped to listen. Most of the shots were coming from the fast-firing Winchesters, but there were more and more Enfields joining the fight. The Confederates had Medina outnumbered, but Steele knew the shooting would bring other Mexicans from the upper camp. There was no way to know how many armed men were there. Steele began to work his way up the hill. If he could get back to the stockade, he might be able to get Helen and her father out during the confusion of the fighting.

But then he heard a voice behind him. "*¡Donde vas! ¡Alto!*" He looked back. It was Medina, aiming his rifle at him. Steele dived to the ground. The shot missed, but it was close. He jumped and scrambled farther up the hill into the darkness. The loose rocks underfoot made him stumble often, but somehow he stayed on his feet and kept running. He could hear Medina crashing through the bushes after him.

Steele kept going higher up the hill, but then he saw several men coming across the hill toward him. One of them was carrying a lantern. Medina yelled to them, "Stop him. Shoot him."

The man with the lantern yelled, *¡allí!*" and pointed a pistol at Steele.

Steele stood up and raised his hands.

The man with the lantern kept his pistol aimed at Steele while he waited for Medina.

When Median arrived, he jammed the barrel of his rifle into Steele's chest. "You shouldn't have done that, Mr. Steele. You have allied yourself with Ramsey and now you must share his fate. Goodbye."

Steele slapped the barrel of the rifle away and dived at the lantern, knocking it out of the man's hand. As it bounced down the hill, Steele rolled away into the darkness. He heard Medina fire three quick shots and knew immediately that at least one of them had hit him in the side. Despite the pain, he was able to crawl away into the bushes as more shots came. They were coming close, but Steele didn't think he had been hit again.

When the shooting finally ended, he heard Medina yelling for someone to bring another lantern. Steele crawled slowly and quietly farther up the hill until he made it to some boulders. He crawled behind them and lay still, trying to catch his breath. He could still hear excited voices down below. He peeked over the top of the boulder and looked down. Men with lanterns were working their way up the hill. He ducked back down and the quick movement caused a sharp pain in his left side. He cautiously touched it. His shirt was wet with blood, but in the darkness there was no way to tell how serious the wound was. He knew he didn't have time to tend to it: he could hear them coming closer.

"Find him!" shouted Medina. "Get that gringo. He must not be allowed to escape."

Medina's voice was close. Steele knew he had to get moving, wound or no wound. He began to crawl again, trying to stay behind the larger rocks, but always moving higher up the hill.

When he came to another cluster of large boulders, he stopped to rest. He could see the flashes of lantern light against the hillside. They weren't giving up.

But then he heard a shot and someone yelled. It sounded like a muzzle-loader. He got up onto his knees and looked over the top of the boulder in time to see a lantern tumbling down the hill. Men were shouting and running. More shots came, but none of them sounded like the Winchesters; it was the deeper thud of the Confederate's Enfields. Had the rest of Medina's little army run off?

Steele watched as the Confederates stormed the hill. Even though the Mexicans held the high ground, the Confederates were clearly the more experienced fighters; they knew how to fire in alternating groups, one group firing while the other group stayed hidden to reload. Despite the superior firepower of the Mexican's Winchesters, they soon gave up and threw down their weapons.

The Confederates quickly surrounded them. One of them knocked Medina down and when he tried to get up, another man hit him in the face with the butt of his rifle. Medina went down hard. The group tightened the circle around him, but then another man forced his way into the center of the circle. Someone held a lantern up high and Steele saw it was Ramsey. He was helping Medina to his feet.

Steele didn't wait to find out what was going to happen next. If Ramsey was now in charge, Steele could only hope he would hold true to his promise of releasing Helen and her father in exchange for his son. Steele's job was to go back to San Diego and try to arrange for that trade. He turned and began moving toward the top of the hill.

When he'd made it over the top, he stopped to assess his wound. It felt like the bullet had torn a furrow along his left side. He'd been lucky, but he was still bleeding. He tore off a piece of his shirt and used it to apply direct pressure to the wound. He wished he could see how bad it was, but there was no time for that; he had to keep moving. Medina's force of Mexicans had been overcome, but there was no way to know what Ramsey would do next. Steele worried that he might send riders to chase him down. The best thing would be to get back to Mesa City as fast as he could. From there he could send a telegraphic message to San Diego explaining Ramsey's proposed hostage trade. But would the U.S. government go along with it? They might not, but there was no point worrying about that now. The important thing was to keep moving. He would stay off the roads in case Ramsey had men out looking for him. He would use the stars to make sure he was always heading straight north and maybe, if he was lucky, he would find a farmhouse.

He took one last look back in the direction of the camp. "Goodbye, Helen," he whispered. "I'll be back to get you. I promise."

Chapter 8

*H*olding the cloth tightly to his wounded side, Steele began to run through the darkness. He tried to hold a steady pace, one that he could maintain for a long time. He thought about detouring back toward the road near the entrance to the camp to retrieve his pistol, but decided it was better to stay away from the road. If Ramsey was going to send somebody after him, he should try to get across the border. Maybe they wouldn't follow him into the United States. Just run, he told himself, just keep running north toward that border.

He soon came to the shallow river they had crossed on the way in. He waded out to the middle and stopped to wash the blood from his wound. In the dim moonlight he could see that it was still bleeding a little, but it didn't seem as serious as he had first thought. He washed the cloth out thoroughly and put it back against the wound. He could only hope the direct pressure would eventually make it stop bleeding. He used his other hand to scoop up water and he drank as much as he could. This would probably be the last water he would find before Mesa City.

He continued on and when he topped another hill, he stopped to look back. The moon was setting in the west, leaving the desert very dark. It was eerily quiet except for the occasional cry of a night bird. If Ramsey had sent riders after him, Steele couldn't hear them coming. Maybe they were sticking to the roads, trying to get ahead of him. Would they be waiting at the border? If so, there was nothing he could do about it. He started to run again, heading straight north, always keeping the handle of the Little Dipper in front of him.

Soon, he was out of the hills and onto flat desert. It was easier running there, but he kept on bumping into cactus in the dark. Mostly they just stuck him a little, but there was one type that was especially troublesome. It was a waist-high cactus with arms that were covered with spiny balls that pulled loose if he even brushed slightly against it. When he tried to pull the balls of stickers off of his clothes, they stuck to his fingers, and every time they touched his skin, it felt like dozens of tiny bees stinging him. He realized there must be some kind of poison in each tiny barb. That type of cactus seemed to grow in thick patches so from then on he made a wide detour whenever he came across them.

After a few more hours of running, he saw the first indications of a purple dawn beginning to spread across the eastern sky. The air immediately seemed to grow a little warmer and he suddenly felt very thirsty. As if in response to the coming dawn, coyotes started yipping in the distance. Despite his situation, he liked the sound of the coyotes. It was a lonely sound, but it reminded him of how much he liked the desert, liked being so far from any type of civilization. It made him think of the time he had been lost in that very hot desert in Arizona. He had almost died there. He forced himself to push those thoughts aside and concentrate where his feet were landing. He wasn't free yet. Men on horses could make up time on the flat desert. Without slowing, he unbuttoned the top few buttons of his shirt and immediately it felt a bit cooler. The breeze from running, plus the evaporating sweat, energized him.

Soon, he began to feel an urgent need for water. The sun was just peeking above the distant mountains, but he was already feeling its heat. He kept moving, looking back often, but there was no sign of anybody back there. He was sure he must have already crossed the border. If Ramsey had sent riders after him, maybe they had turned back at the border. Looking ahead, he saw a wide, flat area that seemed completely devoid of vegetation. It was like a dry lakebed, totally flat, stark white, and shimmering in the increasing heat. He knew if he tried to cross it, he could be seen from miles away. But he was sure Mesa City must lie somewhere in the hills on the other side. He had no choice but to go straight across. He tried to hurry, but he was so weak from thirst and the loss of blood, he found it almost impossible to keep running. He began walking instead, but tried to keep up a good pace. He was feeling very thirsty and now that the sun was providing some light, he could see that his wound was still bleeding. He kept moving, but he realized he was no longer sweating, one of the first signs of severe dehydration. He remembered the wounded soldiers that often came off the battlefield severely dehydrated. In the heat of battle, they often forgot to drink and that could be life threatening. Sometimes they were brought in raving and nearly unconscious. The doctors would inspect them for wounds and if they found none they would move on to the next patient, leaving Steele to try to get the delirious soldiers to drink a little water. Often they refused, swearing they were not thirsty. As he made his way across the dry lakebed, Steele took it as a good sign that he was still very thirsty.

When the full heat of the sun finally broke over the top of the mountains, he remembered the Mexican guard had taken his hat. Not good to be out there in the desert without a hat. Once he made it across the dry lakebed, he should try to find something to cover his head.

Then he thought he heard something. He stopped to look toward the east, shading his eyes with his hand. Something was moving out there. Or was it a mirage? He watched for a few more moments, and then he realized what it was: a cloud of dust, moving toward him. Riders.

He looked toward the north. If only he could make it to those hills before they got to him. He began to run, but it was hard. His legs didn't seem to want to cooperate. He glanced back toward the east. The riders were getting closer. There were a lot of them, at least ten, maybe more. They must have spotted him. They were coming directly toward him, riding out of the glare of the early morning sun. He looked toward the low hills ahead. How far was it? It might be farther than it looked, but he had to try to keep running.

Now he could hear the sound of the horse's hoofs pounding the ground. He tried to keep running, but the dried mud underfoot was cracked and uneven. The cracks formed strange patterns and his mind kept on trying to make some kind of sense of them. He tried to concentrate. He had to make it to those hills.

But then he saw the two riders coming in from his right. They had broken free from the others and were bearing down on him. He heard one of them yell and he knew there was no use in running any farther. He stopped and turned to face them with raised hands.

They rode up fast and the hard-breathing horses came to a sudden stop right in front of him, bringing a shower of dust with them. Steele tried to see if he recognized them, but the bright sun behind them made it hard to see. They were wearing uniforms. Confederates?

One of the men yelled, "Who are you? What are you doing out here?"

They didn't know who he was. They must not be Ramsey's men.

He shaded his eyes with his hand and as the full group arrived he saw their uniforms were Union blue. It was the U.S. Cavalry. Finally, he could stop running. He sat down on the ground and the sudden movement made him realize how dizzy he was.

One of the soldiers wore the insignia of a lieutenant and he had a pistol in his hand. As he brought his horse to a stop, he shouted, "The corporal asked who you are. Answer the question."

But before Steele could answer, someone else in the group of arriving horsemen yelled, "It's him, Lieutenant. It's Steele."

Steele knew that voice. "Rudd?"

Rudd rode up next to Steele and reined in his horse. "Steele, it's me," he shouted. "What the hell are you doing out here? I thought you were supposed to meet the kidnappers. Where's Helen? Is that blood? Are you wounded?"

Steele suddenly felt very tired. How long had it been since he'd slept? He looked up at Rudd and said, "Nice to see you, old fellow. Do you think you could get me a drink of water?"

Chapter 9

*T*he lieutenant gave the order to stand down and as the men dismounted, Steele estimated the lieutenant's force at about a dozen— not enough to attack Ramsey's fortified camp. He also noticed two Indians in the lieutenant's troop. They wore blue shirts, like the soldiers, but the shirts didn't have any of the usual Army markings.

The lieutenant brought Steele a canteen full of water and watched while he drank most of it.

"Damn, am I glad to see you," said Rudd, sitting down next to Steele and clapping him on the back. "But where's Helen?"

Steele took another long drink of water before he answered. "She tried to follow me. Ramsey's got her."

Rudd's eyes widened. "Oh no. Now he's got both of them?"

"I'm afraid so. They were taking me to their camp and she followed."

"Damn," said Rudd. "I knew that girl was going to be trouble. She's so damned . . . headstrong. I was waiting for you in San Diego, like you said, but I had a bad feeling about it. The lieutenant and his men found me at the telegraph office. They'd been to the newspaper and talked to Bailey. We rode out to Mesa City and the man at the livery stable said you'd both gone out and never come back." He leaned closer to Steele and whispered, "They're not too happy you came out here without telling them Kane had been kidnapped."

The lieutenant came and stood over them. "Are you ready to tell me what's been going on out here?"

Steele stood up, but staggered. Rudd caught his arm to steady him and noticed the blood on Steele's shirt. "Holy Christ, you're wounded. What happened?"

The lieutenant turned to shout, "Medic, get over here. Bring your stuff."

The medic arrived and lifted up Steele's shirt to look at the wound. "Looks like the bullet didn't hit anything solid. Tore quite a chunk out of you though. Not much I can do. We need to get you somewhere where it can be stitched up."

"Don't you have a needle and thread?" asked Steele.

"Yes, but . . . "

"Then stitch it up."

"Here? I can't even clean it out properly."

"Just do it."

The medic found a curved needle and some thread. Steele looked away while he did it.

Rudd said, Jesus! Doesn't that hurt?" He grimaced with every stitch.

When the medic had finished stitching and bandaging the wound, the lieutenant sat down next to Steele. "Rudd here told me some crazy Confederate general kidnapped his boss. Is that true?"

"I'm afraid it is," said Steele. "Kane and his daughter are being held in a camp on the other side of the border. General Ramsey wants to exchange them for his son who is being held by the war crimes commission back in Washington."

The lieutenant took off his hat and scratched his head. "Politics, that's all I need."

"So that's what it's all about," said Rudd. "He took Mr. Kane to trade for his son."

"Yes, but it's not that simple. He's got an army of former Confederate soldiers with him."

"What?" said the lieutenant. He put his hat back on. "Oh fine. That's just fine. First it's trouble along the border with the Mexicans and now I've got a bunch of crazy Confederates running around down there."

"They're not crazy," said Steele, "Not in the normal sense anyhow. Ramsey has managed to get a significant number of his former soldiers all the way here from Tennessee. He must have had a reason for doing that."

"A reason," said the lieutenant, frowning. "As if those damn Rebels ever needed a reason to cause trouble. How many of them are in this camp?"

"Assuming they are three or four to a tent, Ramsey could have more than one hundred soldiers with him."

"A hundred?" said Rudd. "Damn. He's got a small army down there."

Steele nodded, still looking at the lieutenant. "And some Mexican militia are in the same camp, led by a Colonel Medina. You mentioned trouble with the Mexicans. They may be the ones who have been causing it. Ramsey was trying to form an alliance with them, but when I left, the two groups were fighting and I was told more Mexican militiamen were on the way there."

"How well armed are they?" asked the lieutenant.

"The Confederates were not well armed at all. They were still carrying their old muzzle loaders. But the Mexicans had brand new Winchester Henry repeaters. Much better rifles than the ones your men are carrying. Those weapons are probably now in the hands of the Confederates."

The lieutenant looked toward the south. "How far across the border is this camp?"

"I don't think you have enough men to attack them," said Steele. "Besides, you would endanger Mr. Kane and his daughter. In hostage situations it's best to try to meet the demands of the hostage takers. My job is to go back to San Diego with the demands and try to arrange for a hostage trade."

"I'll send a man back to Mesa City to send a telegraph message to my superiors about this situation. They'll contact your newspaper about the hostages. But I need you to show me where that camp is. I've got an extra horse for you."

"I can't do that, Lieutenant. You'd endanger Mr. Kane and his daughter."

The lieutenant stood up. "All right. I'll find it on my own. My orders were to go down to the border to find out why the Mexicans are causing trouble. Now you tell me Americans are involved. I won't attack them, but I have to determine what their motives are. If they won't disband peacefully, I'll call for reinforcements."

Steele thought about it. Ramsey would have sentries out watching the roads. What would he do if he saw the Army coming? "All right, Lieutenant, I'll lead you to their camp, but you have to let me go in alone. To secure the safety of the hostages."

"Fine, fine, you can go in by yourself if that's what you want, but I have the responsibility to protect American citizens. You have to tell them any American held against their will must be released immediately."

Steele picked up a stick and began to draw a rough map in the sand. "There's a set of hills north of the camp. I came through there last night." Steele drew a series of upside-down V shapes to represent the hills. Then he drew a small a square to represent the camp beyond them. "The camp is in a shallow valley with high ground all around. There's a river a short distance this side of the hills." He drew a wavy line to indicate it.

"That would be the Tijuana River," said the lieutenant. "It's a few miles on the other side of the border. Just a minute," he said, standing up. "I've got two men who know that area." He waved over the Indians. "Look at this map," he said. He stooped down and put his finger in the middle of the square Steele had drawn. "This is an enemy camp. Hills. Other side of the river. Can you find it?"

Both of the Indians nodded.

"I want you two men to take off your blue shirts and go there. Do not engage the enemy. Scout the situation and report back to me. Understood?"

The two Indians nodded again. The lieutenant waved them away, and they both jumped on their horses and took off fast.

Steele stood up. "I'm ready. Let's go."

"Are you sure you want to ride?" said Rudd. "What about your wound?"

"I want to get back there to make sure Helen and her father are still safe."

Rudd took Steele's arm and drew him aside. "Are you sure it's such a good idea to go back in there? Why don't we just let the people back at the newspaper work out the exchange?"

"My job was to negotiate with Ramsey. If there are to be negotiations, someone will have to be inside that camp to do it."

The lieutenant gathered his troops together. "Listen up, men. This man is going to lead us south. He knows where some renegade Confederates are hiding. They may be the ones who hung that sergeant from Nevada. It's important that you all know we will be operating near the Mexican border. We may run into trouble. If the bugler gives the signal to form a defensive position, I want you to form up fast. Mount up!"

Rudd brought up a horse for Steele. "I brought your backpack and put it in the saddlebag. But are you sure you want to do this?"

"I have to find out what's going on down there. Let's go."

They joined the column behind the lieutenant. Rudd moved his horse close to Steele. "Do you think Helen will be all right? I sure hope they don't get any ideas about . . . well, you know. She's a mighty pretty girl. "

"I had the Confederate's assurances that she wouldn't be harmed."

"Yeah, but what about the Mexicans? I'd hate to think what they might do to her."

Steele could only hope that Ramsey had regained full control of the camp and that he would hold true to his promise to protect Helen and her father. He thought about how Helen had put her hand against his chest there in the darkness of the stockade. He could almost feel her light touch. Would she think he had abandoned her?

As the column moved steadily southward, Rudd soon found more personal concerns. "Damn, Steele, the sun's only been up a couple of hours and it's already getting hot as hell. My butt's all sweaty and I just know I'm getting saddle blisters." He stood up in his stirrups to try to relieve the pressure on his backside, but soon he sat down again, complaining that his legs were not as strong as they used to be. "Did you know I used to be able to ride a horse all day?" He didn't wait for Steele's response. "It's true. I could ride all day without a break."

"It is not a long ride to the border," said Steele, "but it's going to get much hotter."

"Yeah, would you just look at this desert. No shade out here anywhere. I wish I'd thought to bring an extra hat for you. Why don't you take mine?" He took it off and held it out to Steele.

"I'm all right. It's not far."

Rudd put his bowler had back on. "Well, at least you ought to eat something." He reached back into his saddle bag to fish out a bottle of beer and some food. "Want one?" he asked, holding out a bottle.

Steele shook his head.

"You've got to eat anyhow." He forced a sandwich into Steele's hands.

Steele ate the sandwich without noticing what it contained, washing it down with plenty of water from his canteen. He glanced at Rudd and found him happily humming to himself as he ate. He wondered how much weight Rudd had put on since those days of riding for hours. How would he hold up if he had to stay out there in the heat all day?

Steele saw a plume of dust ahead and as riders came closer he saw it was the two Indian scouts returning. They rode up fast, their dust settling over everyone as they came to a sudden stop. One of the Indians pointed back to the south. "All dead."

Steele spurred his horse forward. "All dead? What do you mean? Who's in charge of the camp?"

The Indian looked at him and then at the lieutenant.

"How close were you able to get? Did they see you?" asked the lieutenant.

"No one see. All gone. All dead."

All dead? Was the Indian referring to the dead from the fighting? But what did he mean by all gone? Had Ramsey abandoned the camp?

"You mean there were no guards at the camp?" asked the lieutenant. "They'd all left?"

"All gone. Only dead left."

Steele tried to imagine what had happened. Would Ramsey abandon the camp without waiting for word about the hostage exchange? Or had Medina's Mexican reinforcements come? Had they wiped out all of Ramsey's men? If so, what had happened to Helen and her father?

Steele spurred his horse into a gallop. He heard the lieutenant yell but he didn't look back.

By the time he had topped the first set of hills, his horse was lathered and breathing heavily, but he urged him on until he reached the river. There he allowed the horse to drink while he refilled his canteen. Then he forced the horse back into a gallop until he came to the place where he had buried his pistol. He got off to dig it up.

He got back onto his horse, and keeping the gun in his hand, he rode up the hill toward the camp. As he approached the camp entrance, he noticed some deep wagon tracks and a large number of hoof prints heading south out of the hills.

As he entered the camp, he watched the rocks above for movement, but there didn't seem to be any guards. There was no sound except for the rhythmic shuffle of his own horse's hooves.

But then he saw something ahead in the road. In the glare of the sun it seemed dark and low to the ground. It moved. Steele slowed his horse and aimed his pistol. But then he saw what it was: a vulture, a big one, feeding on the entrails of a dead man. The huge shaggy bird waited until Steele was very close before rising clumsily into the air. It struggled to gain altitude and then began a slow arcing turn overhead, joining several others of his kind that were circling high above, waiting for their chance at a meal of human flesh.

Steele stopped his horse next to the dead man. It was a Mexican, wearing one of the gray and black uniforms of the militia. The bird had opened up the man's stomach, probably at the site of a bullet wound. Back in Tennessee, he'd seen magpies and hawks feeding on dead soldiers. It was a common sight after battles. To the birds, a dead human was just an easy meal.

He rode on, seeing several more dead men as he entered the camp, all Mexicans. Had Ramsey gone and taken his dead with him?

The rows of Confederate tents were gone, and just as the Indian scouts had reported, there didn't seem to be anyone left alive in the camp. The log cabin had been partially burned and was still smoldering. Near the front of the cabin were more dead, again, all Mexicans. Medina was not among them.

Steele tied up his horse and hurried to the stockade. The wooden door was ajar. He leaned inside, his pistol ready. A Mexican in a militia uniform was dead inside on the dirt floor.

"Anybody in here?" he yelled. There was no response. He headed down toward the Mexican encampment. More dead Mexicans were huddled behind some rocks. They must have made their final stand there. No matter how many times Steele had come across such scenes during the war, he always thought about the families they left behind, wives who would never again hold these men, children that would wait forever for their fathers to come home.

He went on and found two more Mexicans lying together near a burnt-out campfire. Both had chest wounds, but both had also been shot in the side of the head. Steele kneeled down to take a closer look. The blood around their chest wounds was dry, but blood and cerebral fluids still leaked from their head wounds. Somebody had executed these two wounded men, and it had not been done very long ago. Did it mean someone was still alive in the camp, hiding? He stood up and looked around, but the camp had the silent and lonely feel of a cemetery. A gentle wind sprang up and rolled a tumbleweed along until it came to rest against the body of one of the Mexicans.

Steele put his gun into his boot holster and walked back to the log cabin. The roof and floor had been partly burned away, but the log walls were mostly intact. He pushed aside some rubble and looked inside. The rifle boxes were gone, of course, and the Tennessee battle flag had been removed from the wall. The Confederates must have left quickly. But why? With the captured Winchester rifles, the Confederates could have easily defended the camp. Apparently, Ramsey was not yet ready for a fight. But where was he going? Steele had seen wagon tracks heading south out of the hills. For some reason, Ramsey taking his men deeper into Mexico.

Steele heard horses coming and moved to the window. The lieutenant and Rudd were slowly leading the Cavalry troops into the camp. Most of the soldiers seemed uneasy, and many, including the lieutenant, had drawn their sidearms.

Steele went out onto the porch. "There's no one here."

Rudd hurried his horse forward. "Helen and her father?"

"There's no sign of them."

The lieutenant put his pistol away and ordered his men to look around.

Steele waited on the porch as Rudd came up to join him. "There were rifle boxes stacked in here. Now Ramsey has them."

Rudd leaned in to look.

The lieutenant came part way up the steps. "What do you think happened here?"

Steele walked to the edge of the porch and pointed towards the stockade. "The two prisoners, Mr. Kane and his daughter, were being kept down there. But they're gone. It looks like Ramsey and his Confederates packed everything into wagons and headed farther down into Mexico. It shouldn't be hard to follow their wagon tracks."

The lieutenant shook his head. "No sir, I can't do that. I can't go deeper into Mexico. I shouldn't even be here"

"I understand that, lieutenant, but I can."

"Alone?"

"A man alone might stand a better chance in Mexico."

"What about that wound in your side? You should come back to San Diego with us to have it looked at."

"Your man taped it up. There's nothing more that can be done about it."

The lieutenant shrugged. "It's your funeral. He went down off the porch, but turned back to Steele. "A lot of dead men here. And for what? Don't they know the war is over?" He shook his head again and mounted his horse. "Assemble the men," he said to his adjunct.

"Aren't you going to bury the dead?" asked Rudd.

"Not my responsibility. The sooner I get my men out of this God-forsaken country the happier I'll be."

Steele turned to Rudd. "When you get back to San Diego, make sure your newspaper is putting all the pressure they can on Washington. The best hope for Helen and her father is to get the government to exchange them for Ramsey's son. If I can find them."

"You're going to go after Ramsey?"

"That's right. I'll follow their wagon tracks."

"What good will that do? You can't fight a hundred soldiers."

"We need to know where Ramsey is in case Washington agrees to the exchange. And I may find some opportunity to get Helen and her father out of there."

"Okay," said Rudd, "if you're going, I am too."

Steele shook his head. "It would be better for you to go back. The lieutenant said there had been trouble along the border. Gringos may not be very welcome in Mexico right now."

"Oh no you don't. If you're going, I'm going, and that's final. This is my big chance to write an important story and I'm not letting it go."

"It could be a hard ride."

"I can do it. You may think I'm just a fat city newspaper reporter, but I was bumping around the West on a horse while you were still over there in your fancy European private school. I can take care of myself."

"Do you have a gun?"

"You bet, I got a big converted Colt in my saddlebags. Why, when I was back in Arizona, I could shoot the eye out of a—"

"Quiet!" said Steele.

"Hey, I was just trying to tell you about the time—"

Steele held up his hand. "Listen." He took out his pistol and looked up into the hills above the camp. "Somebody's up there."

"Where? I don't see anybody."

Steele pointed. "There's a man way up there. See him? In the rocks."

Rudd looked up toward where Steele was pointing. "Oh yeah, now I see him. He's waving at us. Who the hell is that?"

From that distance Steele couldn't see the man clearly. He was sitting on the ground, waving both of his arms. Suddenly, Steele realized who it was. "It's Kane. Tell the lieutenant." Steele started running up the hill.

Chapter 10

When Steele reached Kane, he found him sitting on the ground, leaning on his elbow. His clothes were covered with dust, but he didn't seem to be bleeding. "Are you wounded?" asked Steele kneeling down beside him.

"Naw, I hurt my knee. During the fighting, the guards ran away so we got out of the stockade and made our way up here."

"But where's Helen?"

"I twisted my knee and couldn't walk. When Ramsey's men came up the hill after us, she went back down to meet them. Told them I'd left with you. My brave girl doesn't back down from anybody. I could hear her yelling at them, cussing them out, as they took her back down. They kept on looking for me, but it was dark and they didn't find me under these rocks. She told me to hide so I did. She said you'd come."

"What about the Mexicans? Did you see Medina?"

"I think most of the Mexicans ran off, but I'm not sure. It was too dark."

"Let me look at your leg," said Steele. He pulled up Kane's pant leg and could immediately see that the man's knee was very swollen. "Hard to tell how serious it is, but you won't be able to walk on it for a while."

Kane looked down at his swollen knee and then back up at Steele. "Are you a doctor, as well as a detective?"

"I worked with the wounded during the war." He pushed Kane's pant leg back down.

When Kane saw Rudd and the lieutenant working their way up the hill, he took ahold of Steele's sleeve and pulled him closer. "Two

Indians rode in a while ago. I was afraid to let them know I was up here."

"They're with the Cavalry. Scouts."

"With the Cavalry? But why did they shoot the men that were on the ground?" He glanced down at the lieutenant and Rudd who were getting closer. "They just shot them in the head and walked away," he whispered. "I was afraid they were going to come up here and shoot me too. That's why I hid when I heard your horse coming."

"All right," said Steele. "Don't say anything to the lieutenant." He stood up to see where the two Indians were. They were still down next to the cabin, waiting with the horses. Why would the two Indian scouts would execute the dying Mexicans?

As the lieutenant arrived, Steele said, "Kane has hurt his knee. Help me get him down."

The lieutenant helped Steele get Kane to his feet and they started down the steep hill with Kane between them, hopping on one leg.

Rudd arrived, out of breath. "Are you shot, Mr. Kane? What happened."

"No, it's my damned knee," said Kane. "I twisted it."

"We saw some horses running loose," said the lieutenant. "My men will get one for you."

Rudd looked back up the hill. "Where's Helen?"

"She saved me," said Kane. "She gave herself up to them to save me. They took her away in a wagon. We've got to go find her."

"We can't follow them any farther into Mexico," said the lieutenant.

Kane scowled at him. "You have to. I'll bet I know your commander, young man." He grabbed the lieutenant by the arm. "Listen, you bring back my girl and I can get you promoted to a major."

"Sorry, sir. More likely I'd get demoted to a private. I shouldn't even be this far inside Mexico."

"Damn it man, you can't just leave my daughter in their hands. If anything happens to her I'll . . . I'll . . . "

"Sorry, sir. All I can do is get you back to San Diego."

"I don't want you to take me back to San Diego, I want you to go after my daughter. She's a citizen of the United States and those Confederate rebels have taken her into a foreign county."

The lieutenant removed Kane's hand from his arm. "We'd better get moving, sir. He turned and started back down the hill.

Kane continued to bluster while Steele and Rudd helped him back down the hill. They sat him down on the steps of the cabin while one of the soldiers ran off to find him a horse.

Steele looked at the two Indians who were standing near the cabin. Both had long braided hair and looked enough alike to be brothers. It was hard to tell how old they were, maybe about thirty. They were watching everything that was going on, but they seemed to be doing it covertly, as if they didn't care. Whenever anyone moved close to them, they found a way to casually move away. They never interacted with the soldiers, or with each other; they just waited, silent and watchful.

Kane called Steele over. "Listen, Steele, I don't know what my people at the newspaper said they'd pay you to negotiate my release, but now everything's changed. I want you to find my daughter. I'll pay you whatever you want. Catch up with Ramsey and tell him I'll get his son back, no matter what it takes. Remind him that he promised to keep my daughter safe."

"I'll do my best, Mr. Kane."

Kane looked off toward the north. "If anything happened to her, it'd kill her mother."

"Yes, sir. Tell your wife not to worry. We'll bring her back."

"Good, good. Listen, Rudd, you can't come back without her, you hear me? That's your only job now. Consider yourself on double salary until you bring her back. Have you got money? I'd give you some but those damn Mexicans took everything I had. They even my gold pocket watch."

"I have some money, sir," said Rudd.

"All right then. If you get to a town with a telegraph, you let me know what's going on. I'll stay in San Diego until I hear from you."

"Yes, sir."

The lieutenant brought a horse and helped Kane up. He called his men together and they all rode out fast.

Steele went to one of the dead Confederates and picked up the man's gray felt hat. It had the woven red cord hatband that indicated he had been a member of an artillery division. Steele slapped it against his thigh to knock off some of the dust before trying it on. It fit.

He got on his horse and he and Rudd rode out to the south, following the wagon tracks.

"I've never seen Mr. Kane like that," said Rudd. "He's really worried about Helen. And who could blame him? Who knows what might happen to her."

The wagon tracks led down out of the hills and then turned east.

"Hey, they changed directions," said Rudd. "Where are they going now?"

"They seem to be staying in Mexico, but close to the border."

"I bet they're afraid of the Mexican's. You said that Medina guy had more Mexican militia troops coming. Ramsey must want to run back across the border into the U.S. if they come"

"Maybe."

"Well, if we're gonna catch up to them we'd better get going," said Rudd, spurring his horse.

When Steele didn't follow, he reined back and waited. "Shouldn't we try to catch them? They've got a big head start."

"They won't be moving fast. Look how deep those wagon tracks are. They're heavily loaded. No use in tiring our horses. We'll catch up to them soon enough, and I'd rather we didn't get too close to them while it's still daylight."

"So what are we supposed to do, follow them all the way back to Tennessee?"

"I doubt if Ramsey is heading for Tennessee."

"So where's he going?"

"There's no way to know."

Rudd took off his hat and fanned his face with it. "Aw, hell, maybe he's just running away, hightailing it out of here before the Cavalry comes after him."

"Maybe. But while his alliance with the Mexican militia may not have worked out, he's not the type to give up. He has a plan."

"Are you sure? Maybe he's crazy, just another madman who didn't want the war to end."

"He doesn't believe the war has ended."

"All right, so he doesn't think the fight is over. So why didn't he stay back there in the Mexican's camp and fight the Cavalry?"

"He's an experienced military officer. He will pick his time and place."

Rudd frowned. "Aw, I just don't get it. Why did he bring his little army all the way out here in the first place?"

"That is the important question," agreed Steele. "Why *did* he come to the West? He could have sent that letter to any newspaper in the country. And why did he kidnap Kane? If he really wanted to negotiate the release of his son, there are plenty of officials back east he could have captured, men who are more directly involved in what is going on in the post-war South."

They rode on a ways in silence before Rudd said, "You know, I bet Ramsey just ran out here to get away from that war-crimes tribunal. Then, when he got out here, he hatched this plot to kidnap Mr. Kane."

Steele shook his head. "No, it was all part of a plan he formulated in advance. He had an arrangement with Medina, and his men knew where to come to meet him."

"Okay, so he had a plan. What's he going to do with his little army now that he's got them here?"

"An army is used for fighting."

"Fighting who? Look around. There's nothing here but sand and rocks and cactus."

"That's a good point. He came here to join the Mexican militia. It means that whatever he was planning, he needed a larger force."

Rudd thought about that. Then he said, "Okay, so who was he planning to attack, the Cavalry? In California?"

"He could have waited for the Cavalry to come to him, or he could have taken his army across the border into California. It means he's not ready."

"He must be afraid of the Cavalry. That's why he's running east."

"I doubt it," said Steele. "In the West, the U.S. Cavalry is spread very thin right now. Most units are back in Missouri and Kansas, putting down post-war rebellions there. The few units that are left out here are fighting Indians. Ramsey already has a large enough force to overcome any Cavalry unit in the West, and with those new Winchester military rifles, he has enough weaponry. He has some other plan."

Rudd put his hat back on and hurried his horse to keep up with Steele. "Uh, speaking of plans, what do you plan to do when we catch them?"

"Watch for opportunities to get Helen away from them. But if we can't do that, we need to keep track of where they are in case Kane has success in arranging the hostage trade."

"Okay, we'll just follow them. I sure hope Helen's all right."

"During the war, hostages were well taken care of. If Kane wants his son back, Helen is now his most valuable commodity."

"I sure hope you're right."

They followed the wagon tracks all morning and into the afternoon. The heat of the day continued to build even as the afternoon sun settled farther down toward the western horizon. What little breeze there had been earlier in the day disappeared.

Steele let Rudd ride ahead and pulled up his shirt to see if the riding had reopened the wound in his side. The medic's bandage was dark red, but it didn't seem too wet. He pulled down his shirt and caught up with Rudd.

Late in the afternoon, as they topped a ridge, Steele saw Ramsey's column down in the valley ahead. From that distance, it appeared to be only a long, thin, moving cloud of dust."

Steele glanced at Rudd. He was leaning way forward on his horse and his eyes were closed. "Rudd! Wake up."

Rudd sat up quickly and pulled on the reins, which caused the horse to stop suddenly. He barely managed to stay on by grabbing a handful of mane. "What happened? Are they coming?" He looked wildly in all directions.

"We've caught up with them." Steele pointed down toward the column.

Rudd stood up in his stirrups to see. "Man, from up here it looks like there's a lot of 'em. Are you sure it's only a hundred?"

"It does look like more." Ramsey was keeping his troops together in one long column, moving fast. But it did look like more than one hundred men. Had more soldiers come across the border to join him?

"Well, shouldn't we be heading down there?" asked Rudd.

"No, let's wait a bit. Ramsey will have a rear guard out."

They got off their horses to wait. Far below, Steele could see that the column was approaching a small village."

"Look, they're turning north," said Rudd. "I knew it. They're going back across the border."

"I think they're just avoiding that little town down there. We'll let them get farther ahead, then we'll go down."

They sat in the long shadow of a tall cactus to wait. Rudd drank the last of his water and began to scratch in the sand with a stick. He looked up at Steele. "You know, I've been thinking. Maybe now that Ramsey has his army and those new rifles, maybe he's going back east to try to start the war again."

"I don't think so. Ramsey said when you're out manned, you change tactics. And he also talked about Apaches. He admired their tactics."

"Indian tactics? You mean like hiding in the hills and attacking . . . what? Wagon trains?"

Steele smiled and shook his head. "I think he was referring to their quick strikes, limiting their attacks to remote settlements and retreating quickly. He referred to the Apaches as a guerrilla force."

"A guerrilla force? But he's putting together a regular army."

"I think it just means he doesn't plan a direct confrontation with the U.S. Army. Look here." Steele took Rudd's stick and drew a straight line to represent the border. Then he drew another line below it to represent Ramsey's path.

"What's that, a map?" asked Rudd.

Steele pointed with the stick. "That's right. This is Ramsey's force, heading straight east, below the border. He's avoiding the Mexican towns. He doesn't want to attract too much attention, but he's always staying close to the border. Now what is east of here?"

"Well, if he keeps going east, he'll eventually hit Texas."

"That's right, but it's a long way to Texas. And there's not much before that, no large cities because there's not enough water to support a city. The next major source of water is the Colorado river." He drew a vertical line to represent the river.

Rudd found another stick and used it to point to the river line. "Yeah, but are there any Mexican cities anywhere along that river?"

"Not really, but there is a small city up on the other side of the border. Yuma." Steele used his stick to point to the intersection of the border and the river.

"He's going to attack Yuma?"

"It's possible, but that would call attention to where he is. And it would jeopardize his chances of getting his son back."

"Oh, yeah. Then I bet he must be heading for Texas."

"Only one way to find out. Let's go."

They got up and Steele poured the last of the water into his hat for the horses. Then they remounted and started down the hill in the gathering darkness. Ramsey's column was disappearing at the other end of the broad valley.

By the time they reached the bottom of the long downslope, it was fully dark. In the dim light of the rising narrow moon, Steele saw two horsemen waiting on the road ahead.

"Riders ahead," whispered Rudd.

"I see them."

"Should I get my gun out of my saddlebag?"

"Yes, but keep it under your shirt. Continue riding at the same slow pace. Let me have your hat"

"My hat? Why do you want it?"

"If those are Ramsey's men, they might recognize me from when I was in their camp. But they've never seen you. As we pass them, talk. Be friendly."

"Right," said Rudd, handing over his bowler hat.

Steele put it on and hid the Confederate hat in his saddlebag.

As they approached the two men, Steele saw that they were waiting at a crossroads. One road angled off to the south, but the wagon tracks stayed on the trail that went to the left. "We'll take the right fork," he whispered.

As they passed the two men, Steele kept his head down.

"Evening boys," said Rudd. "Hot enough for ya?"

Neither of the men spoke as Steele and Rudd rode past.

"Do you think those are Ramsey's men?" whispered Rudd. "They weren't wearing Confederate uniforms."

"Ramsey's rear guard. There may be more around somewhere."

Rudd looked back, but quickly turned around. "They're still watching us. Do you think they know we're following them?"

"There's no reason they'd expect two lone Americans to be following them. But they'll report it to Ramsey. They must not have recognized me in the dark. Otherwise . . . "

"Otherwise what?"

"Otherwise you'd have had your chance to show me how good you are with that Colt."

"Jesus," whispered Rudd, looking back again. "What do we do now?"

"We go on into this town as if that's exactly where we were heading all the time. Our horses need water anyhow."

"Yeah, me too. And how about we get some food? My saddlebags are almost empty."

As they rode into the sleepy little town, Steele handed Rudd's hat back to him and put the Confederate hat back on. Several families were out in the street cooking their evening meal over small wood fires. It was a very small town, and most of the houses were made out of vertical sticks lashed together.

The people looked up to watch them as they passed by, but no one spoke to them.

When they came to the center of the town, they came upon a well in the middle of the street. "Let's water the horses," said Steele. "Don't make any sudden movements." He nodded toward what appeared to be a cantina. Several men were in front of the building, watching them. Only one of them was armed, a big man with a crooked nose. He wore a fancy hand-tooled leather holster with a big pistol in it.

"Should I get out my gun now?" whispered Rudd.

Steele shook his head. "That pistol is an old percussion Starr. It might not even work. Let's keep our weapons hidden unless we need them."

The Mexicans continued to watch them when they stopped to water their horses.

"How about that food?" whispered Rudd.

"Do you want to go ask them for food?"

Rudd looked them over. "Guess not. Damn, a person could starve to death."

After their horses had finished drinking, they topped off their canteens and remounted. But before they could ride out, the men came into the street to confront them. The man with the pistol was leading them. *"Paren un momento, amigos,"* he said.

"Apenas de paso," said Steele "We needed *agua. Para los caballos. Gracias."*

"What'd you say?" whispered Rudd.

"I told them we needed water for the horses. I said we were just passing through. Keep moving, but slowly."

But the man stepped into their path. "What you *hombres* doing *aqui?*"

"On our way to the border," said Steele. *La frontera.*" He pointed to the north.

"Shall we make a run for it?" whispered Rudd

"Don't do anything. Keep your hands in plain sight."

"Go home, *Gringos,*" said the Mexican.

"We're going. I'll tell my commander. We won't be back this way."

The man stepped aside and the rest of the Mexicans parted to let them through. Riding out of town, Steele kept his eyes straight ahead but Rudd kept on looking back. "They're still watching us." He turned back to Steele. "That was close. What did they want?"

"They just wanted us to go away. They thought we were part of Ramsey's army."

"So they've been noticing the Confederates passing through?"

"Wouldn't you notice an army riding through your neighborhood?"

"Yeah, I guess so," said Rudd looking back again. "To tell the truth, I'll be glad when we're back in our own country."

They rode out of the town and again picked up Ramsey's trail. It wasn't hard to find, even in the dark. There was still the smell of dust in the air and plenty of fresh horse droppings to mark their path. With only a little light from the crescent of moon overhead, they had to move slowly. Steele stopped often to listen.

After a few hours of slow riding, they crested a ridge and saw numerous campfires in the valley below. They were grouped into a rough circle.

"Looks like they've stopped for the night," said Rudd.

"Shh," whispered Steele. "Your voice carries a long way out here. Ramsey will have posted lookouts."

"What should we do?" whispered Rudd.

"Let's get off the road." Steele pointed toward a nearby cluster of large boulders. "Go slow and try to be as quiet as possible."

Once they were hidden in the rocks, Steele dismounted and handed his horse's reins to Rudd. "Stay here with the horses. I'm going down there."

"You're going to walk right in there? Isn't that a little risky?"

"I may be able to slip into their camp." Steele removed his backpack from the saddlebag and took out the Confederate private's uniform he'd purchased in San Francisco.

As he started to put it on, Rudd said, "Hey, that's a Rebel uniform."

Steele stuffed his clothes into the saddlebag. "That's right. You stay here and keep watch. If I don't make it back, head straight north. Find the Cavalry."

"Don't say things like that, Steele. Are you going to try to get Helen out of there?"

"I don't know if I can. If I'm not back by dawn, get away from here as fast as you can."

"All right," said Rudd. He took out his pocket watch and tried to see in the dim light of the moon. "How long shall I wait?"

"No need to look at your watch. If you see it start to get light in the east, go."

Rudd put his watch away. "Good luck, Steele. Try to bring her back, but don't get yourself killed doing it."

"If you hear gunshots, leave immediately. Understand?"

"Got it." Rudd stuck out his hand.

Steele shook his hand and started walking down the hill toward the distant campfires.

Chapter 11

Steele moved slowly, stopping often to listen. His wounded side was aching, but there nothing he could do about it.

Halfway down the hill, he was lucky to discover a shallow sand wash that seemed to lead down toward the Confederate's camp. He knew he could move more quietly in the sand so he followed it.

As he got closer to the camp, he heard voices. Sentries. He quickly went down on his stomach and didn't move. He held his breath, listening. All was quiet except for the cry of a coyote a long ways off. Then, he heard the voices again and saw the glow of two cigarettes in the dark.

He crawled away slowly, looking for more sentries. He found them where he expected, just within sight of the previous two. Ramsey was maintaining wartime rules, posting sentries very close together all around the camp.

Steele glanced up at the moon. It was now higher in the sky and a little brighter. There was little chance he could slip past the sentries without them seeing him.

He could hear voices from within the camp, rising and falling on the currents of cool air that came up the hill.

He stood up and brushed the sand off of his uniform. He strode quickly toward a position about half way between the sentries.

"Halt. What are you doing there, soldier?" A sentry was instantly on his feet, pointing his rifle at Steele.

"Just went out to take a leak," said Steele, adopting the slight drawl he had heard so often back in Tennessee.

The sentry lowered his rifle. "Next time sing out, damn it. I coulda shot your ass."

"Yes, sir. I'll do 'er, sir. Sorry."

Steele hurried past the sentry, keeping his head down. He skirted the campfires, moving quickly, as if he was on an errand. Most of the men were already stretched out on the ground in their bedrolls. It had been a long day for them. They were probably grateful for the relatively soft sand of the desert.

Avoiding the concentrations of sleeping men, Steele moved quickly through the camp, looking for Helen. At one point he saw an Indian approaching. He quickly turned away and pretended to busy himself stacking firewood. After the Indian had passed, Steele turned to watch him go. He hadn't seen any Indians back in Medina's camp. Had they come here to meet up with the Confederates? Was Ramsey using them as guides, just as the lieutenant had?

Steele kept moving and he soon saw a campfire that was larger than the others. There were several soldiers sitting around it. Was that where Ramsey was? He approached carefully, staying well out of the circle of light cast by the fire. He heard one of the men speak and then laughter.

Steele looked for a way to get closer. Two wagons were parked close by. He circled around behind them and when he was sure no one was looking, he crawled under the nearest one. He waited there and listened to the men talking. He couldn't make out any of the individual words, but they sounded cheerful. It reminded him of the many times he had camped with soldiers during the war. He had learned that soldiers rarely talked about the war, except maybe to talk about their superiors, either fondly or in criticism. They were more likely to talk about home and family, or the weather.

Steele carefully crawled to the second wagon. Now he was close enough to hear their words. They were talking about events back east, about the outrages the North was committing in the South such as placing Negroes, former slaves, in important positions.

Someone said it was time to check the sentries. Steele knew that voice: it was Ramsey. A man stood up, an officer in a double-breasted gray shell jacket. Steele hadn't seen any officers back in the Mexican's camp. Were the other men around the campfire also officers? Had they been waiting there in the desert for Ramsey? If so, it meant Ramsey was not running away from the Cavalry, or even away from

Medina: he was moving toward the east with a clear plan, and he was picking up more men as he went.

Steele started to crawl away, but then he saw something move, very near another wagon. It was someone lying on a blanket. Steele wondered why a soldier would be sleeping alone, so far away from the others. Then the person turned over. There was something about that movement. It was a woman. Was it Helen?

He carefully crawled closer. It was Helen. She was resting against the wagon's wheel, with both of her arms over her head. It looked very uncomfortable. She groaned and tried to turn onto her side and Steele heard the rattle of chains. She was in that uncomfortable position because her wrists were chained to the wagon's wheel.

He assessed the situation. Could he get to her? If he tried to get across the open space between them, the men around the fire would be able to see him if they happened to look up. Should he take the chance? It wouldn't do any good if they both ended up in Ramsey's hands. But he knew he had to try. He waited until he was sure no one was coming, and then he scrambled across to the wagon next to her and crawled under it. He stopped to listen. The men back at the campfire were still talking, laughing. He looked at Helen. He couldn't see her face in the darkness, but she seemed to be sleeping. He was so close he could almost touch her. He wanted to touch her, tell her he was there, but he was afraid she would cry out. Maybe he could put his hand over her mouth, whisper to tell her who it was. If he could get those chains off of her wrists, they might be able to get out of the camp and disappear into the night.

He carefully crawled closer to her. But then he heard somebody coming. He held his breath. The gray-clad legs of two Confederate soldiers stopped very near Helen. Were they looking at her? After a few minutes, they walked on.

Helen turned toward him. Looking through the spokes of the wagon wheel, he could finally see her face. It seemed troubled. She was asleep, but she seemed restless, uncomfortable. She was even more beautiful than he remembered. He had to wake her to let her know he was there. He glanced back at the men around the campfire. They were still chatting. He slowly reached through the wheel's spoke to cover her mouth with this hand.

But that was when he saw the guard. Steele quickly pulled his hand back. The guard a young man in a Confederate private's uniform. He was whittling on a piece of wood. Luckily, the boy was so intent on his carving he hadn't noticed Steele's hand come through the spokes.

Steele moved back farther under the wagon. They must be guarding her day and night. Was Ramsey expecting him to try to rescue her?

The guard continued to carve the small piece of wood. The men at the campfire chatted away. Steele looked back at Helen. She seemed unhurt. Her face was a little dirty, but it was still the same beautiful face he remembered. He couldn't take his eyes off of her. Would she be happy to see him? Of course, she would be happy for the chance to get away, but would she be happy it was him? He knew he should get away as quick as he could, but she was so close. He stayed where he was, listening to her gentle breathing.

He turned onto his side and looked at the guard. There was no way to get to him without being seen by the men at the campfire. Did Ramsey anticipate that he might come to free her? Is that why she was so well guarded?

Finally, Steele had to admit to himself there was no way to free her. He was going to have to leave here there. He wished he could have found a way to let her know he had been there. Then at least she would know that he was nearby, trying to help her. Then he remembered the large white handkerchief Rudd had given him. Would she recognize it? He took it out and crawled close to her. Being careful not to touch her, he carefully placed the handkerchief next to her. A wisp of her blonde hair was in her eyes and he had to force himself not to reach out and brush it away. He crawled away and out from under the other side of the wagon. He stood up and dusted off his uniform before heading straight out into the desert. "Going out to take a leak," he called, waving cheerfully to the nearest sentry. The man looked sleepily in his direction and didn't even bother to wave back.

Steele found Rudd waiting where he'd left him.

"Where's Helen?" Rudd whispered. "Did you find her?"

Steele put his finger to his lips to silence him. He mounted his horse and gestured for Rudd to follow.

They moved slowly over the top of the hill and down the other side. When they were safely away, Steele got down to change out of his Confederate uniform. He told Rudd what he had learned, about how Helen had been chained to the wagon, and how she was being guarded. He didn't mention that he'd left the handkerchief. He was beginning to wonder if that had been a foolhardy thing to do. Was he trying to be the hero, trying to tell her he would come back to save her? The handkerchief might reassure her, but it might also give away the fact that he had been there. If so, Ramsey would tighten his security which would make it even harder to get her out of there. As they rode on, he silently chided himself for putting his feelings above common sense. He hoped she would be able to hide the handkerchief, or at least convince her captors that it was something she'd had with her all along.

"That poor girl," said Rudd. "I sure wish you could have got her out of there."

"I do too," said Steele. "I do too."

Chapter 12

When they were down out of the hills, Steele spurred his horse forward. "Let's go. We have to get ahead of them."

They rode for an hour and then Steele led them back up into the hills.

"What are we going to do here?" said Rudd.

"Wait for them. You should lie down and get some sleep. It will be dawn in a few hours."

"How can I sleep?" complained Rudd. "My stomach is so empty its growling will keep me awake all night."

"I thought you had food in your saddlebags."

"Aw, I ate all that while you were down at their camp. I was . . . nervous."

Steele tied up the horses and found a place to lie down between the rocks. He stared up at the stars, thinking about Helen and how uncomfortable she had looked trying to sleep while chained to that wagon. He couldn't get that image out of his mind. He wondered what she would think when she found the handkerchief. He hoped it wouldn't make her feel worse, knowing he had been so close but unable to free her. She had seemed so small and fragile chained up that way. It showed how single-minded Ramsey was. He was keeping his valuable hostage well guarded, but he was apparently little concerned about her comfort. Steele thought about his drawing of Ramsey. When he finished the eyes in that drawing, he would have to find a way to show the man's particular kind of cruelty, that lack of concern for others except with regard to how they might further his plans.

When the pre-dawn glow of the sun began to spread across the desert, Steele woke up, trying to hold onto the fragments of a dream about Helen. In the dream she was not Ramsey's prisoner. Instead, she was running down a grassy slope toward him, happy and free. She was wearing a light, flowered dress and she was unbelievably beautiful. He suddenly realized he had seen Stacy that way once. They were on a hillside near the ocean. Stacy was happy, running toward him. But it had been Helen in the dream, not Stacy. And in the dream she had been holding something in her hand, bringing it to show him. What was it? A white stick? No, it was a lighted candle. But it wasn't nighttime in the dream. Why was she trying to show him a lighted candle in the middle of the day?

He glanced at Rudd who was still sleeping peacefully, curled up on the ground. He sat up to look at the sky. A few thin salmon-colored clouds radiated out across the eastern sky. Ramsey's men would be just breaking camp. They would be along soon.

He sat up to check his wound. It was aching, but it didn't seem to be bleeding.

He took out his drawing pad and began a new drawing of Helen as she had looked in Ramsey's camp. He tried to make her look peaceful, but he couldn't shake the thought of how troubled her face had been as she slept chained to that wagon. It resulted in a drawing of a very sad Helen.

After a few hours, a dust cloud on the horizon signaled the approach of Ramsey's column. As Steele had expected, they were continuing straight east. As Ramsey's army passed through the valley below, Steele was finally able to get an accurate count: one hundred and eighty men on horseback, several more in the wagons. Their numbers had almost doubled since they had left the Mexican militia camp.

They were too far below to tell the identity of individuals, but a group of four riders were at the head of the column. Steele assumed Ramsey would be among that group. When the wagons came along later in the column, he looked at each of them, trying to spot Helen. In most of the wagons, two men sat on the seat in front of the canvas-covered cargo. That was typical: one man to control the horses, the other to mind the brake. But in one wagon, three people were on the seat. The person in the middle was wearing a white shirt. It must be Helen. Even while traveling, they were keeping her under close guard.

Several outriders rode up and down next to the column. They were methodically checking any potential hiding places near the road. After the last men in the column had passed, two more horsemen came along slowly. Steele suspected they might be the same two men who had been waiting at the crossroad near the Mexican town. He waited until the rear guard was completely out of sight before waking Rudd.

"What now?" said Rudd, blinking. "I just got to sleep."

"They've already passed. We can start after them now."

"Give me a minute," said Rudd yawning. He sat up and put his hand to his stomach. "I'm so hungry I could eat a pine cone." He looked around. "If there were any pine cones in this barren desert."

Steele got the horses ready and when Rudd had finally managed to get up and onto his horse, they started down the hill toward the clear trail Ramsey's column was leaving. Rudd was mumbling to himself.

They reached the valley floor and started following Ramsey's trail. But when they had been following for only a short time, Steele nudged Rudd and said, "We've got company."

Rudd used his hand to shade his eyes from the sun. "Who is it?"

"I can't tell yet. They're making sure to come at us out of the sun. Earlier you wanted to use your pistol. Now would be a good time to take it out."

"Damn, there are bunch of them," said Rudd.

"Only eight."

"Is it Ramsey's men?"

"No, they're Mexicans."

"What do you think they want?"

"We'll soon find out." Steele reached into his boot and took out his pistol.

Rudd took out his Colt. "What if it's that Colonel Medina and his men? Are you sure we want to take them on? They got us outnumbered. Bad."

"It's not them. Hold steady." Steele could see that the approaching men were not wearing the gray and black uniforms of Medina's militia. They were wearing dusty brown clothes that might have once been colorful but were now about he same color as the trail dust that was being kicked up by their horses. They all had on large *sombreros* of varying designs and all were armed.

The Mexicans reined in their horses. Their leader was riding an off-white horse but it was so dusty and mud-caked it might well have been mistaken for a Dun Roan. Under his drooping mustache, the man seemed to be smiling. "*Hola, amigos*. Where you go?"

Steele picked up the glint of a gold front tooth. So far none of the men had drawn their weapons, but one of the men with an old single-shot rifle was pointing it more or less in Steele's direction.

"You lost, *señor*?"

Steel waited, not moving. The Mexican was like a wily old coyote looking them over, deciding if it was safe to move in.

"*Tan muchos hombres*. Why so many soldiers, señor?"

"We will be gone from this place soon," said Steele.

The Mexican leaned forward on his saddle horn. "Why the *pistolas*, señor? ¿*No problema, si*?"

"I got that," whispered Rudd. "He wants to know why we have our guns out. Uh, why do we?"

Steele didn't answer. He was focusing his attention on their leader. If any of them went for their guns, he would have to drop the leader with one shot and try to make a run for it.

The leader held out his hand toward his companions. "They ask me, why *gringos* here? Horses eat grass. Drink *mucha agua*. You pay."

"I don't see any grass," said Rudd loudly, looking around. But he leaned close to Steele and whispered, "Should I give him some money?"

"Don't move," said Steele. "Do not show any money."

The leader took off his sombrero. As if it was some kind of signal, some of the other Mexicans began to slowly move to the side. It didn't take them long to form a semicircle around Steele and Rudd.

"Put away guns, *señor*. No problem."

"We use our guns to signal for help," said Steele. "But I can shoot you in the face if you want me to."

"Face?" asked the man, puzzled.

"*Cara. Uno* bullet, *Su Cara*," said Steele, touching his forehead.

The Mexican laughed one short laugh, but then he grew somber. "*Pero amigo*."

Steele shook his head. "*No amigos*."

The Mexican spit on the ground. His smile was gone. *"Vaya Usted."* He pointed at Steele. "No come back *aquí.*"

"Convenido," said Steele, turning his horse to follow the path left by Ramsey's column. The Mexicans moved aside.

Rudd followed close behind, looking back. "What did he say?"

"He said not to come back. I agreed that we would not."

"That was close. I thought we were dead. Why do all the Mexicans think we're part of Ramsey's bunch?"

"They probably noticed that Ramsey always leaves men behind to trail the column."

"Well, I'm ready to get out of this country. It's dangerous down here."

"Es verdad."

"What does that mean?"

"It means you are right."

Chapter 13

*A*fter another day of following the column, Steele could see that Rudd was so tired he was ready to fall off his horse. Steele felt sorry for him, but knew they had to keep going. With the bandits behind and Ramsey's army ahead, they had no choice but to stay on the trail and keep moving.

Late that afternoon, they topped a hill and saw Ramsey's army in the green valley of the Colorado River below.

"There they are," said Rudd, coming back to life. "Looks like they're stopping. Good. We can finally get some rest." He got down from his horse and immediately sat down on the ground.

Steele could see that Rudd was correct, Ramsey's group had crossed the river and stopped. But why would they stop before nightfall? They'd been moving fast up until now. They didn't seem to be setting up camp so they must be only stopping long enough to replenish their water supplies before heading on east. But then he saw part of the group break off and ride north. "Look, they're splitting up."

Rudd stood up and shaded his eyes with his hand. "Yeah. Hey, they've got two wagons with them. Maybe Helen is in one of them."

"No, only one man is driving each wagon. And the wagons are empty. You can tell by they way they bounce."

"Then they must be going for supplies. But where would they get supplies out here?"

"Yuma. Let's go."

"What?"

"We've got to follow them."

"Follow them? Why? You said Helen's not with them. I'm bushed. Let 'em go." He flopped down on the ground and lay back with his arm over his eyes.

Steele could see that Rudd was near the end of his rope, but knew they had to keep moving. He lightly tapped the bottom of Rudd's boot with his toe. "I know you're tired, but we have to follow them.

Rudd looked up at him, squinting into the sun. "I need some rest, Steele. My butt is wore out and my back is killing me."

"The main group has crossed the river. It means they're going on. But for now, they've stopped. We can use the time to follow the ones heading north. There will be a telegraph in Yuma. We have to contact Mr. Kane and the Army to let them know what's going on."

Rudd sat up. "It's too much, Steele. I'm wore out." He threw down his hat, then, with a little cough, he waved away the dust it had raised. "Hell, we don't even know where they're going for sure."

"That's why we have to follow them. Let's go. There'll be food there."

Rudd thought about that for a second. Then he got up with a sigh. "All right, all right." He grabbed his hat and jammed it on his head. He got up on his horse with a groan.

Steele led the way, hurrying his horse forward. Far below, he could see that Ramsey's men were moving much faster than they were.

"They're going like bats out of hell," said Rudd. "They'll turn those wagons over if they're not careful."

"Look, they're putting out a rear guard." Steele pointed. "Two riders. We'll have to stay up here in the mountains."

Steele urged his horse on and was keeping up a good pace despite the rocky ground. But when he looked back, Rudd wasn't there. Steele turned his horse around and found Rudd a ways back sitting on the ground with a pained look on his face. He got off his horse and hurried to Rudd's side. "What happened?"

"Dumb horse stumbled. Pitched me off."

"Are you hurt?"

"Sprained my wrist, I think."

"Let me look at it." He took Rudd's wrist, moving the hand up and down. "Nothing broken. Anything else."

My back hurts, but that's nothing new."

Steele could see that Rudd needed a few more minutes so he sat down next to him.

Rudd picked up a rock and threw it down the hill. "I guess you learned a lot working in that Army hospital."

"Mostly the doctors treated the serious wounds. And did amputations. The other injuries were left to nurses and assistants, like me. We saw just about every type of injury you can imagine."

"Even hurt backs?"

"Yes, we saw a lot of sore backs. Sometimes the soldiers had to carry sixty pound packs all day, in addition to their weapons."

"Tough."

"It *was* tough on them, especially the city boys, the ones not used to heavy work. They came in all the time with back trouble. Unfortunately we were under orders to send them right back to the front lines, as long as no bones were broken."

"Guess that's what I am too, an out-of-shape city boy."

"You're not in bad shape for a man your age. You just need to lose some weight."

"So that's why you never let me have any food." Rudd grinned. "You're trying to help me lose weight."

Steele smiled back at him, happy to see Rudd was at least finding some humor in the situation. He stood up and held out his hand. "Ready to go?"

Rudd allowed Steele to help him up, but he wasn't ready to get back on his horse. He stretched his back from side to side. Finally, he said, "All right, Sergeant Steele. I'm ready to go back to the front lines. As long as you quit referring to me as a man of your age."

"Agreed," said Steele.

He helped Rudd get back onto his horse and they again started down the hill.

"I can't see them anymore," said Rudd riding up next to Steele. "Should we go down and try to pick up their trail?"

"They're far enough ahead we can go down to the desert now, but we'd better stay well away from their trail until we get closer to Yuma. They'll still have those rear guards out."

"Suits me. As long as we get to Yuma in time to get something to eat. Maybe breakfast. Steak and eggs would be good."

As Rudd continued to mumble to himself, Steele led the way down out of the hills, frequently looking back to make sure Rudd was all right. Once they reached the desert floor, they made better time, even though it was much hotter there. After a few hour's riding, they came to a dusty, rutted road that led into a small town.

"Oh, no," said Rudd. "Another Mexican town. Should I get out my gun again?"

"No need," said Steele, pointing at a faded sign that announced *Welcome to Silver Gulch*.

"Hey," said Rudd. "It's in English. We must have crossed the border somewhere."

As they rode in, Steele could see that the town was long abandoned. The only thing that remained was a scattering of falling-down buildings that had been built out of rocks. Whatever had been used for mortar had failed and most of the walls had caved in. The buildings were now havens for birds and nest-building rodents.

They slowly approached the largest of the rock buildings and it too could have been mistaken for a long abandoned outpost except there was an old man sitting in front on a sagging porch. He was slowly rocking back and forth in a rickety rocking chair. The man waved and seemed friendly, except for the fact that he had a double-barreled shotgun across his lap.

Steele and Rudd stopped their horses in front of him. "Good afternoon, sir," said Steele. "Could we trouble you for a little water?"

"Sorry, gents," said the smiling old man. "Got to haul the water all the way from the river." He gestured over his shoulder with his thumb. "Fraid I can't spare any extra."

"How about food," said Rudd. "Got any food? We'll pay."

The old man looked at Rudd with one eye closed. "Got to bring that in too. Can't spare any of that either."

"Are you out here all alone?" asked Rudd.

"Just me and my old shotgun here. Nuthin' in it but nails and such. But I bet it would hurt some though."

"We aren't going to take anything without your permission," said Steele. "But there are quite a few hoof prints in the dirt. You're not really alone out here, are you?"

"I'm alone right now, ain't I?" The old man paused and then added, "But you're right. My boys are up at the mine." He used his shotgun to point toward the nearby hills. "But they haven't been findin' anything so I 'spect we'll be movin' on soon. Silver Gulch, they used to call this place. Optimistic, I call it. But them two boys like to dig so dig they do."

"How far is it to Yuma? asked Steele.

"Not far. Bout ten miles, I recon. Just follow the road 'til it hits the river, then cross over."

"All right," said Steele. He turned to Rudd. "Only ten more miles. Can you make it?"

"Do I have a choice? There's nothing here and this old man isn't even willing to give a dying man a drink."

"Sorry boys. Nuthin' here but history. This old house, what's left of it anyhow, used to be part of the old Saint Pedro mission. A while back, actually a pretty long time ago, there was a big massacre here. Apaches they say. Wiped out about a hundred Spanish settlers and held a whole bunch more hostages. But nobody paid the ransom so they killed 'em all. They even done in old Captain Don Fernando Medina, the man who first set foot in these parts."

Steele turned his horse and started off down the road.

Rudd followed, grumbling about what kind of man wouldn't even give a person a tiny little drink of water.

Steele hardly heard him. He was thinking about what the old man had said about a Spanish explorer named Medina, the first to explore the area. Could the name be a coincidence? Medina was a common Spanish name, but General Ramsey had said Colonel Medina's family had come from Spain and that they had once held vast amounts of property in the area. Was that why Medina was trying to raise an army? To take back his ancestral homeland?

"You know, Steele, I'm feelin' like I'm about done in," said Rudd. "How long do you figure it will take us to get to Yuma?"

"Not long, but we need to take it slow until we can get these horses some water at the river. We'll make it."

Rudd wiped his brow with his sleeve. "Damn, it's hot. Listen, Steele, if I start fallin' behind, don't leave me. Tie my horse to yours if you have to, but don't leave me out here by myself."

Steele moved his horse close to Rudd's. He patted Rudd on the back and offered him his canteen. "I'm not going to leave you, no matter what."

Rudd drank the rest of the water and slumped forward in the saddle, but he kept going.

Steele could see that Rudd was suffering. His eyes were barely open and his sunburned face was making him look very old. But Steele suspected his old friend was stronger than he knew. If he'd made it that far, he'd make it the rest of the way. Steele rode close to him, making sure he didn't fall off.

By the time they came to the river, the sun was low behind them, casting long shadows. He nudged Rudd to show him they'd made it.

"Finally," was all Rudd said.

They stopped to let the horses drink and Rudd sat down at the river's edge to get a drink and to splash water on his face and neck. That seemed to revive him somewhat.

After Steele had filled the canteens, they got back on their horses and crossed the river. It was only a short ride from there to Yuma. Steele knew Ramsey's riders would have already reached there. "We should slip into town quietly," he said, "in case Ramsey's men are still here. Let's get off the main road."

They rode behind some of the town's outlying buildings and tied their horses to a tree. They walked between buildings and out to the main street. There was no one around and Steele immediately saw why: the people were all gathered together in the middle of the street farther down. They hurried in that direction and Steele soon realized the people were crowding around someone lying on the ground. It could only mean one thing: Ramsey's men had come and gone.

Rudd nudged one of the men and said, "What happened here?"

"Some kind of gang," said the man. "They rode in and shot up the whole town. Took all the money from the bank, the food from the store, and all the guns too. Then they rode right back out again."

"There's no food left?" asked Rudd.

"Nope. They took all the food the general store had, and a bunch of other stuff too. They had a wagon with 'em and they filled it up."

Rudd grabbed the man's arm. "You mean there's no place a man can get a meal in this whole town?"

"Oh, if you're hungry you can always get something to eat over there at the bar. The gang didn't even go in there."

"Thank heaven for that," said Rudd, heading for the bar.

Steele pushed through the crowd. "Let me see if I can help."

At the center of the crowd, he discovered the person lying in the dusty street was a young soldier in a U.S. Cavalry private's uniform. A thin woman in a blue and white dress was cradling the boy's head in her lap. She looked up as Steele kneeled beside her. "Are you a doctor?"

"I had some training in an Army hospital." Steele felt for the young man's carotid artery. "But I'm afraid this boy is dead."

The woman looked at him, her eyes open very wide. "But he can't be. He was talking to me just a minute ago."

Steele stood up. "Does this town have a telegraph office?"

A young boy stepped forward. "Down the street." He pointed. "Is th . . that guy dead?"

Steele started toward the telegraph office, but the boy pulled at his sleeve. "There's another shot guy behind the bank. I'll show you." The boy pulled him in that direction.

Behind the bank building, another crowd was gathering. The boy pushed his way to the center, dragging Steele with him. He pointed to the man lying on the ground. "It's a . . a . . nother soldier. He g . . . got shot too."

Steele could see that it was already too late: the soldier had a fatal head wound.

"They killed the sheriff too," said a man wringing his hands nervously. "When they came out of the bank."

Steele again started toward the telegraph office.

"Hold it right there, Steele!"

Steele stopped. He turned back to see a very short man in a brown plaid suit. The man was pointing a gun at him. But Steele didn't recognize him. How could the man know his name?

"That is your name, isn't it?"

"Yes, it is. Stop pointing that gun at me."

The man cocked his revolver. "I want to know who those men were. They left a letter for you and I want some answers."

"A letter?"

"That's right. He said you'd be along soon enough." The man kept the gun pointed at Steele as he held out a letter wrapped in a white handkerchief.

Steele immediately recognized that handkerchief; it was the one he'd left for Helen. "Was the person who gave this to you an old man?"

"That's right. An old guy in a fancy Confederate officer's uniform. A lot of them had on Confederate uniforms, and they were all carrying brand new repeating rifles. What's going on? Is the war starting again?"

"Let me read the letter," said Steele.

"Not 'til I get some answers. I'm the mayor of this town. Or at least I was 'til today. They took my wife and I want to know why or this damn gun might just go off and blow a hole in you."

"They took your wife?"

"Yes, by God, and some other women too."

"Put your pistol away," said Steele quietly. "I'm sorry about your wife, but I don't think they will hurt her. They've taken other hostages too. That's why I'm chasing them."

The mayor frowned, but he lowered his pistol. "Other hostages? My wife is a hostage?"

Steele put his hand on the man's shoulder. "I'm afraid she is. Let me see the letter."

He handed it over and Steele unwrapped it from the handkerchief. It was from Ramsey.

Mr. Steele.

I know you have been following me. I commend your persistence but do not attempt it again. The two men who failed to recognize you even after my warnings have been punished. They will be more vigilant in the future.

Be assured that your young woman is safe and in good health. I speak with her often. Last night, when she thought no one was looking, she took out this handkerchief to hold it close to her face. Very touching. I think she misses you.

Be warned, do not try anything like that again. The life of your little Helen depends on it.

General C. J. Ramsey

Steele reread that last line. *The life of your little Helen depends on it.* Would he really harm her?

Steele refolded the note and put it in his pocket. He resisted the impulse to smell the handkerchief to see if any scent of her lingered on it. He put it in the same pocket with the note.

"Who's this Helen?" asked the mayor. "Is she a friend of yours?"

"Yes, she is. She is also being held hostage."

"Listen, Steele, I don't care who they were, I just want my wife back. Help me get together a posse and we'll go after them."

"I'm afraid that wouldn't help. He's got something like two hundred men a ways south of here in Mexico, all well armed."

"Two hundred? Oh no. What will we do if they come back?"

"I don't think they will come back. They got what they wanted. Maybe we can get some help from the Army. I have to get to the telegraph office to contact them."

"The Army is a long ways from here. Closest fort is in Tucson."

"Isn't there an Army fort across the river in California?"

"Yeah, there is a fort over there, a small one, but I was told most of them rode out a couple of days ago. Some kind of border trouble out in California. They only left a few of the younger soldiers to guard the fort. Those boys did try to come help us, but they got shot. Brave boys."

Steele immediately realized what had happened. Once that Cavalry lieutenant got back to San Diego and told his superiors about Ramsey's army down below the border, they must have put out a request for help from other units. But how could Ramsey have known that? Did he have a spy in Yuma?

"Maybe I should go after them myself," said the mayor. "They took everything I had in my store anyhow. Maybe they'll take me hostage too. That way at least I could be with my wife."

"They don't need you as a hostage," said Steele. "They will have guards out behind them and they'll just shoot you. I know you're very worried about your wife. We'll try to get her back."

"Damn, I hope they don't hurt her. I don't know what I'm going to tell her sister and her mother back east. They told her she shouldn't have come out here with me."

"Show me where the telegraph office is," said Steele. "I have to send a message back to California."

The mayor shook his head. "I already tried that. It wasn't working. But we sent some men out to see if the wire is down. Maybe it's fixed by now. The telegraph is up at the end of the street. I'll show you."

He led the way to the telegraph office. A crowd was there, milling around outside. A young boy saw them coming and broke free from the crowd to grab Steele's arm. "Do you know what's going on, mister? Why did they take my mother?"

Steele stopped and took the boy's hand. "Your mother will be all right, son."

One of the men stepped forward. He was holding a blacksmith's hammer. "Oh yeah, how do you know? How do we know you're not in with them? Some of them had on Confederate hats like yours."

The mayor pushed the man back. "Now take it easy everybody. I'm trying to get to the bottom of this."

He took Steele by the arm and led him up onto the board sidewalk and into the telegraph office.

A heavy set balding man was sitting in the only chair with his feet up on the desk chewing on a toothpick. "No use comin' in here," he said, not even turning to look at them. "Telegraph's not workin'. I sent a boy out, but he's probably hidin' somewhere."

"If the wire has been cut," said Steele, "it will be on this side of the river."

"That right?" The operator looked at the mayor and jerked his thumb in Steele's direction. "Who's this bird?"

"He's been following them. He says there are hundreds of them down across the border, a whole army."

The telegraph operator frowned at Steele. "Who the hell were those guys? They looked like Confederates, some of 'em anyhow. I saw 'em clear as day. Rode right past here and out to the old mission."

"The mission?" said Steele.

"He means the old mission church," said the mayor. "Out on the north side of town. Somebody said they took a wagon inside the walls."

"No way it could be Confederates," said the telegraph operator tipping his chair back on two legs. "Not way out here. I figure it was a bunch of outlaws, all dressed up to look like soldiers."

"It depends how you define soldiers," said Steele. "The war is over, but they really were former Confederate soldiers. They're still commanded by a Confederate general."

The operator let out a low whistle. "A general? What's he tryin' to do, start the war up again?"

"I think that's exactly what he's trying to do."

"Holy Christ. Wait 'til I get this key workin' again and pass the word down the line."

"You might want to wait until you speak to the Army before you do that," suggested Steele. "No need to start a panic. You said they went to the mission. Who's in charge there?"

"Some old Spanish priest," said the mayor. "People say he's been in this town since way back, before it was even a real town. Only Mexicans and Indians go there. Some Mexicans even come up from below the border. The Indians come in from somewhere out on the desert. Me, I'm a Baptist so I've never been out there."

Suddenly, the telegraph key began clicking.

The operator let his chair drop back down into all four legs with a thump. "Hey, how about that. That boy isn't as lazy as I thought." He listened for a moment and then said, "It's just old Charley down the line. He's wonderin' why I haven't been in touch today." He turned back to Steele. "You know, I should have known something was gonna happen when the line went dead earlier today. Shoulda figured somebody musta cut the line. Cochise did that a couple of years ago when he came through this area stealin' horses."

"The Apaches are operating in this area?" asked Steele.

"Naw, not lately. Haven't seen hide nor hair of 'em since then. I hear he's up in the mountains somewhere over near Tucson. Givin' the Army fits I hear." He picked up his pad and pencil. "All right, bud, let's get that message sent out."

Steele instructed the man to send a message to Kane at the San Diego newspaper office, informing him of Ramsey's raid on Yuma. He told the man to also ask how the hostage negotiations were going.

As soon as the operator started sending the message, Steele stood up to leave. "I want to go out to that mission. How far is it?"

"Not far. Right out at the edge of town."

Steele started toward the door, but turned back. "Is there a stage to Tucson today?"

The man looked at the clock on the wall. "Sure, but you'll have to hurry. It should be comin' through any minute now."

Steele wanted to find out why Ramsey's men had gone to that mission, but he also wanted to make that stage for Tucson. If Ramsey's army was continuing on toward the east, the next main city they would come to was Tucson. That stage would be the best way to get ahead of them.

He was about to leave the office when the telegraph key started clicking again.

"It's for you," said the operator, listening. "He's asking about somebody named Helen."

"Tell him Helen is safe, but she is still held by General Ramsey."

The operator did as instructed and then turned back to Steele. "Who's this General Ramsey?"

But before Steele could answer, another message started coming in. The operator listened. "Kane says, stay where you are. New info about Ramsey's son. Will be arriving soon."

"Tell him I can't wait, I'm going after Ramsey. Tell him to meet us in Tucson."

Steele opened the door to leave.

"Hey, who's paying for this?"

"I don't have any money, but the man you've been sending messages to is Edward Kane. He will pay you when the stage stops here on the way to Tucson."

"Edward Kane?" said the mayor. "The newspaper tycoon? He's coming here?"

"That's right. I'm going to try to catch that stage to Tucson. Would you have somebody take care of our horses? They belong to the Army. They're tied to a tree out west of town."

"Sure, whatever you say," said the mayor. "Hey, is it true that Kane is gonna run for the U.S. Senate? Maybe a man like that can help get my wife back, and the other women."

"I'm sure he'll do what he can. Explain the situation to him when his stage comes through."

Outside the telegraph office, Steele had to push his way through the growing crowd. He waved off their questions as they followed him down the street to the bar.

Inside the bar, he found Rudd seated at a table that was covered with food and bottles of beer. He was surrounded by a crowd of men and between bites he was telling them about the long, harrowing trip they had completed, describing how they had risked their lives to follow the Confederates. He looked up as Steele approached. "Hey, Steele. I was just telling these fellows about you. Tell these guys how we held off a hundred Mexican bandits, just the two of us. They don't believe me."

"Let's go," said Steele.

"But don't you want anything to eat? They make good sandwiches here. And they got cow cheese too."

"If you're coming, bring it along. We've got to hurry."

Rudd gathered up as much food as he could carry and followed Steele out into the street. "You know, Steele, I don't think I can take much more of this horse-riding stuff. My butt is so sore I've got blisters on my blisters."

"You won't have to. We're taking the stagecoach. Ramsey left a message. He knows we've been trailing him so we can't do it anymore. We may be able to get ahead of him by taking the stage to Tucson."

"A stage? That's more like it. If there's room in that stagecoach, maybe I could even lie down for a while. That'd help my back more than anything.

"We've got to hurry. Let's go get our saddlebags."

Steele led Rudd back to the horses and pulled his saddlebags off. He waited as Rudd filled his saddlebags with food and bottles of beer. When he was ready, they hurried toward the stage office. Rudd was more cheerful than he had been for days. "I sure hope the stage is one of those new Concords. I hear they're real comfortable."

Chapter 14

*T*he stage wasn't a Concord, but as they started out on the straight road to the east, Rudd was happy that it was entirely empty. "Now maybe I can finally get some rest." As soon as he managed to find a somewhat comfortable position, he was sound asleep.

While Rudd dozed, Steele made notes in his journal. He wished he would have had time to go to that Spanish mission back in Yuma. Why had Ramsey gone there? And why did he take a wagon there? There wasn't likely to be anything in a mission that would interest Ramsey, let alone something that would require a wagon. Was it a meeting place? If so, why would the old priest allow the mission to be used by a renegade Confederate army? Steele entered his thoughts about it in his journal and put the book down on the seat.

He stared out the window, remembering how Helen had looked chained to that wagon in Ramsey's camp. Why would Ramsey risk his plan to exchange her for his son? Why would he attack Yuma when his son was still in jeopardy back in Washington? And why did he need more hostages if he already had an agreement to exchange Helen for his son?

As they continued on toward Tucson, the sun sank lower in the west and Rudd continued to doze. Steele took out his drawing pad and began a sketch of the sleeping Rudd. He was still working on it when Rudd woke up.

Rudd sat up, rubbing his eyes. He blinked and looked out the window. "Hey, it's getting dark. Where are we?"

"Still on our way to Tucson."

"Okay, let's have something to eat while you tell me why we're going there."

"We're going to Tucson because it's the next town east of here."

Rudd took out some food and two bottles of beer. "You think Ramsey will come back across the border to attack Tucson?"

"It's possible."

Rudd handed some bread and cheese to Steele. "But Tucson is a pretty big town, isn't it? Not a little cow town like Yuma. Ramsey's not going to attack a real city, is he?"

"It seems unlikely, unless he's ready for a confrontation."

"But what about his wanting to trade Helen for his son? Doesn't he care about that any more? Why would he take on the U.S. Army if they're still holding his son?"

"I have been asking myself the same thing. I sent Kane a message. He says he's coming here and he has more information about Ramsey's son. I told him to meet us in Tucson."

"Mr. Kane is coming here? That's great. Maybe he's worked out a trade for Ramsey's son."

"Maybe. But if that's the case, why would Ramsey attack Yuma?"

Rudd held up a hunk of bread. "What about food? Maybe Ramsey's bunch raided Yuma to get food. Maybe they were starving. Don't forget they took all the food that general store back there had."

"Two hundred men do need a lot of food, but they also took a wagon out to the old Spanish mission. That could be why they went to Yuma."

"The mission? What were they after there?"

"Something they needed a wagon for, something important enough to go to Yuma."

Rudd frowned. "Doesn't make any sense to me. Hey, they told me at that bar that Ramsey took some hostages, but only women. Why women?"

"Easier to handle, I suppose. And more highly valued by their menfolk. Hostages are useful only to the degree that somebody wants them back."

"You make it sound so logical, Steele. But if you don't mind my saying so, these are real people we're talking about. People were killed back there. It's more than a game of logic."

Steele looked out the window. "I know people were killed. And men's wives were taken, mothers of real children. But to understand Ramsey we have to be logical about it."

"Logical. Is logic always the answer?"

Steele thought about the question. During the war he'd come to depend on logic as if it was his personal religion. His teachers in Europe had emphasized the need for logic in all situations and Steele had believed them, but war was something that defied logic. He was completely unprepared for the horrors of what he saw in the war, but he soon realized that the only way to stay alive was to depend on calm logic. But now, as he looked out at the bleak desert, he wondered if he had learned that lesson *too* well. Had it left him unable to feel the things others felt?

Rudd interrupted his thoughts. "But I guess that's why you're good at what you do. Me, I guess I worry too much. I worry all the time. About Helen, for instance. I worry about her still being in the hands of that madman. And now he's taken other women too."

"General Ramsey is not a madman. To think so would be to underestimate him. He undoubtedly rose to the rank of general because of abilities he demonstrated in the war."

"And he thinks he's still at war."

"I believe he does."

"All right," said Rudd. "We'll use logic." He hesitated. "Uh, how do we begin?"

"We begin by figuring out what Ramsey is going to do next."

"All right, what do you think he will do?"

"The best way to predict a man's future behavior is by looking at his past behavior."

"I see. Well, he attacked Yuma. Does that mean he's going to attack another city?"

"First, we have to figure out *why* he attacked Yuma. If it was to make a point to the Army, the attack has done it's job. He may not need to do it again."

"Make what point?"

"To show what he's willing and capable of doing. It's almost as if he killed those soldiers and took those hostages to say to the Army, 'Here I am, come and get me.'"

"He wants the Army to come after him?"

"He has to know that will be the main result of his attack."

"So has he forgotten about his son? Why would the government deal with him after he's killed those people in Yuma?"

"That's the hardest thing to understand. Why didn't he wait to find out if Kane was able to work out the exchange for his son?"

"Good question. And what does logic tell you the answer is?"

"It tells me that something has changed and Ramsey knows it. I received a telegraphic message from Kane saying the situation with regard to Ramsey's son had changed. Somehow Ramsey must have already known it."

"So what has changed?"

"Maybe the government won't, or can't, do the exchange. At least not at this time."

Rudd munched on an apple while he thought about that. "I bet it's politics. I bet those politicians back there wouldn't even consider it. They don't think anything that goes on out here in the West is all that important anyhow. They only think about getting reelected and they know there aren't enough votes out here to matter."

Steele looked out the window into the darkness of the lonely desert. "If that's so, then he will attack again. To be sure he has their attention."

"So what happens when we get to Tucson? Do we just wait there to see if he comes?"

"No, we head south down toward the border to try to find him."

"Uh oh, that means horses again."

Steele smiled. "At least this time on the stage will give your backside a bit of a rest."

Rudd groaned. "I knew this was too good to be true. Damn, back on a horse again. You'd think we were some kind of cowboys. Okay, say we go south from Tucson to look for him. How do we find him? It's a big desert."

"We won't have any trouble finding him. As we have learned, when a force of that size goes through, everyone in the area knows about it."

"Well, if we end up down in Mexico again, I hope we don't run into more bandits. We were lucky get out of Mexico alive last time." Rudd began searching through his saddlebags again. He found an egg and pulled it out. He held it up happily. "Want a boiled egg?"

Steele shook his head and looked out at the passing desert thinking about Ramsey down there in Mexico. He and his men were from Tennessee, but they were learning about the Southwest and the desert as they went. A smart commander would learn as much as he could about the environment in which the battles were going to take place. He would study the terrain, just as he studied his opponent. Ramsey said he admired the desert-dwelling Apaches, and he had two Indians with him. What was he learning from them?

Rudd was soon asleep again and despite the swaying and bouncing of the stagecoach, he slept soundly through the night. Sitting up, Steele managed to doze a little, but he woke with a start after yet another troublesome dream. In the dream, a soldier suddenly loomed up in front of him. Half of the man's face had been shot away, but the remaining half grinned at him. Steele had tried to go help the man, but his way was blocked by women and children, all with terrible wounds, all wanting his help.

Steele stared out into the darkness, realizing that everyone in the dream had been wearing strange gray and black uniforms, even the children. The dream reminded him of the wounded civilians he had seen at Chattanooga when Colonel Wilder's Union artillery shelled the town from across the river, accidentally hitting the civilians' homes. Had Ramsey been in Chattanooga at that time?

Rudd slept on, despite the bouncing of the stage over the rough road and the dust that constantly seeped up through the floorboards.

The sky in the east was just beginning to lighten with the approaching dawn, when they rolled into Tucson and slowed. There were a surprising number of people on the streets.

Rudd sat up, rubbing his eyes. "Are we there yet?"

"We're just coming in."

Rudd looked out the window. "What are all those people doing out there? It's not even light yet?"

Before Steele could answer, two soldiers rode up and yelled to the driver to stop. A young corporal looked inside. "One of you named Steele?"

"You're supposed to come with me." He wheeled his horse around and yelled to the stage driver. "Follow me."

"What's going on?" yelled the driver. "Why is everybody running around?"

"Just get moving," said the corporal.

The driver cracked his whip and the stagecoach lurched forward. With the corporal and the other soldier riding ahead, they rolled through the dirt streets fast, forcing people up onto the board sidewalks.

The stage stopped in front of a fort with a surrounding wall constructed out of large logs. The gate was open, but two armed sentries stood guard in front. Steele noted the large number of armed soldiers that were patrolling the walkways above the walls. The fort seemed to be on alert.

As they got out, the driver was still asking questions. "Why does the Army want to talk to you guys? What's going on in this town?"

"We don't know any more than you do," said Rudd.

The two sentries stood aside as the corporal led them inside the fort.

Steele saw that there was a fairly large main building made of adobe with a tile roof. The stars and stripes were flying on a low pole in front of it. There was one other building, a long, narrow adobe building that looked like it might be barracks.

Inside the main building, the corporal knocked on the frame of the commander's open door. "Major Carter, those men from Yuma are here."

"Send 'em in."

The soldier stood aside and Steele and Rudd entered the office. A burly man in a Cavalry major's uniform was seated at the desk. Two junior officers stood behind him. The major had the stub of an unlit cigar clamped into the corner of his mouth. He was looking them over, not smiling. Steele noticed a telegraph message on the desk.

"Sit down," said the major, pointing to the chairs in front of his desk.

"I'll stand, if you don't mind," said Rudd, rubbing his butt to show how sore it was.

Steele also remained standing.

"Which one of you is Steele?"

"I am," said Steele. "What has happened?"

"I'll tell you what happened, your so-called General Ramsey has sent us a message. No, not a message, a threat. It came in just a little while ago, sent from Nogales, a town down in Mexico, just across the border." He picked up the telegraph form from his desk and handed it to Steele.

The message was brief and to the point:

I spared Yuma but Tucson will pay the price for your treachery.

This time he had signed it with his full name, General C. Jacob Ramsey.

Steele reread the message. What treachery was he referring to? And if he really was planning an attack, why give the city advance warning? Was he trying to instill panic? The more he reread the message the less Steele understood it. The message didn't make any demands. It didn't say anything about hostage negotiations. For some reason, Ramsey must have decided to demonstrate what his army of former soldiers could do. He handed the message back to the major. "So he's coming."

"Coming? What the hell you talkin' about?" The major shifted his cigar to the other side of his mouth.

"This message is from a former Confederate general named Ramsey. His men attacked Yuma. I'm sure you've heard by now about what happened out there."

The major stared at him, chewing on his cigar. "Yeah, we heard about it. Some bandits raided the town, all dressed up pretty in Confederate uniforms. They said you knew what this was all about and that you were on the stage on your way here." He pointed to the telegraphic message. "So you think this is the same guy who attacked Yuma?"

"It is," said Rudd. "We know it is. We followed him all the way to Yuma and he attacked the town with a whole bunch of his men and he took all the food and–"

"Right, right, we know all about that," interrupted the major. "A raid on the town. Hostages taken. We got plenty of telegraph messages about it. I think everybody in the damn country got messages about it. Your so-called general has got everybody all riled up. The mayor thinks this character is gonna march right into Tucson. He's insisting we declare martial law. I say nonsense. This is no little podunk Yuma. No bunch of misfits is going to ride in here and attack this town."

"He's not *our* general," said Rudd. "And he's not so-called. He was a real general in the real Confederate Army. He's got a lot of soldiers with him and they–"

"Wait a minute, wait a minute," said the major. "We heard they were all dressed in Confederate uniforms, but what would a real Rebel general be doing out here?"

"He was a Confederate general," said Steele. "General Jacob Ramsey. During the war, he was the commander of a Confederate regiment in southern Tennessee. He's now wanted by the war-crimes tribunal and that may be why he's out here. We've been following him for days. The last time we saw him he was down in Mexico with–"

"This crazy message is from a real Rebel general?" The major waved the message in Steele's face. "Did you see what it said? I spared Yuma. What's that supposed to mean? They didn't burn the place down? Why would they do that? And why was it sent to the mayor of this town and not to me? I think your General Ramsey is a complete madman. He's got the mayor and half this town in a panic, but he doesn't scare me." The major threw down the message.

"So you've had no reports of Ramsey being in this area yet?" said Steele.

"What do you mean, yet? You really think he's gonna come marching down Main Street? Not likely. We got a full garrison here, Steele, all experienced Indian fighters. So a bunch of renegade Rebels snuck across the border for one raid. So what? They ran right back down to Mexico where we can't get 'em, didn't they? I say they've had their fun and that'll be the end of it. This message is just tryin' to scare us."

"You may be right," said Steele, but it would be wise not to discount the possibility that he means what he says."

The major used his cigar to point at Steele. "If he thinks he can take us on, let him come. We don't scare easy, bub."

"If you're not worried, why are the soldiers in this fort on alert? There's something more you're not telling us."

The major looked at Steele, chewing on his cigar. "Yeah, well, maybe it's somethin' and maybe it isn't, but don't let it get beyond this room. It's those damn Texans. They're acting up again. I got word from El Paso that some of those crazy Goddam Rebels over there have been diggin' out their raggedy old Civil War uniforms and putin' 'em on again. A bunch of 'em were spotted headin' this way. Can you believe it? Here we kicked them Reb's asses in the war and now they think they can get up out of the dirt and try to take us on again. One little raid into some sleepy little Arizona town by some crazy old Rebel grayback and some of those Texans get riled up and think the war's startin' all over again."

"War is a state of mind," said Steele. "Ramsey knows that. If he can convince enough people that the war is not really over . . ." He decided not to finish his thought. "Do you have any idea how many Texans are heading this way?"

"Oh, who knows. And what makes you think they're coming here? Maybe your General Ramsey is headin' over there to Texas to meet up with them."

"That is possible, but if I could ask, Major, how many men do you have?"

"I've only got a hundred and sixty-two right now, but I can deputize every man and boy in this town if I have to."

"Men and boys against hardened Civil War veterans? The Confederates are armed with the latest weapons, Winchester Improved Henry rifles."

Major Carter looked hard at Steele. "Impossible. We can hardly get any of those out here ourselves. Where would he get them?"

"Somebody may be supplying him through Mexico. They might even have a cannon. I saw a large weapon crate in a camp in western Mexico. Ramsey was allied with a group of Mexican militia there. Commanded by a Colonel Medina. He may have been getting the weapons through him."

"Did you say a cannon? You think they're draggin' a big old cannon along with them? I'll believe that when I see it. I was told that every cannon in this country has been taken inside Federal armories, because of all the trouble they're havin' back east."

"It could be a small cannon. Possibly from Europe."

"Europe? Now wait a minute. What are you saying? That this crazy general has help from Europe?"

"I read that the Winchester company has been selling most of their newer weapons to Spain."

"Spain? What the hell do I care about Spain?" The major stood up and angrily threw the stub of his cigar toward the spittoon in the corner. It missed. "Maybe they have some fancy new weapons, but they've never dealt with the 6th Cavalry."

Chapter 15

*T*he major abruptly ended the interview, saying he had to go calm down the mayor. Steele and Rudd left the building and found a carriage waiting for them at the front gate. The driver said he had been instructed to take them directly to the newspaper office.

As soon as they were seated inside the carriage, Rudd said, "I'm tired of all this, Steele. Running around telling everybody what we know. I'm putting my foot down. I'm hungry and I'm tired. If they want any more information, they have to feed us and find us a room."

At the newspaper office, a thin, nervous-looking young man was waiting for them at the front door. "You Rudd?" he asked. "From the San Francisco office?"

"That's right," said Rudd, "although it seems like forever since I left there."

The young man turned to Steele. "So you must be Steele, the detective. Mr. Kane telegraphed us about you. He wants you both to wait here for him. He's coming."

"He's already on his way?" asked Rudd.

"You bet he is. He said to tell you he's hired a special coach and he'll be here by tomorrow."

"That's all he said?" asked Steele.

"That's it. Just said you two were to wait here for him. Boy, his coming sure has got everybody running around this office like chickens with their heads cut off."

"Hasn't he ever been here before?" asked Rudd.

"Are you kidding? Mr. Kane come here to Tucson? We didn't even think he knew we existed. We're putting together a special edition about the war rumors to welcome him. Do you think he'll like that?"

"Probably," said Rudd, "but if you think he'll like that, wait until he sees the story I'm going to write. Get me a copywriter. I've got the real truth of the matter right here." Rudd tapped the side of his head.

"Is it about what happened out there at Yuma?"

"It sure is. I was just there and I know all about it. We've been following that guy for days. Haven't we, Steele?"

The young man turned to Steele. "What guy is he talking about?"

"I'm afraid Mr. Rudd won't be able to tell you many of the details just yet."

"He won't?" said the young man.

"He won't?" said Rudd.

"I'm afraid not," said Steele. "All he can say is that an unknown group of men attacked Yuma."

"Wait a minute," protested Rudd. "My job is to report the news. I've been wearin' out my butt following Ramsey for days and days and now you're saying I can't report what I saw with my own eyes?"

"Yeah," said the young man, "why can't he report what he saw with his own eyes? Uh, who's Ramsey?"

"It's up to you," said Steele, meeting Rudd's eyes. "You can write your story, but you have to be careful what you say. Anything you write will end up in his hands, and possibly in other people's hands back east. Give him too much information and it could endanger Miss Kane and the others."

"Miss Kane?" asked the young man. "There's a Miss Kane? Besides Mr. Kane? Is she coming too?"

"Never mind," said Rudd, waving off the question. "But I can write up an eyewitness report about what happened out there in Yuma, can't I? About how this . . . unknown group came in and, well, nobody knows exactly who they were, but they . . . uh, came in and shot up the town. There were dead soldiers lying right in the middle of the street."

"Wait, wait," cried the young man, "let me get a copywriter. So it's true what we heard? Somebody said they took women away with them. Is that true too?"

"I'm afraid so," said Rudd.

"Oh, God," said the young man, "who knows what those bandits will do to those women. We should get that in the story too. I'll be right back with a copywriter. And I've got to alert the layout people about this too."

As the young man hurried away, Rudd leaned close to Steele and whispered, "Why can't I tell them it was Confederates?"

"Because that is undoubtedly what Ramsey expects you to do. You heard what Major Carter said about how some of the Texans reacted when they heard about the attack on Yuma. Ramsey may be trying to stir up that kind of response."

"I see what you mean. Okay, I'll just say a large group of outlaws hit Yuma. But what about the Confederate uniforms? People are talking about that."

"Rumors."

"Right. Just rumors. I won't even mention that detail. Maybe we can turn the tables on the general, make him think somebody else is getting credit for what he's doing."

"Good idea. While you're filing your story, I'll go find some horses."

"Now, come on, Steele. Don't even mention horses to me until I get a good night's sleep,"

"Do you think Helen and those other women hostages will get a good night's sleep tonight? We have to ride south toward the border to find out if Ramsey is heading this way."

Rudd held up his hands. "All right, all right. I get your point. Go get the horses. Tell them the newspaper will pay. Do you have any money on you?"

"No, the Mexicans took it back at the their camp."

Rudd took all of his money out of his pocket and carefully counted out half of it for Steele. "Just give me time to file my story. Then I'll go to the hotel and reserve us a couple of rooms. That way I can fall right into bed when we get back."

Steele smiled as he turned away. Rudd was a complainer, but he was trying hard to hold up.

Steele asked directions to the stables and as he headed that way he thought about what the major had said about troublemaking Texans. Were the former Confederate soldiers from Texas donning their uniforms and heading toward Tucson because they'd heard about what happened in Yuma, or were they coming to meet up with

Ramsey? Either way, Tucson could be in a lot more trouble than the major would admit.

Passing a hardware store, something in the window caught Steele's eye. It was a powerful looking pair of field glasses. He went in and bought them.

At the livery stable, he asked the owner to pick out two good horses. The man wasted valuable time trying to get Steele to buy the horses, but finally agreed to a pay-by-the-day arrangement. When Steele said the newspaper would issue him a payment voucher, he agreed without argument. Apparently the newspaper had a good credit rating in the town.

Steele started to put his saddlebags on the horse, but the man still had ahold of the reins. "Now listen," he said, "I don't want you taking these horses anywhere near the mountains. If you do, them Indians'll come down and take 'em away from you. That happens and I'm gonna charge your newspaper for 'em. Full price, you hear me?"

"Where are the Indians supposed to be?" asked Steele.

"Who knows? Up in the mountains somewhere. That's all I know." He jerked his thumb toward the northeast. "And I hope you ain't plannin' to head out to Yuma neither. I hear there's some kind of trouble out there too."

"What kind of trouble?"

"Some bandits attacked the town. That's what people are sayin' anyhow. Everybody is all riled up 'bout it. I talked to one guy who said he heard it was a bunch of Confederates, but I 'spect it's just them Mexicans again. They've been doin' all kinds of border town raids lately."

"Is there a Spanish mission in this town?" asked Steele as he mounted the horse.

"Yeah, out west of town. But no use goin' out there. They don't speak any English."

"One more thing, can you tell me how far it is down to the border?"

The man handed him the leads of the second horse. "It's a fair piece of ridin'. If you're headin' down there you won't make it before dark."

"Thank you for the information," said Steele turning his horse to head back to the hotel.

At the hotel, there was no sign of Rudd. Steele tied the two horses to the hitching post and went inside to ask if a Mr. Rudd had checked in. They told him he had and gave him a room number, but when he knocked at that room, there was no response. He went inside and found Rudd sound asleep. He hadn't even bothered to take his boots off. Steele wished he could let him sleep for a while longer. He felt a great weight of tiredness in himself, but he knew there was no time for sleeping as long as Ramsey still had Helen and the other women hostages. He woke Rudd with a nudge. "Time to go, Rudd. I've got the horses out front."

Rudd rolled over to face the wall. He mumbled something unintelligible.

"Maybe I'd better go alone. Let you get some sleep."

With great effort, Rudd swung his feet to the floor. "I'm getting up. Just a little worn out is all." He got to his feet and stood by the bed rubbing his back. "Do we have time to get something to eat? I told the newspaper we were on a special mission personally authorized by Mr. Kane and I . . . uh, persuaded them to sign some vouchers for us. We can eat all we want. For free."

"I'm afraid we don't have time for that. It's quite a ways down to the border."

"Now I'm sure you're trying to starve me to death. But it won't work. I've still got a little food left." He grabbed his saddlebags and followed Steele out of the room and down the stairs, mumbling all the way.

Steele offered to help Rudd up onto his horse but Rudd waved him off. "Just give me a second. I'll make it."

Once Rudd was mounted, Steele led the way south out of town.

"Looks pretty peaceful," said Rudd. "Maybe he's not coming."

"He had a reason for sending that warning message."

"Maybe he's going to attack somewhere in Texas."

"Would he want to attack the only people of the West who joined the Confederacy?"

"Ah, I see what you mean." Rudd was silent for several minutes as they rode on. Then he said, "But what if we meet Ramsey's men coming up from the border? I mean how long you figure it will take them to get this far?"

"If they continued to travel as fast as they were when we last saw them, I would expect them to get here later tonight. Ramsey's main column can't be moving very fast with all those loaded-down wagons, but he might send faster riders ahead. If so, they could already be out here somewhere."

Again, Rudd was silent. The road was empty and there was no sound except for the repeated rhythm of their horses' hooves in the dirt. Finally, he said, "Uh, you know, Steele, we're kind of out here all by ourselves. We may not see them coming" He stood up in his stirrups to look ahead.

"That's why I bought these," said Steele. He reached back and pulled the new field glasses out of his saddlebag." Take a look."

"Hey, nice. Where'd you get these?"

"I just bought them in town. They seem very powerful."

"They sure are," said Rudd as he adjusted the focus. "Man, I can see things a mile away."

They rode on as the sun dropped below the western horizon. Rudd was enjoying himself looking through the field glasses. "Hey, wait a minute," he said, raising his hand and bringing his horse to a halt. "There's people on the road ahead."

"How many?"

"They're kickin' up a lot of dust." He lowered the field glasses." Maybe we'd better hide."

"Let me see."

Rudd handed the glasses to Steele who quickly readjusted the focus. It was a large group, all on foot, moving slowly. "It's not Ramsey. It's civilians."

"Not Confederates? Thank goodness for that. Why do you think there's so many of them on the road?"

"I don't know. From their dress, I'd say they're farmers. One of them is leading a cow."

"A cow? What the hell?"

When the farmers arrived, Steele saw that they were led by an old man who was followed closely by several children. A young boy was leading a scrawny cow. A group of women brought up the rear, some of them with babies in their arms.

Steele called to the old man. "Where are you going?"

The man and the boy kept their eyes on the ground and walked quickly past them. The women did the same, passing by in silence.

Before long, a Mexican couple came along. A young girl hid behind the woman's skirts.

Steele called to them: "*¿Ustedes vieron hombres en uniformes? ¿Uniformes grises?*"

The man shook his head and they hurried on.

"What did you say?" asked Rudd.

"I asked them if they'd seen any men in gray uniforms."

"Maybe they didn't understand you. How did you learn to speak Spanish, anyhow? You said you'd never been to Mexico before."

"I learned it in school. In Rome."

"That's the problem, they speak Italian in Rome."

"I learned both Italian and Spanish there. Those people understood me, but they're afraid to answer."

"Maybe they just don't trust strangers."

"I saw this kind of thing during the war," said Steele. "All through the war there were refugees on the roads, whole families packed into wagons with all of their possessions. When I asked them where they were going, many were afraid to answer, suspicious of anyone who spoke to them. If they did respond they just said they didn't know where they were going. Anywhere, as long as it was away from the fighting."

"I bet some of them were heading out West. A lot of people came out here to get away from the war."

"That's true," said Steele. "I saw quite a few abandoned homes, especially in the border states. Missouri and Arkansas. At first people just moved out of the way of the battles, but eventually they learned they couldn't predict which way to run. By the end of the war, large areas along the border had been completely abandoned. Good homes were standing empty."

"Didn't they go back after the fighting had moved on somewhere else?"

"They weren't allowed to go back. The Union Army found out some of the people in that area were harboring border raiders so they went in and burned down all of the houses and barns."

"Jesus, what happened to those people?"

"No one knows."

They rode on, meeting more and more people. A tiny wagon approached, drawn slowly by a single donkey. An old man was seated in the wagon, urging the donkey forward with a switch.

Steele turned his horse and fell into pace alongside the cart. "Where are you going, sir? Why are all these people on the road?"

The old man spit tobacco juice into the dirt before looking up at him. "They're runnin', son, runnin' scared."

"What are they running from? Have you seen soldiers?"

The old man looked at him. "Guess you ain't from around these parts."

"No, we just arrived. Did someone tell you to go to Tucson?"

The man spit again. "This mornin' my neighbor comes and says, 'Here they come again.' So I hitches up old Becky and off we go again. Damn Army don't do nuthin' to help us. They stay in their fort up in Tucson, when it's down here we need 'em."

"So this has happened before?"

"Yep. First it's the Indians and now the Mexicans been comin' across the border again. Raidin', stealin'. This time my neighbor heard it was a whole bunch of 'em. It's enough to make a man pack up and go back to Indiana."

"Did your neighbor see soldiers? Men in gray uniforms?"

"Yep, gray uniforms, that's what he said. Carryin' some kind of fancy new rifles. Get out fast, he says. Didn't have to tell me twice. I got out. Same as most of the others."

"Thank you, sir." Steele wheeled his horse around and rejoined Rudd to tell him what the man had said.

"So Ramsey's army is already here," said Rudd.

"It appears that at least some of them are."

"They must be raiding the farms near the border for supplies."

"It doesn't seem likely he could get much from these farmers," said Steele. "Besides, he should be well-stocked with supplies from that raid on Yuma."

"So why are the people so scared?"

"That man said Mexicans had been raiding their farms lately. Maybe they were already scared."

"Hey, look," shouted Rudd, pointing to the south.

Steele saw what Rudd was pointing at. Fires. Quite a number of them, lighting up the evening sky all along the horizon.

"Holy hell," said Rudd. "He's burning these people out."

From the number of fires, Steele knew it was not one force bearing down on a settlement and burning them out; it had to be small parties of soldiers fanning out across the entire area, setting fires as they went. "They're not after supplies. They're setting fires to instill panic."

"But why?"

"Let's go find out." Steele spurred his horse into a gallop.

"Wait!" yelled Rudd. "Why are we going toward them? Shouldn't we be going the other way, to get the Army or something?"

He yelled something else, but Steele couldn't hear what it was. He slapped his horse with the reins to keep it running. If the raiders were quickly setting fires and moving on, they could disappear back into the night as quickly as they had come. He had to get there before that happened to find out if they really were Ramsey's men.

When he topped a small hill, he found himself close enough to see individual buildings burning in the gathering darkness. He slowed his horse to a walk. The raiders were burning everything, homes, barns, even small outbuildings. Steele tried to determine the direction they were heading, but there was no apparent pattern to the fires. They seemed to be everywhere, lighting up the night sky with an orange glow.

Rudd caught up and rode next to Steele. "He's burning them all out. The man has no mercy."

Steele pointed. "Look, down there. A new fire just starting. That's where they'll be." He again spurred his horse into a gallop.

"Not again," shouted Rudd. "Wait for me."

When Steele came to a dry ravine that looked as if it would lead him closer to the burning homestead, he turned off the road and followed it. He glanced back to see if Rudd was following. He was, but not very quickly.

When he reached the bottom of the hill, Steele could see men on horses riding from building to building, setting them afire with torches. He jumped down from his horse and waited for Rudd. When he arrived, Steele said, "Stay here. I'm going to try to get closer." He handed the reins of his horse to Rudd. "If I don't make it back, go tell Major Carter what's going on here."

"No, don't do it," whispered Rudd. "There's nothing we can do here. Let's just go back and tell Major Carter."

"I have to find out who it is. I won't be long." Steele turned and hurried down the ravine, staying low and close to the sandy wall. As he had hoped, the ravine was leading him closer to the burning buildings. So close, that soon he began to hear shouts from the men who were lighting the fires. He scrambled up the wall of the ravine and found himself only a few hundred yards from the burning homestead. Three men on horseback had finished setting the buildings on fire and had gathered together. Steele could see them clearly: they were not wearing gray Confederate uniforms, but the gray and black uniforms of the Mexican militia he'd seen back at Medina's camp. Did it mean Medina was still alive? If so, how would it serve his purpose to burn out the small farmers who'd built homesteads along the border? Was he trying to draw the Army down from Tucson?

Suddenly, one of the men stopped and pointed in his direction. Steele ducked down. They couldn't have seen him in the dark, could they? Then he heard one of the men yell, *"Un reflexión, allí."*

A reflection? In the dark? Then Steele realized what it was: Rudd must have been watching them with the field glasses and the Mexican spotted a reflection of the fires from the glass.

Steele slid down the bank of the ravine and ran back toward where he'd left Rudd. He soon heard the pounding hoofs of horses up on the rim of the ravine. They were coming fast. He flattened himself against the side wall and they pounded past him, the light of their torches dancing in the darkness. They hadn't noticed him down in the ravine; they were going after Rudd.

Steele began to run again and was almost back to the horses when he saw Rudd ahead, trying to mount his horse. But the horse had panicked at the sound of the approaching horsemen and was moving sideways away from Rudd who was desperately hanging onto the saddle horn, cursing the horse, even as the Mexicans bore down on him.

One of the Mexicans pulled out a pistol and Steele heard one shot. Rudd lost his grip on the horse and fell. The Mexican closed in, ready to finish him off. Steele got there and jumped toward the Mexican just as he leaned down from his horse to put a bullet in Rudd's head. The Mexican was knocked off his horse and the shot went wild. Before the man could recover, Steele scrambled under the startled horse after him and tore the gun out of his hand. The man swung wildly, but Steele avoided the blow and hit him hard in the face with the butt of the gun. The man went limp, but before Steele could get up, he heard another shot that kicked up the sand next to him. The horse reared up over him and then bolted and ran off down the ravine. Steele quickly threw a handful of sand onto the torch that lay burning on the ground and crawled away into the darkness.

He lay very still, trying to catch his breath. The other two Mexicans dismounted and approached carefully. They held their torches up high, shading their eyes as they peered into the darkness. Lighted by their own torches and also blinded by them, they were easy targets. Steele threw away the Mexican's pistol and pulled out his own little Remington. "¡*Alto!*" he yelled. "¡*Vuelvae!*"

But they did not retreat. Both men instantly fired in his direction and then ducked for cover. Foolishly, one of them didn't drop his torch; Steele could still see him, crouching behind a bush. The man fired twice more in his direction and one of the shots came very close. Steele aimed for the Mexican's midsection and squeezed the trigger. The man cried out and fell backward. Steele swung his gun toward the other man, but he was crawling away fast, whimpering a breathless prayer that mentioned the Holy *Madre del Dios* over and over. Steele put his gun back into its boot holster and got up.

"Are you hit?" whispered Rudd.

"No, are you?"

"No, I'm all right. But, Steele, those weren't Ramsey's men. They were Mexicans."

Steele ran to his horse. "Let's go. We've got to get out of here before the others come."

"Sounds good to me," said Rudd. "It's damn dangerous out here." Rudd tried to get up onto his horse, but he was still having trouble getting the excited animal to hold still. Steele caught hold of the reins and forced the animal's head down while Rudd mounted. Then he got up on his own horse and kicked it into a fast run back toward the road with Rudd close behind.

They started back toward Tucson at a gallop, but soon they had to slow down because of the many slow-moving refugees on the road.

Rudd rode up next to Steele. "Who were those guys back there?"

"Mexican militia," said Steele. "The same uniforms that I saw in Medina's camp back in Mexico."

"But why are they burning everything?"

"They must be trying to draw the Army down here. Then they'll run back across the border."

"But why would they do that? What's the point?"

"A diversion."

"A diversion? You mean trying to draw the Army away? From what?"

"It could mean Medina is still working with Ramsey. His job could be to draw the Army down here while Ramsey sneaks across the border somewhere else."

"I thought you said Ramsey and Medina fought each other back there at that camp."

"They did, but war makes for some surprising alliances. Do you remember reading about the alliance General McCulloch was forced into during the war?"

"No, who's that?"

"Never mind. The point is Ramsey will work with whoever he needs to if it helps him accomplish his goals. I should have known it. He spoke to me about it, said if I wanted to understand the future of warfare I should learn about the art of alliances. He quoted Napoleon about alliances of the weak against the strong. We've got to get back to Tucson to warn the Army."

They continued back toward Tucson as fast as they could, often being forced to the edge of the road to go around slow-moving groups of refugees that were also heading that way. As they neared Tucson, they came upon an old iron-wheeled wagon that was slowly clattering its way toward Tucson. It was overloaded with people: children, old men and women, mothers with babies in their arms. Rudd pointed at them and whispered, "I really feel sorry for these people. They're getting burned out of their homes and they don't even know why. They're just getting caught up in--"

A bright flash lit up the dark sky ahead. "What the hell?" said Rudd.

The wagon slid to a stop, forcing Steele and Rudd to also stop.

They all watched the northern horizon in silence. Soon, there came a low rumble, then more flashes.

"Lightning?" asked Rudd.

Steele shook his head. "There's not a cloud in the sky."

Then there came another flash, and then another, followed by a rumbling that seemed to roll across the desert towards them.

"We've got to get there fast," shouted Steele as he spurred his horse into a gallop. "Let's go."

"Wait," yelled Rudd. "What's happening?"

"Artillery!" shouted Steele over his shoulder. "Tucson's under attack."

Chapter 16

Steele and Rudd rode hard toward Tucson, but they were soon slowed again by a family that had stopped their rickety wagon in the middle of the road to watch the bright flashes in the sky. The younger children seemed to think it was some kind of fun entertainment and were making sounds of delight with each new flash and rumble.

As Steele carefully guided his horse around the family, Rudd brought his horse up next to him. "How do you know it's artillery?"

"Once you've heard artillery, you never forget it. Those are exploding shells, the kind that go off on impact."

Steele again spurred his horse into a gallop, but they soon began to meet people running *away* from Tucson. Steele had seen that all too often during the war: sometimes the refugees didn't know which way to run.

A few miles farther on, they came upon a man swinging a lantern to try to stop them. "Don't go that way!" he shouted. "There's some kind of battle going on there."

Steele and Rudd went on past the man, but when they tried to pick up the pace again, they almost ran down a young boy in the dark who was trailing after the family, leading a fat pig on a rope.

"We've got to get off this road," shouted Steele. "Follow me!"

"Not again," said Rudd. "Why is everybody else running from danger and we're always heading toward it?"

Steele guided his horse out into the desert, heading toward the artillery flashes that were coming from the hills west of Tucson. It was slow going through the rocks and the cactus, but eventually they made it high enough into the hills to see the city far below. There were numerous fires burning in the city. There in the darkness, listening to the hard breathing of his horse, Steele had a strong memory of seeing the nighttime shelling of a town in Virginia; this had the same strangely detached feeling of unreality.

Steele stopped his horse and Rudd came up alongside.

"The shelling has stopped," said Rudd, "but it looks like half the city is on fire."

Steele listened for any sound in the darkness, but heard nothing. He was sure they were close to where the shelling had come from. How could they have gotten away so quickly?

"What do you think they were shooting at?" asked Rudd. "The fort?"

"The fires are too widespread. They weren't aiming at any particular target."

"Maybe they're just bad shots."

"No, this was Ramsey's demonstration of what he can do."

"So you think this was Ramsey? How could he have gotten here so fast?"

"His main force may not be here yet. This was probably a small group, using Medina's diversion to get their cannon up here. They fired randomly at the city and moved out."

"Jesus," said Rudd. "Look at those fires go. Those poor people."

Steele slapped his horse with the reins. "We've got to get down there. There will be wounded." The horse struggled to find footing, but Steele kept it moving.

He heard Rudd's cry from behind: "What if it's an invasion? Doesn't artillery usually precede an invasion?"

"Ramsey isn't ready for that," said Steele over his shoulder. "He told me when the weak are up against the strong they should use guerrilla warfare."

"Guerrilla warfare?" said Rudd. "With cannons?"

"Guerrillas strike quickly and then retreat," said Steele. "A lightweight cannon is the perfect tool for that."

"The perfect tool, he says," mumbled Rudd. "An army is out here shooting cannons and we're up here all by ourselves."

The trip back down out of the hills was slow because they often had to work their way around rocky ledges. Other than the sound of their horses, the night was very quiet.

But then, Steele heard Rudd cry out. He looked back to see Rudd's horse running up the hill. He went back and found Rudd sitting on the ground. He was rubbing his knee and cursing nonstop.

Steele dismounted and hurried to Rudd's side. "What happened?"

"Eyes. There were two eyes out there looking at me. Big yellow eyes. It was like they were glowing in the dark."

"Probably a mountain lion."

"A mountain lion? Oh, my God, it must have been ready to spring at me, and my horse knew it."

"A mountain lion is not likely to attack a man on a horse, but your horse must have smelled it and reared."

"Yeah, well now I got cactus thorns in my butt, as if I didn't have enough problems in that vicinity from being on a horse all day every day."

Steele helped him to his feet. "We have a lot more to fear from the two-legged animals than the four-legged ones. Your shout may have been heard by Ramsey's men if they're still nearby. We'd better hurry and find your horse."

Rudd followed, limping. They found the horse a short distance away. But as Rudd tried to remount, Steele stopped him. "Wait. Listen."

"What is it?" whispered Rudd.

"Somebody's coming. Horses."

"Oh, Christ! I knew we shouldn't have come up here. If it's Ramsey's men they'll kill us for sure."

Steele pulled out his pistol. "Shh. Get behind the rocks."

They squatted behind some large boulders and suddenly, a voice came out of the night: "Who's up there? I'm warning you, I've got a dozen men coming right behind me. Give up now or we'll start shooting."

"I think it's the Army," whispered Steele. He called out: "It's Drew Steele and John Rudd. We're known to your commander, Major Carter."

That caused some discussion–three or four voices, all talking at once. Then someone said, "Let us see you. Come out with your hands up."

"I'm not going out there," said Rudd. "It could be a trick."

Steele put his gun away. "I'm coming out. Make sure your men don't shoot."

He walked out with his hands up. One of the men lit a bright Dietz lantern and held it up high. As Steele walked forward into the circle of light, someone said, "That's one of the guys who was at the fort earlier today."

A soldier in a lieutenant's uniform came forward into the light. "What the hell are you doing out here, mister? Don't you know there's been an attack on the city?"

"That's why we're up here," said Steele. "We were looking for them. I need to talk to your commander right away."

The lieutenant ordered one of his men to take Steele and Rudd back down to Major Carter.

"I'll get our horses," said Steele.

Rudd stood up. "My butt's so sore I'd rather walk," he grumbled. But when Steele brought him his horse, he reluctantly climbed aboard.

The soldier led them down the hill, holding up a lantern. The light helped them make fairly good progress going cross-country directly back to Tucson.

As they entered the town, they began to see people running through the streets in panic. Steele had seen many such scenes during the war: fear was driving the people to run, but they didn't know where to go. They seemed to be running in all directions at once, impeding the fire brigades who were trying to get to the fires. Steele could see that the exploding shells had done their job, creating panic and starting fires over a wide area. And he knew there was more fire to come as sparks from the out-of-control fires blew to buildings that had not been hit directly. Even adobe buildings were catching fire when burning embers fell onto their thatched roofs.

People noticed the soldier in the lead and yelled questions at him: "What's going on? What should we do?" The soldier ignored them and forced his horse through the crowd. Steele and Rudd followed close behind.

As they made their way through the chaos, Steele couldn't help but be impressed by the effectiveness of Ramsey's plan: a short barrage, probably from a small single cannon, had created more panic than an attack with all of his forces could have. Raiders riding into a town and shooting it up would cause fear, but that was something Westerners had seen, or heard about, before. An artillery attack was something else. Unlike the people of the South, westerners had never seen war; they had never been forced to deal with the wartime reality of exploding shells falling out of the sky. Steele was sure it was Ramsey's plan to teach them about that.

Rudd pointed out a woman who was sitting on the edge of the board sidewalk. She was cradling a young child in her arms. Steele stopped his horse and got off to see if he could do anything for her. He saw immediately there was nothing he could do for the child; it was dead. The woman seemed dazed, but uninjured.

Steele called to the soldier who was leading them. "I've got to try to help."

"No, sir," said the soldier. "My orders are to take you directly to Major Carter."

"These people need help," said Steele, dismounting. "I'll talk to the major later."

"If you're going to help, then so am I," said Rudd.

"But what should I tell Major Carter?" said the soldier.

"Tell him we'll be there as soon as we can." He turned to Rudd. "These horses need food and water. Go see if the stable is still standing."

"Okay," said Rudd, taking the reins of Steele's horse. "I'll be right back."

Farther up the sidewalk, Steele saw a man wearing a long white coat who was tending to injured people. He assumed it must be the town doctor. A harried nurse was trying to help him. Her crisp white uniform had been spoiled by smears of blood and black smudges of soot from the burn victims.

Steele hurried toward them.

As Steele got closer, he saw the doctor was treating a man with a serious shrapnel wound in his neck.

Steele touched him on the shoulder. "Doctor?"

The doctor didn't look up. "Go inside and wait. Can't you see I've got my hands full here?"

"Doctor, my name is Drew Steele. I had some experience treating wounds during the war."

The doctor turned to look at him. "By God, we could sure use the help. My name's Harrison, but no time for formal introductions. I'm having them bring all the wounded here to this bar. The ones that can walk are already inside." He turned to the nurse. "Take this man inside to look at the wounded in there."

The nurse led Steele through the swinging doors into the bar. She wiped the sweat from her brow with the back of her hand as she looked around the room. "We've got wounded all over the place. I don't know where to begin."

"I'll look at the most seriously wounded first." He noticed a young man laid out on a poker table. A crowd of men were gathered around him, staring as they drank from their beer mugs.

Steele pushed his way through the crowd to the boy. The men let him through, but they didn't move any farther than they had to. They seemed to be fixated on the gruesome scene before them. He felt for the boy's pulse. There was none. "Some of you men take this boy out of here. He's dead."

The men just looked at Steele, beer mugs in hand.

"Either help or get the hell out of the way. And get me some hot water."

One of the men came to life. He finished his beer in one gulp and said, "I bet I can get some hot water over at the barber's."

"Get it," said Steele. "As much as you can find. And bring some more lanterns over here. I need more light."

Several of the men put down their beers and hurried to gather up lanterns. "I'll go next door," said one. "I bet the Silver Dollar's got more lanterns."

Steele turned to the nurse who was staring at him in amazement. He took her aside. "Put some of these men to work bringing me the most seriously wounded. Put the first one on this pool table and line the others up on the floor next to it."

"Yes, doctor."

Steele decided not to correct her misassumption that he was a doctor. It might be better if the wounded thought he was.

Within minutes, Steele had organized a treatment system. The nurse brought a scalpel and some stitching thread and Steele did the best he could with those limited tools. A few people had suffered shrapnel wounds and some had serious burns. But most of the injuries seemed to have been caused by panic; there were a number of broken arms and other injuries caused by falls. Many of the victims were confused, unable to understand what was happening. As Steele treated a man with a shrapnel wound to his leg, the man seemed more interested in finding out what had happened to the town than what was wrong with his leg. "What's going on, doctor? Has the war started up again?"

Steele assured him that it had not, but he wondered if he was telling the man the truth.

Hours later, most of the wounded had been treated. The nurse was bandaging the last of them when the owner of the establishment arrived and got very upset that his bar had been turned into a hospital. He demanded payment for the amount of beer that had been drunk in his absence. After a few men came forward to pay, he calmed down and even brought out food and water for the victims.

The doctor came in wiping his face and neck with a bloody rag. "Well, that's the last of them outside. How's it going in here?"

"We've got all of them stabilized," said the nurse. "This doctor knew just what to do."

The doctor turned to Steele, nodding his approval. "Well, doctor, looks like you've got things under control in here."

"I'm not a doctor," said Steele. "I worked in a Union Army field hospital."

"Hey, how about that? I worked in a Confederacy field hospital. Where were you stationed?"

"Tennessee."

"I was in Virginia. Got sent down there right out of medical school. They cut down our training to one year and then they sent us right to the front where we got our real education. Anyhow, thank heaven you came along when you did. This is a bad situation. Cannon shells coming down out of the sky. It's like being back in Virginia all over again. Nobody seems to know who is behind it."

"I believe the artillery fire came from Confederate soldiers," said Steele.

The doctor looked doubtful. "Confederates? Our boys? All the way out here?"

"We've been following them for days," said Steele.

"Well, in a way, I'm not really surprised," said the doctor. "I'm getting letters from back home saying there's talk all over the South now about fighting back. They're all saying somebody has to do something about the North's repression. Things are bad down there, real bad. It's like the blockade is still going on. No jobs, not enough food, and nobody seems to be able to do anything about it. Everybody just sits around blaming the North. I came west to get away from that kind of thing. Who knew the damn war would follow me here?"

Before Steele could reply, Rudd rushed in through the swinging doors. He was no longer wearing his suit jacket and his white shirt had smudges of blood and soot all over it. His shirt sleeves were rolled up to the elbows. "Oh, there you are, Steele." He turned to the doctor. "I think that's everybody, Doc. 'Cept the dead ones, of course. What should we do with them?"

"I'll take care of it," said the doctor heading for the door. "I suppose I've got to do death certificates." He glanced at Steele. "It does feel like war again, doesn't it, Steele? Come by my office and see me when you get a chance. You can tell me about these wandering Confederates and we can reminisce about the good old days of . . . bloody warfare." He gave Steele a rueful smile and hurried out.

As the doctor left, the young soldier that had escorted them into town came in. "Major Carter is still waiting for you, sir."

"I guess we'd better go see him now," said Rudd. "This young man came back to get us, but I put him to work carrying people. He said it 'bout broke his back. Mine too, that's for sure. Dead people sure are heavy."

Steele rolled down his sleeves. "All right, I'm ready."

"Thank you, doctor," said the nurse.

"I'm not a–"

"I know," she said reaching out to touch his hand, "you're not a real doctor. But we all thank you anyhow."

Steele wasn't sure what to do with her delicate little hand so he shook it firmly.

"Can we go now?" said the soldier.

Steele patted the nurse's hand before releasing it. He turned to follow the soldier out into the street.

The town had calmed somewhat, but a large number of people were still milling about, talking with great excitement. As they headed for the fort, Steele saw the full extent of the damage. Many houses had been hit and some were still smoldering.

"We had to dig a lot of people out," said Rudd. "We heard a woman crying under that one." He pointed toward a burned-out building. "Her husband was tearing at the burning wood with his bare hands. Said his wife and little girl were in there. I tried to get him to stop, but he wouldn't so we helped him dig until we found them. His wife got burned some, but I think she'll be all right. Then we found the little girl. Poor little thing. She was wearing a nice pink dress. Wasn't hardly dirty at all. Like she was all dressed up to go to church or something."

"Was she dead?"

Rudd continued to stare at the smoking ruins.

"Did she survive?" asked Steele again.

Rudd turned to look at him with tears in his eyes. "Huh? No, she was already dead by the time we got to her. Hated to see that. I guess she couldn't breathe under there."

They continued to walk toward the fort in silence. It was Steele's first chance to think since he'd stopped to help the doctor. Seeing the destruction all around, he thought about General Ramsey, the man who was responsible. He remembered his first impression of Ramsey. He had looked like a tired old man, ready for retirement. But the destruction all around proved the general was not yet ready to give up the fight. He had ordered the shelling of the city, knowing innocent people would die. A general with wartime experience knew better than anyone how much suffering and death an artillery attack would bring. And yet Ramsey had done what no wartime commander had done at any time during the war: he had deliberately attacked innocent civilians. It was now clear what Ramsey's plan was: he was going to show the world a new kind of war, a war that would involve every man, woman, and child.

Chapter 17

At the fort, the soldier had to convince his fellow soldiers inside to open the gate. Steele could see that many of them were young and they looked very frightened as they pointed their rifles through the gate at Steele and Rudd. They seemed to be expecting some kind of further attack, maybe even from these two strangers. The young soldier patiently explained that Major Carter was waiting for them and the gate was finally opened.

Once through the gate, Steele saw there was little damage inside the fort. Only two buildings had been hit and they were not badly damaged. Clearly, the fort had not been the main target of the artillery attack.

The soldier led them to the commander's office where they found Major Carter at his desk, surrounded by officers all talking at once. One officer was insisting that troops would soon come, following up on the initial artillery attack.

Steele pushed through to the major's desk. "I don't believe there will be a ground attack tonight, Major."

All of the officers turned to look at him.

The major stood up and took the stub of his cigar out of his mouth. "Where have you two been? And what do you know about this?"

"I believe it was a quick round of cannon fire to create panic," said Steele. "They won't do anything else tonight."

The major jabbed the air in Steele's direction. "You don't know what you're talking about, mister. This was a planned artillery attack. I was at the Wilderness and at Petersburg too. We always used artillery to soften up the enemy before an attack."

"And I was at Blue Springs," said Steele, "where General Jones used only two cannons, firing in sequence, to make Major Carpenter retreat to the woods because he thought an attack was coming. It gave Jones time to move his army across the river before Carpenter could cut him off."

"Blue Springs? You mean Blue Springs, Tennessee? What do I care about that? We are about as far from Tennessee as we can get and I've got artillery fire coming down on my wooden fort."

"Yes, sir. I know you've been attacked, but as I've been trying to tell you, you're dealing with General Jacob Ramsey. He was a field commander under Bennett in Tennessee, as was Jones. General Ramsey would certainly be aware of how Jones used his artillery in that campaign."

"So you're saying he's just trying to scare us?"

"That's right, but it may have also been to cover his movements."

The major threw his pen down on the desk. "So what am I supposed to do? Sit here and wait to see if you're right?"

"It might be worth while to send some men out to look for Ramsey."

"I've got men out all over the mountains west of town."

"We've just come from there," said Rudd, stepping forward. "We saw your soldiers chasing their tails in the dark. And I saw a mountain lion out there too. It came at me and almost–"

"It's true, Major," interrupted Steele. "We were south of the city when we saw the flashes from up in the foothills. We rode up into the western mountains to try to find the cannon, but it was already gone. They fired off several salvos and moved out fast."

"You went down south toward the border?" asked the major. "What were you doing down there?"

"We were looking for Ramsey, of course," said Rudd.

"You must have been pretty sure he was coming."

"Damn right we were," said Rudd. "And now a lot of other people know he's coming too. They're burning farms down there. Last night the roads were filled with farmers, whole families, running this way, at least until Ramsey's attack started. Then they just stood in the middle of the road, confused."

The major shook his head and sat down hard. "I know all about that. Scared people running all over the place down by the border. I sent thirty men down there to check it out, but I expect it's just the usual trouble. Mexicans sneaking across the border to rob the ranchers."

"It *was* Mexicans," said Steele. "It was that militia group I told you about, dressed in distinctive gray and black uniforms. They were setting the fires, but they were not stealing. I think it was another diversion to keep you from detecting the Confederates as they came across the border."

"Mexicans I know about, but wearing some kind of uniforms? That's a new one." He turned to look at his officers. "Those border raiders are gettin' mighty fancy, aren't they? Wearin' uniforms now."

"The Confederates may be coming across the border in small groups," continued Steele, "to avoid attracting too much attention. I would look for them east of here."

"East? But that cannon was firing at us from up in the western mountains."

"That's why I would expect Ramsey's main column to be in the east. Aren't there more mountains to the east?"

"Yeah," said the major. "Bigger mountains. He turned to his officers. "All right, get going. Send some men up into the Rincons. See if you can find anything that looks like a Confederate." He waved them out of the room.

After the officers were gone, the major gestured toward the chairs in front of his desk. Rudd sat down heavily, but Steele remained standing.

The major pointed toward the east with his thumb. "If your General Ramsey is heading up into those Rincon mountains, he's in for big trouble. They're crawlin' with hostiles. Apaches. They come down to attack the ranches around here and then they disappear back up into those mountains."

"It's possible Ramsey is going there specifically to join with them," said Steele.

"What?" The major looked at him, his mouth hanging open. "Why would you say a fool thing like that?"

"General Ramsey spoke admiringly of Cochise and his guerrilla-like tactics."

"You think he's trying to join up with old Cochise? Either you're crazy or he is. That Cochise is not gonna let a white man anywhere near his stronghold. Those mountains are his territory. He knows everything that moves up there, every lizard and snake."

"For days I've been trying to figure out where Ramsey was heading," said Steele, sitting down. "Now that you've told me the Apaches are in the mountains east of here, it all seems to fit. Ramsey spoke about guerrilla warfare, about striking fast and getting out fast. He spoke of alliances of weaker forces against the strong. He spoke admiringly of Cochise and the Apaches. It makes sense that he's trying to form an alliance with them, just like he did with that Mexican militia group."

"I don't buy it," said the major, shaking his head. "An alliance between Confederates and the hostiles? I'll believe that when I see it."

"Ramsey has been moving east for days, staying on the Mexican side of the border, but constantly heading in this direction. If he's turned north now it means this is where he wants to make his stand, not with frontal attacks, but with the kind of quick strikes and fast retreats you saw tonight."

The major took the cigar out of his mouth. "But why here?"

"Guerrilla warfare," said Rudd loudly.

They both turned to look at him.

"I mean, don't guerrillas always fight and then run off to hide in the mountains? I bet those eastern mountains are pretty close to this city, aren't they?"

Steele turned back to the major. "Rudd is correct. That's exactly what guerrilla fighters do. The nearby mountains and a potential alliance with the Indians make it likely he's planning more strikes against this city. Although Tucson is not a large city, it's well-known back east. Much has been written about this area, and about Tombstone. The stories of western shootouts and bank robberies and such are very popular back east in the newspapers and penny novels. Attacks on this city might well give Ramsey exactly the kind of publicity he wants. He could be hoping it will encourage more Texans to come here to join him."

The major chewed on his cigar with obvious irritation. "That's all I need. More Texans. Well, if that's his plan, we'll be ready for him. He'll find out what we're made of here in Arizona. Them Texans will find out too."

"You said you only had one hundred and sixty-two men."

The major shrugged. "Ramsey doesn't know how many men I have."

"I suspect he does. It would be easy to send a man in here to assess your strength."

The major banged his fist on the desk. "Let him come, by God! He'll soon see why we whipped those Rebs in the first place."

Chapter 18

*O*n the way to the hotel, Steele thought about Major Carter's brave words. Although the major had apparently seen action in the war, Steele suspected that few of his men could say the same. Even if they were experienced Indian fighters, they would never have been tested by a real army. How would they react if they had to face seasoned Confederate troops led by an experienced general? Steele was sure they would be put to that test sooner or later.

At the hotel, Rudd said he was ready for a nice hot bath, some food, and a good night's sleep. But before he could decide which he wanted first, the desk clerk came running over to hand him a message.

Rudd read it and said, "It's Kane. He just arrived. We're supposed to go over to the newspaper office to see him right away."

"Let's go," said Steele, starting toward the door.

Rudd didn't move. "Wait a minute, Steele. I'm tired. I mean really tired. Don't you think Mr. Kane could wait until I at least got a bath?"

"Go ahead. I'll go talk to him while you have your bath. He's probably very worried about his daughter. "

Rudd looked longingly up the stairs, as if that bath was pulling at him. But finally he shook his head and turned back to Steele. "No, no, I'm coming. Christ, a man can't even take a few minutes to wash up around here. I bet I'm starting to stink pretty bad. And I'll probably never get a minute to find a bite to eat either."

Rudd cheered up considerably when they arrived at the newspaper office to find Kane seated in the editor's office, eating. He was surrounded by almost all of the newspaper's employees. Kane saw them arrive and waved them into the office. "Get in here, you two," he yelled. "Where's Ramsey? Did you find him? Did you see Helen?"

"Ramsey's still got her, Mr. Kane," said Rudd. "But Steele saw her. She's not hurt." He turned to one of the other men. "Would you mind if I had some of that chicken? It looks mighty good."

The man pushed the platter of chicken toward him.

Kane sent the newspapermen away, saying, "Do like I told you and get that special issue out right away." As the men hurried out of the office, Kane turned to Steele. "Where is Ramsey now? I need to talk to him."

"We think he's nearby," said Steele.

"Nearby? What the hell does that mean? I hope you didn't lose track of him."

"We stayed with him," said Rudd, his mouth full of bread and baked chicken. "We followed him for days and days, until he attacked Yuma."

"Yeah, they told me all about what happened when I came through there. They had some kind of ridiculous band out there to meet me at the stage stop while we were changing horses. They were blaring away while I tried to talk to the mayor. He said the Confederates came in and took his wife, along with some other women."

"You're right about that, Mr. Kane," said Rudd. "We got there right afterwards and it was bad. They killed the sheriff, and some young soldiers. Then we came here and Ramsey bombarded this town with some kind of cannon and a whole bunch of people got killed. I helped with the wounded. Steele did too."

Kane glared at Steele. "So you were helping with the wounded while my Helen was still out there somewhere, suffering who knows what at the hands of that madman."

"I saw her. She was unharmed at that time."

"What did she say? Did you tell her I was coming?"

"I wasn't able to talk to her."

"They had her all chained up, Mr. Kane," said Rudd. "And there were guards. Steele couldn't do anything about it."

"So you just left her there?" He was ignoring Rudd, looking hard at Steele.

"I regret very much that I was unable to get Helen out of Ramsey's camp. But I didn't want to do anything that might endanger her. I agreed with you that the best hope was to go along with Ramsey's plan to exchange her for his son."

Kane looked at the floor and shook his head. "I'm afraid we've got a problem there." He looked up at Steele. "Ramsey's son is dead. They'd already killed him by the time I got back to San Diego."

"Oh no," said Rudd. "What happened?"

"Nobody's quite sure. The Army says he was shot trying to escape, but there seems to be some . . . troublesome details. The Southern newspapers are saying it was a conspiracy to kill him because they couldn't catch his father." He looked at Steele for several seconds before he asked, "What do you think Ramsey will do when he finds out? You don't think he'll hurt my little Helen, do you?"

Rudd was also looking at Steele, waiting for an answer.

Steele now understood Ramsey's motivation for the attack on Yuma, and the angry, threatening telegraph message he'd sent warning Tucson that they were next. "He already knows. That's why he attacked this town. There will be no dealing with him now. When they killed his son, they killed his only reason to negotiate. I expect at this point his only goal will be to keep fighting, to prove the war can still be won."

Kane jumped up. "But what will he do with Helen? Listen, Steele, you've got to get word to him. He must need money for his cause. You find him and tell him I'll pay anything to get her back."

Steele shook his head. "He won't have any use for money now. He'll only want revenge."

Kane began to pace, his face pale. He stopped in front of Steele. "You think he's going to kill her?" His voice was almost a whisper.

"There's no reason for him to do that," said Steele. "A man like Ramsey doesn't kill without a reason. He will most likely keep her for some other purpose. Remember, he also took other women hostages in Yuma. He might be planning to use her and the other women as human shields. That was common during the war."

"Did it work?" asked Rudd.

"Rarely. Usually the hostages paid the price."

Rudd looked shocked and started to say something, but Kane cut him off: "Well, I'm not going to sit by and wait for him to kill my only remaining child." He shook his finger at Steele. "You're the expert. You know all about these Rebel generals. Do something."

Steele waited for Kane to calm himself a bit before he spoke. "Ramsey may still want to get Washington's attention. He may still have use for a hostage, someone more valuable than Helen." He paused, looking at Kane for a response. The man didn't seem to understand what he was suggesting, so he went on. "He might be willing to trade Helen for you, for a more . . . important hostage."

Kane stepped back as if Steele had slapped him in the face. "Me?"

Kane resumed his pacing. He stopped and turned back to Steele. "Even if he would trade her for me, he'd probably just kill me, wouldn't he?"

"You would be in great danger," agreed Steele, "but you might be safer than Helen is. You would give him a more valuable bargaining tool, assuming he still wants to influence events back in Washington."

Steele watched the man pace. Was he not willing to put himself in peril, even to save his own daughter? Steele began to wonder if he should offer himself as a trade for Helen. Ramsey might want to get rid of her. He had other human shields now. Maybe he'd like someone to talk to, someone who'd appreciate his war strategies, his self-perceived military genius. It could be worth a try. "If you don't think it's a good idea, I might offer myself as an exchange for her."

Kane spun around to look at him. "You? What would he want with you?"

"It's worth a try."

"It's not that I'm not willing," said Kane. "But I don't know what my wife would do without me. And there's my business to think about. My employees."

"I understand, sir. I'll go try to find him. I might be able to find a way to get Helen out. If not, I'll offer myself in trade for her and see what he says." He started toward the door.

Kane grabbed his arm. "No, come back and sit down here. What are you trying to do, shame me into this?"

"No, sir, I just--"

"I'll do it. I have to. My wife said she'd . . . Well, anyhow, find this General Ramsey and tell him. Tell him if he'll let Helen go, I'll give myself up to him."

"I'll convey that offer to the general," said Steele. "But first we have to find him."

"Well, get going and do it. You too, Rudd. Who knows what that madman might be doing to Helen right now."

"We think he's hiding in the nearby mountains," said Steele. "But there's no use going out at night. We'll start looking for him at first light."

"Well, it won't be long before dawn now, will it?" said Kane, pulling out his pocket watch. He held it out to show Steele. "Time is passing, Mr. Steele. I want you to find him. You *have to* find him. Tell him I've agreed to be his hostage, as long as he lets Helen go. That's your only job now. Nothing else matters." He turned to Rudd. "You stay with Steele until he finds Ramsey. Then you get back here as fast as you can to get me."

"Yessir, I'll do it, sir. I'm not all that tired, really."

"While you boys do that, I'll go talk to the Army. Whose in charge here anyhow?"

"That would be Major Carter," said Rudd, grabbing a few more pieces of chicken before getting up. "It's only a short trip up the street. I'll tell them to get you a carriage."

"It might be dangerous for Helen if the Army finds Ramsey before we do," said Steele. "Tell them to give us at least one day before they go up there."

"I'll tell them that," said Kane. "And I'll tell them a lot more. The Army took my son and now by God they'd better cooperate with me to get my daughter back. I have important friends in Washington. Where is this Major Carter?" He punched his fist into his other hand. "I'll light a fire under his ass, believe me, I will." He charged out the door, ignoring the newspaper employees who tried to talk to him.

Rudd grabbed some of the food and hurried after him. "It's just down the street, Mr. Kane. Only a short carriage ride."

"Forget the carriage. I'll walk." He stormed out the door, but stopped on the board sidewalk. "Where do I go? Point me in the right direction." But he didn't wait for instructions, he started off down the street, but in the wrong direction.

"Uh, it's that way," yelled Rudd, pointing to the north.

Kane turned around and stomped off down the street in that direction.

"The fort is all the way to the end of the street," called Rudd. "You can't miss it. And don't you worry, we'll find Helen and bring her back, won't we Steele?"

Steele looked toward the eastern sky. There was just a hint of the coming dawn. "We might as well get started, Rudd. As Mr. Kane said, it'll be dawn soon."

"Nope," said Rudd, stuffing the food into his pockets. "First we got to rest. I hardly made a dent in that bed. And besides, we need a bath. They've got a good bath room there, nice hot water, and it's on the same floor as our rooms."

"You go take your bath and meet me in front of the hotel. I'll go get the horses."

"Damn it, Steele, don't you ever slow down? Just give me an hour, okay? And don't get me that same horse. I want one that isn't always trying to throw a man off. You hear me?"

"I hear you," said Steele, "but you may have to explain it to the horse."

"Very funny," said Rudd. He headed for the hotel, holding one hand to his back.

Steele watched him go, wondering how much longer Rudd was going be able to hold up. He had to admire Rudd's willingness to keep going, even though he complained about it.

As he walked to the stables, Steele's thoughts again turned to Helen. Did she know what had happened to Ramsey's son? Had Ramsey told her? Was he taking it out on her? He remembered how uncomfortable she had looked trying to sleep with her hands chained to that wagon wheel. If they really were in the nearby mountains, he hoped Ramsey was at least letting her rest more comfortably.

When Steele arrived back at the hotel with the horses, he was surprised to find Rudd waiting on a bench out front. He was brushing his bowler hat and he was wearing a different suit.

"Are you sure you want to continue wearing a suit?" asked Steele. "It's going to be hot again today."

"Got to keep up appearances, don't I? I want to show these small-town folks how a gentleman dresses."

"Suit yourself. Let's go."

Rudd didn't even complain as he mounted his horse. "Sure felt good to take a bath," he said as they started out. "Woke me right up. Maybe I'm getting to be like you. Don't hardly need any sleep at all." As if to demonstrate his new-found energy, Rudd urged his horse into a fast trot and rode right past Steele to take up the lead. Steele watched him go, happy to see him so rejuvenated, but he could not help but worry about what another day in the saddle would do to both of them.

Just beyond the last outlying houses east of town, they passed a small detachment of soldiers, standing guard. Steele was surprised that they hadn't been stopped for an identity check. He leaned toward Rudd and said, "They're not checking people."

Rudd looked back. "Should they be?"

"During the war, civilians in the war zone were always stopped. Men were often held overnight while their identities were verified. The lack of such measures means the major is still not taking the threat seriously."

"I see what you mean. Ramsey could be sending in men to find out what the town is up to."

"That's right. The major has been fighting Indians. They're used to being able to recognize their enemy."

"Speaking of Indians," said Rudd, "the major said there were a lot of them up here. Maybe I should keep my gun handy."

"We may well see Indians, but it doesn't mean they'll be hostile. Nevertheless, if you see a large group of them coming rapidly toward you, it might be a good idea to go in the other direction." Rudd's startled look made Steele smile. "Especially if they're wearing war paint," he added.

"If we run into anything like that, you'll only see the back side of me," said Rudd, not smiling. "I can move fast when I have to."

As they rode away from the town and into the hills, the sky in the east began to gradually grow lighter. It was already getting warm, but Steele knew it would be much hotter when the sun rose over the top of the nearby mountains. He looked back down toward Tucson. Except for the town's few street lanterns it still looked dark and quiet, as if the town itself was sleeping peacefully, as if the artillery attack had never happened.

Steele led the way up into the mountains, always watching the ground for tracks. If the artillery attack had come from west of town, it only made sense that the rest of Ramsey's soldiers would have moved through to the east. But by the time the sun broke over the top of the mountains, they had seen no tracks.

When they came to a sandy area, Steele got down from his horse. "Have you noticed these parallel streaks?"

Rudd got down to look. "No, but I see them now. What do you think they are?"

"It could be somebody dragging bushes along to obscure tracks."

"Uh, yeah, maybe, or it could just be the wind. I bet it gets plenty windy up here."

Steele kneeled down and drew a circle in the sand with his finger. "Look at this depressed area in the sand. The regular streaks run right through the dips. Wind would pass over it. Steele stood up and looked toward the higher mountains in the distance. "Let's head up there. We'll ride about thirty yards apart. Look closely at any sandy areas we come across."

After a few hours of riding at a slow pace, always heading up toward the higher mountains, Steele stopped and called to Rudd. "Come look at this."

When Rudd arrived, Steele got down and pointed out two sets of streaks in the sand coming in from two different directions.

Rudd got down for a closer look. "Looks like groups meeting up."

"That's what I was thinking It could be Ramsey's artillery team, coming up to rejoin the main group."

Rudd looked nervously in all directions. "Uh, maybe it's time for us to turn back."

"Not yet." He got back on his horse and continued on with Rudd lagging behind

After another hour of riding, Rudd came up next to Steele. "It's getting hotter and hotter and we haven't found a damn thing. Isn't it time we headed back?"

"Just a little farther. We're almost to the end of this valley. It will be interesting to see if the streaks change direction once we're out of it."

Rudd snorted. "Interesting, he says. As if riding all day in this heat is great fun."

At the end of the valley, the streaks did turn upward into a wide sand wash. A short distance farther on, Steele got off his horse and knelt down next to some rocks. "Look here. Hoof prints. The streaks lead to here, then these few hoof prints, and then the streaks pick up again only a few feet ahead."

Rudd got down to look. "So they *were* covering their tracks. But why did they miss these?"

"Remember, they came in last night. They must have been staying in one line, dragging bushes behind the last horses. The bushes must have hit the rocks and skipped over these few tracks."

"But what about their cannon? Doesn't a cannon have great big wheels? Wouldn't it leave deep tracks? All I see here is some horse hoof prints."

Steele used his finger to draw a circle around one of the tracks. "These are not tracks from a horse's hoof. See how much narrower this one is?"

"Yeah, so what?"

"Mules. The front of a shod horse's hoof is wider, and the hoof wall is thicker."

Rudd leaned closer to see what he was talking about. "How the hell do you know that?" But before Steele could answer, he said, "I know. Books, right?"

Steele shook his head. "No, from walking the roads of Virginia and Tennessee behind convoys of horses and mules. During the war, mules were widely used to carry the heaviest loads. Look how deep these mule tracks are. They were carrying something heavy."

"The cannon? Can a mule carry a cannon?"

"Not an ordinary cannon. But I recently read that lighter-weight field artillery pieces are being developed in Europe, some that can be entirely disassembled."

Rudd thought about that. "But what makes you think those tracks are from Ramsey's men? It could be anybody."

"Why else would somebody be up here?"

"Maybe it was Indians. The major said there are Indians all over the place up here."

"Indians don't shoe their horses."

"Oh. Didn't know that." Rudd scratched the back of his neck. "So if this really is Ramsey we're following, where's he heading?"

"There's only one way to find out. Let's go."

Rudd flopped down on the ground and began to fan his face with his hat. "Just give me a minute."

Steele went to his horse and got the field glasses out of his saddlebag. He adjusted the focus and scanned the mountains ahead. His eye was drawn to a sheer cliff farther up the mountain. It was hundreds of feet high, and mostly unbroken. With the sun in the western sky, the smooth rocky face of the cliff seemed dark and ominous. It looked unclimbable, sheer and smooth. Not likely anyone could get up there, certainly not men on horses.

Then he noticed some unusual rock formations at the base of the cliff. He readjusted focus of the field glasses and saw a strange rock column that stood like a sentry just in front of the cliff. Looking farther to the west, he saw another towering pair of columns. They almost appeared to be leaning against each other, like drunken friends holding each other up. He wondered how such rock columns could have been created. Maybe they had originally been part of the cliff and the softer rock between them had gradually eroded away.

Steele lowered the field glasses. The cliff was still several miles away. He wondered if it was worth a ride up there to take a closer look.

Rudd shaded his eyes and peered in that direction. "What are you looking at?"

"There's a high cliff up there. I think we should ride up and take a closer look."

"Let me see."

Steele handed Rudd the field glasses.

"Looks like a straight up wall of rock," said Rudd. "I don't think anybody could get up there. Let's forget it." He handed the glasses back to Steele.

"There may be an opening somewhere," said Steele. "I think we should go look."

But then he saw something. A flash of light. "Wait a minute. Something is reflecting the sun up there."

Rudd shaded his eyes again. "What? What did you see?"

"A flash of light. Up on top of the cliff. It could be a signal mirror."

"A signal mirror? Way up there? Who's signaling?"

"Somebody could be using flashed signals to report our movements."

"Report to who? Shouldn't we maybe get out of here?"

"If we can see the flash from here, they must be signaling somebody down in this area."

"Jesus," said Rudd, looking in all directions. "Is it Indians?"

Steele looked through the field glasses and spotted a line of dust rising up into the sunlight. He refocused the glasses until he could see them clearly: horses, maybe six or seven of them, coming fast. He saw another reflection amidst the galloping horses and this time he knew it wasn't a mirror; it was gold colored and he knew immediately what it was. "Riders coming," he yelled. "Get on your horse. Fast!"

Steele stuffed the field glasses into his saddlebag and jumped onto his horse. He kicked it into a gallop and looked back to make sure Rudd was following. He was, but he was having trouble getting his tired horse to run. Steele slowed and when Rudd finally caught up, Steele used his reins to slap the rear of Rudd's horse. It responded, moving a little faster, but it seemed to be struggling under Rudd's weight. Steele hurried his own horse to draw alongside.

"Damn, damn," shouted Rudd. "I knew it. It's Indians, isn't it?"

"I can't see who it is yet," yelled Steele, "but they have those new Henry repeating rifles. I saw the sun reflecting off of the gun's brass frame."

"Oh no. I hope we can outrun them." Rudd kicked at his horse, but it barely responded.

Steele stayed close, whipping Rudd's horse whenever it faltered. Rudd was leaning forward, hanging on tight, even though his horse wasn't moving all that fast.

Steele looked back and saw that their pursuers were gaining on them. Whoever it was, they were riding better horses than the old stable horses he and Rudd were on. The riders had raised their rifles over their heads, and even at that distance, the brass frames of the rifles reflected bright yellow flashes in the sun.

Steele looked ahead and saw a rocky ridge a short distance up the hill. He turned his horse in that direction. "This way," he yelled. He reached down into his boot and pulled out his Remington. He aimed it back toward the riders and fired off two quick shots, just to let them know he was armed.

"They're too far away," yelled Rudd. "You'll never hit them from here."

When they reached the ridge, Steele jumped down and caught the reins of Rudd's horse. "Take your saddlebags and run for those boulders." He tied the horses to a bush and grabbed his own saddlebags. He saw that Rudd had taken cover behind a large boulder and he ran in that direction just as the first shots came. They all hit higher up the hill. He dived behind the nearest boulder just as several more shots tore into the dirt nearby.

"Are you all right?" yelled Rudd from his hiding place. "Are you hit?"

"I'm not hit," Steele yelled back. "Do you have your colt?"

"Yeah. Should I start shooting? They're still a ways off."

"No, wait until they get closer."

"But you tried to hit them."

"That was just to let them know we're armed. And I'm hoping the Army might be close enough to hear the shots. Get ready, Rudd. Rest your pistol on the rock and be sure you have a good target before you fire."

"All right. Maybe we can take a few of them with us before they get us. If I can stop my damn hands from shaking."

"Don't think about yourself," yelled Steele. "Don't think about anything except what you're aiming at. You said you once won a shooting contest. Make one of them your target. Nothing else matters but that target."

Steele pulled the box of pistol bullets out of the saddlebag and replaced the two spent shells. He peeked over the top of the boulder and as they got closer, he saw it was Indians. They seemed young. They were shirtless and they all had what looked like smears of paint on their faces. "It is Indians," he yelled to Rudd, "but only six of them. Stay down."

A series of shots from the Indians glanced off of a boulder just above him and whined off into the distance. Steele hoped their shooting high meant they were not very experienced with those new rifles yet.

Then he heard Rudd fire three times. "No," he yelled. "They're still too far away. When they get closer, aim toward the leader's torso. Aim low. If you miss him, you might still hit his horse."

He cocked his own gun and rested it on top of the rock. Several more shots came from the Indians and he involuntarily ducked. He steadied himself and waited, watching them come. He took careful aim at the Indian who was in the lead, still waiting. He knew he had to make every shot count in case it turned into a siege. The Indians were getting close enough to see them clearly. They were very young. He took aim at the leader, but before he could fire he heard Rudd shoot and the Indian's horse went down. The rider rolled and scrambled away into some nearby bushes.

"I got him!" yelled Rudd. "By God I got him."

The rest of the Indians veered off. They galloped a short distance away, and then they grouped together, getting ready for another charge.

Steele heard Rudd fire again and again, but he knew it was a waste of bullets: at the distance it would take a lucky shot to hit anything. Rudd finally stopped firing.

Steele realized Rudd's gun must be empty. "Reload quickly," he yelled. "How many bullets do you have with you?"

"I don't know," Rudd yelled back. "I just threw a handful into my saddlebag."

The Indians began their charge, firing their rifles as they came.

"Have you reloaded?" shouted Steele.

"I . . . I keep on dropping the damn bullets. I can't stop my hands from shaking."

"Quit thinking about your situation. Think only about what you have to do. If we can hit a few more of them, maybe they'll give up."

The Indians were closing in. Steele knew he couldn't do anything more for Rudd; either he would stand his ground or he wouldn't.

Steele rested his gun on the top of the boulder and aimed at the lead Indian who was shouting and shooting as he came. As he got closer, Steele saw that the boy had white stripes painted on his chest, as if to represent the wings of an eagle. Steele aimed carefully at the point there the bird's wings intersected the center line of the boy's chest and squeezed the trigger. When the bullet hit, the young man looked surprised, and for a moment, it looked like he would keep coming, but then he fell backward off of his wildly running horse and rolled a short distance, arms flopping loosely like a child's rag doll. Then he lay lifeless, face down in the dust. The other Indians veered off as soon as their leader went down.

"Are you all right, Rudd?"

"I'm okay. Are they gone?"

"For now, but they'll come again. Are you ready?"

"I . . . I guess so. Tell me when they're coming."

Steele kept his eyes on the Indians. For the moment, they were keeping their distance.

Then the young brave who had fallen into the bushes stood up and began to back away. Steele pointed his gun at him, but didn't shoot.

There was fear in the young Indian's eyes, but he didn't run. He had his rifle in his hands, but he kept it pointed at the ground as he backed away. Finally, he turned and ran to the other Indians. One of them helped him up onto the back of his horse and the entire group turned and rode away fast.

Steele stood up and saw why the Indians had left: a large group of riders was coming up the hill, moving fast. It was the Army.

Rudd saw them too. He stood up and started waving.

"Careful," shouted Steele. "They don't know who was shooting up here."

Rudd ducked back down behind the rocks and started waving his handkerchief.

When the troops arrived, Steele saw they were led by Major Carter. The major had his pistol out, as did several of his officers who were close behind him.

Steele stood up and put away his own pistol.

"I might have known it would be you two," said the major. "Kane said you were poking around up here. Can't you two stay out of trouble?"

Rudd popped up from behind his rock. "It was Indians, Major, a whole bunch of them."

"I see a dead horse," said the major. "And one dead Indian. That's all."

"There were a lot more than that," insisted Rudd. "We just about got killed."

The major got down from his horse and walked to the dead Indian. He poked at him with his boot. Young troublemakers. Look at that war paint."

"They were young," said Steele, "but they were organized. Someone up in the mountains was signaling to them with a mirror."

"A mirror? That's a new one. Well, you boys can relax now. We won't see any more of that bunch."

Steele walked to the dead warrior and picked up his rifle. He handed it to the major. "I told you they had new Improved Henrys. This is the same weapon I saw the Mexican militia group carrying."

"Well, how about that?" said the major, examining the gun. He ejected a shell. "And in good working order. Now where the hell could this young buck have got his hands on a rifle like this?"

"As I suggested earlier, General Ramsey wanted to form an alliance with the Indians. Can you think of a better way than to give them brand new repeating rifles?"

"The major looked at the gun. I'll believe your Indian alliance theory when I see it. More likely this hostile killed somebody and took it off him. The Indians around here call these yellowboys. They like the shiny brass part." He turned away and started back to his horse.

Steele caught his arm. "Major, someone up on top of a high cliff was signaling to these Indians. You should at least go up there and see who it was."

The major jerked his arm free. "There's nothing up there. No way to get up. Everybody knows that. And if this Indian was really getting signals from somebody, it was probably his renegade friends, not rampaging Confederates. I've sent men up here many times to look for Indians. If they're here, they stay out of sight. They're smart. They only attack fools who come up here by themselves. If you would have talked to me before you went off half-cocked, I could have told you that. Now maybe you'll listen." He turned away and told his men to mount up.

On the way back down to the city, the major rode ahead, surrounded by his officers. Steele and Rudd rode along behind, ignored.

"Maybe the major is right," said Rudd. "Maybe that Indian stole that gun somewhere. I'd hate to think of a white man giving weapons like that to Indians."

"No, they were all carrying those rifles. All new, all the same unusual model I saw down in Mexico. They could have only come from Ramsey."

"So, Ramsey is arming the Indians. Why? To get them to attack Tucson?"

"When he's ready."

Rudd thought about that. "You know, if Medina is still working with the Confederates, Tucson could be attacked by three different groups. The Mexicans could come up from the border at the same time Ramsey and his Indian friends come down from the mountains."

"Not a very comforting thought, is it?" said Steele. "Ramsey told me the future of warfare was alliances of the weak against the strong. He seems to be trying to prove his point."

"Then heaven help us against the weak," said Rudd.

Chapter 19

By the time they reached Tucson, it was almost dark. The major and his troops turned off toward the fort without a word to Steele and Rudd.

When they reached the stable, Rudd slowly and painfully got off his horse. "That's it," he said. "I'm never getting on one of these critters again. I've got enough saddle sores to last me a lifetime." He held up a hand to stop Steele from responding. "Don't say it. I know we haven't found Helen yet. We have to keep trying. At least let me get a good night's sleep before we go out there again."

"Why don't you get some rest," suggested Steele. "I'll go tell Kane what we learned."

"But we didn't learn anything."

"He needs to know that. It will only take a few minutes."

"All right, all right, I'm coming. But then it's a bath and food for me. Or maybe food first, then a bath. I'll have to think about it."

At the newspaper office they found the major, arguing with Kane.

"This is my daughter we're talking about," said Kane. "As long as she's–" He stopped in mid-sentence when he saw Steele and Rudd at the door. "Here they are now. Why don't we ask them?"

Major Carter wheeled around and scowled at them.

"The major says you boys got yourself in a bit of trouble up there in the mountains," said Kane. "He thinks you're interfering with his operations."

Rudd stepped forward. "We were following your orders, Mr. Kane. You said we should try to find Ramsey and convince him to exchange Helen for you."

The major turned back to face Kane. "You're planning to exchange yourself for your daughter? Why wasn't I informed about this?"

"There was no need to inform the Army," said Kane. "It's a private matter."

"Private matter? There are no private matters in a situation like this. I have to be informed about everything that's going on, you hear me?"

"I will do what I have to do to get my daughter back," said Kane calmly. "So far I can't see that the Army has done anything to help."

"Listen Kane," said the major, leaning over the desk, "I got Mexicans attacking farms down by the border. I got Indians chasing civilians off the mountain. And now I got you interfering with the U.S. Army, running your own operation out of your damn newspaper." He turned to look at a large map on the wall. "And where did you get this map? It looks military."

"I have my sources," said Kane.

"The major is right," said Steele. "We should be working together to get Helen back."

"So you admit you were wrong," said the major.

"Yes, we were wrong not to send word that we would be out there looking."

"Well . . . all right then. See that you do so in the future."

Steele walked to the wall map. "This is where we went today." He tapped the map. "We saw what we think was a signal from on top of a cliff. Then we were attacked by Indians who were carrying the same new Winchester rifles we saw at Ramsey's camp."

The major joined him in front of the map. "We already knew the hostiles were up there. Once we followed a bunch of 'em almost up to that cliff, but then they disappeared. Nuthin'. Not even any tracks."

"We saw tracks," said Rudd. "Mule tracks."

"Mule tracks? So what?" said the major.

"Mules are for carrying heavy loads," said Steele. "Such as a cannon."

The major shook his head. "Now you're gonna start in again about some little cannon. I'll believe that too when I see it."

Kane got up and came to join them in front of the map. "So does it mean Ramsey is up there?"

"I think he is," said Steele. He turned to the major. "Have any of your men been up on top of that cliff?"

The major shook his head. "I told you before. There's no way to get up there. We've tried. Besides, there won't be any Indians anywhere near those cliffs. Supposed to be magic, or sacred, or some damn thing."

"I can't believe my ears," said Kane. "You know the Indians are up in those mountains, but you haven't you gone up there to root them out?"

"You get me enough troops and I'll do it, Kane. Until then, I've got bigger troubles down by the border."

"I could contact the governor of this territory. He could order you to go up there and find my girl."

The major got red in the face. "Go ahead. I don't work for the Governor. How I do my job is none of his concern, and none of yours either."

"Well, you work for the President, don't you?" said Kane. "I know the President personally. I'm sure he'd be interesting in knowing the Tucson contingent of the U.S. Army is doing nothing to help my daughter."

"He already knows we've got trouble out here, believe me. I been getting telegraphic messages from Washington all day. And I can tell you he's a lot more worried about the Mexicans than a little trouble with Indians, or with some crazy Confederate general. But even if the President himself told me to mount up, we wouldn't be able to find those hostiles up there in those mountains. Believe me, we've looked. They're like ghosts once they get up there."

"You mentioned trouble along the border," said Steele. "Has there been activity other than the fires we reported to you?"

"Just the usual kind. Not your concern. Mexicans acting up is all. You think your General Ramsey is trouble? He doesn't have anything on those Mexicans. They've been giving us trouble since the treaty of forty-eight."

"I don't care about Indians or Mexicans," said Kane. "All I care about is my daughter."

"We'll find her, Mr. Kane," said Rudd. "Soon as we get some sleep we'll go out and look for her again."

"Sleep!" shouted Kane. "Do you think my daughter is getting any sleep? Her mother is worried sick. I've got three telegraph messages from her since I got here. Do you think she's sleeping nights?"

"I think Rudd's right," said Steele. "You should get some sleep too, Mr. Kane. It's not going to do you any good staying awake worrying. We'll go back up there in the morning."

"You're all crazy," said the major, heading for the door. "Bound and determined to get yourselves killed." He stopped by the door to add, "If you go back up there, you're on your own. This time I won't be there to save you. With all the trouble down by the border, I'm spread too thin as it is. I've asked Washington for reinforcements and when they get here we'll start looking again. That is, if you can show me any real evidence your crazy Confederate general is really up there."

"The next thing you hear from Ramsey will be another attack," said Steele.

The major just shook his head and left without responding.

"He's no help," said Kane. "Now what am I supposed to tell my wife?"

"Tell her we'll find her," said Steele.

"Yeah, well, I tell her that in every message I send. But she just keeps saying, 'when?'"

Chapter 20

*B*ack out on the street, Rudd said, "Do you think Mr. Kane will really get in touch with the President?"

"Maybe that's exactly what Ramsey wants him to do."

"What? Why would he want that? The President might send more troops out here."

"I'm sure he's under a lot of pressure to do exactly that. But how many troops could he spare? With all the recent trouble in the South, what troops he still has in uniform have probably been sent down there."

"Yeah, well, I've got troubles of my own," said Rudd. "If I don't lie down soon, my back is gonna probably give out completely."

"Why don't you go back to the hotel. There's nothing more we can do until morning."

Rudd's face lit up. "Really? You don't need me?"

"I'm going to talk to the doctor. I'll come get you in the morning."

"Not too early, I hope."

"Not until dawn."

Rudd walked away grumbling. "Dawn. Not until dawn, he says. It's practically dawn now."

Steele asked directions to the doctor's office, hoping he would be there despite the late hour. On the way, Steele saw quite a few people in the streets or on the board sidewalks, talking in small groups. It was as if the recent events had made them unable, or unwilling, to go to sleep.

When Steele knocked at the doctor's door, he opened it immediately. He was wearing spectacles and carrying a book.

"I'm sorry to bother you at this time of night," said Steele, "but I'm worried that there might be another attack. I'm especially worried about the civilians that live near the fort."

"Civilians? Aren't we all civilians now?"

"Is doesn't feel like it to me. It feels more like the war, all over again."

"Let's hope it's not all that drastic," said the doctor. "Nothing we can do about it tonight anyhow. Come in and sit a spell."

They moved to the parlor that adjoined the doctor's treatment room. As Steele sat down, the doctor cocked his head to the side. "You seemed to sit down a might gingerly, there, Steele. Back bothering you?"

"No, I was wounded in the side a few days ago. It's still a little stiff."

"What? A few days ago? Why didn't you ask me to look at it?"

"It was stitched up in the field. I haven't had much time to even think about it since then."

"Well, pull up your shirt and let's have a look."

Steele did as he was told and the doctor looked closely at the wound. "Doesn't seem to be any infection. You're lucky. But you're going to have a hell of a scar there. Never seen such a clumsy job of stitching."

"We were in a hurry."

"Never good to hurry stitching. " He pulled Steele's shirt back down. So tell me what you know about these renegade Confederates. You still think that's who shelled the city last night?"

"I'm sure of it. Let me tell you how all this started." Steele told him about the kidnapping of Kane and how they'd been following Ramsey's group all the way from western Mexico.

The doctor listened thoughtfully. "But why did they come here? If they'd been staying down there in Mexico until now, why did they decide to come across the border here?"

"I believe he came here to try to form an alliance with Cochise."

The doctor looked at him over the top of this spectacles. "Cochise? Form an alliance with a white man. Not likely."

"That's what the major said. Nevertheless, I believe that's why Ramsey came here. He told me he admired the tactics of the Apaches."

"Well, it doesn't seem like they'd want to hook up with any white men after what they've been through, but who knows how an Apache thinks? Hey, here's an idea. You should go out and talk to old Jed McNeil. He told me he'd met old Cochise once. He knows a lot about the Apaches. Hires them to work on his place. McNeil has a ranch out north, not too far from the mountains. I used to go there to treat his wife's tuberculosis."

"How do I find his ranch?"

"I'll draw you a map."

The doctor found a piece of paper and was in the process of drawing the map when they heard the first shell hit. The explosion shook the entire building.

The doctor jumped up. "Jesus! Not again." He grabbed his bag and headed for the door. Steele picked up the map and followed him. More explosions shook the house and the doctor stopped. "Wait! We'll need extra bandages and tourniquets." He went back and pulled open a drawer. "And take some of those surgical needles and thread too. You handle the stitching and I'll do the cutting, okay?" Without waiting for an answer he rushed out the door.

Steele followed, but he was wondering if maybe he should try to get up into the foothills before the attackers got away. They might lead him to Ramsey and Helen.

Out in the street, frightened, screaming people were running toward them, away from the shelling. Steele and the doctor had to constantly dodge people who were blindly running through the dark streets.

The sudden flashes of light tore through the darkness, followed instantly by the sound of the explosions. But Steele realized the shells weren't making any sound as they came in. It was obviously not one of the Civil War Howitzers. Those shells made a distinctive whistling sound. It had to be a rifled gun of some kind, probably a breech-loader.

He was still trying to decide whether to ride out to find the cannon when the doctor grabbed his arm. "Hey, what's wrong?" he yelled. "I thought you'd been through this kind of thing during the war." Another shell hit and the doctor automatically ducked even though the explosion was some distance away.

"I'm thinking I should get out there and try to follow them. They could lead me to Ramsey."

"No, there'll be wounded here. I need your help."

A horse suddenly came out of the darkness, running wild. Steele had to hold up both hands and yell to make the horse change it's path. It went by fast, barely missing them.

"Damn, that was close," said the doctor. He hurried on down the street.

Steele followed the doctor, trying to stay close to him despite the chaos in the street. As they ran toward the explosions, Steele realized they were coming from the area of the fort. This time Ramsey must have decided to hit the Army directly. People were running in the other direction, driven by fear. In the panic, some of the slower ones, especially the women and young children, were getting knocked down.

Suddenly, two men on horseback came out of the darkness, bearing down on them. Steele pulled the doctor out of the way as they galloped by. Unfortunately, a woman and her young boy were not so lucky. The horses ran them down and galloped on, hardly slowing. The boy got up holding his arm, but the woman didn't move. Steele and the doctor ran to her.

"She's unconscious," said the doctor, "but she's breathing all right. Just knocked out, I think."

A riderless horse tore past them and disappeared into the darkness.

"We've got to move her out of the street," said the doctor.

Steele gently picked the woman up in his arms, and with the doctor's hands under her head and neck, he moved her to a nearby board sidewalk and laid her down there.

"I think we have to leave her," said the doctor. "There will be more serious injuries than this." He stood up and shouted at the people running past. "Stop, stop. Some of you help us. This woman needs help."

But no one stopped. They ran on into the night, too frightened to listen.

But then the shelling stopped. Steele stood up. It seemed strangely silent. "There won't be any more firing," he said to the doctor. "They'll be scurrying back to their mountain hideout."

After the doctor finally got some people to stop to help the unconscious woman, they ran toward the fort. As they approached, Steele could see that the damage was extensive. One of the log walls surrounding the fort had been blown away and several buildings inside the perimeter were aflame. Ramsey's cannoneers had been very accurate.

Major Carter was there, apparently unhurt. He was organizing a party of soldiers to dig out the wounded from beneath a collapsed and burning building. "Get this barracks put out first," he yelled. "There are men in there. Snap to it!"

While the doctor went to set up a makeshift treatment center in one of the undamaged buildings, Steele helped treat the men the major's group was digging out of the barracks.

He found some singed blankets and laid the injured men out on the ground well away from the flames. "Have your men bring the worst of the wounded here," he shouted to the major. "The ones who are bleeding. Put the other's over there." He pointed toward another building that was only slightly damaged.

"I thought you were a detective, not a doctor," yelled the major.

"I worked in an Army hospital during the war," said Steele. "Hurry. First we have to stop the bleeding then we can assess the other injuries."

The major quickly organized a team to bring the injured to Steele. Steele treated the ones he could and sent the rest in to the doctor.

Rudd soon arrived and hurried to Steele's side. "The explosions just about knocked me out of bed. Can I help?"

"Do you have a strong stomach? asked Steele.

"I suppose so. I can eat just about anything."

"Then go inside and help the doctor. He will be doing the amputations in there."

"Amputations?" Rudd hesitated. "Uh, maybe I could help you here."

"Hurry!"

Rudd hurried off to help the doctor while Steele did what he could to set bones and stop the worst of the bleeding. He moved from man to man, assessing injuries, stitching up wounds, showing each man how to apply direct pressure to their own wounds to stem the flow of blood. Whenever a man died, he removed the tourniquets and bandages for reuse and then called to the major's men to take the body to the back wall of the fort, out of the way.

Eventually the fires were put out and there were no more men to treat. How many wounds had he bound up? He couldn't remember. How many had died? At least a dozen, maybe more. He sat down next to a man whose arm was severely damaged. Steele had stemmed the flow of blood from the man's shattered arm and had been coming back to the man to loosen the tourniquet from time to time. But now, as he examined the man's arm more fully, he realized that it was not going to be possible to save it. He left the tourniquet in place and asked, "How are you feeling, soldier?"

"My arm hurts real bad, doc. Can't you do anything?"

"They will be taking you in to the doctor soon, private."

"Will he fix up my arm, doc?"

"He'll do the best he can, soldier. Just rest easy." Steele thought about how many men he'd said those words to during the war. And now it was happening all over again. Why? Ramsey must know that an attack on an Army fort would surely draw a swift response from the government. Did he believe the Army was so tied up dealing with the post-war trouble down in the South they wouldn't be able to respond?

With the search for the injured completed, the major walked over to Steele, wiping his forehead with the back of his shirt sleeve. Steele noticed he was no longer wearing the jacket of his uniform. His white shirt was dark with blood, sweat, and soot, but he still had his cigar planted firmly in the corner of his mouth.

"We've got all the fires out now," said the major. "And I think all my men are finally accounted for. They hit us hard, didn't they?"

"They did," said Steele.

The major took the stub of his cigar out of his mouth, looked at it, and threw it to the ground. "This is not like it was back in Virginia, not the same at all. We had a perimeter back then. No way the enemy could get close enough to surprise us."

He looked at Steele, as if he expected a response. When Steele remained silent, he said, "So, you think this was your Confederate general again?"

"I expect so."

"I just got word that the two sentries I had stationed out that way were found dead. Throats cut, both of them. Never even had time to draw their sidearms. Indians, I expect."

"I'd better go help the doctor," said Steele.

"Come see me in my office, as soon as you finish helping the doctor. I guess we'd better talk about this crazy general of yours."

"I'll be there as soon as I can."

Steele found the doctor sitting on the floor of his make-shift hospital, sewing up what was left of an unconscious man's leg. He looked up at Steele. "Am I glad to see you, Steele. Come here and take over."

Steele sat down beside him and took over the stitching. "You must be exhausted, doctor."

"I'm not all that tired," said the doctor, standing up. "It's just my back. We ran out of tables so I had to do a lot of this kind of thing sitting on the floor. My back is killing me." He stretched his back as he watched Steele work. "Hey, nice stitches there, Steele. Where'd you learn to do it so . . . pretty?"

"I didn't get to do much suturing on the living, but I got a lot of practice sewing up the dead. The officer in charge of the field hospital wanted the bodies to look nice before they shipped them back home."

The doctor laughed a short harsh laugh, almost a cough, as he turned away and went to work on the next patient.

"Where's your nurse?" asked Steele.

"She's up in my office," said the doctor, "patching up the walking wounded. I got word there were a bunch of civilians up there waitin' for me so I sent her up to tend to them."

Steele nodded and went back to work.

After a few minutes, Rudd came through the door. "This is all I could find, doctor." He held up a ruffled woman's petticoat. "But the lady said she'd just washed it."

"It will have to do," said the doctor. "Start tearing it up. I need long strips, about six inches wide."

Rudd did as he was told, focusing on his work.

"Glad to see you're all right," said Steele.

"Oh, hi there, Steele. Didn't see you sitting there on the floor. Yeah, I'm all right. The explosions woke me up and I came running."

"He's been very helpful," said the doctor.

"How are you holding up?" said Steele.

"My back's a little tired. Sure could use something to eat, though."

"That's a good idea," said the doctor, pausing his sawing half way through an unconscious man's leg. "When you get that cloth ripped up why don't you go get us all something to eat."

"I'll do it," said Rudd happily. He increased the pace of his cloth ripping and was soon finished. "How about if I go back to the hotel restaurant and have them make us up some sandwiches?"

"I'll eat anything you bring back," said the doctor.

I'll be right back," said Rudd, hurrying out the door.

"He's been a big help," said the doctor. "He's a good man,"

"He is," agreed Steele. "A very good man."

Chapter 21

*I*t was well after dawn when the doctor finally suggested they all go to get some sleep. Steele and Rudd went outside and stood under the shade of the building's porch. The fort felt strangely quiet. There were no soldiers to be seen except for a small group working to rebuild the collapsed outer wall.

"I'm so tired I think I could just lay down right here in the dirt and go to sleep," said Rudd.

"Better try to make it back to the hotel," said Steele, patting him on the back.

"Aren't you coming?"

"I am, but Major Carter said he wanted to see me. I'd better go to his office. Then I'll head back to the hotel."

"You're not going to try to get me on a horse again are you?" said Rudd, putting a hand to his back.

"The doctor told me about a man named McNeil who's supposed to know a great deal about the Apaches. I want to go out to his ranch to talk to him. But you don't have to go if you don't want to."

"If you're going, I'm going," said Rudd. "Just let me get a few hours of sleep before I have to get back on that damn horse."

"I'll come wake you when it's time to go," said Steele. With a smile, he added, "I'll bring your favorite horse."

Rudd groaned and rubbed his backside. "Forget the horse. I'd rather walk."

Rudd continued to complain as he walked away and it made Steele smile again. Despite his complaints, Rudd could always be counted on. He had again worked hard to help the wounded, when many others hadn't. He was a good man, just as the doctor had said.

Steele felt the tiredness in himself. The long night of tending wounds had been physically and mentally draining. They had saved quite a few soldiers, but as always, it would be the faces of the dead that he couldn't get out of his mind. He had seen hundreds die during the war, and those faces often came to visit him at night in his dreams. He had long since accepted that they would always be with him. He shook his head to push away such thoughts.

Back at the fort, he found Major Carter at his desk. He was alone, which was surprising.

"I expected to find you in some kind of war council," said Steele. "Where are all your officers?"

"Everybody's out looking for that cannon. I'm not letting anybody sit around on their duffs until we find it. If your General Ramsey is up there, we'll ferret him out. Now, have a seat."

Steele sat down. "And what if they do find him? The last time I saw Ramsey's column he had almost two hundred men with him. And you said you knew of more coming in from Texas to join him, and you've got even fewer men now than you than you had before."

The major chewed nervously on his cigar. "I'm sending messages to Washington every few hours. I hope this attack on my fort finally stirs them into action. They keep saying they're sending me reinforcements, but if that's so, where are they?"

"Are your reinforcements coming by rail?"

"Supposedly, but I can't get a clear timetable about when they're gonna get here. By the way, Washington says we're not supposed to tell anybody it might be Confederates that attacked us. Just a bunch of border raiders, that's what they want people to believe."

"What do you believe, Major? Are you finally convinced that General Ramsey is behind these attacks?"

"I guess so, but I don't understand what he thinks he's doing. Maybe he does have a bunch of crazy Confederates with him, and maybe he has made friends with some renegade Indians, but these attacks are just going to mean a quicker end to him. Maybe he does have some kind of fancy new cannon, but it won't do him any good when my reinforcements get here. I lost a lot of good men last night and he's going to pay for that. I'm going to find him and I'll guarantee you we won't need any war crimes tribunal to deal with him. Out here we know how to take care of things ourselves."

"You said two sentries were killed outside of town last night. Where were they stationed?"

"Up in the hills, northeast of town. I had men spread all across those hills, but maybe they were too far apart. Tonight we'll be ready for 'em. I can assure you of that. This time we'll have a real force out there. All night."

"Then they won't come tonight. Ramsey is adopting guerrilla tactics, hit and run. He won't confront a large force."

"He'll have to deal with me sooner or later. If Washington sends me enough soldiers, we can take care of this situation in no time. I told 'em this was something completely new out here, not as simple as rounding up hostiles. I told 'em if they'd have given me enough men in the first place, we wouldn't have this problem. But no, last month they sent a thousand men up north to chase the Cheyenne around. A waste of time, I say. Those Indians'll just run back across the Canadian border, the way the Mexicans run back into Mexico."

"Let me ask you something, Major. Do you know a man named McNeil? He's supposed to know a great deal about Indians."

"Sure I know McNeil. But he won't tell you a damn thing. He accused me of persecuting the Apaches. Can you believe that? The hostiles come down out of those mountains and kill innocent people and he accuses me of persecuting *them*."

"I'd like to talk to him," said Steele. "The doctor told me McNeil has been hiring Apaches to work on his ranch. He may have heard something about Confederates working with the Indians."

"Yeah, I heard he was hiring Indians. But I can't believe he'd hire any Apaches."

"I just want to talk to him. The doctor seemed to think McNeil had met Cochise."

"What? If he's seen Cochise, he should have come right in here to tell me about it. There's a price on Cochise's head, a big price. Tell you what, if McNeil knows anything about Cochise, then I want to talk to him too. You think your Confederates are a problem? The big problem for the ranchers around here has always been the Apaches. I'll take you out to McNeil's place later this afternoon, as soon as we have this place secured. I'll find out what he knows about Cochise or know the reason why."

Chapter 22

Steele left the fort and went back to the hotel. He located the hotel's bath room and was gratified to discover there was no one else there. While a Chinaman filled one of the tubs with hot water, he sat on a bench and thought about Major Carter's words. If the major was able to convince his superiors to send reinforcements, what would Ramsey do in response? Would he go into hiding, or continue to attack? It was possible he had already accomplished what he wanted with the two artillery attacks. The town was in a panic and the fort was in ruins. It wouldn't take long for that news to get back east.

The hot bath helped him relax and it took some of the aches and pains out of his muscles. He decided to go to his room to try to get a few hours of sleep.

In his room, he sat on the bed, wondering if he still remembered how to sleep. He decided to lie down for a quick rest. He didn't bother to take his clothes off.

But he couldn't sleep. He stared up at the ceiling, thinking about Helen. What was she doing right now? What was she going through? Was Ramsey still protecting her, as he had promised?

He awoke with a start and sat up quickly. What time was it? He felt like he hadn't been asleep very long, but he had dreamed. He could only remember fragments of the complicated dream: in some kind of fog, or smoke, he had come face to face with a young girl. She seemed lost. She was calling his name, but whenever he tried to run toward her she disappeared into the smoke again. When he tried to go to her, he found himself trying to climb a very steep hill. No matter how fast he ran up that hill, he could never catch her.

He pulled his boots on, wondering if the girl in the dream represented Helen. It would make sense: in the dream, the girl was lost and couldn't hear him. But what was the smoke ? Smoke from a battle? The dream left him with an uneasy feeling, as if there was something he had forgotten to do.

He pushed away the remnants of the troublesome dream and realized that for the first time in many days he felt hungry. He decided to go down to the hotel's restaurant.

He bought a newspaper in the hotel lobby and took it into the restaurant where he ordered a meal of hot soup and bread. It tasted very good. He thought about sending for Rudd, but decided to let the man sleep a little longer. He was just finishing his second bowl of soup when Rudd came thought the door. He looked much rejuvenated.

"There you are, Steele," said Rudd, sitting down. "I hardly recognized you sitting here at a real table and eating like a civilized person. What's good to eat?"

"I had the soup. It was quite good."

"Soup? Are you kidding?" He leaned closer. to whisper, "Listen, Steele, don't forget we're on the job. The newspaper is paying. At least have a steak or something."

"The soup was fine," said Steele, turning back to the newspaper.

After Rudd had ordered the soup *and* a steak, he asked, "Hey, is my story in there? Let me see."

Steele folded back the newspaper to show him.

"Hey, I finally made the front page. How about that?"

"It's a good story," said Steele.

"Well, thanks," said Rudd as his meal arrived. "I did work rather hard on it."

"I can see that. There are several other stories about the situation, and some eyewitness reports about the artillery attack. No mention of Confederates."

"I'll bet that was hard on Kane, not to be able to publish such a big story."

"This other front page story, right next to yours, is about the people killed and injured in the artillery attack. It's very . . . graphic."

"Let me see," said Rudd.

Steele handed him the newspaper.

Rudd looked at the story only briefly before handing it back. "I bet that's Kane's story. Lot's of gory details. He knows what sells newspapers."

Steele put down the paper. "While you finish eating, I'm going to go out to that old mission."

"You think something's going on out there?"

"It's possible. I'm still wondering why Ramsey went to the mission in Yuma."

"Those old places are mostly used as churches, aren't they? Maybe they went to that one in Yuma to pray for forgiveness."

"Very funny. I'll be back soon. The major has agreed to take us out to meet McNeil."

"Now wait a minute. I didn't say I wasn't going with you. Shoot, Steele, just when I finally get to sit down for a good meal, you're ready to go gallivanting off again. Can't it wait until I'm done eating?"

"Go ahead and finish. I won't be long."

"Hang on, hang on. I'm coming. Can't break up a good team like us now, can we?"

Steele waited while Rudd quickly ate as much of the steak as he could wolf down. Then he stood up and began stuffing bread into his pockets until they were bulging.

He followed Steele toward the door, but suddenly changed his mind and hurried back to the table. He soon rejoined Steele in the street, happily eating a hastily-made sandwich of steak trapped between two large hunks of bread. "What do you expect to find at the mission?" he asked between bites.

"I don't know. But Ramsey always seems to strike when he's near one of them."

"Could be a coincidence, couldn't it?"

"Could be," said Steele. He got up onto his horse. "Ready?"

Rudd patted his horse's neck. "Ah, my trusty horse," he mumbled.

Steele smiled at the self-derisive humor and waited while Rudd, with some effort, mounted while still holding his sandwich.

As they started out, Rudd brought his horse alongside Steele's. "Let me ask you something, Steele. Don't you ever laugh?"

"Time enough for that after we get Helen and the other hostages back." Steele spurred his horse forward. But as they rode out past the small Mexican shacks at the edge of town, he was still thinking about

Rudd's question. He used to laugh when he was with Stacy; in fact, they laughed often. Had he changed that much without her? Would he be any different if she came back? He shook off those kinds of thoughts and hurried his horse forward.

When they came to the dilapidated adobe outer walls of the old Spanish mission, Steele couldn't see any sign of life inside. Two of the old buildings were obviously unoccupied, apparently now used as roosting places for a handful of scrawny chickens. But there was a solid gate made out of new boards at the entrance, and quite a few hoof prints leading up to it. Beyond the gate was a courtyard completely empty except for a dusty stack of firewood and a broken-down old wagon.

They rode up to the gate and Steele pushed at it. It was secured with wire, wrapped several times around the gatepost.

"¡Vayas!" It was a man's voice, shrill and full of agitation. The voice had come from a window on the second floor of the main building.

"What did he say?" asked Rudd.

"He said go away."

"Maybe we should," said Rudd, turning his horse. "That voice didn't sound friendly."

"I want to talk to the father in charge," called Steele. "Deseo hablar con el padre."

"No aquí. Vayas."

"What did he say?" asked Rudd.

"He still says go away."

"What if he shoots us? Every Mexican we've met so far wants to shoot us."

"If he shoots us he'd have to pray for forgiveness. He's inside a church."

"Now he makes a joke," said Rudd. "Come on, let's get out of here. This old place gives me a bad feeling."

"In a moment," said Steele. He turned back toward the mission and called, "Who is in charge here? I want to speak to whoever is in charge."

"Nadie. Go away." Suddenly the barrel of a Winchester rifle began to edge out of the window.

"Look out!," yelled Rudd. He took off fast back down the road.

Steele guided his horse behind the shelter of the adobe wall. He reached down into his boot and pulled out his pistol. "Why would you have a rifle in this church?" he yelled. "And why isn't there a priest here?"

"*No hay un padre aquí. Vayas.*"

Steele expected a warning shot, but none came. There was no way to tell how many men were inside the mission or how heavily armed they were. He decided there was nothing he could do about it for the moment. He put his gun away and turned his horse to catch up with Rudd.

Rudd was waiting a ways down the road. "Jesus, Steele, that was close. Why would a Mexican be guarding that old mission with a rifle?"

"Did you notice that rifle? It was one of the new Winchester Henry's."

"Seems like everybody's got 'em now. What does it mean?"

"That man could have been one of Medina's militia. We'd better go tell Major Carter."

Back at the fort, they found the major waiting impatiently at the gate next to his horse. "Where in the hell have you two been?" He said, chewing on his cigar. "If we're going out to McNeil's we gotta get moving. I don't have all day to do this."

"We were out at the old Spanish mission," said Rudd. "Somebody pointed a rifle at us."

"Is that right?" said the major. "I've been getting complaints about that place from the Mexicans. They say church services have been cancelled for the past two Sundays."

"And you haven't gone out there to investigate?" said Rudd.

The major scowled at him. "You think it's my job to take the Mexicans to church? I've had my hands full." He mounted his horse. "But if you say somebody pointed a rifle at you, I'll send some men out there to talk to 'em when we get back."

"You might also notify the Cavalry in Yuma, and in California and Texas. Better have them check any mission that's near the border."

"Why, you think it's got something to do with this Confederate business?"

"The rifle that was pointed at us was another one of those new Winchester Henrys."

"More of those, eh?" Suddenly silent, the major led the way out of town and onto a dusty road that wound its way up into the hills. He seemed lost in thought, but Rudd made up for it by talking the whole way, telling the major all about the close calls they had had while following Ramsey down in Mexico. He related a very exciting version of how they had confronted the gang of Mexican bandits, with guns drawn, and how they barely escaped with their lives.

The mention of Mexican bandits seemed to bring the major out of his thoughts. "The trouble with those Mexicans is they don't seem to understand that this is our country now. We fought 'em in the Mexican-American war twenty years ago and they lost. So why don't they just go home and quit making trouble."

"Are they still burning farms down by the border?" asked Rudd.

"Yeah, and we've got reports of them raiding other homesteads, from here to El Paso. They're leaving the Mexican farmers alone, only attacking the white ranchers. I thought we had 'em under control and now this new bunch is at it again."

"The new bunch?" asked Steele. "Is it the militia we told you about, the ones in the gray and black uniforms?"

"I guess it's them. All dressed up fancy. I sent some troops down there, but the raiders just ran right back across the border like they always do. My orders are to not chase 'em into Mexico. How am I supposed to keep 'em in check if I they just run right back across some imaginary line on a map?"

"Isn't the Rio Grande river down there?" asked Rudd. "That's not an imaginary border."

"The Rio Grande forms the border between Texas and Mexico," said Steele, "not Arizona."

"Oh." Rudd frowned and took off his hat to fan himself. "Getting hot isn't it?"

They rode on in silence until Major Carter pulled back his horse to ride next to Steele. "What did the doctor tell you about McNeil?" he asked.

"Only that he thought McNeil might know something about where Cochise was."

"Yeah, well, maybe he does and maybe he doesn't. But getting anything out of old McNeil will be like pulling teeth."

"He's not cooperative?"

"Cooperative? He's the opposite of cooperative. Contrary old bastard. But never you mind, if he knows anything about Cochise, I'll get it out of him. I can have him locked up if necessary."

"We aren't going out there to arrest him, Major. I just want to find out what he knows about the Apaches."

"If he knows anything, he'll have to tell me," said the major, spitting into the dirt. "It's his duty as an American."

When they arrived at McNeil's ranch, a somber old Indian came out to take their horses. The major demanded he go tell his boss that he had company, but the Indian just slowly led the horses away without a word.

They headed for the main house, the major in the lead. "I'll bet that one's an Apache," he whispered. "I can smell 'em."

Before the major could knock on the huge, hand-carved front door, it opened and a tall unsmiling man with gray hair greeted them. "Ah, Major Carter. What brings you to my house? It's been a long time."

"Not so long, NcNeil. Don't you remember? I came out here after your wife died. You wouldn't even talk to me."

"If I did that, I'm sorry, Major. It was a hard time for me after Sarah died. A hard winter altogether." He turned to Steele. "And who did you bring with you? Guests? I don't get many guests anymore."

"This is Steele," said the major, "and the other one is Rudd. They're from California."

McNeil shook their hands and led them inside. He walked next to Steele. "So you're from California, Mr. Steele? What brings you men to Arizona?"

"We work for the San Francisco Morning-Herald, Mr. McNeil. Rudd is a reporter and I'm a private detective. I asked Major Carter to bring us to meet you."

"A private detective, eh. Don't think I ever met a private detective before. Now why would a San Francisco detective come all the way to Arizona to see the likes of me?" Without waiting for an answer, McNeil led them to an expansive room with many windows and a huge fireplace. He gestured for them to sit in the large leather-covered chairs.

"We've been following a man named Ramsey," said Steele, "a Confederate general. We followed him all the way from western Mexico and now we think he's here, hiding in these mountains."

McNeil's dark eyes watched Steele as he spoke. Steele tried to determine whether or not the man was surprised by his words, but neither his face nor his eyes gave much away.

"You said a Confederate general, Mr. Steele. Don't you mean a former Confederate general?"

'That's the trouble," said Rudd. "He doesn't seem to think the war is over. He's got an army and he's been attacking towns in Arizona. Yuma, and now Tucson."

McNeil looked at Major Carter. "Yes, I heard about the attack on the town, but I never heard anybody say it was done by Confederates."

"We don't know for sure who it was," said the major. "These boys did follow some old Confederates here, so maybe it was them. But that's not why I came out here today. I want to know what you know about Cochise. There's talk in town you may have met him."

McNeil ignored the major's comment and turned back to Steele. "What makes you think this General Ramsey is hiding in the mountains?"

They all stopped talking as a tall, very thin Indian brought in a pitcher of liquid and glasses. He placed the tray on a small table next to McNeil.

"Thank you, Nan."

The Indian left without a glance at any of them.

"It's a kind of tea, gentlemen, " said McNeil pouring the liquid and passing a glass to each of them. "I don't know what's in it, but the Indians say it's good for us. Here's to your health." He lifted his glass and drank about half of the liquid.

Steele sipped at it. It didn't taste too bad, but Rudd made a sour face when he tried it.

The major didn't even pick up his glass. He was scowling at McNeil.

"By the way," said McNeil, "the man who served us is named Nantan. I believe it means good communicator, but if so I don't know why they named him that. He rarely speaks. But he's a good man. Been with me for more than a year."

The major made a scoffing sound and McNeil glanced at him. "Major Carter doesn't believe an Indian can be a good employee, but he's wrong. I'm running this ranch with their help. I couldn't do it without them."

"That's because nobody else will work out here with them around," said the major.

"I was unable to get any other help even before I began hiring them."

"That's because they would've scalped any competition."

McNeil kept his eyes on Steele, refusing to look at the major. "That's ridiculous. They are hard workers, and they are peaceful. Unlike my former employees, they don't even fight among themselves."

"The doctor in town told me that you had a good relationship with the Indians," said Steele. "That's why I wanted to meet you."

"You mean it wasn't because of my gracious Irish manner?"

"No, sir," said Steele with a smile. "The doctor didn't tell me about that."

For the first time, McNeil also smiled. "Very tactful, Mr. Steele. I know I'm not the best of company since my Sarah's been gone, but I am happy to have guests, especially ones who traveled so far to get here. It has been many years since I visited San Francisco. By the way, when you see the doctor again, tell him hello from me. He was a comfort to my late wife."

Steele took another sip of his drink and put it down on the small table next to his chair. "Let me get right to the point, Mr. McNeil. The reason we have been following General Ramsey is because he kidnapped a woman named Helen Kane. Ramsey is holding her as a hostage."

"Would this Helen Kane be any kin to the Mr. Kane, the newspaper man who is often in the news? I hear he may run for the United States senate."

"Yes," said Rudd, leaning forward. "He's my boss, the owner of my newspaper. I write about him all the time."

"I may have read your stories then, Mr. Rudd, if they are ever reprinted in the local newspaper."

"Well, I wouldn't know if my stories ever, uh, get this far. But they're popular in San Francisco."

McNeil turned back to Steele. "But why did you think I would be able to help you find this girl? I know nothing about it."

"If you know where the Indians are, you have to tell us," said the major. "Do the Apaches have anything to do with these Confederates? Your tame Indians must be telling you something."

"Tame Indians? How insulting, Major. They are simply men, like you and me."

"Mr. McNeil, let me explain," said Steele. "I spoke with General Ramsey at his camp in western Mexico. He said he admired the Apaches and I got the feeling he might try to form an alliance with them. It's possible the general has come to these mountains to meet with Cochise. The doctor thought if anybody knew where Cochise was, you would."

McNeil took a sip of his drink, and for the first time he broke eye contact with Steele.

Steele wondered if he was looking away while he decided how to respond. He decided to push a little harder. "In fact, the doctor thought you had met Cochise."

"Listen, McNeil," said the major, "if you have any idea where that murderin' redskin is it's your duty to tell me."

McNeil turned to him, no longer smiling. "Is it my duty to tell you how to find and murder peaceful Indians, Major? People you are trying to forcibly move off their land?"

The major stood up abruptly. "What a bunch of crap. That Cochise has killed more white men than any other Indian in this territory. And white women too. He's killing your kind of people, McNeil, white people. Where the hell is your loyalty?"

McNeil jumped up to confront him. "How many innocent Apache women and children have you and your men killed, Major? What about Queen Creek?"

"You know I wasn't at Queen Creek, McNeil. But if I had been–"

"Gentlemen, please," said Rudd, standing up and stepping between them. "This isn't getting us anywhere." He turned to McNeil. "Sir, Helen Kane is an innocent young woman. She did nothing to deserve being kidnapped. All we're trying to do is get her back. Her poor mother is worried sick about her. Can't you help us?"

McNeil shook his head. "No, I'm afraid I can't, Mr. Rudd. But you're right. We should act like civilized men about these . . . disagreements. Please, come and join me for some lunch. I have a woman who cooks for me. Wonderful food."

"Probably Indian food," said the major.

McNeil nodded. "Yes, it is Indian food, but also they have many Spanish influences in their cooking. I think you may enjoy it."

The major looked away. "I doubt it."

"Sounds good to me," said Rudd with a grin.

McNeil led them into a large dining room with a long table that appeared to have been cut from one piece of wood and polished to a fine sheen. It was set with glasses, colorful plates, and fine silverware. "Sit down, sit down," said McNeil. "Can I get anyone something stronger to drink?"

"Do you have any beer?" asked Rudd. "I sure could use a beer in this heat."

"I'm afraid I have no way to keep beer fresh out here, Mr. Rudd. But I have some fine bourbon."

"Maybe after we eat," mumbled Rudd.

The major took him up on his offer, but Steele declined.

McNeil was filling the major's glass when the same thin Apache who had served the tea came in with a platter of tortillas and a large bowl of what looked like vegetables in a red sauce. After the Indian had placed the food on the table, McNeil whispered something to him and he hurried away.

"Use the tortillas to scoop out some of this," said McNeil, pushing the bowel toward Rudd. "I think you'll like it."

Rudd did as he was instructed, rolling up the tortilla and dipping it deep into the bowel. But after one bite he put his hand to his mouth. "Hot," he exclaimed, fanning his mouth with his free hand. "Maybe I'd better have some of that bourbon."

"Try eating some more tortillas," suggested McNeil as he poured bourbon into Rudd's glass. "That works better than liquid."

Steele noticed the old Indian standing in the doorway before anyone else did. The man was dressed as any cowhand might be, with a worn, but clean, dark shirt, leather pants, and scuffed boots. The only Indian attire he wore was a leather headband that had odd symbols burned into it.

McNeil noticed him. "Ah, Eskamin, come in, come in."

Steele noticed the major had put his hand to his sidearm.

McNeil stood up and held out his hand toward the Indian. "Gentlemen, let me introduce one more guest. This is my new range rider and friend, Eskamin. I'm afraid he doesn't speak much English. But he does speak some Spanish and if you like I can do a bit of translating." He waved the Indian over. "Come, Eskamin, *venga, juntese a nosotros.*"

Eskamin came to the table and sat down in the empty chair without a word. He sat very still, keeping his eyes down.

Still standing, McNeil lifted his glass, as if he was about to make a toast. "Because of your mention of a female hostage, Mr. Steele, I have asked Eskamin to join us. Regrettably, he too has been victimized by hostage taking. We should be honored to have Eskamin at our table. He was a great chief of the Apache people. Although he is getting on in years now, he is still considered to be a great chief by many of his people." He picked up the decanter of bourbon and turned to Eskamin. "Here, give me your glass. Drink with us."

"Now wait a minute," said the major, "you know you aren't supposed to provide any Indian with liquor, let alone an Apache."

McNeil ignored him. The Indian picked up his cut-crystal glass and handed it to McNeil without a word or a change of expression.

Steele did note that the Indian had understood McNeil's request for his glass. He wondered if Eskamin might understand more English than McNeil realized.

The major shook his head in disgust while McNeil poured the glass half full and went on as if he hadn't heard the major's warning. "Eskamin's job is to ride out to look for newborn calves. It's lucky for us that he was here because he happened to bring one in last night."

Steele watched the Indian as he sipped at the bourbon. Was he drinking, or just pretending to drink? The Indian kept his eyes down, not even looking up when McNeil made reference to him.

McNeil took a drink from his own glass and went on. "Eskamin led many of his people to safety when they were attacked by the Army. I'm told he was a close friend of Cochise, that they rode together in the old days. But of course he won't speak of that."

"Mr. McNeil, I asked earlier if you knew where I might find Cochise," said Steele. "If Eskamin knows where he is, it would be a great help to us. You see, Helen's father has agreed to become the general's hostage in exchange for her. I too am willing to become the general's prisoner if he will agree to release Helen and the other women hostages he is holding. But to propose this exchange, we first have to find Ramsey. I wonder if Cochise might know where he is."

McNeil took time to think about Steele words before he answered. "I have met many of the Apaches, Mr. Steele, and have been a guest in some of their lodges. But they value their . . . privacy." He glanced at the major. "And their independence. I must honor their wishes."

"But I'm sure Eskamin could help us," said Steele, turning to face the Indian. "He must know where Cochise is. *Es Verdad?*"

The Indian looked briefly at Steele, but quickly lowered his eyes.

"I must apologize for my friend," said McNeil. "I've never seen Eskamin talk to a white man, except for myself. You have to understand what he has been through. You spoke of this young woman held captive by renegade soldiers. If anyone can understand your anxiety, it is my friend Eskamin here. When he was the leader of his people, he fought the white man when they tried to force his people off of their land. But when he learned of the great numbers of white men that were coming to Arizona, he finally agreed to lead his tribe to one of the new reservations. The government made many fine promises to him. But when they didn't keep their promises, Eskamin led some of his braves off the reservation. They went back to their ancestral lands, land they had been living on and hunting on for many centuries. The Army chased after them, but the Indians hid high in the mountains near here."

"Now listen here, McNeil," said the major, "there's no need to go over all this again. It was before my time out here. A young lieutenant was in charge back then and he knew very little about Indians."

"Nevertheless," insisted McNeil, "it was your Army that put the lieutenant in charge of managing the Indians in this district. He was the commander at the fort and he was supposed to oversee this entire territory. And his superiors must have approved his taking members of Eskamin's family as hostages, including the women and children."

"The Army held his family hostage?" asked Rudd.

"Indeed they did," said McNeil. "The lieutenant put out the word that he would begin to kill Eskamin's family, one by one, if he did not bring his braves back to the reservation."

"The U.S. Army?" said Rudd. "Kill hostages? They wouldn't do that, would they?" He looked at the major who was staring toward the window.

Steele was watching Eskamin who was still sitting very quietly, as if the conversation had nothing to do with him.

Rudd turned back to the major. "Major, is what he's saying true?"

When the major didn't respond, McNeil answered for him. "I'm afraid it is true, Mr. Rudd. The lieutenant started with the old men and when they were all dead he executed a few of the old women. He was ready to start killing the children when Eskamin finally came in and gave himself up to save them."

Rudd frowned at Major Carter. "Major, how could the U.S. Army do such a thing? Tell us it isn't true."

The major shrugged. "McNeil is distorting the facts. Those so called old men were not as old as all that. They were fully capable of killing. They had undoubtedly killed many white men in their time."

"And the old women?" said McNeil. "How do you respond to that, Major? None of the hostages, men or women, were ever charged with any crime and you know it. There was no trial, not even an official hearing. They were simply shot, one by one, in order to force Eskamin and his braves to give themselves up."

"It was a time of war," said the major. "The hostiles knew that. Martial law was in effect."

"So you're justifying the killing of women hostages?" asked Rudd.

"Of course not" said the major. "It was unfortunate that . . . other means were not tried first. But these things happen in a time of war. Remember, the federal government had declared the Apaches to be hostile to our nation's interest. Besides, the lieutenant was dully punished for his actions."

"Reprimanded and transferred," said McNeil. "I heard he wasn't even demoted. Just sent to some insignificant post back east. Probably so the press couldn't find him."

"Well, I can find him," said Rudd. "Or at least my newspaper can. We'll report this atrocity. Didn't the local newspaper report it at the time?"

"Yes, Major," said McNeil. "Tell us, why wasn't the local newspaper allowed to report it? What was it you said when you came here to take over? Something about not wanting to inflame the situation?"

"Long time ago," said Eskamin quietly.

They all turned to look at him, but he was still staring down at the table. He showed no indication that he had spoken at all, but they had all clearly heard his words. Steele wondered if he was trying to tell them he wanted to forget about it. Or was he saying he didn't want white men talking about it? In any case, it was now clear that he understood more English than McNeil had suggested. Everyone at the table was silent, realizing they had been speaking about him as if he wasn't there.

McNeil was the first to break the silence. "I'm sorry to bring up such a painful memory, my friend. You are right. It was years ago. Please, everyone, let's not speak further of such bad times. Everyone eat. Eskamin, my friend, eat. You are my guest."

Rudd pushed the bowl of food toward Eskamin and held out the platter of tortillas. The old Indian took only one tortilla. He folded it carefully and placed it on the edge of his plate.

"Let me tell you how Eskamin came to work for me, "said McNeil. "After he gave himself up, he languished in a terrible one-room prison on that reservation for many years. His solitary prison, which was made out of rocks and had a tin roof, was hot in the summer and cold in the winter. Often, he was left to almost starve. I had heard of his plight and when I requested workers be brought here from the reservation, I specifically asked for him. But they refused to let him go. Finally, after years of trying, a few months ago a friend of mine at the reservation convinced them to agree to a test work program for him. They released him into my custody. So far he has done his job very well. I believe he will become one of my best employees." He lifted his glass. "Here's to a brave man, a survivor."

Steele and Rudd raised their glasses in tribute, but the major pointedly continued to eat, ignoring them.

If Eskamin understood the nature of the toast he didn't respond. He was looking at the major.

"Now, back to the purpose of your visit," said McNeil putting down his glass. "Mr. Steele, you spoke of renegade Confederates who have captured this young woman. Is she your woman?"

"I only met her recently. I have been employed by her father to find her and bring her back to California."

"But I think I see something in your eyes when you speak of her. You care for her, do you not?"

Steele was taken aback by the question. How did he feel about Helen? He hadn't known her very long, but he had to admit he thought about her often. He had been trying to maintain his objectivity, trying not to let his emotions get in the way of his task, but he wanted to answer the man honestly. "Yes, I do," he said quietly. "After this is all over, I hope we will–"

"So I was right," interrupted McNeil, smiling broadly. "I thought I detected something in the way you spoke of her. Well now, I may be a foolish old man, but we can't ignore love, can we?" He turned toward Eskamin, still smiling. "Maybe we should help this young man get his girl back. All he wants to do is negotiate an exchange for her. You, of all people, can understand that, can't you Eskamin?"

Eskamin shook his head. He didn't take his eyes off of McNeil.

"Come now, what could it hurt? Maybe you could arrange a meeting in some neutral place. Cochise is a fair man. If he knew the young woman's friend here was waiting nearby, maybe he would help us find her."

Again, Eskamin shook his head.

The major glowered at Eskamin. "Speak up old man. If you know where Cochise is, tell us now!"

Eskamin ignored him. He kept his eyes on McNeil.

"I bet I can convince him," said the major reaching down to draw his sidearm. "Give me five minutes alone with this bastard and I'll have an answer." He waved the gun in the direction of the Indian.

McNeil jumped to his feet. "Major Carter! I will not have such behavior in my house. Eskamin is my guest, as you are.

Ignoring all of them, Eskamin calmly picked up his tortilla and took a bite of it.

"I insist you give that pistol to me," demanded McNeil. "I should have made you remove it when you came in."

The major kept his gun in his hand, glaring at Eskamin. "If this redskin thinks he can defy me, he's got another think coming."

From somewhere under the table, McNeil pulled out a small revolver. He pointed it at the major. "Major Carter, this is my house and I set the rules here. Give me that gun."

"Don't point that pea shooter at me, McNeil," snarled the major. He turned to point his gun at McNeil.

"Wait! No!" yelled Rudd.

Steele acted quickly. He grabbed the barrel of the major's gun and pushed it down. The shot sounded very loud in the room and the glasses on the table jumped as the bullet lodged in the tabletop. The major tried to pull the gun away, but Steele kept a strong grip on it.

"Jesus!" said Rudd. "You could have killed somebody."

"Let go of my gun, you son of a bitch" shouted the major. "I'm warning you."

But Steele didn't let go. "I think you should do as Mr. McNeil says," he said calmly. "We don't need guns to resolve this."

"And I'm telling you to let go of my gun right now." The major jerked at the gun but Steele held it tight. The major was getting red in the face.

Steele quickly reached out and dug his thumb into the major's wrist, pushing down hard on the main tendon.

The major yelped in pain as his hand involuntarily released the weapon.

Steele handed the gun to McNeil.

"That was a mistake, Steele," growled the major, rubbing his wrist, "and I won't forget it. You accosted an officer of the United States Army. I could have you jailed for that."

"I'm sorry, Major," said Steele. "I was just trying to keep things from getting out of hand. I'm sure Mr. McNeil will gladly give you back your pistol as we leave."

"Of course I will," said McNeil putting both his gun and the major's down on the table. "Sit down, Major. This man has done you a favor. He kept you from doing something you would regret later. The trouble with you, Major, is that you have been fighting Indians so long you have come to see them all as the enemy. And since that idiot, General Crane, put a bounty on their heads, everyone else is starting to think of them that way too."

The major was still rubbing his wrist. "General Crane only put that bounty on Apache warriors. And he was right to do it. The citizens of this district are fed up with the constant Indian raids."

"So when those citizens bring in a scalp for payment, how do you know it was a renegade and not a squaw?"

"So that's it, isn't it, McNeil? You'll always side with the Indians. You're nothing but a Goddammed Indian lover. I knew it before I came out here today, but this proves it. Everybody around here knows what you are and they're all getting mighty tired of you protecting the hostiles."

McNeil smiled and shook his head. "It's small minds like yours that cause the real trouble. You'll never understand that Eskamin here is as human as you or I. He is my friend and I would trust him with my life long before I would trust a man like you. I'll show you." Abruptly, he slid his small pistol toward Eskamin.

The Indian caught it before it stopped moving. He picked it up and looked at it. He did not point the gun at anyone, but neither did he put it down.

"Now, Eskamin, you have the pistol," said McNeil. "Tell the major you don't want to hurt him, or anyone."

Eskamin turned to face the major who immediately put up his hands and said, "See here, man, I have nothing against you personally."

But the Indian turned back to McNeil. "You my friend."

"Of course I am," said McNeil. "You know that."

Startlingly, he brought the pistol up to point it at McNeil. Steele was on the other side of the table and knew he couldn't stop him. But why was he pointing the gun at McNeil, his friend, his employer? The Indian's face remained calm but he was pointing the pistol directly at McNeil's chest. "You no take these men to Cochise," he said.

"Now listen here, Eskamin, I wasn't planning to do that. I just said you should arrange a meeting with Cochise." He pointed toward Steele. "I just wanted to help this man find his girl."

"No meet with Cochise. You promise."

"I only promised Cochise to keep his location a secret. No one needs to know that. This man loves that girl. We should help him."

"No. You promise."

"All right now, Eskamin, you've made your point. Now give me that gun."

"You must promise."

"No, Eskamin, I will not make such a promise. And if you are still my friend you must now give me that gun."

"Am I friend? You promise?"

"Of course I am your friend. Haven't I always been your friend? Didn't I help you get off that stinking reservation?"

"I your friend too, McNeil. I promise," said Eskamin. Then he shot McNeil in the chest.

Both Steele and the major moved toward Eskamin, but the Indian swung the gun around to face them.

Steele looked back toward McNeil who seemed confused, unsure of what had happened. He reached down to touch the place on his chest where the bullet had gone in. He tried to get up out of his chair, but sank to his knees and then fell onto his side.

Rudd jumped up and ran to him.

"Give me the gun," said Steele, holding out his hand toward Eskamin.

The Indian turned to face the major, pointing the pistol at him. "Tell all," he said. "Tell them. Anyone can kill enemy, but I kill friend. Then they know too. White man promise no good. All Apache must learn. White man sick in heart."

"Come here quick, Steele," cried Rudd. "You've got to do something. McNeil's hurt bad."

Steele hurried to McNeil's side. As he assessed McNeil's injury, he heard the major say, "You won't get away with this, Indian. We'll hunt you down."

"No hunt," said Eskamin.

Steele looked up just as Eskamin put the pistol down on the table and turned to walk out of the room.

But before he made it to the door, the major reached across the table and grabbed the gun. "Stop right there, Indian."

The Indian stopped, but he did not turn around.

Steele's shout of "No!" came simultaneously with the shot. Eskamin fell to the floor, shot in the back of the head.

"Jesus," yelled Rudd. "The man was unarmed."

"He was going for help," said the major. "He'd bring all the other hostiles down on us." He stood looking down at the Indian's body. Then, as if he'd suddenly remembered something, he ran out the door, shouting, "Damn, McNeil's other redskins. They'll be gettin' away."

As Steele turned back to McNeil, he heard two shots from outside, but he knew there was nothing he could do about that. He tore away McNeil's shirt. The bullet had gone in just under his rib cage on the left side. It must have missed his heart because he was still conscious. Steele used part of the torn shirt to apply direct pressure over the wound. McNeil looked up and whispered hoarsely, "He didn't understand. Our fault. Too many years and . . . too many . . . injustices."

"Don't try to talk," said Steele. "I may be able to slow the bleeding until the doctor gets here."

"No matter," whispered McNeil. "She's . . . waiting for me."

"Don't talk like that," said Rudd. There were tears in his eyes. "Steele here can help you. He learned all about wounds during the war."

"Doesn't matter . . . anymore," murmured McNeil. A trickle of blood leaked out of the corner of his mouth.

"Just relax," said Steele, but he knew bleeding from the mouth was a bad sign. He looked up at Rudd. "You'd better ride back to town to get the doctor."

McNeil reached up to take Steele's wrist. "No. I'm ready. Just . . .bury me out . . . next to Sarah. She's . . . waiting . . . there."

"I understand," said Steele.

McNeil was still holding tight to Steele's wrist. "Cochise. He's up in the mountains. He may be . . . able to help you. Look for . . . two columns . . . of rock. One leaning . . . against the other."

"Two rock columns?" repeated Steele. "I think I know the place."

McNeil looked up at Steele and smiled. "If you love that girl . . . don't ever let her . . . get away. Life doesn't mean anything . . . without them. They . . ." He hesitated, coughed once, and let out a long breath. He didn't take another breath in. His eyes stared lifelessly up at the ceiling.

It was a stare Steele had seen many times at the Army hospital. "He's gone."

"Damn," whispered Rudd. "Damn, damn."

Just then, the major hurried back into the room. "Murderin' redskins got away." He stopped and looked down at McNeil's body. "Dead?"

Steele nodded.

"It's your fault, not mine." The major was still holding the revolver. He shook it at Steele. "If you wouldn't have taken my gun away I could have taken care of that Indian before he did this."

"It's too late for that," said Steele standing up to confront the major. "I'm not going to argue with you about who was at fault here.

If you want to arrest me, then do so. Otherwise quit threatening me with that pistol."

The major hesitated.

Rudd stepped forward. "Steele was only trying to calm the situation down. It wasn't his fault that McNeil got killed. What that Indian did was between him and McNeil."

"Yeah, well, maybe McNeil got what he deserved," said the major. "And another thing, the next time you put your hands on me I'll–"

"You'll do what?" said Steele moving up close to the major's face. "There is no need for next time, Major. I'm right here in front of you now. What is it you want to do?"

Rudd put his arm between them. "Now hold on. McNeil is lying dead right here at our feet. Don't you think we should figure out what to do with him?"

Steele hesitated, then nodded in agreement. "You're right. I'm frustrated because I couldn't do anything to stop it." He turned back to Major Carter. "Put away that gun, Major. You know you aren't going to do anything with it. Does McNeil have family in town?"

The major shook his head and put the gun down on the table. He picked up his own revolver and jammed it back into his holster. "How would I know? I'm not his keeper." But then he looked down at McNeil's body and shook his head. "No," he said more quietly, "I don't think he has family around here anymore. I think his daughters both got married and moved back east somewhere."

"Would anyone know where they are?"

"Maybe the doctor."

"Would you ask him when you get back to town?"

"I guess I could do that. But what about you? Aren't you going back too?"

"No, Rudd and I will bury McNeil next to his wife. That's what he asked us to do. Then we'll bury Eskamin and go try to find Miss Kane. Tell Mr. Kane we've gone to look for her."

"You two are going up there alone again? You'll get yourselves killed. Those pet redskins of McNeil's will have alerted Cochise by now and he'll be waiting for you. Wait until my reinforcements arrive from back east. They should be here soon. Then you can go up there with us. We'll flush 'em out."

Steele shook his head. "We'd prefer to go on our own, Major. Remember, we're trying to arrange a peaceful exchange for Kane's daughter. If we can accomplish that, we'll let you know what we find out."

"Well, you go right ahead then. It's not on my head if you get killed. Me, I'm gonna–"

A rumble that sounded like distant thunder stopped him before he could finish the thought. He ran outside, followed by Steele and Rudd.

There wasn't a cloud in the blue sky. They stood there in front of McNeil's house looking back down the hill toward the city. Another rumble, quickly followed by a third."

"Artillery again?" said Rudd.

Steele shook his head. That' not artillery. It sounds like dynamite." He turned to the major. "I'd get back to your fort if I was you."

"What? You think it's some kind of attack? In the middle of the afternoon?"

"Didn't you say nearly all of your men were out looking for the Confederates? It would be easy enough for somebody to ride right into town with dynamite in their saddlebags."

"I don't believe it," said the major. "Why would they want to blow things up?"

"To show they can," said Steele. "To instill terror. It's how guerrillas fight, with ambush and sabotage. In eighteen-twelve, when Napoleon attacked Russia, the Russian guerrillas hid in the hills and attacked him at will, often just to show what they were capable of doing."

"Jesus Christ!" shouted the major. "The Confederates are attacking my fort and you're lecturing me on the Goddam Napoleonic Wars." He ran for his horse and galloped away.

They watched him go. "Let's find some shovels and bury these men," said Steele.

It took some time to dig the holes. They buried McNeil next to his wife's grave and Eskamin some distance away. When they were finished, Rudd said, "Do you think we should say some words?"

"Go ahead," said Steele.

"Uh, actually, I've never exactly done it before."

"Just say what you're feeling."

"Well, all right." Rudd thought about it for a minute. Then he said," Well, we . . . feel real bad that Mr. McNeil here had to get killed by his Indian . . . friend. He seemed like a good fellow. We hope he rests in peace here by his wife. And the Indian too. And . . . well, I guess that's all. Amen."

"Let's get moving," said Steele, putting his hat on.

"Maybe we should rest up for a while. We could stay here until morning. I'm sure McNeil wouldn't mind."

"Are you sure you want to stay here all night? The Indians will know we're here."

"Uh, maybe you're right. But what about those Indians that attacked us the last time we went up into the mountains?"

"The major said he had soldiers posted all over the mountains now. Hopefully, the Indians have retreated to their hideout until the soldiers go away."

"I don't know, Steele. We barely got away with our scalps that last time."

"What choice do we have? McNeil told us where we might find Helen. We have to go there and look."

"All right, but if we see any sign of those Indians we have to run for it. Agreed?"

"Agreed. Now help me find something to carry water in."

"I'll try to find some food, too," said Rudd.

"Fine, but don't take too long. I think I know the place McNeil was talking about. When we were up there before I saw two towers of rock similar to those he described."

As soon as they had found and filled four canteens and Rudd had filled a burlap sack with food, they rode up into the mountains. Steele pushed the pace until they were high above the town.

Rudd pointed at Tucson, far below. "Looks peaceful enough down there," he said. "I hope nobody got hurt in those dynamite explosions."

Steele didn't reply, but he also hoped people had not been killed. Because most of the soldiers were out searching for the cannon, the dynamite might have been more of a demonstration of the town's vulnerability than a real attack. The major had admitted that the fort had been left mostly unguarded. Ramsey's spies would know that and use the opportunity to strike. Still, Steele wondered why Ramsey would have carried out such an attack in broad daylight. Setting off dynamite bombs at night would create more panic.

For some time Rudd was silent as they rode higher up into the hills. Then he said, "You were telling the major about Napoleon. So what happened? Did those Russian guerrilla tactics work against him?"

"Napoleon had complete control of most of Europe. No army was able to stop him. When he invaded Russia with six hundred thousand men, the Russians didn't try to stop him either. Instead, they used guerrilla tactics. They burned their own cities ahead of him and destroyed any supplies that would help him. When winter came, the Russians constantly attacked him, but after quick strikes, they quickly retreated back into the wilderness. In the end, it did work. Napoleon gave up and went back to France, but not before losing two thirds of his men to the guerrillas and to the Russian winter."

Rudd let out a low whistle. "Man, that is some story. Did they teach you about that stuff when you were a student in Europe?"

"Yes."

"I wish I would've studied harder when I was in school. Mostly they wanted us to learn a trade and I was, uh, bored I guess."

As they rode higher into the mountains, the day grew hotter. They didn't see any sign of Indians, or the soldiers Major Carter sent up into the mountains. As the afternoon's long shadows began to indicate the coming dusk, they began to encounter more difficult, rocky terrain.

"Do you know where we're going?" asked Rudd.

"See that cliff in the distance?" said Steele, pointing. "That's the same cliff we saw yesterday, even though we're coming at it from a different direction. That's where I saw the two rock columns."

"Still a long ways off," said Rudd. "It'll be dark before we get there." He reached back into his saddlebag and pulled out some of the food he found at McNeil's house. He took a bite of something that looked like dried fruit and held some out toward Steele.

Steele shook his head and spurred his horse forward.

They rode on, constantly working their way higher into the mountains. Finally, Steele saw the cliff in the distance. The setting sun turned the cliff-face pink, then dark red. In the last light of the evening, Steele marked the path toward the cliff in his mind. They would have to make their way up there in the dark.

Once it was completely dark, they were often slowed by rocky ridges they had to find their way around. Despite the slow going, Steele wanted to keep moving. He knew the bright moon they had seen the night before would soon come up, making it much easier to pick a good path through the rocks.

"You know," said Rudd, riding up next to him, "I keep thinking about that Indian shooting Mr. McNeil. He said McNeil was his friend, but he shot him anyway. It doesn't make sense."

"I guess he wanted other Indians to know that white men are not to be trusted, even if they appear to be a friend."

Rudd thought about that. Then he said, "Did you believe what McNeil said? That the army even killed the old women hostages?"

"There wouldn't be much point in threatening to kill hostages if you weren't willing to go thorough with it."

Rudd looked at him and shook his head. "Damn, Steele. I wish you wouldn't say things like that. I mean, what with Helen still being held hostage and all."

"That's why we have to find her quickly. If the Indians at McNeil's ranch have warned Cochise that we are looking for him . . ." He left the thought unfinished.

As they worked their way farther up into the mountains, Steele noticed that the cooling night seemed to be putting Rudd to sleep. He slowed to ride next to Rudd's horse and when Rudd got so sleepy he almost fell off his horse, Steele reached over to steady him. Rudd stopped his horse and shook his head.

"Here," said Steele. "Try drinking some water." He handed Rudd his canteen.

Rudd drank some of the water, but still couldn't seem to clear his head. "I'm sorry, Steele, but I can't seem to stay awake. I'm trying, but my eyes keep on closing even though I don't want them to."

"We should keep going at little farther. I don't think those rock columns are too far ahead."

"All right, I'll try to keep going, but don't be surprised if I fall off this damned horse."

When the bright moon came up, Steele saw the two columns in the distance, close to the base of the cliff. Both of the columns were about the same height, connected to each other at the top, as if they were leaning against each other for support. He turned back to look for

Rudd, but he couldn't see him. He rode back a ways and discovered Rudd's horse had stopped and was nibbling at a bush. Rudd was leaning forward against the horse's neck, sound asleep.

As Steele approached, Rudd sat up with a start and nearly fell off his horse. He recovered his balance and said, "Oh, it's you, Steele. I must have been having a dream. I was in a feather bed and there was this fine lady and . . . well, anyhow. . . you know what I mean."

"Yes," said Steele. "I know. But keep your voice down. We're close to the cliff. I saw the two rock columns I think McNeil was referring to. Let's rest here for a bit." He got down and tied his horse to a bush.

After Rudd had stiffly climbed down from his horse, Steele tied the horse to another bush. By the time he turned back, Rudd was already lying on the ground on his back, his hat over his face. "Sorry," he murmured. "Sleepy." Within seconds he was snoring.

Steele turned back to the horses. He poured some water into his hat, first letting Rudd's horse drink, then his own. As the horse lapped at the water, he looked up at the stars. The familiar stars that made up the Scorpius constellation were still high in the sky. It meant they had several more hours of darkness. If the Indians were up on that cliff, they would be watching. They would have to get up there before it started to get light. He could only give Rudd a few minutes of sleep before they had to push on.

Steele sat down on the ground near Rudd and drank some water. Then he lay back and listened to the night sounds, crickets and a pair of owls calling to each other.

But then the crickets suddenly stopped. Steele sat up to listen. The mountainside was very quiet. He stood up and walked a ways up the mountains to get away from the sound of the horses nuzzling the ground as they searched for anything edible. When he was well away from the horses, he stopped and stood still in the darkness. He listened for any sound that might indicate someone was out there. Something had passed in the night, something unusual enough to stop the crickets. Was it the Indians? Were they coming?

Chapter 23

*S*teele took out his gun, and strained to see through the darkness. There were no sounds and nothing was moving in the immediate vicinity.

But then he heard a distant sound that was so familiar, and yet so unlikely, that for a moment he doubted he had even heard it. He turned to look down toward Tucson. Then the sound came again, unmistakable if you had ever heard it before; it was the chatter of a Gatling gun, a linked series of overlapping shots that, from a distance, always sounded like a ferocious gun battle being fought with many identical guns.

But then it stopped.

Steele waited, listening. Why had it stopped? And why was there no return fire?

Then came the echoing sound of an artillery shell exploding, followed by more repeated bursts from the Gattling gun and some return fire from small arms. Were they attacking the fort?

He reached down to shake Rudd. "Wake up, Rudd. "They're attacking Tucson again."

"That's good," muttered Rudd. He rolled over and was immediately asleep again.

Steele shook him again. "Rudd, you've got to wake up. We've got to go."

Rudd opened his eyes. "Go? Go where? He sat up. "Damn, I just got to sleep. And I was having a dream about that mountain lion. I couldn't hardly sleep a wink thinking it was gonna creep up and eat me."

"We've got to move. Quick."

There was another explosion in the distance and Rudd quickly sat up. "Now I hear it. It's that cannon again, isn't it?"

"Yes. If we hurry, we might be able to catch them before they make it back to their hideout."

Rudd got to his feet stiffly, holding his back.

Steele was already up on his horse, waiting.

After a few tries, Rudd managed to get up onto his horse.

Steele led the way, but Rudd soon caught up. "This time it sounds like a real battle. Who's fighting?"

"It might be an attack on the fort. It sounds like the same cannon, but I heard a Gattling gun."

"A Gattling gun? Out here in the West?"

Steele stopped his horse and held up his hand. "Listen. The cannon has stopped, but it sounds like the battle is still going on."

"That doesn't make sense," said Rudd. "If the battle is still going on, why would the artillery stop?"

"I agree. It doesn't make sense. It could have been another diversion."

"A diversion? From what?"

"I don't know," said Steele, "but I do know we have to get up to that cliff as fast as we can."

"Maybe we should wait for the Army," said Rudd.

"No more talking," whispered Steele. "Your voice carries a long way out here."

When he came to the place where they'd seen the mule tracks the day before, Steele dismounted and waited for Rudd.

When Rudd arrived, he said, "Go hide in those rocks up there. I'll get some bushes to wipe out our tracks."

Rudd quickly headed up the hill.

Steele broke off a branch and brushed away their tracks. Then he led his own horse up the hill after Rudd. He found him quite a ways higher, squatted down behind some large boulders. Steele tied off his horse and got his field glasses out of the saddlebag and began to scan the valley below. Nothing was moving down there.

But he didn't have to wait long before he spotted them coming slowly up the mountainside, all in a single line. "Here they come," he whispered.

As they drew closer, Steele refocused the field glasses and saw that the line was being led by two Indians on paint horses. Next came a Confederate leading two heavily-loaded pack mules. Two more Confederates brought up the rear.

"What do you see?" whispered Rudd.

"Five of them."

As he watched the men go by, Steele tried to judge where they were heading. Were they going to turn up toward the two rock columns?

They went on across the hillside and just when it seemed as if they would continue in that direction, they came to a ridge and turned up toward the cliff. If McNeil was right and Cochise's hideout was somewhere up near those two rock columns, it meant Ramsey had been able to form an alliance with them. Another alliance of the weak against the strong, and the weak were getting stronger.

"I'll try to follow them back to their hideout," whispered Steele. "See those two rock columns up there? Go back down and tell the Army that's where I went."

"Got it," whispered Rudd. "Should I head back now?"

"Not yet."

Soon, as Steele had expected, two more Indians came along, dragging branches behind their horses to obscure the tracks. They too stuck to the same path along the rocky part of the slope until they came to the ridge where they turned up toward the two rock columns.

When they were gone, Steele turned to Rudd. "Now you can go. You'll probably meet the Army coming up to look for that cannon. Bring them, but be sure they give me enough time to get to Ramsey. If he accepts the exchange of Helen and the other hostages for her father and let's me go, I'll meet you and the Army by those two rock columns."

"But what if they shoot you before you can tell them about Kane's offer?"

"If that happens, there will be nothing you can do about it. You'd better get going."

"All right, but try not to get yourself killed." Rudd started to get on his horse, but hesitated. "I almost feel like I shouldn't leave you alone up here. We've . . . been through a lot together."

"Yes we have," said Steele. "We've been a good team."

"Do you really think so? I mean maybe you'd of done better without me tagging along."

"I couldn't have made it this far without you."

"Well, thanks for saying it anyhow," said Rudd. He put out his hand.

Steele shook it and clapped him on the shoulder.

Rudd got up on his horse and leaned down to whisper, "Tell Helen hello for me when you see her. Tell her I . . . we all . . . miss her."

"I will," said Steele. "Go slow and stay on the rocky ground as much as you can on the way down. So your horse doesn't kick up too much dust."

"Got it," said Rudd. "Do you want to take some food with you?" He reached back toward his saddlebag.

"I won't have time for that," said Steele. But when Rudd frowned, he added, "But thanks for watching out for me. I appreciate it."

As he watched Rudd ride out of sight, he realized it was the first time they had ridden off in separate directions since this had all started. He was sorry to see his old friend go. Despite his complaining, Rudd was honest and reliable. His high-pitched voice, his unhurried pace, and even his constant hunger were familiar, and in a way, comforting.

Steele looked up to see the Scorpius constellation just going below the western horizon. He put his field glasses into his saddlebag and pulled out his Confederate uniform. He quickly changed into it. He stuffed his clothes back into the saddlebag and started up the hill.

Chapter 24

As Steele worked his way steadily higher up the slope, he glanced up at the moon. It's light was going to be a problem. They would have lookouts up on top of that cliff, watching for any movement. Hopefully, they wouldn't be expecting one man alone, specially not one on foot.

The closer he got to the cliff, the more cautiously he moved. He stopped frequently to listen for any sound, but the desert was quiet other than the crickets that were gradually getting back into their nightly chorus. There was a slight breeze coming down off the mountain and it felt good in the warm night. He looked up at the cliff. It seemed even higher and darker in the pale light of the moon than it had in the sunlight.

When he reached the foot of the cliff, he moved carefully along next to the rock wall. The two rock columns were a short distance below, but the wall of the cliff nearest the columns was smooth and unbroken. Had McNeil given him the wrong information? Maybe the man's memory was clouded. He searched all along the base of the cliff and although the moon was bright there didn't seem to be any opening. It was as if men and horses had disappeared into thin air.

He continued to search the base of the cliff, but he began to suspect he had gone too far. He had found no canyon, no passageway through the cliff, only smooth vertical rock. There were a few cracks in the rock wall, but nothing wide enough for a horse. It would be difficult even for a man to climb up there. He must have missed something. He retraced his steps, looking carefully at every crack and crevice. Nothing. He looked back down the hill at the rock columns that stood like two giant sentries bowing to each other. What were they trying to tell him? McNeil had said to go to the two rock columns. This had to be the place. But he could see every inch of the rock wall, except one place where cactus grew thick right up to the cliff wall. He recognized that type of cactus: it was the type with the painful little balls of spines he had run into when he was escaping from the camp in Mexico. No one could have gone through that thick cactus patch, and even if they could, there was nothing but sheer rock beyond it.

Still, where else could they have gone? He decided to take a closer look. He got down low and saw that there *was* a meandering little path under the cactus plants, but it was so narrow it could only have been used by small critters like rabbits or porcupines. No horse could have gone in there. The sharp barbs on that type of cactus would be just as painful for a horse. But he did notice quite a few of the cactus balls lying under the plants. What could have knocked them off? He looked carefully at the ground. It was completely smooth. If this was a path for small animals, why were there no tracks of any kind?

Steele stood up and looked at the field of cactus again. He tried to imagine pushing a horse through there. It seemed impossible. But then he had a thought: what if they had something to cover the front of their horses? What if they used a specially-made covering to protect the horses, maybe some kind of thick leather blanket?

He found a stick and used it to push aside one of the cactus plants. He was able to push it quite a ways to the side and when he released the pressure the cactus sprang right back into its original position. He realized that if you could get a horse to push through there, the cactus would move right back into place.

Moving very carefully, and using the stick to push aside the cactus, he tried to slip through sideways. But the cactus balls came off the plants and stuck to his clothes. Every time he moved, some of them worked their way through the cloth and he felt the sharp pricks of the barbs as they pierced his skin. He backed out and used the stick to pry them off. It wasn't easy: some of the barbs had penetrated his skin deeply and didn't want to let go. And even after he got them off, each little pinprick continued to sting.

He looked back at the cactus patch and then at the sheer cliff beyond. There must be something behind that cactus patch. There was nowhere else they could have gone.

He gathered some stones and laid them out in the shape of an arrow pointing to the cactus. If Rudd came back with the Army, he hoped they would notice it.

He broke off a branch from a nearby bush, took a deep breath, and reentered the cactus patch. He used the branch to push aside as many of the cactus as he could, but he was stuck often. Wincing at the many little needles of sharp pain, he gritted his teeth and kept going. He told himself the stings wouldn't last long.

Halfway though, he began to see hoofprints. So this *was* where they had gone. Once they were behind the cactus, they hadn't bothered to cover their tracks.

Then Steele saw what he never would have expected: a tunnel, leading under the cliff. It must have taken years to dig it. Had they also planted the cactus to hide it? If so, it must have been done many years ago.

He took out his pistol and moved cautiously down into the hole. The tunnel was just big enough to get a horse through. It explained how Ramsey's cannoneers could disappear so quickly.

It was completely dark in the hole and the air seemed close and musty. He could hear the echo of his own breathing. He moved forward, feeling along the walls in near total darkness. When he saw the dim glow of moonlight outlining the other end of the tunnel ahead, he stopped to listen. Silence. He moved forward and looked out. The tunnel had led him through the cliff face and into a narrow crevice in the rock. Sheer walls loomed on both sides.

He started to move forward, but then he heard something. He froze, listening. He heard nothing, but just as he was ready to start again, he heard voices, maybe twenty yards ahead. He waited, not breathing. The voices came and went, apparently picked up by the wind. He moved closer until he could hear them clearly. It was Indians, speaking quietly in their own native tongue. This was the Indian hideout, just as McNeil had said. But was Ramsey with them?

He moved back and looked up at the sheer rock on both sides. Was it possible to climb up there? He could see a few potential handholds, dark shadows in the moonlight. It was worth a try.

He took off his boots and his socks and stuffed them down inside the front of his shirt. Then he began to climb, making sure he had one good handhold and one good foothold before each move up. He made good progress until he forced his hand into a crack and immediately heard the frightening rattle of a rattlesnake. He pulled his hand back out fast. Too fast. It caused him to lose his grip and he slid back down several few feet. He grabbed desperately at the rock until he was finally able to catch hold of something, a spindly plant. He jammed his other fist into a narrow crack and held on. He flattened himself against the rock and waited to see if anyone had heard. He looked up toward the top of the cliff and saw a dark shape. Someone was looking down. He got the impression of someone with long hair. Probably an Indian. All he could do was stay where he was and wait. The rattlesnake continued to rattle. It sounded very loud in the night. Finally, the man went away.

Steele waited several more minutes before beginning to move upward again. He climbed somewhat to the side, angling away from where he had seen the man up above. Eventually he made it to the top and crawled over the lip. He found himself on a narrow rock mesa. He looked back down and was surprised to see how high he was above the cactus patch he'd come through. The desert beyond seemed flat and pale in the moonlight.

He crawled away from the edge of the cliff into some bushes. Lying on his back, he pulled his boots back on. He lay there, listening. He heard voices, but they were not close enough to tell if they were speaking English or not. He crawled toward the voices until he came to an overlook. He could hardly believe what he saw: there a narrow valley with at least a dozen campfires burning all along it. Beyond the little valley was a rocky slope that led up to more cliffs.

He crawled forward just a bit more and saw a man standing next to the closest campfire. He was wearing a Confederate uniform. So the Confederates were here. Was Ramsey down there somewhere?

Steele could see that there were two separate groups. The largest group was just below him, probably the Confederates gathered around a handful of scattered campfires. Beyond the fires, he saw a reflection. Was it water? It looked like it might be a small pond. Farther up the valley, there were more fires. Was that where the Indians were? He couldn't see where Helen and the other hostages might be.

He began to work his way down into the valley, following a brushy crevice. He moved slowly, making sure not to dislodge anything that would give away his presence. Halfway down, he stopped. The voices were clearer now.

Then he saw someone move past the closest fire. It was a woman. For a moment, he thought it might be Helen, but then he realized it was an older woman with dark hair. She was wearing a long dress. She must be one of the hostages taken at Yuma, but she seemed to be moving around the camp freely. In fact, she appeared to be bringing food to the men. If the women were being allowed to move about that freely, he hoped he might be able to find Helen.

Steele thought he heard a sound from behind. He turned and caught the glint of a knife just as an Indian lunged at him. He ducked and scrambled away, hearing the knife strike the rock behind him. The Indian was up again quickly, screaming a high pitched, angry wail and diving at him again with that long knife. Steele rolled away, but then he started sliding. He grabbed for some kind of handhold, but found himself falling, tumbling down the steep rock face.

He landed on his back, hitting the ground hard. He tried to scramble to his feet, but only made it to his hands and knees. He couldn't seem to get a full breath. He shook his head, trying to shake off the dizziness.

When he noticed some small rocks falling from above, he looked up to see the Indian standing on the rocks above him. He was pointing down at Steele and yelling something in his own language.

Steele struggled to his feet, but he was still unable to catch his breath, and now he was noticing a sharp pain in his side. He suspected he might have some cracked ribs, but there was no time to think about that now. He backed into the thick bushes and pulled his pistol out.

Voices were coming closer. Steele turned to point his gun in that direction, but then he lowered it; what good would it do him against a whole camp full of Confederate soldiers and Apache warriors?

The first man to push through the bushes was a Confederate private carrying a torch in one hand and one of the new Henry repeating rifles in the other. He lifted the gun to point it at Steele. Steele raised both of his hands and said, "Don't shoot. I have an important message for General Ramsey." He kept his hands high in the air, but he still had the little pistol in his right hand. The soldier was watching that pistol and Steele was watching the soldier's trigger finger on the rifle.

The soldier looked confused. "Who are you? And where did you get that uniform?"

"Same place you did," said Steele, smiling.

That seemed to confuse the man even more, but it had kept him from shooting. The standoff ended when a voice from behind the man said, "Wait. Don't shoot. I know this man."

Steele recognized that voice: it was Ramsey.

The general pushed though the bushes. He was dressed in a splendid light-blue Confederate frock coat, clean and crisp as the day it had been made. A number of medals lined the left breast of the uniform and they caught the torchlight as he moved forward. The general was smiling broadly as he looked Steele over. "Well, Mr. Steele, there you are. I've been expecting you."

Chapter 25

*R*amsey came forward to extend his hand. "Welcome to my humble camp, Mr. Steele. I was sure we would meet again."

Steele grabbed the old man's hand, but he didn't shake it. Instead, he pulled him close and spun him around. He put his arm across Ramsey's neck and pressed his pistol against the side of his head. "Nice to see you again too, General. Now tell your men to stay back. I just came to get Helen. Let me take her and the other hostages out of here and I won't bother you anymore."

His words seemed to amuse Ramsey. He chuckled. "Now is that any way to greet an old friend? He tried to turn his head to look back at Steele."

"Stay still, General. I will shoot you."

"Think what you are saying, Mr. Steele. You don't want to shoot me. We have so much to talk about."

"Just let me take the women out of here. You don't need them now. Your son is dead."

"I'm afraid the situation is more complicated than you realize, Mr. Steele. While I fully understand your concern for the sweet Miss Helen, there are some things we need to discuss. Come, let us sit by the campfire and have a quiet conversation."

More Confederate soldiers were pushing through the bushes. They all had their guns pointed at Steele.

"Tell your men to stay back, General."

Ramsey held up both hands. "Lower your weapons, men. Mr. Steele is merely upset about his woman. He'll calm down soon."

Steele put his lips close to Ramsey's ear. "Listen, General, you know you don't want to die before you see your plan through. Give me the hostages. That's all I want."

Ramsey continued to try to turn his head to look back and as Steele increased the pressure against his neck he lost his balance and almost fell backward. Steele had to hold him up. It wasn't difficult: under his splendid general's uniform, Ramsey was a frail old man, easily controlled. But as frail as he was, Steele could see that he still had control over his men. They had all lowered their weapons, but they didn't back off. They stood waiting for his next order.

Ramsey let out a deep sigh. "We seem to be at something of a standoff. But I understand you better than you think, Mr. Steele. I know you are not going to shoot me. That won't help your Miss Helen. Let us sit down and talk about this like gentlemen."

"I didn't come here to talk, General. I brought a proposal. If you let Helen and the other hostages go, I will stay to be your prisoner in exchange."

"A brave offer, Mr. Steele, but of what value would you be to me? A hostage must have negotiable worth."

"I understand that, but if you let the women go I also have a promise from Helen's father that he'll become your hostage again."

"Now that is a more interesting offer. How unfortunate that Miss Helen is already gone. I'm sorry. I truly am. She was a sweet girl. I enjoyed talking to her."

"Gone?" Steele pressed the gun hard against the general's head. "You're lying, Ramsey. You wouldn't give up your most valuable hostage."

"Be careful with that little pistol, Mr. Steele. You're hurting me. But it's true, I'm afraid she is no longer in my hands. Release me and hand your little revolver to my men. Then I will explain where she is."

"What have you done?" Steele pushed the barrel of the pistol even harder against Ramsey's head.

"Now, now, be calm, my boy. I have not laid a finger on her pretty little head. She has just gone . . . elsewhere. If you remove that strange little pistol from my temple, I will gladly explain. Otherwise, I will have to tell my men to shoot you."

"I don't need to remind you that if they shoot me you will also die instantly."

"You don't want to do that. If I die at your hands, I will become a martyr. My name will be a rallying cry for all those who believe in my cause. But you will also be dead and you will never learn what happened to your precious Helen."

Steele could hardly believe how calm Ramsey was acting. Was he really prepared to die? Few men could honestly say that.

"Good, I can see that you are thinking about my words. Come, let me show you around my camp. You will see that she is no longer here."

"All right. let's go," said Steele. "You lead the way." He released Ramsey, but kept his gun pointed at the back of his head.

The soldiers fell back as Ramsey led him through the bushes and into the camp. Steele was surprised to see how many men Ramsey had with him. They lined a path before them, some with the old Enfield rifles, but many with the new Winchesters.

"Notice that we have a good source of water," said Ramsey pointing out the small pond that reflected the flickering firelight. Steele saw reeds growing at one end of the pond and there were frogs croaking there. It meant it was a permanent water source.

"I have men positioned all along up there," said Ramsey, pointing toward the top of the cliff. "In addition to the Indian scouts you encountered. The sharpshooters stay up there all of the time, near the edge of the cliff. If we are attacked, they will already be in their sniper positions, ready to shoot down at the enemy. As you surely know, a good defensive strategy can be just as effective as a sound offense."

"I don't care about your strategy," said Steele. "Keep moving."

"But of course you do. You told me yourself you've been studying the war. You undoubtedly have been reading those ridiculous books written by the West Point generals who think they won the war. I think we have much to talk about. Many things have happened since we last talked."

When they arrived at a row of tents, the general stopped. "And this is where our women live. I think you'll agree, they are relatively comfortable here."

"Very kind of you to make them so comfortable after you took them hostage and brought them all the way here from Yuma," said Steele. He looked at the group of women who were squatted down in front of the tents tending two large blackened pots hung over a bed of glowing coals. "And I see that you are now referring to them as *your* women."

"Yes," said the general, "we like to think of them that way. Technically speaking, of course, they are still hostages, but here they are free to remain near their tents or go to . . . shall we say . . . socialize with the men. It is up to them. They cook their own food and sometimes they are nice enough to share it with us. They do as they want. As you can see, they are not restrained. It's not necessary to restrain prisoners here because there is no escape from this little valley. The ancestors of my new friend, Chief Cochise, chose this place well. He tells me he has warriors posted at strategic points all around us. Even I don't know where they all are, but I do know they are very, very watchful."

Steele could see that Helen wasn't among the women but he called out to them. "Where is Helen? Helen Kane. Have any of you seen her?"

One of the women, an older woman with graying hair, gazed at him for a moment before replying. "No, she's gone. Are you Drew Steele?"

"Yes, I am."

"She talked about you often, Mr. Steele. I'm sorry."

Steele turned back to Ramsey. "Why did she say she was sorry? What have you done with Helen?"

Ramsey turned to face him. "It's quite regrettable, Mr. Steele, at least from your point of view. But you see, Cochise has a son who is quite . . . aggressive. It was he who convinced his father to make an alliance with us. His name is Napiche and he took very keen notice of the beautiful Miss Helen. In fact, the young man was quite taken with her. Eventually he demanded her as payment for his cooperation, in addition to the fine new rifles of course. What else could I do? She was given as a token of my sincerity."

"You handed her over as if she was an animal to be traded." Steele pressed his gun against the old man's back. "I should kill you right now."

"But you won't, will you, Steele? The strategist in you understands the necessity for such things." Ramsey turned to face Steele, ignoring the pistol. He leaned close and whispered, "If Napiche was so naive as to be willing to make such an exchange for a mere woman, then he might be manipulatable in other ways. You see the advantage it gives me."

"You speak of strategic advantage. It sounds more like revenge to me. You did it after you found out your son had been killed."

"Revenge? For my son? My heroic son? Not at all, Mr. Steele. It was done because it had to be done. I needed that alliance. All my plans depend on it."

Steele met the general's steady eyes. Was Ramsey actually expecting him to understand, maybe even to appreciate his clever tactics? It was clear the general only thought of people in terms of advantage and disadvantage: to him, Helen was merely a pawn, a tool to be used to accomplish his purposes. But it meant there was still hope. Helen might still be nearby.

Ramsey was staring at him, waiting, as if he still expected Steele to agree, to compliment him on his wisdom. Two uniformed soldiers moved closer, their Winchester rifles aimed at his head. Steele knew they would fire immediately if he either shot Ramsey or tried to run. He had to make a decision. He had to think like Ramsey; he had to think strategically: there was a time to attack and a time to retreat. If Helen was being held nearby, he might be able to find some way to get her out. He turned and threw his pistol into the pond.

The two soldiers rushed forward to grab Steele's arms, but the general waved them away. "Now that's better, my boy. I knew you were an intelligent man."

"Did I have another option?"

"No, I'm afraid you did not. Given the situation, you made the wise decision. As I said to you once before, you would have made a good officer. I would have been proud to have you under my command."

"As you said, General, you had to think strategically. If the girl was what the Indian wanted, then why not use her?"

Ramsey smiled and shook his head. "So, now you are going to pretend to agree with my tactics. There is no need for such pretence. I know you cared for the girl. But you must see my position, whether you agree with it or not." He put his hand on Steele's shoulder. "Such are the obligations of war, my boy. But come, let us sit and talk for a while. Are you hungry?" He gestured toward the large cooking pots in front of the women's tents.

Steele shook his head.

With his hand resting on Steele's shoulder, Ramsey led him back toward the campfire. When they were seated, Ramsey asked his men to give them some time alone. The men got up and melted into the shadows. However, the two soldiers who had been following them stayed nearby, their rifles constantly aimed at him.

From a hand-carved box at his side, the general removed a clay pipe and filled it with tobacco. He pulled a twig out of the fire to light it and sat back to look at Steele, puffing contentedly. "You seem to have a penchant for small hidden weapons, Mr. Steele. Do you have others?"

"No."

"I'll accept your word as a gentleman on that," said Ramsey, puffing on his pipe as he studied Steele. "By the way, speaking of weapons, I'm sure you are curious about the weapon that brought the meaning of war to the fine citizens of Tucson. The cannon came all the way from Europe. It is a rifled German field piece, breech loading and very accurate. It's lightweight enough to be disassembled and carried on two pack mules. A remarkably effective tool for a fast-moving guerrilla force. Would you like to see it?"

Steele didn't answer. He waited, watching the general smoke his pipe. He did want to see the cannon–it was undoubtedly a fine weapon. But he didn't want to participate in the general's game of nonchalant conversation with his prisoner. It was too much like a cat toying with a trapped mouse. Was Ramsey keeping him alive just long enough to tell him about his clever strategy and his fancy new weapons of war?

"Tell me, Steele, how is the town reacting to their introduction to my kind of warfare? I'm very curious to know."

"The people of the town are quite unnerved, but you didn't need me to tell you that. I'm sure you have your spies."

"And I expect Major Carter is beside himself, isn't he?" said Ramsey, smiling. "Tell me, Steele, was the major in the war? Does he have any sense of strategy at all?"

"I believe he was at Petersburg in '64, probably with Wilson's raiders."

"Just as I suspected. A horse soldier. And he must have come late to the war, when it was safe to gather medals and promotions so he could go home a hero. I suspected as much. Tell me, is he cowering in his little wooden fort, hiding there as he waits to learn from whence the next attack will come?"

"I'm not privy to his plans," said Steele.

"Oh, but I expect you are. I'm told you have been a regular visitor to his office, and that you used your considerable medical skills to help his wounded soldiers. Very commendable, Mr. Steele."

"There were wounded civilians there also. Many were killed."

"Ah yes, unfortunate. But those are the exigencies of war, my boy. Now, as a student of such things, you must admit that it was an effective tactic."

"Attacking civilians? They were innocent people."

"Innocent? No, no, Mr. Steele, I hardly think so. The Westerners are a smug people, living quite comfortably in their little domiciles, reaping the benefits of their corrupt government. They have been living well off their ill-gotten gains, mindless of the sacrifice of their brethren of the South and the Indians from whom they took this land. Now they must pay for those benefits. It's only fair. They must pay."

"No honorable officer would have thought to bombard innocent civilians, not even during the darkest days of the war."

"And that was their mistake. The so-called leaders of the Confederacy did not bring the war to the people of the North. General Robert E. Lee sat up there on his fine horse and told us to fight an honorable war. He failed to realize there is no such thing as honor in war. I told him that. Bring the war to the people, I said. Make them pay and they will soon realize how much they have to lose. Our leaders did not make the people of the North understand the gravity of what Mr. Lincoln and his cronies were up to. I saw it then and I see it now. The fat and comfortable of the North were able to sit in their fine houses and go to their fine parties as if there was no war going on at all. Lincoln and his co-conspirators were able to convince them that the war was all about slavery. That was their ruse and it was easy for those in the North to get rich off the war while their brothers and sisters in the South suffered."

"That was quite a speech, General. You should have taken up politics."

"Maybe I will, my boy. When all this is over, maybe I will."

"You see yourself as a hero of the new South, do you?"

"Of course. And I am. If I survive this endeavor, I will enjoy seeing those fools grovel at my feet. When the South has risen again, when we have victoriously driven the Federals back to their serpent's lair in Washington, I will be carried back to my beloved Tennessee as the savior of a country, the man who showed them the way. But wait." He held up his hand. "Before you argue, or try to find some clever insult in a futile attempt to anger me, let us change the focus of our conversation to more pleasant things. For example, we could discuss how modern weapons can be effectively employed in my new approach to warfare."

"Does it really matter what I say, General? Why don't you just tell me what you're going to do with me?"

Ramsey looked at him, silently puffing on his pipe. Then he shook his head and looked away. "Too bad. I was looking forward to talking to you, a student of the war. But I'm afraid my time now runs short. It is regrettable that you must die, but I understand you, Steele. I know you would try to overcome me, even in the face of obvious defeat. And I know you would try to find your Helen and take her away from here. I cannot allow that. It would anger Napiche and he might begin to question our fragile alliance."

"So why haven't you killed me already?"

"There was no need to kill you right away. I thought we could have at least one quiet and uncontentious discussion before your time came. But let us agree to have no regrets. We all must go to see our maker sooner or later. You and I will meet again in the afterlife. Sometime, somewhere, I will fight my last battle. Then I will go to my Lord and Savior. He will welcome me and I will sit by His side and look down upon the world of men. And when that time comes, you and I will be friends again, up there." He pointed to the sky. "We will ride the hills of the hereafter together."

"So you expect to be welcomed up there, do you?" Steele mimicked the general's pointing at the sky. "Despite your deeds here on earth?"

Ramsey smiled pleasantly. "Of course. I have done my duty as a soldier, and as a patriot. I have shown unrelenting loyalty to my country. I fully expect to be rewarded for that."

"You have a very different view of such things than I," said Steele quietly.

"Ah yes, I was told you were an educated man. As a result, you force yourself to believe in reason, in science. But you will see the truth when it is your time. There is a higher power and a higher meaning to all this. You will look down from above and see how insignificant you were. You will wait for me and then we will sit together up there and be friends, not combatants, observing how it all plays out down below."

"And how do you think it will play out, General? You think you have a perfectly defensible hiding place here in the mountains, but it is also a trap. Eventually you will be found and the Army will lay siege to this place."

"Now, now, do you take me for such a fool, Mr. Steele? The Army has been looking for this secret place for years. I'm sure you must have sent your friend Rudd for help, but I expect by now my Indian allies have intercepted him. Their task is to roam and watch. No one comes or goes in this area without Cochise knowing about it. And what he knows he tells me. I'm afraid your friend is no more. By now one of the young braves will have his scalp hanging from his belt."

Was he bluffing? Steele had neither seen nor heard any Indians as they approached the cliff. But they had approached from the north, not from the direction of the city. Maybe the young warriors had intercepted Rudd on his way down. Steele felt a strong pang of regret for bringing Rudd into this. Had poor Rudd ridden all that way, suffered saddle sores and gone without food and sleep, just to die on a lonely mountainside in Arizona?

"Ah, I can see from your silence that you *were* hoping for rescue, weren't you? Unfortunately, there will be no one coming to save you. Even if the Army did learn we were up here, they could do little about it. My men can hold out for as long as necessary. It would be something of a siege, but in the end it would be as futile as McClellan's foolhardy attempt to capture the peninsula."

"Surely you know that in a siege, history favors the attacker," said Steele. "In fact, it's odd you mention the peninsula. Some of the fortifications used by Magruder were left over from the defensive positions of the British during the Revolutionary War. Remember? The Colonists successful siege against Cornwallis there helped to determine the outcome of that war."

Ramsey stroked his beard as he looked at Steele. "You certainly know your history, my boy. But no one has ever had such a completely defensible position as this. If the Army was to attack this place, history would remember how long my brave men defended it. It would become one of those significant moments in history, a rallying battle that would unite the Confederacy, just as the last stand of the Texans at the Alamo united them against Santa Anna. I expect they would build a monument at the base of the cliff."

Steele shook his head. "History will not remember this place. History will remember the siege at Vicksburg. It, along with Gettysburg, will rightfully be remembered as the two battles that signaled the turning of the war in favor of the Union. Your little renegade army here will not even rate a footnote."

Ramsey was no longer smiling. With more than a touch of irritation beginning to show in his voice, he said, "You are wrong, Mr. Steele. While those poorly planned and ineptly executed battles you mentioned were the turning point in the *eastern* theater of the war, history will remember me as the one who refused to let such incompetence result in the end of a proud and glorious country. The *western* theater, the ground upon which we now stand, will be remembered as the place where it all began again, where the new confederacy of Southern and Western states showed the real path to renewed glory. Here is where it will begin, Mr. Steele. This forlorn mountain, surrounded by the dry desert and cactus, will be known as the birthplace of the new Confederacy."

"So is that the point of all this? Is that why you gathered your renegade army here? To have someone build a monument to you? Surely you didn't bombard and kill the innocent citizens of Tucson just for that."

"Can it be that you have failed to grasp the significance of all this? And you think of yourself as a man of reason. Look around you, Mr. Steele. See how my force has already grown."

"So you have a few more men. How will that help you, cowering up here in the mountains?"

"Do not try to bait me, Steele. Surely you must understand that this little force is only the advance guard. We are the emerging voice of the new South and we will be heard. We have already been heard. Our rallying cry out here will lead to a thunderous roar that will be heard across the country. What you don't understand is that I have already accomplished my purpose."

"By forming an alliance with a band of renegade Indians? You tried to form an alliance with Medina's militia and that didn't work. What makes you think your alliance with the Indians will work any better?"

"What makes you think my alliance with Colonel Medina didn't work?"

"I saw the results back at your camp in Mexico. Many died back there, on both sides."

The general nodded thoughtfully. "Sometimes disputes and misunderstandings have to be worked out with . . . aggressive methods."

"So you *are* still working together, but as separate forces. I saw how his soldiers set fires along the border to distract the army while you moved north. And tonight there was an attack on Tucson. That must have been Medina's force, in concert with your little German cannon. But I don't see what that was supposed to accomplish."

Steele watched the general as he calmly dragged a twig out of the fire to relight his pipe. When it was lit, he leaned back and looked at Steele. "Are you still attempting to gather information, even at this late hour?"

"I'm just curious. If you're going to kill me anyhow, what does it matter?"

Ramsey continued to look at Steele for some time. Then he said, "I will satisfy your curiosity, my boy. There's no reason not to now. Tell me, have you studied the tactics of Napoleon?"

"I've read a little about that period."

"And did he not form alliances with his neighboring countries while he built up his armies?"

"So these alliances are only temporary while you build up your forces? Do you plan to turn against the Mexicans when you're finished with them, just as Napoleon turned against his ally, Spain."

"It is not so simple, Mr. Steele. You always jump to the most obvious conclusion. There are alliances and then there are alliances."

"What does that mean? Are you referring to Napoleon's brother, Joseph? Does Medina have political ambitions in Mexico?"

"Very astute. Indeed he does. In fact, Medina plans to be the next President of Mexico, based on his recapture of at least some of the stolen Arizona and California territory. Oh, how I wish you and I could have worked together. You have a fine mind for military strategy."

"So Medina has political allies in Mexico, and I assume, also in Spain. They are the ones supplying you with weapons, using the old Spanish missions."

"Now your mind is racing ahead. In fact, the real truth is much larger than you realize." He smiled and leaned closer. "Why do you suppose I came all the way out here to form these alliances? Did you really think my goals had anything to do with this worthless desert?"

"So you do plan to take your fight back to the South. Then what is the purpose of your attacks on Yuma and Tucson? Are you trying to draw the Army out here?"

"Yes, of course, but it is more than that. Think about the need for coordination in war. The Mexicans and the Indians are but two groups that stand in opposition to the fragile Federal government. I say fragile because that government cannot stand now that we have successfully eliminated Mr. Lincoln."

"So you plan to bring other groups into your alliance?"

Ramsey shook his head. "Not plan, Mr. Steele, planned. It has already been accomplished. The Mexicans were among the last to be added. What the Federals didn't foresee was the extent of the unrest in the South. Due to the injustices of the occupation, many former soldiers were eager to find a capable leader to take up the fight again. I built my alliances carefully before I came out here. There is a secret network of Confederate officers already in place throughout the South. They are reorganizing, bringing together their most loyal men. They are waiting in the hills, from Tennessee to West Virginia, ready to strike. They have been preparing and training since the end of the war. By now, they have all learned to use the fine new weapons I have provided."

Ramsey sat back and puffed on his pipe, waiting for Steele's response. He seemed genuinely proud. He must have been waiting for an opportunity to tell someone about his glorious plan. Steele knew it meant the general didn't intend to keep him alive much longer. The only way he could extend his time was to keep the general talking. As long as he was alive, he might get a chance to at least pass the information along to someone. Maybe he could get word to Helen through the other women hostages. Then, when the Army came, she could warn them about Ramsey's plan.

"Thinking it all through, Mr. Steele?" said Ramsey, interrupting his thoughts. "You look troubled."

"I'm trying to decide if what you say could be true. It sounds like the hopeful dream of a defeated patriot. Do you really think you can restart the war? Even if you could mount your style of guerrilla warfare with some quick strikes to scare the people back east, how can you hope to coordinate all those disparate groups when you couldn't even keep Medina's Mexicans in line?"

"Colonel Medina's militia, and my other disparate groups, as you call them, are all allied in our opposition to a corrupt and illegal government in Washington. That is all the coordination we need. Every man is loyal to that cause, and they all know I am the one to lead them to victory."

"I keep thinking about the soldiers you say you've been gathering together back in the South. It sounds like a bunch of disgruntled men who can't face defeat. I can imagine them back there, hiding in the hills, sitting around campfires just like this one, polishing their beautiful new weapons and talking about how heroic they were back in the good old days of the Civil War."

"It matters little now what you think, Mr. Steele. The wheel is already in motion. The final phase took place yesterday when nearly all of the Federal Army units that are still under arms back East were loaded onto trains to head this way. They think they are coming west to deal with Mexican border raiders and a troublesome band of renegade Confederates somewhere in Arizona. But they are actually being led away from where the real fighting will be. That was why a few of the fine citizens of Tucson had to die, to be sure the Federals would act. As soon as we received confirmation that the trains were moving this way, my network of sympathetic newspapers and linked community groups began passing the word throughout the Confederacy. Tonight I will take a few of my most trusted men and go to Texas to coordinate the next phase of my new type of war. It is set to begin in two days, on the anniversary of my greatest victory at Chickamauga Creek."

"Your great victory at Chickamauga Creek? How can you call it a victory when it cost the Confederacy eighteen thousand men? That little stream is still known as the river of death. In the end, all it did was help force Lincoln to replace Rosecrans with Ulysses S. Grant. After that, you never had another significant victory in Tennessee."

The general was no longer smiling. "River of death? How dare you use that phrase in front of me? If it was a river of death it was because it flowed with the blood of Granger's troops, not mine. If Longstreet had done what I said . . ." He stopped and spat into the fire. Then he turned back to Steele. "But that is all in the past. It matters little now, and I will speak no more of it. Such things are best left to the book-writing puppets and magazine braggarts. *My* history, the history of my real victories, will begin two days from now, as soon as I arrive in Texas to coordinate the attacks. At my command, all of my allied soldiers will strike as one. From the Cubans in Florida to the Basques in Louisiana, they will all strike at the same moment. The loyal sons of the Confederacy have been waiting for this moment. I have far more men in uniform than you can imagine. The Federal's repressive *reconstruction*, as they call it, provided all the recruiting incentive I needed. Medina's Mexicans and my Indian allies will keep the Federal troops busy here in the West while my guerrillas take over key positions in the east. My well-trained soldiers will work in concert with my new allies to begin a new kind of war, something the world has never before seen, a war of coordinated terror. We will bring panic and fear to the fat and complacent city dwellers of the North. They will all feel my wrath. Units are already in place in the woods and fields near their largest cities. They all have those remarkable little German cannons and you have seen what that type of weapon can do to a city. We will bring them all to their knees."

"And who will profit from that, General? Does whoever is supplying you with weapons and money really want the North defeated? We both know there are no arms manufactures in the South or in the West."

Ramsey nodded, smiling. "So, you begin to understand."

"I understand who would benefit by arming you. The war profiteers. They can pretend to sell weapons to Spain, knowing they will come back to you through Mexico. The Northern war profiteers were nearly put out of business when the war ended. It makes sense they would be eager to supply you with those brand new weapons. They want you to extend the war so they can continue to make those huge wartime profits. If you have any success at all, they know the war will start again so they can go back to selling weapons to both sides. And this time they will also get to sell additional weapons to Spain and Mexico. But one thing puzzles me, General, how can you justify lining the pockets of the very people who helped defeat you?"

"As much as I doubt the sincerity of your question, Mr. Steele, I will answer it. In the end, my most satisfying victory will be over them, the greedy vultures who feed off of the victims of war. One of our first targets is to be the arms manufacturers themselves. Skilled teams of night fighters are ready to sweep into their factories and carry away their equipment and their technicians. We will build our own secret factories in the new Confederacy. We will become arms merchants ourselves, but we will supply only our allies. We will immediately cut off the flow of weapons to the Federals and any nation that might consider supporting them."

Steele realized that an attack on the weapons manufacturers was the most dangerous aspect of the general's entire plan. Small groups of guerrillas hiding in the hills would be very difficult to root out, but they would not pose that great a threat without a good supply of weapons. If Ramsey could continue to put an unlimited number of weapons into the hands of any dissatisfied former soldier who agreed to join his guerrillas, he might well begin a long war of unpredictable attacks and retaliations. Napoleon's failure in Russia proved you cannot defeat guerrillas on their own ground if they have access to enough weapons.

"I see by your silence that you have finally begun to understand the brilliance of my plan, Mr. Steele. You are undoubtedly realizing that the soldiers of the North have already gone back to their farms and factory jobs. Their so-called military leaders have all taken off their uniforms to become fat and lazy politicians. Many of their political leaders have abandoned their posts to go on the lecture circuit where they tell the people how brilliant they were in defeating a poorly prepared and poorly led Confederacy. The people of the North are completely unprotected. We will sweep over them like a plague."

"No, General, that is not what I was thinking. I was thinking your plan is doomed to fail. It is far too grandiose to have any chance of success. You are depending on widespread and uncoordinated groups to act in concert. As you yourself saw at Palmyra Crossing, things change during a battle. Strong and decisive leadership must react to those changes immediately."

"Wheeler was a fool at Palmyra. He should have had a contingency plan in case the Federals discovered he was at the river. Besides, this will be a very different kind of war. In this war, I will be totally in charge. There will be but one man directing it all, a military man, not some overweening, untrained politician elected by less than a majority of his own cohorts. That is the true genius of my guerrilla war, Mr. Steele, the alliance of many different individual groups, acting independently, with one military mind to direct it all."

Steele looked away. He understood that Ramsey's kind of war could be effective. But he also understood that Ramsey's own ego had created the flaw in his plan: by setting himself up as the sole coordinating authority he had introduced a vulnerable link in the chain. Paradoxically, even though he was the one remaining Confederate general still willing to fight, he was garnering too much power and control in his own hands. If Steele could find a way to stop him, the general's entire plan would be halted before it even got started. Steele looked at Ramsey. He was only three feet away. Without a weapon, he might not be able to kill the general, but with a quick strike, he might be able be able to at disable him. He glanced at the two guards. They were still watching him closely, their rifles ready. By the time he looked back at Ramsey, the general had drawn his pistol. He was smiling, as if to say he could anticipate Steele's every move.

"Lost your tongue, have you Mr. Steele? Well, I can't blame you. There is nothing you can do and therefore nothing you can say. And I regret this is to be the end of our very interesting discussion. I must now go to meet with my men before I leave for Texas. I expect my brief artillery attack on Tucson will have accomplished its purpose of drawing Major Carter's little force up into these mountains. Colonel Medina's men will be waiting there to annihilate them. As soon as the Cavalry is wiped out, Medina will have his way with the fine citizens of Tucson. It will be the first Western city to once again be under the flag of Mexico."

Steele shook his head. "You don't really mean to tell me you think Medina can hold a city the size of Tucson. You said yourself more troops are already on their way west."

"Medina only has to hold Tucson for a short time and the news of war in the West will flash across the entire continent. Across the world. It will be the rallying signal that will unite the disaffected in the South and elsewhere. It will bring them all together like nothing else can. Medina will lose Tucson eventually, but the battle will have served my purpose."

"It won't work, General. The rest of the country pays little attention to what goes on in the West, unless it has to do with outlaws or gold discoveries. They will see it for what it is, a bunch of troublesome Mexicans coming across the border to plunder. Another minor flare up out West, a bother, not a war."

Ramsey looking thoughtful. Then he smiled. "You are trying to aggravate me, aren't you? But you are wrong. The country *will* take notice when they learn it is the Confederate Army that is in action in the West. They will take notice because my chain of loyal newspapers in the South are ready to report the story the moment my plan begins."

"Does anyone still read the disaffected voices of Southern newspapers? The people of San Francisco closed down the Secessionist Press when they continued to print anti- unionist news. The same thing happened throughout the country."

"I'm afraid I have no more time for your quibbling, Steele." He tapped the burnt tobacco out of his pipe and stood up. "I will give you a few minutes to make peace with your maker, then I will come with five men. I will give you the honor of a full military firing squad." He signaled to the two guards and they came forward. "Take Mr. Steele to the punishment pole. Tie him securely there. If he tries to say a word to you, gag him. Do not take your eyes off of him. I will bring a firing squad in a few minutes."

"So you're going to murder me?" said Steele, standing up. "What happened to your sense of military order? If you really do represent the new Confederacy, I should be considered a prisoner of war."

"A prisoner of war, Mr. Steele? I'm afraid in a guerrilla war there is no such thing. A true soldier in my kind of war will expect to fight to the death. Next you will be asking for a formal trial. But I ask you, did they give my son a trial? He was a hero of the Confederacy and they shot him down like a dog."

"You don't know that, general. I was told your son was--"

"Silence. I do not wish to speak of my son. He is dead and they will all pay. I am the law here and the sole authority. You came in the night dressed as a spy and you shall be executed as a spy. Good night, Mr. Steele."

Ramsey walked away and the two guards led Steele to a pole in the middle of a clearing at the upper end of the camp. The larger of the two guards tore off Steele's shirt and pushed his face up against Steele's. "You are an insult to this uniform," he growled. "I will enjoy watching you die."

He roughly pulled Steele's hands back and tied them together behind the pole. Then he put a leather cord around Steele's neck, pulling it so tight against the pole it left him barely able to turn his head. That guard took up a position nearby to watch him while the other man fetched wood to start a fire. Once the fire was going, they sat down, but they never took their eyes off of Steele. Steele wondered if either of the men had ever been tied to the pole, maybe as punishment for some minor transgression against Ramsey's orders. He decided to try speaking to them. "Listen, men, did you know Ramsey plans to leave you here while he escapes? You'll die on this mountain, you and all the others. You should get out of here before it's too late."

Both of the guards jumped up and ran toward him. The big man struck Steele in the side of the head with the butt of his rifle. There was an intense flash of pain and for a moment all Steele could see was a confusing blur of movement. His ears were ringing as he felt them force a gag into his mouth. He blinked his eyes to try to clear them, but it didn't work. He felt blood running down the side of his head onto his shoulder. It felt cool in the night air.

By the time his eyes cleared, the two guards were back sitting by the fire, their rifles resting across their legs. Steele tried to slide down the pole so he could at least sit down, but the leather around his neck was too tight. He kept his eyes on the guards, feeling the throbbing pain in the side of his head.

The two guards calmly stared back at him. After a few moments, the big one raised his rifle to point it at Steele. "Bang," he whispered.

Steele turned his head to the side as much as he could to get the pressure off his Adam's apple. Then, keeping his eyes on the guards, he began to strain against the leather cord around his neck, hoping the combination of sweat and constant pressure might loosen it a little. Eventually the leather did stretch just enough to allow him to turn his head back and forth. The guards didn't notice; they were talking in low tones, both poking at the fire with sticks. Steele looked off toward the flickering firelight of the Indian campfires in the distance. Was Helen there? He wondered if someone had told her he was in the Confederate camp. He hoped so. At least she would know he had come to try to save her.

He relaxed his muscles as much as he could and let the ropes hold his weight. The rough wood of the pole dug into his back, but he tried to ignore it. His ribs ached, but he knew pain didn't really matter now. Ramsey would soon come to kill him.

Being careful not to show any movement that the guards could see, he began to work at the ropes around his wrists. He could feel that they were bound very tightly behind the pole. How much time did he have? The General would probably want to slip out of the camp while it was still dark. Steele glanced up at the stars. Only a few hours before dawn. He worked at the rough ropes, but he wasn't having much success. His wrists were feeling raw.

He was still working on the ropes when he heard the first shell go over. He recognized it immediately as a shell from a Parrott cannon, making its familiar sound, like the planing of a board in a sawmill. He closed his eyes and waited for it to hit.

The shell exploded against the hillside beyond the camp, creating a flash that was bright even behind his closed eyelids. The sharp shock wave blew past him and reverberated back again from the cliff. It meant Rudd had gotten through to the Army and they had come back and found the tunnel. The major would use normal wartime tactics, cannon fire followed by a swarming attack.

Steele opened his eyes to see the reaction of the two guards. They were both on their feet, but they seemed frozen in place, unable to decide what to do. The second shell hit much closer and the guards ran for the protection of the rocks. As more shells came, Steele saw that many of the Confederates were running toward the cliff. Were they going to fight? Or were they just heading for cover?

Between explosions, Steele could hear rapid gunfire from Ramsey's snipers up on top of the cliff. More and more shells screamed in. Most of them exploded farther up the hill, but a few were hitting in the middle of the camp sending the Confederates running in all directions.

Another shell sailed over his head and hit against the mountainside, then another hit a short distance to his right, then another farther on. Steele realized the major was using a spread pattern to cover the entire area. Sooner or later, the firing pattern would work it's way back to where he was and that would be it for him. Smoke was enveloping the entire camp. He heard the gunfire from the area of the cliff intensify. Soon, it was almost constant and there was answering fire that was just as intense.

A shell hit close behind him and Steele felt something hot against the back of his shoulder. He'd been hit, but with his hands tied there was no way to determine how serious the wound was.

Another shell hit even closer and he was amazed he hadn't been hit by shrapnel again. He gave up pulling at the ropes; his wrists were raw and the ropes were just too tight. All he could do was wait and listen to the shriek of the incoming shells and the explosions that followed. Major Carter was using artillery to soften up Ramsey's position. A sound strategy, but one that was mindless of the safely of the hostages. The major would undoubtedly say the lives of a few hostages could not be allowed to hinder a surprise attack. He would go by the book. Thousands had died in the war in the name of sound strategy so what were a few more deaths?

More and more shells came and Steele knew it was only a matter of time before one of them got him. As he thought about it, he realized it wasn't a bad way to die. After all, he should have died many times during the war. He had been lucky too many times. Hopefully, the major would be able to overcome Ramsey and his death would be one of the last deaths in this particular war. As he calmly watched and listened to the sounds of exploding shells all around him, Steele didn't regret the decisions he had made in his life. He could not be sad about his intentional search for danger and adventure, even though it had led him to this moment. He had followed the battles during the war to try to understand why men did such things, but he had to admit he also found something there that attracted him, something that pulled him back to it, again and again.

He thought about Stacy off there in Europe. She would miss him, but she would do all right without him. He thought about his parents in London. Would they ever learn what had happened to him?

He thought about Helen. If he had one regret, it was that he hadn't been able to save her. McNeil had used his final breath to say, 'If you love that girl, don't ever let her get away.' If only he could have had some time to get to know her better. She was a beautiful young woman, full of life. He hoped she would survive this and that the Army would rescue her from the Indians.

He sensed somebody behind him. Was it Ramsey come to kill him? Then suddenly, his hands were free. Someone had cut him loose. He tried to turn and peer through the smoke and the darkness to see who it was but the leather strap around his neck prevented it. He strained at the leather. But then it was also gone.

He ripped the gag out of his mouth and turned to see who had freed him. There was so much smoke he could only see that it was a lone figure standing there in the dark, holding a long knife. Then he heard her voice. "You didn't come, Drew. I waited and waited. Why didn't you come?"

Chapter 26

*T*he smoke cleared and he saw her. It was Helen, alive and apparently uninjured. He reached out to pull her to him, holding her tight, not wanting to let her go.

Another shell landed nearby and Helen tried to push him away. "Let me go, Drew. We're going to get killed if we stay here."

Steele looked at her, smiling. He couldn't stop smiling. She looked fine, dressed in a thick, colorful robe-like dress that left her shoulders bare. Oddly she looked somewhat older, and very tired. But that didn't matter. She was alive and she was right there with him. "You look beautiful," he said.

She ducked as another shell exploded in the middle of the pond, but Steele hardly noticed it. All he wanted to do was look at her.

She took his hand and pulled him. "Come on. We've got to get out of here."

She led him past the pond and up the steep slope. They stumbled over rocks and low shrubs in the darkness and the smoke, but they kept going. Steele's ribs hurt and his shoulder where he'd been hit with shrapnel was probably bleeding, but that didn't matter; he was alive and he was with Helen.

She seemed to know where she was going so he let her lead. Eventually, they made it far enough away from the explosions to stop and catch their breath. Leaning forward and gasping, Helen put her small hand against his chest and looked up at him. "One of the other women told me they'd caught you. I knew they'd tie you to that punishment pole. If you weren't going to come save me, I figured it was up to me to save you."

Now that they were away from the smoke, he could finally get a better look at her. The moonlight cast her face in shadows, making her appear very sad. All he could think to do was to grab her and kiss her. So he did.

She didn't resist, but she pulled away sooner than he would have liked. "We have to keep going, Drew. Napiche will come. He's the chief's son. He ran off to fight when the shelling started, but I know he'll come looking for me."

She tried to pull Steele farther up the hill, but he held her back and took her face in his hands. "Ramsey told me what happened, Helen. I'm sorry. I'm so sorry. I wish I could have found you sooner."

"But you didn't, did you? After I found that handkerchief that night, I thought you would come back for me. When no one was looking, I took axle grease from the wagon wheel and put it on my wrists. It wanted to have those shackles off when you came for me. But they were too tight. I was so sure you would come back, I pulled and pulled until one of them finally came off, but it hurt my wrist."

She held out her arm to show him. Steele couldn't see very well in the pale moonlight, but he ran his fingers along her wrist and felt the wounded flesh. It made his heart ache to think of her pulling with such ferocity against the cold steel of the shackles. He kissed her wrist gently and whispered, "I'm sorry, Helen. I should have found a way to rescue you."

She leaned against his chest and put her arms around his waist. She started to quietly weep. "Why didn't you come, Drew? I waited for you. I waited so long."

""I'm sorry," he whispered. "Ramsey sent the handkerchief back to me with a warning to stay away. He said he'd kill you."

She pulled back and wiped her eyes with the back of her hand. "He's a cruel man, but he pretends not to be. He came to talk to me all the time, acting like he cared about me, talking soft like he does. The night I pulled off one of the shackles, he came and discovered it. I was bleeding, but he put those terrible things right back on me, even tighter. He didn't care how much it hurt. When we were on the move, he came to talk to me almost every night, saying he was my friend, talking on and on about his dead wife, about his stupid son. But all the time he was planning to give me to that animal."

"Yes," said Steele softly. "He told me he liked to talk to you. But I think he's gone crazy. He's planning to start the war all over again."

"The hell with him, the hell with the war." She took Steele's hands. "Come on. Let's go up higher and forget about them. Let them all kill each other off. I don't care."

She started up the hill, and for the first time, he noticed she was barefoot. He caught her arm. "Helen, you don't have any shoes on. It's rocky up here. And there's cactus. Maybe we should wait here."

She looked down at her feet. "I don't need shoes. My feet are getting tough. Napiche won't let me wear shoes. And he only lets me wear this . . . robe thing. There's nothing under it so anytime he wants to he can . . . " She turned away. "I don't want to think about him . . . anymore. I don't want to think about him ever again."

As she led him farther up the hill, Steele thought about what she had been through. She had been the daughter of a rich man, living a pampered life. Would she ever be able to find her way back into that life again? Would the sadness and anger that now marked her face ever go away?

They continued on up the rocky slope until they were well away from the valley. Steele stopped to look back down toward the camp. The fighting was still going on, but there was no way to tell who was winning. He wondered if Ramsey was still alive. As long as the battle continued, Ramsey wouldn't be able to escape through the tunnel and he'd said there was no other way out. But was that true? Maybe the Indians knew another way.

"Come on," said Helen. "There's no use looking back. There's nothing you can do down there."

Climbing ever upward in the cool night with Helen's hand in his, Steele began to feel almost peaceful. Despite the distant booming of artillery and the frequent crack of rifle fire, he was with Helen and that was all that mattered for the moment. She led him higher and higher, as if she was trying to get so far away she wouldn't have to think about any of it ever again.

But soon they came to a sheer cliff. They moved along the base of it until they came to a ledge that overhung a deep canyon. There was no way to go on. Below them was a sheer drop of hundreds of feet. Was this what Ramsey was thinking about when he said there was no way out?

Steele pulled Helen back from the edge. "We'll have to wait here until it gets light. Maybe we can find a way out in the morning."

She shook her head. "Napiche said there is no way out, no way for me to escape. He said this little valley is a magical place, created by the ancestors."

Steele led her to a place between the rocks that was sheltered from the cool night breeze. They sat down and huddled together. "Our biggest problem is that there's no water up here," he said. "If Ramsey can hold out against the Army for a long siege, we'll have to go back down to get water."

Helen shook her head. "I'm not going back down if Napiche is still alive. I'd rather die of thirst."

Steele didn't know what to say, so he just held her. She was trembling, but he knew it wasn't because she was cold. He held her close against his bare chest and kissed her hair softly. Finally, she started to cry, quietly at first, but then harder, crying and moaning, rocking in his arms. He just held her tight, hoping she would be able to cry away all of the pain.

Then the shelling suddenly stopped. She lifted her head to look in that direction. "They've stopped. What does it mean?"

"It means the Army will attack now."

At first there were only a few shots, then more and more, until it sounded like everyone down there was firing all at once. Steele knew it meant Major Carter's troops were trying to fight their way into the valley. Because Ramsey had such a clear defensive advantage, it was smart of the major to try to fight his way in before the dawn came.

Helen looked back at him. Her eyes glistened with tears in the moonlight. "Have you seen my father? Is he all right?"

"Yes, he's in Tucson. He was fine the last time I saw him, but he's very worried about you."

"Is his leg all right? He hurt it back at the Mexican camp."

"Yes, it's fine now. You know, Helen, he loves you very much. He offered to exchange himself for you."

"He did? But I'm not really surprised. He was really brave when we were being held down there in Mexico. Are you sure he's all right? Ramsey told me he'd attacked the city with some kind of wonderful cannon. He gloated about it, said he had the whole town in a panic. Were many people hurt there?"

"I'm afraid so. Many were hurt and some were killed, both soldiers and civilians."

"He said he was going to do that. He didn't care how many–"

"Wait," whispered Steele. "Something moved down there."

They both leaned forward to try to see what it was. Steele couldn't see anything except bushes and rocks on the mountainside below. Maybe it had just been a rabbit, or a bush sent tumbling in the gentle breeze.

But then something in the shadows moved. It looked like a man, crouched down, moving slowly up the slope. The figure stopped near some rocks, but after a few seconds, he started moving again, coming up, heading right toward them.

"It's him," whispered Helen. "It's Napiche. I knew he'd come. He's not a normal person. He's . . . " The shadow rose up. Had he heard her?

"Ay-lin? Donde está?"

Helen grabbed Steele's arm. "It is him. Don't let him get me, Drew. I won't go back with him. I'll jump off that ledge before I'll go with him. I swear I will."

"Don't move," whispered Steele. "Stay right here." He stood up.

"No, don't go" she whispered, trying to pull him back down. "He'll kill you."

"Do you still have that knife?" whispered Steele.

"What?"

"The knife. The knife you used to cut me loose."

"No. I . . . I don't know where it went. The explosions . . . I guess I dropped it somewhere."

"Ay-lin," came the voice again. *"Vuelva!"*

"That means get back here," she whispered. "He says it to me all the time. He can't even say my name right. Aylin, he calls me. He won't let me get ten feet away. He's afraid the other warriors will want me and he'll have to share me. His old wife hates me. She beats me. When I try to fight back he takes her side and hurts me. He . . . "

Steele didn't want to take his eyes off of the shadow below, but he glanced at Helen and saw that she had pulled her knees up, as if she was trying to curl herself into a ball. "Listen, Helen," he whispered. "I'll try to stop him, but he may have a weapon. If he kills me, you have to go with him. It will only be for a little while. The Army will come for you. Do you understand?"

"No, I won't go back with him. I'll kill myself first. I mean it."

Steele took her by the shoulders. "Helen, listen to me. You have to stay alive. Promise me you'll stay alive."

She seemed calmer, now staring at him. "Will you promise?" he repeated.

She slowly shook her head. "No, I won't go with him." Her voice was remarkably steady and calm. "It doesn't matter if the Army comes. What do I have to go back to? I'm . . . soiled. No man would want me now."

Steele glanced back down at the shadow. It was beginning to work its way up toward them. "Ay-lin? *Donde está?*"

Steele cupped her chin in his hand. "Oh, my beautiful girl, don't you know any man would want you? I want you. You are still the same beautiful young woman you were before. No matter what happens, you have to stay alive. Think of the future. Think of your parents. Your mother misses you very much."

That made her break down and start crying again. She put her hands over her face and rocked back and forth, crying so hard she could hardly catch her breath. She reached out blindly to cling to Steele's hands. "Stay with me. Don't go."

Steele looked back at the figure who was still coming up the hill. "Alright," he whispered. "We'll face him together." He pulled her to her feet. "Does he speak English?"

"A little," she said, wiping her eyes as she tried to stop crying. "Mostly Spanish . . . I think."

Steele kept Helen behind him as he turned to face the approaching figure. When the man got close, he stopped and stood very still, looking at them.

Steele could see him clearly in the moonlight. Napiche was not a big man, but he had a knife in his right hand and he looked very strong. He was dressed in a loose fitting, open shirt. He had long dark hair, held by a headband.

Steele called out: "She doesn't want to go with you. *Ella no quiere ir con uste*d. I won't let you take her."

Napiche did not reply. Instead, he held out the knife and went into a crouch. He moved to the side, stealthy, like an agile animal. Steele decided his best chance was to get close, use his size and strength to try to get the knife away from him.

The Indian began to move in, maintaining his crouch. He feinted once with the knife, but Steele didn't react; he held his ground and kept his eyes on the silver gleam of that blade in the moonlight. The Indian jabbed again. Another feint, then he began to move closer. Steele tried to slowly move back, but discovered Helen close behind him, hindering his movement. "Helen," he whispered. "Move away from me. Stay back."

He felt her move away. He glanced back and saw that she was moving toward the exposed ledge. "No," he whispered. "Don't go out there."

She continued in that direction.

The Indian was moving slowly forward, forcing Steele to also retreat toward the ledge. Napiche was holding the knife out as he came, ready to lunge forward for a quick thrust, but Steele saw that his palm was up. It meant when he struck, the blade would be vertical. If it hit Steele in the chest that way, it wouldn't go between his ribs, and if the man's first strike didn't penetrate his chest, he might be get ahold of the Indian. But Steele knew he would have to act at the same instant the knife came, making sure the blade hit him in the upper chest, not the stomach. The Indian was young and he looked nervous. Steele could only hope he didn't have enough experience to turn the blade sideways as it hit.

Steele saw the flash of the blade as the Indian lunged at him. When he felt the knife make contact with his chest, he fell backward and at the same time he grabbed for Napiche's loose shirt. He felt pain as the knife made contact with his ribs, but he was able to get a good grip on Napiche's shirt with both hands. He let himself fall backward, pulling the man down with him, but he kept his knees up between them. As soon as he felt the Indian falling forward, he kicked out hard with both legs and Napiche was sent flying over his head. Steele quickly flipped over and saw that Napiche was on his stomach, desperately trying to keep from sliding off the ledge. Steele watched as the man found a crack in the rock and for a moment it looked as if he might somehow be able to save himself. But then Helen was there. She picked up the Indian's knife and moved slowly forward, holding it high. As she advanced on Napiche, she was murmuring something. It got louder and louder until Steele could hear the two words she was repeating over and over: "Never again. Never again. Never again."

Steele jumped up and shouted, "Helen, no." But it was too late. She swung the knife down at the Indian's hands, but missed and struck the rock, causing a spark in the night. She lifted the knife again and the Indian held up his hand to ward off the blow. That movement caused him to lose his grip and he slowly began to slide backward over the edge. He scratched desperately at the rock, as if he might dig into it with his fingernails. But he couldn't stop sliding; he went over the edge, but didn't begin screaming until he was halfway down. In the night, as the sound of his scream faded away, it sounded like the forlorn wail of an animal in anguish. When the cry was suddenly cut off, Steele knew the man had hit the rocks far below.

Helen was teetering on the edge, looking down into the darkness, still holding the knife. Steele moved carefully forward, making sure he didn't startle her. When he was close enough he stepped forward and got his arm around her waist. He firmly moved her away from the ledge and back to where they could again sit down against the rock wall. Her hands were shaking as he gently pried her fingers loose and took the knife away from her. He placed it on the ground and turned back to comfort her.

She cried against his shoulder for some time before she managed to recover. Then she sat up and touched his chest. "Oh, Drew, is that blood? Did he stab you?"

"I don't think it's serious.

"Oh no, let me see."

"Put some direct pressure on it," he said. "They took my shirt, but that handkerchief should still be in my pocket."

She pulled it out and folded it. He took the handkerchief and pushed it hard against the wound, trying to stop as much of the blood flow as he could. "It's too dark to do anything about it tonight," he said softly. "We can look at it in the morning."

She put her head down on his lap and let out a long sigh. "Lets just stay here forever, can't we? Let's not ever go back."

Steele stroked her hair, watching the setting moon. As it moved down closer to the western horizon, it began to take on a rusty color. Despite his injuries, and despite what they had been through, the sight of that colorful moon gave him a peaceful feeling. He looked down toward the camp far below, but it was too dark to see what was going on down there. There was an occasional sound of a rifle shot, but the fierce fighting seemed to have ended. Steele hoped it meant the Army had taken the camp. He let his hand rest on Helen's shoulder, hoping she might be able to fall asleep. With his other hand, he kept the pressure on his wound and tried to stay very still. Soon, her breathing became shallow and regular. He didn't move. Sleep would be the best thing for her now.

But then the shelling began again.

Helen first twitched in her sleep, then sat up abruptly. "What is it? Is he coming?"

Steele patted her hand. "No one is coming. We're safe."

Helen put her arms around his neck and whispered, "Talk to me. Please. Don't let me go to sleep again."

"There's nothing to be afraid of now. No one knows we're here. We can just stay here and wait until morning."

With the flash of the next exploding shell, he could see her face clearly: her eyes were wild with panic. She winced with the sound of each new detonation.

"Helen, relax. We're safe up here."

But she continued to stare at him with that wild look. "You said you wanted me. Do you really want me? I mean, after . . . what that . . . man . . . did to me?"

"Of course I want you. I've always wanted you, from the first time I saw you. You're still the same beautiful, troublesome girl that was so irritated with me back in San Diego." He smiled and touched her cheek.

But she pushed his hand away. "No, I mean do you still want me the way I am now, the way a man wants . . . a woman?"

He took her hands in his and kissed them. "Of course. I felt . . . that way about you when we were out by the hot spring. You soaked your shirt in the water. Do you remember?"

She nodded and put her forehead against his chest. "I remember. But I'm not . . . the same as I was then."

"You are the same. Exactly the same."

She looked up again. "But Drew, you don't know the things that man did to me. He forced me to . . . do things. The first time . . . I bled, but he wouldn't stop."

"It doesn't matter. That's all over now."

"Do you mean it? You'd still want to make love to me."

"If that was what you wanted." He looked into her eyes.

"Then make love to me now. Right now. I have to know."

"Maybe now is not the time, Helen. We'll have plenty of time to be together when we get out of here."

"But what if we don't? What if the Army fails and Ramsey comes up and captures us again?"

"I won't let that happen, I promise. Why don't you lie back down and rest."

"So you won't make love to me? You don't want to?"

"I didn't say that."

"Then prove it to me. Prove you care about me." She stood up and began taking off her gown.

"Helen, wait." He got up onto his knees and held her hands to try to stop her. But she slapped his hands away and continued to undress. She dropped her garment to the ground and stood naked in front of him. In the soft moonlight, her body was more beautiful than he could have imagined. But was this really what she wanted? As if in response to his silent question she took his hand and began to move it over her body. He didn't resist. Then she sat down beside him and began kissing his neck, pressing her body against him. She held onto him and wouldn't let go. She whispered, "Please."

He made love to her as gently as he could, at first feeling only her response, making sure it was what she really wanted. But soon he began to lose himself in the feel of her body beneath him. He forgot about the fighting, the sound of explosions and gunfire in the distance. He let himself go down and down until he was lost in the feel of her, aware of nothing but the smell of her hair, the warmth of her sweat mingling with his, the sound of her excited breathing in his ear.

Chapter 27

Sometime in the night, despite the constant gunfire from down below, Steele fell asleep. When he woke up sometime later, Helen was holding him close. He gently moved her arm aside and sat up. She murmured something, but didn't awaken. The moon had gone down, leaving the mountainside in total darkness. There was complete silence. Was the fighting over? Had the Army successfully stormed the camp? He couldn't see any torches moving around down there; more likely both sides had exhausted themselves. The Army must have pulled back to wait for daylight.

The night had grown much cooler so he found Helen's garment and gently put it over her. He lay back down next to her to wait for the dawn. He stared up at the stars and listened to her breathing, wondering if later, after this was all over, they would lie together somewhere safe and comfortable while he listened to the sweet sound of her peaceful breathing. He hoped that dream would come true.

The next time he opened his eyes, it was still dark but there were streaks of pale gold in the sky above the mountain peaks to the east. He sat up and looked at Helen. Her blonde hair was all in a tangle and he reached down to brush it away from her face. He was happy to see that her sleeping face had lost some of the trouble that was there before. As he watched her sleep, he suddenly realized he was happy. It wasn't a feeling he was used to. Strange, he thought, to have such a feeling, given that Ramsey and his army of Confederates might be down there looking for them. He and Helen were stuck on the side of the mountain with no food or water. If the Indians were still in the valley below, they would eventually come looking for Napiche, their chief's son.

He lay back down next to Helen and the movement brought a sharp pain in his chest. He'd forgotten all about the knife wound. And he could also feel the shrapnel wound, sharp and troublesome behind his shoulder. He realized he hadn't once thought about either wound during the night.

He looked up at the gradually lightening sky, realizing that he had, for the moment, at least, somehow escaped death again. How many times had he been close to death? Was that why he continued to seek out danger? For the feeling of aliveness and clarity that came with survival?

He glanced over at Helen and discovered she was awake and staring at him. "Is it all right? I mean, was it all right that I asked you to . . ."

He gently put a finger to her lips. "It was what we both wanted."

She smiled and stretched, causing the robe to slip off of her. She didn't seem to notice. Suddenly she sat up. "Oh, your knife wound. Did it hurt when we . . . ?"

"No, I'm fine."

"Let me see." She touched his chest. "It's not bleeding, but it's all swollen. Does it hurt?"

"Not much."

She shook her head and frowned. "It's lucky the knife didn't go in farther. You could have been killed."

"He didn't know to turn the blade sideways. He hit a rib."

"So to kill a person with a knife you have to turn it sideways?"

"Yes, if it's a strike to the upper chest or back."

"Oh, Drew, you talk so calmly about it. Where did you learn . . . such things? Have you killed someone before? I mean, before . . . last night."

He looked at her, not sure she really wanted to hear the answer.

She started to say something else, but stopped and turned to look down the hill. "Listen, there's no fighting. Is it over?"

"I'm not sure it is. They may be waiting until the sun comes up." He took her hands in his. "Listen, Helen, I don't want to leave you, but I have to go back down there. Ramsey's got plans to go to Texas to coordinate a new war of guerrilla attacks back east. I have to make sure he doesn't get away."

She shook her head. "No, you can't, Drew. It doesn't matter to us what he does. Stay here with me."

He looked into her eyes. "You know all I want to do is stay with you, but Ramsey has to be stopped. Maybe he's already been killed, but I have to go back down there and find out. Then I'll come right back here, I promise."

She shook her head again, more forcefully this time. "No. If you're going, then I'm going with you. I don't want to be alone again. I . . . can't."

He saw the fear and confusion in her eyes. She held tightly to his hands, refusing to let him go.

"All right, we can go down together. But only until we get close to the camp Then I have to go in alone."

She got up and he watched her as she got dressed.

When she noticed, she smiled and shook her finger at him. "You're looking at me, just like you did back there at the pond in California. I thought you were watching what was going on down there."

"Oh, sorry," he said, also smiling. "I was looking at something far more beautiful."

He got up and dressed quickly while she watched him. Then he picked up Napiche's knife and led the way down the mountainside.

As it began to get lighter, he could see men moving around down in the camp, but it was still too dark to see which type of uniform they were wearing.

But then something caught his eye. "Get down!" He pulled Helen behind some boulders rocks.

"What is it?" she whispered. "I don't see anything."

"Something moved. Over there on the other side of the hill, in those bushes." They waited, watching for any movement, but there was nothing. He began to wonder if it might have been an animal, maybe a deer. But then he saw it again. Something was moving up the hill in the dim pre-dawn light.

"It might be Ramsey," he whispered. "I've got to go see. You stay here."

"No. I'm coming with you." She stood up.

"All right, but stay behind me." He moved across the hillside toward the bushes, moving cautiously with Helen close behind. But he hadn't made it far when he saw the muzzle flash, and at almost the same instant, he heard the gunshot. He felt something hit his leg and he found himself sitting on the ground.

"Oh, no," cried Helen. "Are you shot?" She fell to her knees next to him.

He pulled her down behind some rocks. "Stay down. Don't move." Where had the shot come from? He peeked over the top of the rocks, but couldn't see anybody anywhere on the mountainside. The shot must have come from somebody hiding in the bushes, where he'd seen the movement.

He looked down at his leg. In the dim light, it looked like the bullet had hit just above his knee. Hopefully it had hit only muscle and not the bone. He looked back toward the rocks just as an Indian suddenly stood up. He was a very thin old man with flowing white hair. He was flanked by two young braves. Despite the pain in his leg, Steele's first reaction was to be impressed that the Indian had hit him at that distance. Maybe the old man had intentionally shot low to wound him. He assumed he would soon find out. They would soon come to finish him off. He hoped they wouldn't hurt Helen. "When they get here, don't tell them about Napiche. Say you haven't seen him."

But the Indians did not come. The old Indian handed the rifle to one of the younger braves and they turned away. They quickly went on up the hill and disappeared from sight.

Helen stared at his leg, her hands over her mouth. "Oh God, Drew, you're bleeding. What should I do?"

"Tear away the cloth. Let's see how bad it is."

She did as he instructed and he saw the neat hole where the bullet had gone in just above his left knee. But there was also an exit wound on the back of his thigh and that was good. At least the bullet was not lodged in the bone. But the bleeding would have to be stopped. He quickly took the lace out of one of his boots. Then he found up a short stick and used it to twist the string tighter and tighter around his leg above the knee. Gradually the bleeding slowed.

Helen was weeping and shaking uncontrollably. "What should I do, Drew? I don't know what to do."

"Let's just wait here a minute. If the Indians were escaping, the fighting down below may be over."

"But your leg. What shall we do?"

He touched her cheek. "It's not that serious. Don't worry. When the bullet goes clear through, the patient usually . . . " He stopped. A man had just stepped out of the bushes. He was coming across the hillside toward them, moving slowly. He was carrying one of the new Henry rifles.

They watched him come, and soon Steele recognized him. It was Ramsey.

Helen grabbed Steele's arm. "Oh, my God, Drew, it's Ramsey. He's coming. What should we do?"

"Find the knife. I dropped it when I was hit."

She quickly found the knife and held it out to him.

"No, you take it in case he comes after you. Go down and try to find Major Carter. Tell him Ramsey is up here. Tell him Ramsey is trying to get to Texas to coordinate guerrilla attacks back east."

"No, I won't leave you."

"Helen, listen, this is important. You have to get to the Major. If Ramsey gets away, the war could start all over again. A new type of war. Many innocent people will be killed. It's up to you to stop him."

She glanced toward Ramsey. "But he'll kill you."

"If he does, there's nothing you can do about it. You can't help me here. Go! Stay behind rocks as you go down so Ramsey won't be able to get a clear shot at you."

She stood up, tears filling her eyes. She hesitated, but then seemed to make up her mind. She turned and started to run down the hill. She fell once, but was quickly back up and running. She turned back for one last look and raised her hand before she disappeared behind a field of large boulders.

Ramsey arrived and leaned on his rifle, panting. He was no longer wearing his general's frock coat and his fancy pleated white shirt was torn and dirty. He looked down at Steele. "So there you are, Mr. Steele, lying on the ground like a wounded squirrel. That was quite a good shot, wasn't it?" He held up the Henry rifle, admiring it. "These lovely weapons are quite accurate."

"A little low," said Steele.

"Oh no, I meant to take the legs out from under you. If I had wanted to kill you, I could have, believe me. I was known to be quite a good shot in my younger days."

"You're not the one who shot me. I saw the man who shot me. It was an Indian. Your old eyes are much too far gone to hit anything at that distance."

Ramsey shook his head, smiling. "You never miss a chance to provoke me do you? Well, do you think these old eyes can hit you from this distance?" He lifted the rifle and aimed it a Steele's chest.

"I doubt even you could miss at this range. And it would be very much like you to shoot an unarmed man, wouldn't it?"

Ramsey was no longer smiling. "An executed man is always unarmed, isn't he? But here now, let's not be angry at the last moment." He turned to look down the hill. "Now where has your little Helen run off to? Gone down to fetch help for her man, has she?"

"She ran off," said Steele, turning his attention back to his leg wound.

"Oh no, I don't believe she would leave you, Mr. Steele. I saw her go. I'll bet she's hiding down there. You see, I know she cares for you very much. She told me herself during our little conversations." He again looked down the hill. "Come on out from behind those rocks, my dear," he shouted. "You can't stay in there forever you know."

Steele hoped Helen would be able to gradually work her way down the hill without Ramsey spotting her. If she got far enough away, he wouldn't be able to hit her, even with that very accurate rifle. He had to try to hold Ramsey's attention until she made it. "What happened, General? Did your grand plan fail? You probably weren't expecting artillery, were you?"

"Oh, but I was." Ramsey sat down on a rock and leaned forward on his rifle. "Of course I knew your Major Carter would try to soften us up with artillery. But I expected to be gone by then. Somehow he found the entrance even though he never could before. But be that as it may, once he found us, I knew he would do things by the book. Major Carter is very predictable. Despite his artillery attack, my men could have held him off. They are well trained and brave to a man. We had the high ground. We could have held off an army ten times the size of Carter's little force. But you see, the main advantage of artillery lies not in its destructive force but in its psychological effect. That is every soldier's weak point, fear. But my men did not fail me. It was the Indians. The chief's son, Napiche, ran off somewhere and after that the others seemed to think we had brought down the forces of their gods upon them. 'You have violated our sacred place,' that's what their old medicine man kept on yelling at me. As if it was I who had sent the artillery shells instead of Major Carter. When that fool Napiche up and disappeared into the night, some of his young friends gathered together and attacked us from the rear. The next thing we knew we were fighting Indians on one side and the U.S. Army on the other. My men could have won a fair fight, but as I'm sure you know, winning a war on two fronts is next to impossible. But no matter, Major Carter doesn't know where I've gone. My friend Cochise was showing me a secret way out of this valley. He was leading me out, but I was unable to keep up. Amazing an old Indian like that can move so fast. But when he realizes I have fallen behind, I'm sure he'll come back for me."

Steele shook his head. "Cochise won't be back for you. He shot me to keep me from following him and he doesn't want you following either. He's leaving you to your fate."

Ramsey looked back up toward the top of the hill. "Impossible. We had an agreement. I am his only hope to overcome the U.S. Army."

"You were too old and too weak to keep up, General. You'll never find your way out of here now."

Ramsey shook his head. "He will come back. You'll see. Then I will dispose of you and go on to Texas to lead my army of guerrilla fighters to victory."

Steele shook his head. "You have no more alliance, general. The Indians turned on you, just as the Mexicans did. Remember your lecture about Napoleon? You forgot that he too learned the danger of fighting a war against your enemy with your so-called friends at your back."

Ramsey nodded thoughtfully. "It is true, alliances can be fragile. But my plan will win out in the end."

"What plan, General? When you don't arrive in Texas to lead your pack of dreamers, they'll just go back to their homes and families."

"No, once again, you are incorrect, Mr. Steele. Even if Cochise doesn't come back, the plan will go forward without me. No one will be able to stop them because no one knows the plan except you and you will soon be dead."

"But you must be there to direct it. Isn't that right? How could they hope to succeed without your guidance?"

"Such sarcasm doesn't suit you, Steele. While I agree that my leadership may have been crucial to an early victory, my men will persevere and in time they will overcome the weak and unmotivated Federals. My plan to take away the North's weapons manufacturing capability will go forward, as will the artillery attacks on the cities. That alone may be enough to cause the corrupt government in Washington to collapse. That will leave the Confederacy free to reorganize and reemerge with such momentum that nothing will be able to stop it."

Steele again shook his head. "You miscalculated with regard to your alliance with the Indians, just as you did with the Mexicans. You miscalculated about how quickly and how effectively Major Carter could mount an attack against your mountain stronghold. It seems to me you've made one miscalculation after another. And what about the war profiteers? You sacrificed your fine principles by accepting weapons and money from them, but surely you must understand they will turn against you as soon as your men attack their factories."

The general looked toward the east. Steele suspected he was thinking about what was going on back there. Was he starting to have doubts?

"When the cause is great enough," said Ramsey quietly, "the ends justify any and all means." He shook his head as if to shake away any doubts. "But none of it matters to us now, does it? In the end, the Confederacy will prevail, with or without me. Justice demands it."

"So," said Steele quietly, "if you believe the Confederacy is going to rise again without you, what's the point of shooting me?"

"Why, you should be honored, Mr. Steele. As I promised, you are to have a starring role in the last act of this drama. You will be the last man to be killed in this place, a place that will be remembered long after we are gone. We will be written about, you and I. For as long as men discuss war and keen strategy, your name and mine will be inextricably linked. We will go down in history together."

"After you kill me, do you plan to make a glorious stand here on this hillside? Perhaps you see yourself holding out against them, just you and your fine new rifle."

"Maybe I misspoke about you being the last to die, Mr. Steele. If you are right and my friend Cochise does not return to lead me out of here . . . well then, you will be the second to the last man to die here. I will be the last. I will give no one else the satisfaction of killing me. I will shoot you with this fine rifle and then, if your Major Carter comes before I can escape, I will use it on myself. I will forever more be known as a martyr to the cause, then, as I promised, you and I will go together to meet our Lord and Savior. We will have great adventures up there, you and I."

"Do what you will," said Steele. "But I don't believe we'll see each other beyond this life."

"Well," said Ramsey, standing up, "there is no point in arguing about it. We shall know soon enough." He lifted his rifle and aimed it at Steele's chest.

Just then, Steele saw Helen creeping up behind Ramsey. She was moving very silently in her bare feet. If only she could get closer . . . "Before you shoot me, General, I have one last request."

Ramsey hesitated, then lowered the rifle. "And that is?"

"I want to know why you abandoned your son."

"I did no such thing."

"But you did. You came all this way to demonstrate a new type of warfare. Why would you deny your son the chance to participate in such a glorious campaign? Why would you leave him behind to be tried by the Federals as a war criminal?"

"My son," said Ramsey, nodding thoughtfully. "My heroic son. I wish I had time to explain it all to you, Mr. Steele, but I can't have you stalling for time, can I?" He again raised the rifle, but hesitated and once again lowered it. "I will give you one thing, you have been a worthy adversary. I will admit that I admire your courage, your persistence. I could have used a man like you. And I will even admit that I even feel . . . shall we call it . . . regret that you will not be able to spend more time with your lovely Helen. Many times, when I looked upon her, I regretted that I was not a younger man. If I were, I might well have vied with you for her favors. But be that as it may, it is time for us to explore the next realm." He raised the rifle.

But Helen was already behind him. She whispered, "Go by yourself, old man."

Ramsey got a curious look on his face, a mixture of surprise and mirth, as if he had just thought of something very funny. He tried to lift the rifle to shoot Steele, but it seemed too heavy for him.

Steele scrambled forward and took the gun out of his hands, and as Ramsey sank to his knees, Steele saw the handle of the knife protruding from his back.

"I did it right, didn't I," said Helen. "I turned it sideways." He voice sounded almost calm, but her hands were shaking.

Steele caught Ramsey as he started to fall. He gently laid the man down on his side.

"Helen?" said Ramsey. He turned his head to look at her. "How could you do this to me? After all our wonderful talks in the night."

"Wonderful talks!" She shook her finger at him angrily. "You mean while I was chained to a wagon wheel and forced to listen while you rambled on and on about your glorious career, your brilliant strategy."

Ramsey turned his head to look at Steele. "A woman scorned is a dangerous woman" he said with a grim smile.

Steele looked at the knife protruding from Ramsey's back. It had gone in between his ribs, just as Helen had intended, but from the angle of the knife handle, it looked as if it had struck something solid and been forced upward. It probably hadn't even punctured the lung. Ramsey would undoubtedly survive.

"How does it look . . . Steele? Will I . . . die?"

"It is serious, General."

There was fear in Ramsey's eyes. "Won't you . . .pull . . . it out?"

"It's better not to. Pulling it out without a surgeon at hand could cause even more damage."

"It doesn't matter. I know I'm going to die here. I can feel it coming. If I could ask one small . . . favor. Don't leave me for a while. I don't want to die . . . alone."

Helen sat down next to him. "We won't leave you. You don't deserve our pity, but we'll wait here with you until the end."

He looked up at her with tears in his eyes. "I wish you wouldn't have done that, Helen. I had begun to think of you almost like a daughter. How could you stab me in the back like that? Aren't you sorry now?"

She shook her head. "No, I'm not sorry. You were about to shoot my man. I love him. What would you have done in my place?"

Ramsey looked at Steele. "She's too good for you, Steele."

"That's the one thing we agree on, General." Steele looked down the hill. Now that the sun was up, he could see men moving around down there and they were wearing Union blue. He got up onto his knees and pointed Ramsey's rifle into the air. He fired two quick shots. Soon, the soldiers were running up the slope in their direction. He sat back down in front of Ramsey.

"I don't mind dying here," said Ramsey. "I'd rather die in battle than at the hands of that . . . war crimes tribunal." He looked up at Steele with tears in his eyes. "I'll be waiting for you, Steele, in the glorious hereafter. Along with my dear wife and my son."

"You never finished telling me why you didn't bring your son out here with you."

Ramsey looked off into the distance. "My son. My . . . heroic son." He closed his eyes.

"His son was not a hero," whispered Helen. "He was a coward."

Ramsey opened his eyes. "Please don't say that, my dear. Back then I thought he was a . . . He wasn't . . . what I wanted him to be, but I see the truth now. My son was a hero, in his own way. A true patriot."

Helen shook her head. "That's not what you told me, General. During those nice long talks we had while I was your captive, you told me your son was a coward. That he ran from battle."

Ramsey was quiet for some time. Then he said, "It's true, I did say that. But I was wrong. I should have forgiven him. I was too . . . harsh back then. I told my men I would shoot any man who turned and ran. And then when my own son was the first to run, I couldn't go through with it. I stood him up in front of the men and put a gun to his head. I even pulled the trigger. You know what he did? He fainted. He wasn't even man enough to face his own death. At the time, I regretted that I hadn't put a bullet in that gun. I was . . . so ashamed of him I sent him away, back to Mississippi, to hide under the beds of women. I sent him to his old maiden aunts just to get him out of my sight. But now I know it wasn't his fault. It was . . . my fault. I must have . . . brought him up wrong. I was ashamed of him and he knew it. That's why he ran when he was under fire and . . . it must have been why he . . . gave himself up to the war crimes commission. He wasn't afraid of the war, he was . . . afraid of me."

"But you could have brought him out here to redeem himself," said Steele.

"I didn't even ask him to come. I thought he would be afraid when the fighting started, that he would get in my way. And now he's . . . dead. They killed him because of me."

Steele looked down the hill and saw the major and several soldiers approaching, followed closely by Rudd.

"Hey, look, it's Steele!" yelled Rudd, pointing. "And Helen's there too. They're alive."

Somehow, Rudd managed to arrive first, red-faced and out of breath. He rushed to give Helen a big hug that must have taken her breath away too. Then he took off his hat and fanned himself with it, leaning over with his hands on his knees, breathing hard. When he had finally recovered enough to speak, he said, "By God, you made it, both of you. I was worried sick about you. On my way down to Tucson, some Indians started to chase me, but luckily the major and his men were coming up. They ran 'em off and I brought the major up to the cliff. We saw your arrow there on the ground and when somebody started shooting down at us, the major set up his cannon and started firing. I couldn't make him stop. I thought you were both goners."

"We were waiting for you," said Steele, smiling. "We were hoping you would bring us something to eat."

"Oh damn," said Rudd. "I should have." He turned to the major. "Didn't I tell you they'd be hungry? I told the doctor that too. He's down there patchin' people up."

The major looked down at Steele. "Looks like you got yourself all shot up, just like I knew you would."

"You were supposed to wait to see if I could get Helen and the other hostages out before you attacked," said Steele.

"Well, you didn't come out so I figured you were already dead."

"And the other hostages? Did you figure they were already dead too?"

"Ramsey had to be stopped," said the major. "A lot of lives depended on it. And besides, we didn't know who was up here. All we knew was when we found that secret tunnel somebody started shooting at us. We figured it was either Indians or the Confederates. Turned out to be Confederates. No Indians around." He turned to Helen. "But if this young woman here is Helen, then she looks just fine to me." He lifted his hat, and made a little bow.

"No thanks to you," she said, turning away.

The major shrugged and looked down at Ramsey. "And this must be the infamous General Ramsey. Why, he's just a shrunken up old man."

"Quite ungracious of you, Major," said the general, calmly looking up at him. "Unfortunately, I am unable to stand up and challenge you to do me the honor."

"What does that mean?" said the major. "A duel? Pretty funny. You must be living in the past, General. This is not your fancy plantation society. Out here in the West we know how to take care of the likes of you."

Helen stepped forward to face him. "Just shut up, can't you? Don't you see this man is dying?"

"Well, maybe he is and maybe he isn't," said the major, but a lot of my soldiers died because of this man. If I could get a few minutes alone with him I'd—"

"Please stop talking and do something useful," she said. "Can't you see Drew has been shot too?"

"I can see that. But it's only a leg wound. Not even bleeding all that much. Anyhow, we'll get him down to the doctor. We'll take the general down too, even though we should just leave him up here for the coyotes." He waved his men forward.

"If I could ask one question," said Ramsey. "What happened to Colonel Medina? He was supposed to be keeping you busy."

"You mean those damn Mexicans?" The major laughed a short, harsh laugh. "Somehow they got their hands on a fancy new Gatling gun. Used it to shoot up the town. Then they robbed some stores and took off back for Mexico, like they always do. Now if you'll excuse me, I've got a bunch of crazy Confederates to round up." He again tipped his hat to Helen and started back down the hill.

"I'd stand up and surrender my sword to you," Ramsey yelled after him. "If I had a sword."

Helen glared at him. "You two deserve each other." She turned her attention to Steele, getting his arm around her shoulder. Rudd took the other side and together they stood him up.

"Just leave me here," said Ramsey. "I'd rather die here than in captivity."

"You aren't going to die," said Steele, "not from that knife wound anyhow. We'll get you down to the doctor and he'll patch you up. You didn't worry much about holding others in captivity. Now you'll get your opportunity to learn what it's like when we turn you over to the war-crimes tribunal."

"All's well that ends well," said Rudd, beaming. "We're all alive and we're all here together. Let's get down off this mountain. I found your horse and there's still some of that good dried fruit in your saddlebag, unless those damn soldiers found it and ate it all."

That made Helen laugh, but she hid her smile behind her hand. Steele, who had his arm around her waist, gave her a little squeeze of silent communication between them. As they slowly started down the hill, he wondered how many more quiet moments of mutual understanding they would share together. Many, he hoped.

Epilogue

*I*t was a sunny day in San Francisco. The early morning fog had burned off and Steele was sitting at his desk, rereading a letter from Helen. At first she had resisted her father's plan to get her out of the country, but when Steele had suggested she start school at the Escole de Paris and said he would come there to be with her after she got settled in, she finally agreed. Her letters were full of joyful ramblings about the freshness of ideas in the exciting culture of Paris. From her letters, Steele could see that she was also very interested in the debates about women's rights that often took place at the college. He had the odd thought that if she ever went across the channel to London, she might run into Stacy. How different they were, and yet they had both ended up in Europe, both interested in women's rights.

Suddenly, Rudd burst into his office carrying an armload of newspapers. He dropped them onto Steele's desk, nearly upsetting the open inkpot. "Look at these Southern newspapers, Steele. Mr. Kane gave them to me. They're reporting on the rounding up of Ramsey's men, but wait 'til you see what they're saying about the general. Every newspaper in the South is making him out to be some kind of hero."

Steele had already been out early that morning to get the local papers. They were also reporting on the trouble back east and on Ramsey's appearance before the war crimes tribunal. But unlike the Southern newspapers, they were mostly poking fun at the general's pompous oratory.

"Can you beat that, Steele? The Southern papers are saying he shouldn't be held up as a war criminal but as a war *hero*. They're crying for his release. Fat chance of that."

"What are they saying about his escapades in Arizona?" said Steele. "Do they think he should be forgiven for the people he killed there?"

"Not a single mention of that," said Rudd. "It's like what happened out here in the West doesn't matter."

Steele picked up one of the newspapers. It was the old Secessionist Press, now reborn as an anti-Federalist weekly based in Mississippi. It had a front page editorial about Ramsey's trial. Steele quickly scanned it and found that the editorial was more about criticism of the North's reconstruction policies than about Ramsey. It said the North's attempt to find General Ramsey guilty of war crimes was nothing but a pretense to "wave the bloody shirt," and once again remind Southerners that they had started the disastrous war and were therefore to blame for all the death and destruction.

Steele put down the newspaper. "There's still no mention of the arms merchants that were supplying Ramsey and Medina with money and weapons."

"Not a word," said Rudd. "There were a few early reports about the Army posting guards at their factories because of the trouble down south, but nothing since then. Of course Colonel Medina is still shooting off his mouth down in Mexico City, vowing to take back the land the United States stole from Mexico twenty years ago. You can tell he's going to base his campaign for the Mexican presidency on that. But he never mentions Ramsey or the Confederates."

"I expect you had something to say about all that in your column today."

"Damn right I did," said Rudd. "Same as I've been trying to tell them every day." He folded back the Morning-Herald to show Steele his column. Then he began to read from it. "It is time to end this ridiculous chatter about General Ramsey being a hero of the old South. He was a kidnapper and a rogue who ordered the killing of innocent people in Arizona. I was there and saw it with my own eyes. I helped dig some of the poor victims of General Ramsey's mad adventure out of burning buildings when I was there in Tucson. Regardless of what he may or may not have done during the Civil War, he must pay for his dastardly crimes in Arizona, like any other murderer." He slammed the newspaper down on the desk and waited for Steele's response. "Well? What do you think? Did I tell it right or not?"

"You made your point very well," said Steele.

"Well, somebody has to. If this using Ramsey for political purposes goes on, they might not even convict him."

"I expect they will convict him," said Steele. "And they will sentence him to death, just as they sentenced all the others to death. But notice none of those prior sentences have been carried out."

"So they'll just throw him in prison?"

Steele nodded. "I hope they don't execute him. That would be giving him exactly what he wants, martyrdom. Once his trial is over and he's in prison, the nation will soon forget him. The last battle of the war is finally over and they want to forget it ever happened. Someday, they might even quietly release Ramsey."

"Well, he's an old man," said Rudd. "Maybe he won't live that long."

Steele didn't reply. It was true that Ramsey was old, but his oratory on the stand showed he still believed his actions in Arizona were necessary and just, and that the fight for his beloved Confederacy had to go on. A man who burned with that much belief in his own purpose might live very long indeed. Steele couldn't help but wonder if he might someday be called on to contend with the general again.